Dauntless

Dauntless

Alan Evans

HODDER AND STOUGHTON
LONDON SYDNEY AUCKLAND TORONTO

This is a work of fiction set in the framework of events at the time. The characters are all fictitious and in particular those of Finlayson and Edwards are not based on any real person.

British Library Cataloguing in Publication Data
Evans, Alan, *b. 1930*
  Dauntless.
  I. Title
  823'.9'1F   PR6055.V13D/
  ISBN 0-340-25305-3

Contents

My thanks to:

Squadron Leader Gordon Hyams, DFC, who flew Short Seaplanes in that war.

Anina Kaplan and the Staff of the Museum of the History of Tel-Aviv-Yafo, particularly Michaela Golderthal.

The Hagana Museum, Tel Aviv.

All those people who helped me in Israel and Deir el Belah, and the Arab gardener and gentleman at the British Military Cemetery at Deir el Belah.

The staffs of the National Maritime Museum, Imperial War Museum, Public Record Office, Royal Geographical Society, Royal Air Force Museum, Fleet Air Arm Museum and the library at Walton-on-Thames.

But as always – any mistakes are mine!

In 1917, after three years of war, Britain barely survived a U-boat campaign that threatened to starve her into defeat. The French army mutinied, Russia was torn apart by revolution and the battles in France and Flanders only resulted in enormous slaughter. So the British government sought in desperation for a victory to off-set the succession of disasters.

The enemy stretched from Germany on the North Sea through Austria-Hungary to Turkey and her Ottoman Empire in the Middle East. That empire was rotten, the army its only strength. If Turkey could be defeated then Germany would lose an ally and, instead, face the drain of war on another front, because an attack could be launched on her through Turkey.

The Turks fought two British armies, one in Mesopotamia and the other, the Egyptian Expeditionary Force, in Palestine. If that army in Palestine, which had driven the Turks back from the Suez Canal and through the desert of Sinai, could drive on northward and cut the line of supply between Turkey and her army in Mesopotamia then the Turks might throw in their hand.

It was a big 'if'. But the decision was taken: a victory was needed and Palestine had to supply it, and soon. That was the task facing the Egyptian Expeditionary Force and its commander, General Allenby, in October 1917.

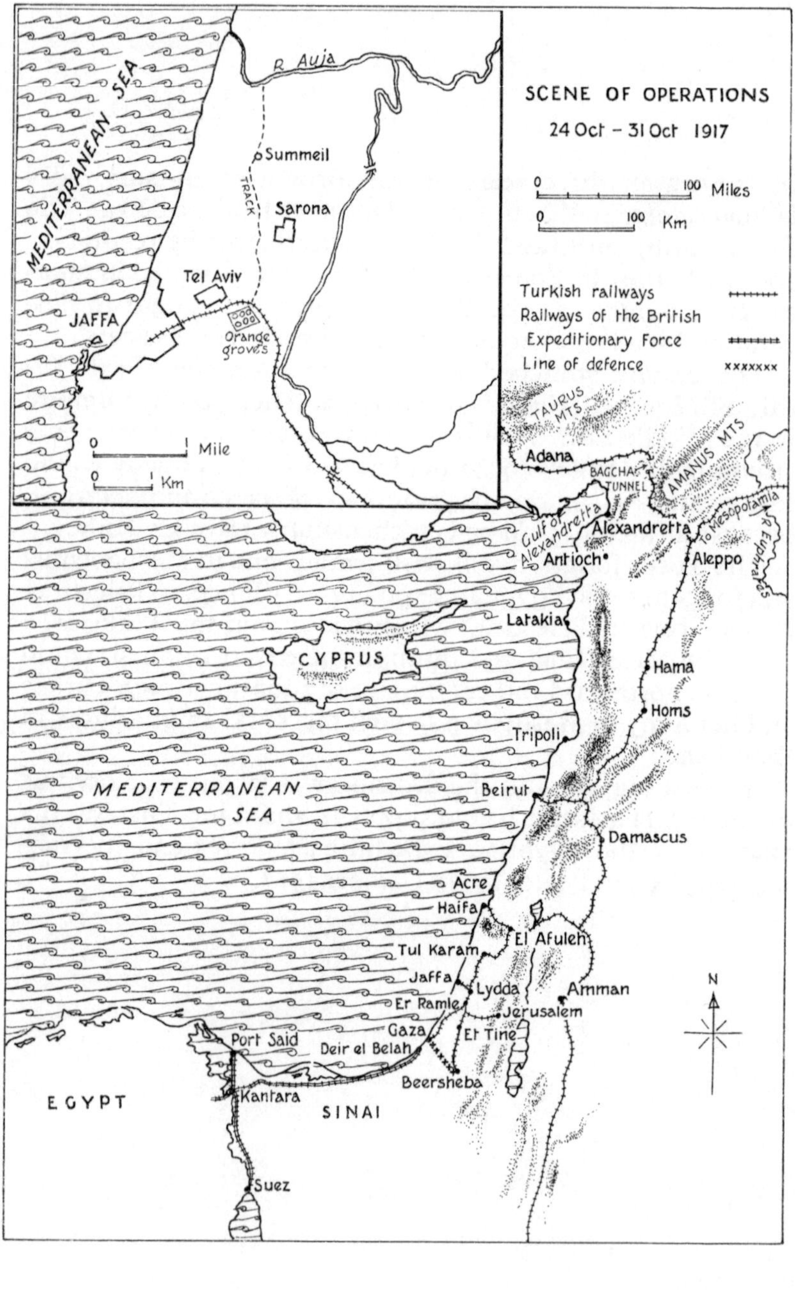

SCENE OF OPERATIONS
24 Oct – 31 Oct 1917
0 100 Miles
0 100 Km
Turkish railways
Railways of the British Expeditionary Force
Line of defence
MEDITERRANEAN SEA
R. Auja
Summeil
TRACK
Sarona
Tel Aviv
JAFFA
Orange groves
0 1 Mile
0 1 Km
TAURUS MTS
Adana
BAGCHE TUNNEL
AMANUS MTS
Gulf of Alexandretta
Alexandretta
To Mesopotamia
R. Euphrates
Antioch
Aleppo
Latakia
CYPRUS
Hama
Homs
Tripoli
MEDITERRANEAN SEA
Beirut
Damascus
Acre
Haifa
El Afuleh
Tul Karam
Jaffa
Lydda
Amman
Er Ramle
Jerusalem
Gaza
Et Tine
Port Said
Deir el Belah
Beersheba
EGYPT
Kantara
SINAI
Suez
N

I

Make or Break

24.10.17.

Commander David Cochrane Smith pencilled the date at the top of the notepad and it triggered the thought: Allenby's army would attack the Gaza-Beersheba line in a week, on the 31st. It would be a battle vital to the entire future of the war. Thoughtfully, he laid the notepad down and stared out across the water.

He stood right in the stern of H.M. Seaplane Carrier *Blackbird*. Until the war, she had been a fast cross-channel packet. Now she had accommodation for four Short seaplanes in the big barn of a hangar the dockyard had built on her after end. His own ship, the light cruiser *Dauntless*, cruised a quarter mile to starboard. Both ships were on a course almost due south, with the coast of Palestine lifting above the eastern horizon, the morning sun blazing out low over the sea from that coast.

Smith's figure in the white drill trousers and shirt was slight, seemingly frail, but that was deceptive. He was thin-faced, not handsome, the pale blue eyes watchful under the peak of the cap. He was probably as happy as he would ever be. He had a command and considered himself lucky, and he was grateful to Rear-Admiral Braddock who had been sent out to organise convoys to combat the menace of U-boats in the Mediterranean. He was a friend. Smith had few friends, and was bleakly aware of it. But Braddock had asked for him, got him the command of *Dauntless* and had given him *Blackbird* as consort. Smith and his seaplane carrier were to

9

act in support of Allenby's army, while Braddock concentrated on convoys.

Smith suspected the old admiral had fought to get this command for him, and he was right. Smith was unpredictable. He had won two bloody but decisive actions, one in the Pacific and one in the North Sea, but in the first he had outraged a neutral government and created diplomatic uproar, and in the second had again broken the rules, defied his immediate superior and even unofficially 'borrowed' a monitor from her anchorage in Dunkerque Roads. There were many who said he was a hot-head and a rebel, and Braddock admitted there was some truth in the charges, but he had won his fight all the same.

Now Smith stood aboard *Blackbird* and told himself that this was make or break for him. He was far from a conventional naval officer, brought up in a village shop in Norfolk by adoptive parents – a retired chief petty officer, Reuben Smith, and his wife, Hannah. He had no knowledge of his true family, no background at all, a mystery to his contemporaries and to himself. His career had been chequered, the long routine of service life highlighted by successful actions, but marred by scandal. Now he was convinced his professional future hung in the balance. If he made a success of his part in Allenby's campaign then his critics would be silenced and he would have a professional future, would go forward on the flood-tide of victory. And there *would* be a victory. There had to be. The allies needed it in this third year of war and Allenby had been sent out to get it. Smith dared not think of the alternative.

The carrier had reduced speed to ten knots and was slowing still as one of the Shorts was wheeled out of the hangar, its big, box-like floats resting on a trolley. It stood fifteen feet high, a biplane with its wings folded back, but now it was clear of the hangar the riggers swung out the wings and rammed the locking pins into the sockets on their leading edges. The Short changed from a nesting bird to one ready to fly, wings spread. Smith saw Lieutenant Chris Pearce checking that those pins were secure, as he always checked since the day he had been about to take off and had seen one hanging loose.

Chris was a pilot as well as captain of *Blackbird*, a tall, good-looking young man who had worn an engaging grin when Smith first met him, three weeks before. But since those early days he had gone downhill and now he looked drawn and edgy, tired. Smith was startled. He had not seen Chris for days: he had worked him and his crew hard but still he should not look as worn as he did. It added to Smith's recurring doubts. Pearce had come to him with reports of near-brilliance. But his was a highly-strung brilliance and, in Smith's short experience of him, he had proved increasingly nervy and erratic.

He had four flying crews on board, but he was flying himself today. He drove himself hard, as if needing to prove something. Now Pearce turned, lifted a hand signalling that he was ready and Smith joined him, took the leather flying helmet and climbed up into the Short. That was all the flying gear they needed in these last days of the Mediterranean summer. He put notepad and map on the seat of the observer's cockpit. Pearce stood in the pilot's cockpit in front of him, reaching up for the hook on the derrick purchase dangling on the end of its wire. The armourer passed up the 16-pound anti-personnel bombs to Smith, four of them and each no more than a foot long. "All we've got left, I'm afraid sir."

Smith listened to his instructions as he set the bombs down on the floor of the cockpit, the Lewis gun on its Scarff ring-mounting nudging his back. He nodded his readiness as Pearce looked round questioningly.

Pearce faced forward, lifted a hand, the winch hammered and the derrick lifted the Short and swung it out over the side to hang above the sea. Events moved rapidly now. *Blackbird* was used to launching a seaplane in forty-five seconds. The Short dropped down to the sea off *Blackbird*'s port quarter and seamen standing on her wide rubbing strake used long poles to boom off the fragile seaplane from the steel side. For a second it dangled less than a foot above the wave-crests slipping beneath the floats as *Blackbird* steamed slowly ahead, then Pearce yanked the toggle release that slipped the hook and the Short smacked down on the sea. *Blackbird* pulled away, increasing speed now the seaplane was slipped.

'Short' was a deceptive term, being the name of the firm that made it; the Short was forty feet long and the wings spread sixty-three feet. And 'floatplane' was a more accurate term than 'seaplane', because besides the two big floats under the mid-section there was a smaller float at each wing tip and another on the tail. The Short sat back on the tail float now it was on the sea. Shorts were big, ungainly birds but reliable. They flew and flew.

Pearce turned the tap on the compressed air cylinder in his cockpit, and under the thrust of the air the pistons of the Maori engine kicked and it fired. Pearce ran it up, taxi-ing then shoved forward the big wheel that topped the control column until the tail float lifted off, and hauled back on the wheel as the Short reached flying speed. There was just enough broken water to unstick the floats and the Short rose into the air. Pearce eased it around in a gently-banking turn until they were headed towards the distant coast and still slowly climbing. Ten minutes later they crossed the coastline at fifteen hundred feet.

Allenby's orders had been short and to the point. The government had sent him out from France to capture Palestine. The land lay under Smith now; this would be the battle-ground. Behind him was the sea, to his left and far to the north was Syria, ahead the Hills of Judaea lifted in a blue wall to the east and on the right, in the distant south, was the desert of Sinai. Palestine had been fought over for thousands of years and soon would be fought over again. And as never before.

The Turks had ruled here for centuries and when the war started they advanced through Sinai and threatened the Suez Canal but were beaten back. In the last year the British army under Murray fought its way through the desert of Sinai and the way was hard because the Turks fought hard. Now they had with them the German Asia Corps under Kressenstein, five thousand of them, all specialists and scattered through the Turkish formations to supply a technical stiffening to the courage already there. It was the German engineers who had built the Gaza-Beersheba line.

The Short turned south, following the thread of the railway

and pointing its nose towards that Gaza-Beersheba line sixty-odd miles to the south. Beersheba was the fortress at the southern end of the Hills of Judaea, while Gaza stood on the northern coast. The German engineers had strung fortifications across the thirty miles between and they boasted the line was impregnable. Now Allenby had taken over from Murray. The Germans knew he would attack the Gaza-Beersheba line and believed he would fail. But he had no choice except to try. Allenby's army crouched ready on one side of the line, Palestine lay on the other, and he had his orders: take Palestine.

Braddock's orders to Smith were simply: harass the enemy.

"Harass the enemy." *Dauntless* and *Blackbird* had raced up and down this coast from Gaza to the Gulf of Alexandretta, three hundred miles to the north, for the last two weeks. *Dauntless* shelled installations and any troops seen, drove the coastwise traffic of dhows and small craft into the shallows, then sent armed boarding parties in the motor-boat to set them afire or blow them up. *Blackbird*'s Shorts reconnoitred and bombed the railway whenever they could. A railway track was a difficult target to hit and, when it was, any damage could be made good in a day, but any delay meant a break in supplies to the enemy army. Palestine's roads were poor and few. The railway that ran down from Alexandretta to the Gaza-Beersheba line was the sole slender artery sustaining the enemy there. So the enemy defended it and the flights over the railway were met by gun-fire or the Fokker fighter planes of the Asia Corps.

This was not Smith's first flight in those two weeks because he needed to see for himself – he could not always stand by and send others. So here he was with Pearce, looking for trouble and ready to make it; hence the four 16-pound bombs. He knew these were all that remained after the Shorts' repeated bombing attacks. Trouble was not hard to find. A week ago one of the Shorts was hit by gun-fire and forced down in the shallows off the coast. Again Smith had sent an armed party in the motor-boat, this time to lift the pilot and observer out of the surf. They had been very lucky.

The Short droned on at a steady sixty knots and the old Arab town of Lydda slid under the port wing. The Turks had a garrison a mile or so north of it, but Smith saw no troops on the move. The railway ran on southwards. Smith stood up and leaned to one side to peer ahead, round the radiator of the water-cooled engine, like a laundry basket a foot square, which was mounted right in front of the pilot's cockpit. There was no train in sight. The spur line coming up from Jaffa on the coast swung southwards to angle towards and finally join the main line at Lydda station, a half-mile south of the town itself. The junction of the lines formed a V which held the green of a wood but that was still ahead of them. Also ahead of them, and a mile south of the station, was a German anti-aircraft battery.

Pearce had not forgotten this and the Short was banking away to steer well clear of the guns, turning eastwards towards the coast and picking up the line of the railway to Jaffa. Smith saw Pearce scowling, pushing up the goggles to rub at his eyes irritably. Smith stood up again with the bombs rolling about his feet, smacked the pilot's shoulder and pointed at the steel ribbon of the track running across the green of the plain and the trailing plume of grey-black smoke some seven or eight miles ahead. Pearce pulled down the goggles, peered in the direction Smith indicated and the scowl was wiped away by a grin. He eased the nose of the Short down in a shallow dive. It was the train that ran once a day from Lydda down to Jaffa and back again, or had until *Dauntless* and *Blackbird* shelled and bombed it. Now it was trying again, puffing down to the coast, pottering along at around fifteen miles an hour, while the Short was making close to eighty knots and dropping out of the sky towards it.

Smith groped down by his feet as he watched the train coming up – six, seven, eight trucks, all of them loaded, then the tender stacked with logs of wood because the Turks were short of coal, and the engine, its tall chimney belching out the smoke that carried down along the side of the track. There were men on the footplate of the engine. The Short was down to two hundred feet or so, sweeping forward over the train. Smith could see the dark faces turned up to him.

He was standing again, holding the bomb over the side of the cockpit, yanking out the pin and seeing the fan of the tail start to revolve. He let it go as the locomotive raced back towards him, the footplate flashed beneath and he saw a soldier there with a rifle at his shoulder.

The Short was past in a blink and tearing away ahead of the train as the bomb burst, in front of the engine but wide of the track. Smith groped for another as the Short's nose lifted, the port wing dipping in as tight a turn as the unwieldy craft could produce, and the nose pointed once more at the train.

Smith reminded himself that the Short wasn't overtaking the train now but closing it and he had to allow for their increased combined speeds. He worried at the pin, got it free and let the bomb go. He squirmed around in the cockpit, banged his head on the breach of the Lewis and swore, swore again as he saw the bomb fall ahead of the train and wide again. He'd botched it. Next time . . . He reached down, felt his fingers on the pin and took care not to grip it, lifted the third bomb.

He remembered the armourer aboard *Blackbird*, macabrely humorous. "You pulls out the pin, sir, and lets the bomb go. See, sir, once you pulls the pin, the fan has a habit o' revolving and after two or three turns that bomb'll go off if you cough. There was one feller got excited and let the pin go an' kept the bomb. That didn't do no good. Not to him, anyway."

Smith grinned briefly, remembering the tale. Now Pearce had turned the Short and they were overhauling the train again. It was steaming more slowly still as it climbed the long slope up the hill before the left-hand turn at the crest and the run down into Jaffa. Sand dunes on the right of the track and orange groves on the left, the train sliding up at him, beneath him, the engine coming up – now!

The bomb burst in the dunes, hurling up sand, yards from the track though level with the engine.

One to go.

The Short was banking right-handed above the crest of the hill. Smith caught a quick, wheeling glimpse of Jaffa a mile or more down the slope on its own small hill, a lean tower and a minaret standing above the walls of the old town perched on the edge of the sea. Then the two ships, far out at sea, patrolling. And then the smaller township, just half-a-dozen neatly laid out, criss-crossing streets, deserted now, that lay a half-mile below the crest and the same from Jaffa. That was where some Jews had moved to from overcrowded Jaffa back in 1909 to build a town of their own. What was it? – Tel Aviv. And all the time he scanned the sky, head turning. He checked in that turning, stiffened, then tapped Pearce's shoulder.

The Short levelled out and Pearce twisted around in his seat, flying the Short with one hand, making downward thrusting gestures with the other.

Smith pointed and Pearce peered in the direction Smith indicated, sought and found what Smith was pointing out. It was like a small black insect, high in the sky and coming up from the south where the German Asia Corps had an airfield at Et Tine. But Pearce put up his thumb, then made the downward thrusting gesture again. So he thought there was time to finish the attack.

Smith hesitated, then nodded. He was a novice observer while Pearce was a highly-experienced pilot and he didn't want to let the train off the hook.

Pearce turned away and the Short's nose tilted down steeply as he set it diving. The crest of the hill seemed to flick at the floats. Then the nose came up and Pearce was flying it down the track, the floats only a dozen feet above it, the orange groves blurring green past the starboard wing tip.

The train was stopped.

Smith saw the tiny figures of men leap from the footplate and scurry towards the groves, but his attention was all for the locomotive and the track with the twin steel rails right under him.

For the last time he yanked out the pin and let go the bomb. The engine flashed beneath him and in that instant the bomb burst. Looking past the tail of the Short he saw the dust rising ahead of or under the engine, he could not tell which but waited as the Short turned, climbing slowly now. The dust blew away like the smoke that trailed from the tall locomotive chimney and Smith saw the bomb had fallen short of the train but on the track. There was a hole now and twisted rails.

That was enough. This was yet another day when the train would not arrive at Jaffa, when the repair gang under its German foreman would have to come out from the station at Lydda to repair the track, when the crew of the train had been harried and frightened. That was in the letter and the spirit of the orders given to Smith. Harass the enemy . . .

Pearce lifted the Short over the crest, then sent it plunging down across the long slope of rolling sand-dunes to the sea. Smith turned around and gripped the Lewis, checked that it swung freely on its Scarff-mounting, cocked it and peered up through the ring sight at the German plane diving down after them.

Far out of range, but for how long? Smith glanced over his shoulder and saw they were over the sea, levelling out close above the waves and heading for the ships that were hull-up over the horizon and seen bows-on as they closed the shore. On board *Dauntless* and *Blackbird* they had spotted the Short and were coming to meet it.

Smith swung back to peer astern, squinted up at the Fokker monoplane and wondered uneasily if they had hung on too long. If it came to a fight the seaplane would have no chance, being slower and far less manoeuvrable than the Fokker.

It was just in range of the Lewis now but Smith was not an expert shot and so he waited, watching the black aircraft astern, as it seemed to swing slowly from one side of the Short's rudder to the other, and closing, steadily closing. He took his eyes off it for a moment as he felt the Short tilt into a banking turn to starboard and he saw they were near to *Blackbird* and she was stopped. Pearce was turning into wind to set the seaplane down, and *Dauntless* was steaming on, starting to turn to patrol around the carrier.

He swung back to peer over the tail, could not see the Fokker, searched frantically but for only a split-second because the Fokker was boring in from his left hand, cutting the corner of the turn the Short had made. He pivoted in the cockpit, swinging the Lewis around, got the Fokker in its sights, lost it, brought the sights on again – and fired as the German fired. He did not know where the burst from the Lewis went to, he saw no signs of a hit on the Fokker but splinters were snapping off the tail and fuselage of the Short, something cannoned off the Lewis sending the shock jarring up his arm, fabric ripped loose from the fuselage and streamed on the wind. The Short was sinking, slowly, and the Fokker snarled over them and away. Smith tried to whip around to follow it with the Lewis but was too slow in turning in the tight cockpit. He saw the Fokker climbing and turning to come back at the Short again. They were skimming the surface of the sea, Pearce was rubbing the heels of the floats into the short waves and breaking the tops of them in unflung feathers of spray that briefly rose higher. They misted around Smith as the floats dug in, then dropped away and the Short was down, taxi-ing towards *Blackbird*.

He was aware that *Dauntless* was firing her three-inch anti-aircraft gun and her Vickers machine-guns were rattling madly. He could see her to his right and astern of the Short. The Fokker was closer, flying through a sky pocked with the bursting shells from *Dauntless*, but that firing ceased as the Fokker dived at the Short.

Smith had a little more time, was a little more ready, breathing controlled, the gun steady in his hands and on the Fokker that filled the big ring sight.

The Short was a sitting duck.

He swallowed at the thought and fired.

He thought this time the burst had scored, was sure he saw pieces flying from the Fokker that swerved and showed its side before it straightened again. But now the German pilot could fire only one brief burst and then he flashed over Smith's head again, was turning and climbing and the Archie from *Dauntless* was bursting around him. He bore a charmed life, plunged down towards the sea but only to level out there and escape more quickly. He fled away, wings rocking, headed towards the shore and pursued by the fire from *Dauntless*. Then that stopped as the gunlayer lost the target tucked right down on the surface of the sea.

Smith found he was sweating, but it was not from the heat of the sun, even though that baked him in the open cockpit now that the wind of passage had ceased. They were coming alongside *Blackbird*, Pearce edging the Short in with the engine ticking over in pulsing bursts. Smith secured the Lewis with shaking hands and wiped the sweat from them on the front of his white shirt. *Dauntless* had launched her gig and it was pulling towards *Blackbird* and the Short. He could see Leading Seaman Buckley, who had served with Smith in the Pacific and the Channel, at the helm, face turned towards the seaplane. Smith forced a grin. That might reassure Buckley who was a seaman and not an airman, suspicious of the seaplanes and distrustful of Smith's ability to look after himself. Smith could see the look on Buckley's face now, half-anxious, half-irritated at Smith getting involved in a fire-fight with a German fighter plane. Smith grinned again. Buckley had a certain licence because of long acquaintance, dangers and hardships shared.

The Short was close under *Blackbird*'s lee now. The derrick was swung out and dangled its wire rope with the purchase block and its hook at the end of it. A heaving line was secured to that hook and a seaman on *Blackbird*'s deck held the rest of the heaving line. Smith saw men standing out on the wide rubbing strake along *Blackbird*'s side again with the long spars ready to hold the fragile Short from running against the carrier's steel hull. But he watched the seaman with the heaving line attentively. Any other observer who missed that line when it was thrown could expect hard words, because it meant the line had to be recovered and thrown again while all the time the carrier lay stopped, which was wasteful of time and effort, and often dangerous.

So Smith dared not miss it himself.

The seaman threw the line, snaking it out across the ruffled sea between the carrier and the seaplane. It fell on the fabric aft of the cockpit and slithered away but Smith dived after it, sprawled precariously along the fuselage with his head towards the tail, grabbed at it and caught it. He worked back into the cockpit, then clambered past Pearce to haul in the line and thus bring down the hook of the derrick purchase. The slip-stream from the propeller pushed at him but he snatched at the purchase block, hooked on to the ring on the upper wing and lifted a hand. As the derrick took the strain the Short's engine died.

"Sir!" That was Buckley's deep Geordie voice.

Smith looked down and saw the gig alongside the Short with the bowman holding on to the portside float. He glanced at Pearce and told him, the words sounding strange in the silence after the engine's dying, "We cut it too fine, Chris."

"Well, we got back, sir." Pearce was breathless and he fumbled with the strap of the flying helmet, not looking at Smith.

"With a hell of a lot of holes and just by the skin of our teeth." Smith paused, then asked softly, "Is anything wrong, Chris?"

"No, sir. Nothing."

Pearce was lying. "This isn't the time nor the place," Smith murmured, "but if you'd like to have a talk—"

"No, sir! There's nothing. Everything's fine." Pearce was quick in his denial, the words jerked out of him.

Now Smith said ruthlessly, but for Pearce's sake, "You look dog-tired and you're on edge. Maybe you're trying to do too much. When you're not on the bridge or flying you're down in the hangar. You're driving yourself too hard." He paused, then: "I don't want you flying again for a while."

Pearce looked at him now, startled, and protested, "Sir! I'm *all right*! It was just that blighter looked a lot further—" His voice was rising but it cut short as he saw Smith watching him and the men in the gig looking up curiously.

Smith said quietly, "You see what I mean." He stood up and swung a leg over the side of the cockpit, picked up the map and notes and dropped his helmet on the seat. "That's an order. No flying." He went down into the gig.

As the bow man shoved off the winch hammered aboard *Blackbird*. Smith sat in the sternsheets of the gig and watched, head turned, as the Short was swung up and inboard, then lowered on to the trolley that waited on the deck. Now they could fold the wings and shove it into the hangar that filled the after half of *Blackbird* from just abaft her second funnel to within fifty feet of her stern. The Short was on that last clear patch of stern deck now. The hangar made her a queer-looking ship. Some wag aboard her had quoted: "There was an old woman who lived in a shoe . . ." *Blackbird* did look a bit like a floating boot but she could make twenty knots and Pearce swore that once you got some way on her she handled like a destroyer. He also admitted that in a strong wind and at slow speed the slab-sided hangar acted like a sail and made her tricky to handle.

Smith turned and faced forward as the gig closed *Dauntless*. She was a light cruiser, commissioned only two years before. Of four thousand tons, she was four hundred and fifty feet long and no more than forty in the beam, slender, graceful and fast; she had steamed twenty-nine knots in her trials and could still do so. Her class of ship was originally built with a pole fore-mast but now that had been replaced by a tripod mast like a battleship's. So in the North Sea those of her class in the Harwich force were known as Tyrwhitt's Dreadnoughts, after the Commodore. That was only a joke because they were a long way from being Dreadnoughts with armour no more than a three-inch thick belt round the hull and only an inch on the deck. She mounted three 6-inch guns, one forward of the bridge and two aft.

Smith was delighted with her, gained fresh pleasure from each sight of her. He knew she had her faults, that to give her speed she was lightly armoured, and when steaming at speed it was hell's own job to work the forward 6-inch because of spray and the seas breaking inboard. He forgave her those, not turning a blind eye to them as a man might to the faults of a beautiful woman he loved, but acknowledging them and re-membering them. Because *Dauntless*'s faults, particularly her lack of armour, could possibly be the death of him and the three hundred and fifty men aboard her.

But that was a million-to-one chance in these waters. The nearest enemy ships were the battle cruiser *Goeben*, light cruiser *Breslau* and the heavy cruiser *Walküre*. All three of these were bottled up in the Sea of Marmara and had been since the early days of the war when they had been caught in the Mediterranean and fled through the Dardanelles to seek sanctuary with Turkey. They flew Turkish colours, were ostensibly Turkish ships, but their commanders and crews were German. They were locked in the Sea of Marmara, an imprisonment that unfortunately tied down a force of British capital ships, there in the Aegean, solely to guard against a break-out, maintaining the weary vigil week in, week out; year in, year out.

Buckley ran the gig neatly alongside *Dauntless* and Smith, grabbing for the dangling ladder, started to climb. On deck a party under the command of Lieutenant Griffith waited to hoist in the gig. A long, dark, soft-spoken Welshman, Griffith had made a brave reputation in the Dardanelles as a forward observer ashore, calling down the fire of the ships in support of the troops. Now he asked, "Any luck, sir?"

Smith answered, "Caught the train on its daily run from Lydda to Jaffa."

"Again? They must be getting fed-up. Give 'em a fright, sir?"

"Not as bad as that Fokker gave me." He grinned at the laughter and climbed up to the bridge.

The two ships headed southwards with *Dauntless* leading, following the line of the coast, searching hopefully for targets for the guns. The land south of Jaffa was sand-dunes, some of them a hundred feet high, stretching inland like a low mountain range, barren, empty. Two hours later the coast was greener and they were passing Gaza, the coastal end of the Gaza-Beersheba line. Smith remembered hearing that the German engineers had settled in at Beersheba to the extent of building themselves a beer-garden. He grinned. There was confidence for you.

Two monitors were anchored five miles out, low in the water like crocodiles, and lobbing 6-inch shells into Gaza as part of the build-up to Allenby's attack. A silver speck in the sky inland and south of Gaza was the observation balloon of Number 49 Balloon Section which was overlooking the

Turkish positions. There was a direct telephone line from the observer swinging in the basket below the balloon to the naval signalling station set up on the shore, so all corrections of the fall of shot could be passed quickly to the monitors. Smoke and winking flame marked the land artillery with Allenby's army, also pounding Gaza. From the ships they could see that army stretching all the way back to the small man-made harbour at Deir el Belah, ten miles to the south, and beyond. A pall of red dust hung permanently over the land, churned up by the hooves of eighty thousand horses, camels and donkeys. This army had built its own railway all the way from Kantara on the Suez Canal as it fought its way across Sinai, and Deir el Belah was its forward railhead. As it laid the railway it also laid a pipeline, so that a large part of its water came from Egypt. It was an army with a tough confidence in itself. Not cockiness; it respected the Germans and Turks for the fighters they were, but it had fought them from Egypt across Sinai into Palestine and beaten them, albeit narrowly, all the way. It was ready to beat them again.

The same mood of confidence ran through Smith's command. There were only six days now to Allenby's attack. Smith was not looking forward to it with eager anticipation because attacks, raids, battles, line-strengthening operations, whatever name you gave them, their first result was a casualty list. But this time the end should be, *had* to be different, not a tragic failure like the Dardanelles nor an unending, murderous struggle like that in France and Flanders, counting losses in millions of wounded and dead, and the gains in scant yards of churned and blasted earth. This time they would achieve a victory, driving the Germans and Turks out of Palestine and bringing nearer the end of the war, the end of the killing, and *Dauntless* and *Blackbird* would play an important part. These last weeks they had proved themselves an efficient team and morale was good.

And yet . . . Smith knew the attack would go in on the 31st, though that was a secret not shared with the rest of his command who only knew it must be soon. But Kressenstein the German commander also knew that it must be soon and would have his own plans. Smith did not speak his doubts aloud, but three years of war had left him wary of over-optimism. Now, as the two ships steamed south, headed for Port Said, he was uneasy.

Adeline Brett, twenty-one years old, small, pretty and blonde, climbed out of the thick oven-heat of the Number Two forward hold of the steam tramp *Morning Star*. The marine sentry, rifle with bayonet fixed slung over one shoulder, turned the key in the padlock and swung open the gate in the barbed wire. Adeline passed through and stood on the deck for a moment, blinking in the strong sunlight after the gloom of the hold, relishing the breeze. The white cotton shirt and drill trousers were plastered to her body with sweat. They were men's naval issue that she had laboriously tailored to fit her but not very well; they were still too big. Now she eased them from her skin and pushed at the dank tendrils of hair clinging to her brow, held up her face to the wind. That was the wind of passage; *Morning Star* was making all of her best speed of twelve knots, smoke billowing from her single funnel, sparks and coaldust and soot raining down aft. The old ship was alone on an empty sea that reflected the sun's glare like a mirror. And she was running for her life.

The girl shivered and hitched at the canvas medical haversack slung from her shoulder and hanging heavy against her hip. She remembered that first dawn at sea when the thump of the explosion and the commotion on deck had brought her running from her bunk to the rail of the *Morning Star*. There she watched wide-eyed as the old destroyer, their escort, back broken by the torpedo, sank in minutes. *Morning Star* had not stopped to help survivors or invite another torpedo. She had run, was still running. And somehow, miraculously, the German submarine had lost her.

Adeline Brett smiled at the young marine sentry with his flat, sailor-like cap on top of his cropped head, and started aft, passing under the bridge and going to her cabin in the superstructure. She had to show an example, that had been instilled into her from childhood. She walked lightly, rope-soled sandals on her feet, near-silent on the deck. In the cabin she opened the haversack, checked its contents and made good its deficiencies of bandages, dressings and pills from a chest she dragged out from under the bunk. Adeline Brett was a nurse.

At the beginning of her career she had cycled down from the big house in Hampshire to the little cottage hospital, just a young girl of good family helping out. But when the war came she went to France where an army surgeon, a veteran of the Boer War and the North-West Frontier, took a liking to her and schooled her. From France she went as a member of a small volunteer team to Gallipoli and then, with what was left of it, to Salonika. There the war and disease took its toll and within a month the team had disintegrated, the others shipped home and she was left alone. Then she found this strange, unhappy battalion.

Now she worked quickly, neatly, packed the haversack so it was ready again, snapped the straps through the buckles and hung it on a hook. She turned the taps to run water into the basin, stripped off the shirt – and saw a flicker of movement at the scuttle as she turned, a crew member's head withdrawn. She swore a soldier's oath and yanked the curtain across.

She washed, worrying about the men of the battalion imprisoned below, dried her face and looked at herself in the small mirror, her reflection shivering with the vibration of the old ship's engines. It was a face burned by the sun, far thinner than that of the young girl of the summer of 1914, the puppy fat of adolescence honed from her by the last three years. She was a woman now. Briefly she wondered at her presence in this tiny, shabby cabin. In that long-ago summer she was the schoolgirl daughter of a rich man, meeting and mixing with the wealthy and famous, one of her uncles a press baron and another in Parliament. She led a leisured, comfortable life, the darling of the big house with its servants, horses and cars. Looking back at that girl was like looking at a stranger, another person in another, incredibly happy existence. Now she was the sole woman aboard this ship and caring for four hundred infantrymen locked away behind barbed wire. So her thoughts came back to those men and her lips tightened, she

thrust away the past and turned away from the mirror. She
consoled herself that by nightfall they should be safe in the
harbour at Port Said.

2

The Battalion

Smith was in his cramped little hutch of a sea-cabin at the back
of the bridge, a seven-foot steel cube holding a bed, a small
desk and a chair. His report lay before him unfinished as he
brooded over Pearce, wondered what ailed him. Should he ask
for *Blackbird*'s captain to be relieved, order him on leave,
request a medical report? But any one of these could prove
damaging to Pearce's career and up to now it had been outstanding. Besides, Pearce's performance of his duties was
adequate. Yet that was not good enough for Smith, a bitter
disappointment after the glowing reports he'd had of Pearce
but equally his disappointment was no grounds for drastic
action. You could hardly relieve a man of his command because he was not outstanding. But Smith should be able to rely
on him totally, and he could not. Something was wrong,
eating away at him, the way he reacted to Smith's questioning
showed that, but whatever it was he was determined to keep it
to himself. Chris had a wife in Cairo he had not seen for weeks
but it could not be that; there were men in these ships who had
not seen wives or families for years.

Smith sighed with frustration, then picked up his pen. They
were bound for Port Said and with luck there would be shore
leave for all of them and that might work a change in Pearce.
Now the report had to be finished before they reached port to
be handed to Admiral Braddock.

Port Said was barely two hours away when the messenger
came running from the wireless office aft. Smith took the
signal, left his desk and the report and went through to the
chart house next door.

"There's a steamer in trouble," he said. "Engines broken down on her way to Port Said. There's a convoy coming down from the north but we're closer and ordered to assist. Course?"

He handed the signal to Henderson the navigator and watched as he plotted the position of the ship on the chart.

Henderson muttered, "*Morning Star*. What's she doing out there on her own?" He pointed at the signal. "And R.D.F. indicates a U-boat in that area!"

A Radio Direction Finding report meant that stations ashore had picked up signals from a U-boat and its approximate position was where the bearing of the signals to the various stations intersected. Smith thought that had probably been the previous night when she had surfaced to charge batteries and could rig her wireless aerial. She must have gone from that area now or she would not have passed by a target like *Morning Star*. But she might well return.

Smith said dryly, "Could complicate things a bit." As he went out on to the bridge he, too, wondered why a solitary ship lay out there without escort.

Dauntless altered course and *Blackbird* followed in her wake, both ships increasing to twenty knots. Even so it would be dusk when they came up with *Morning Star*. When they were still fifty miles away Smith ordered *Blackbird* to launch a seaplane and the Short went booming off across the surface of the sea to lift into the air and go scouting ahead, disappearing over the horizon. It was sent to find *Morning Star* and patrol around her, watching for the U-boat.

Close on two hours later they sighted the Short again, flying in a wide circle at the centre of which lay the steamer. *Morning Star* grew from a speck until they could see her as a tramp of three to four thousand tons: three 'islands' of fo'c'sle, superstructure and poop, with well-decks between. As the sun sank, *Blackbird* stopped to recover the Short but *Dauntless* went on, slipping towards the tramp at ten knots. There was a sea running now, her bow nodding as she rode it.

Ackroyd, the first lieutenant, was on the bridge. Square-shouldered and square-faced, a dour Yorkshireman, he was a 'salt-horse', impatient of fools and paperwork. He already had enormous respect for Smith, who had proved himself a seaman and kept the two ships in almost continuous action for the last two weeks. Ackroyd expected that from what he had heard of the man. But the other rumours of unconventional behaviour, insubordination and scandal, made him wary. Now he said, "Signal from *Blackbird*, sir. The Short reports smoke, probably the convoy, to northward."

Smith nodded, eyes on the ship ahead.

Ackroyd muttered, "What's that row?" He lifted his glasses then said incredulously, "That's wire strung around her hatches and bridge!" Faintly across the sea came the sound of yelling. Then a light flashed from the bridge of the *Morning Star*.

The signal yeoman read: "S.O.S. . . . . Prisoners . . . escaping."

Ackroyd said, "What the hell? *Prisoners?*"

Dauntless was coming up astern of *Morning Star*, would pass her within a cable's length. Smith saw through his glasses what looked like barbed wire laced around her foredeck and bridge and a milling crowd just forward of the bridge, not distinguishable as individual men but a heaving, swaying lump of humanity. He let the glasses fall on their strap and snapped, "Send the sea-boat! Armed!" And as he dashed back to his cabin: "I'll go!"

In the cabin he discarded the glasses, snatched the Webley pistol on its belt from the drawer and buckled it around him, slid down the ladder and ran aft. *Dauntless* was stopped, the way coming off her and pitching in the swell, the cutter already in the sea and her crew gone down into her. He glanced across at *Morning Star* and saw flickering spurts of flame, heard the rattle of rifle-fire. For a moment he stared, then grabbed for the dangling line and dropped hand over hand, turning on the line as *Dauntless* rocked. He caught a fleeting glimpse of *Blackbird* manoeuvring ahead, making ready to pass the tow to the disabled tramp steamer. He wondered, suppose the U-boat turned up while they were trying to take the ship in tow and he was involved in this business, whatever it was? He swore as he dropped into the boat and fell across a thwart. Buckley, holding the line, a rifle slung from one shoulder, apologised: "Sorry, sir."

Smith answered, "Not your fault." Pushing past him Smith snapped at the midshipman in the sternsheets, "Get on with it! Shove off! Oars!"

He sat down with a thump. The cutter thrust away from *Dauntless*'s side, the oars dug in and she headed for the *Morning Star*. He saw the midshipman was Bright, the lumpish one whose clothes were too small for him so the buttons of his jacket strained and his trousers were perpetually at half-mast. Bright? A misnomer? He was the one always falling over things, always bewildered, all at sea. The cutter soared and plummeted as she closed the *Morning Star*. All at sea? True enough today. Smith grinned at his own bad joke but he said, "Smart work, Mr. Bright. You were very quick." He had been.

"Th- thank you, sir."

The evening was cool but Smith saw the boy was sweating, red-faced. Nervousness? Smith murmured, "You're doing very well. Lay us alongside." A little encouragement would not come amiss.

The side of the *Morning Star* was hanging over them now as she rolled. Heads showed over her bulwarks and a Jacob's ladder spilled down to swing above the sea and be grabbed by one of the cutter's crew as Bright yelped, "Oars! Hold her off, there!"

Smith scrambled over the thwarts and pushed between the men to get at the ladder, hung on to it and started to climb. The ladder swung as *Morning Star* rolled. Down in the boat they were holding the bottom of the ladder but Smith was still jerked out over the sea then thrown in against the rusty, riveted plates. He climbed steadily, aware that there had been shooting aboard this ship only minutes ago, that the Webley was in its holster and while the boat's crew were armed there was nothing they could do to help him. Then he saw the faces above him, one topping a seaman's blue jersey and bareheaded but the other wearing the round cap of a marine. He swung a leg over the rail as the marine held out a steadying arm. The marine held a rifle with bayonet fixed in his other hand.

Smith stood just under the bridge. A quick glance aft showed a little group of seamen peering forward. He turned. There was the hold, all the covers on except the two nearest to him and there was the barbed wire. It was strung in a fence across the deck and around the hold and marines were posted by it, a guard on the wired-in hold, rifles with bayonets fixed held across their chests at the high port. Two more marines sat on the deck, one of them wiping at a bloody nose and the other nursing his right wrist. Smith took it all in with one sweeping glance that returned to rest on the captain of marines who stood before him, saluting.

Smith returned the salute and the marine said breathlessly, "Brand, sir."

"Smith. Commanding *Dauntless*. I heard firing a minute ago. What's going on?"

Captain Brand was a muscular young man, broken-nosed. His was a face that might easily break into a wide grin but now he looked a tough nut.

He said, "The prisoners tried to break out."

Smith asked, "Germans? Turks? Where are they from?"

"Salonika, sir. They're—"

"Bulgarians?" In this wide-ranging war an Allied army was fighting the Bulgarians in Salonika in the north of Greece.

Brand dabbed at a cut on his forehead that welled blood and said hesitantly, "They're not *exactly* prisoners, sir, though my orders were to treat them as such in every respect." He saw Smith's exasperation and finished quickly, "They're British soldiers, sir."

British! And not *exactly* prisoners? Smith could see *Blackbird* ahead of *Morning Star* and going slowly astern, closing on the bow of the tramp where a party waited on the fo'c'sle to take the tow. *Dauntless* was patrolling out there, a wraith of a ship in the gathering gloom and there was still the U-boat – but he prompted, "So they tried to break out?"

Brand wiped again at the blood that streamed from the cut on his forehead. "We're quartered right aft. I heard the shouting and ran forward with a few of my men and found the prisoners out on the deck and fighting with the sentries, trying to break past them to get aft, or so it looked. I ordered the men with me to fire over their heads."

Smith said, "And that drove them below." He was staring past Brand at the wire strung around the hold. It had been torn down in a gap of six feet or so.

Brand said flatly, "It did not. More of them kept coming up out of the hold and they were shoving us back and we couldn't get room to use the rifles. But then the major came running up. He got them below again."

"Major?" Smith asked, "What major?"

"Taggart, sir. He's the only officer with them and he's in the hold with them now." Brand paused, then added, "God knows what would have happened if all of them had got out. They'd gone mad!"

"All?" Smith asked, "How many men are you holding below deck in this ship?"

"Close on four hundred, sir." And as Smith turned to peer at him Brand said defensively, "I had my orders, sir."

Smith said, "I want to see."

Buckley and a half-dozen men from the cutter were behind him now, rifles held across their chests, peering suspiciously about the deck. They followed him as he walked to the gap torn in the wire and picked his way through the trodden tangle of it strewn on the deck. There was blood on the wire and the deck. At one side of the gap was a door in the wire, closed and padlocked. There a ladder poked its top rungs out of the hold and Smith moved to it, hearing Brand coming behind him and ordering one of the marines, "Run aft and get some wire to mend this."

Smith leaned over the head of the ladder and peered down into the hold below. He said, "Four hundred men in this hold and the other one forward?"

Brand said, "Yes, sir." He explained, "The dockyard at Malta worked through the night to fit some bunks and hooks for slinging hammocks. There wasn't a troopship available and we had to sail the next morning to embark the battalion at Salonika."

Smith said, "It's a poor substitute for a trooper."

Brand said honestly, "It's bloody awful, sir."

"What did she last carry?"

"I don't know. But she's been a cattle-boat before now."

And still was. Smith stared down into the hold. The ladder led down steeply to the tween-decks. The only light was from the small blue bulbs, police lights, scattered sparsely around the sides of the hold.

He called, "Major Taggart!" His voice echoed in the hold, came back to him a hoarse whisper. He saw faces turned up towards him, faces so close together they were like a mosaic, their eyes catching what light there was.

A voice answered from below: "Yes?"

"I am Commander Smith. His Majesty's cruiser *Dauntless*. I'm coming below."

"Right you are."

Smith swung onto the ladder and started down into the gloom, descending to the 'tween-decks, and the smell of packed humanity rose up around him. The ladder ended in a small clear space of deck, where a score of men were drawn up shoulder to shoulder in four ranks. An officer stood bareheaded in front of them, only a shade taller than Smith but broader, deep-chested, black-haired and black-browed. His tunic hung open, thrown on hurriedly, but the insignia on the cuffs was that of a major. He stood to attention. "John Taggart. Major, Composite Battalion."

Smith held out his hand but stared past him at the other men beyond those who stood drawn up in ranks, the men on the bunks that were built in tiers, four above each other, crouched or perched on the edges of the bunks with backs and heads bent below the overhang of the bunk above. More men squatted on the 'tween-decks and another ladder led down into the hold still further below. Smith saw blue lights down there also, glistening on faces slicked with sweat like oil.

He ran with sweat already. The inside of the hold was airless and humid with the heat of bodies. He asked the major, "Captain Brand only knows your men tried to break out. Can you add to that?"

Taggart was angry, curt. "Two or three of them were standing on the ladder getting a lungful of clean air. Then the girl screamed for help and—"

Smith broke in; "Girl? What girl?"

"This one!"

The voice came from behind and above him and he spun on his heels to see her coming down the ladder, to step on to the deck beside him. She was small, her blonde hair cut short and curled, dressed in a pair of men's white drill trousers and a man's white shirt that hung around her and made her seem even smaller than she was.

Taggart said, "This is Miss Adeline Brett. She's the nurse attached to us. In fact, apart from a dozen orderlies who are little better than stretcher-bearers she's the only medical help we have."

She glanced up at Smith, saw a man surprisingly young for the rank but with a hard eye, and labelled him a career officer, ruthless. She asked coldly, "You command the cruiser? And so you command here?"

And when Smith nodded assent to both questions: "Then you must do something for these men."

It was more order than request, given in a tone that was used to issuing orders. Smith was used to taking them but not from a slip of a girl. He said shortly, "I understand this – disturbance began when you screamed for help."

The girl's brow, lifted fractionally.

"Did it? I know I did scream and I'm sorry. I'd been here in the hold to see to a man who had fallen from the ladder. I was walking aft to my cabin when a man grabbed me. I clawed at his face and pulled away, and because it was a shock, I screamed. But that was stupid. I lost my head for a moment." She thought she was passing it off coolly, and was glad. At the time she had been terrified.

Smith saw the shirt was torn at the neck and showed a white shoulder.

Taggart asked quietly, "Who was it?"

Adeline Brett shook her blonde head. "I don't know. It was dark under the superstructure. He ran away aft."

Taggart growled, "One of the crew!"

"Obviously." The girl did not seem interested. She carried a small haversack slung from one shoulder and now she hitched it around and tugged at the straps that held down the flap. "I came to see if these men need attention. With your permission, John?"

Taggart nodded and she moved to the front rank of the men fallen in behind him, pulled cotton-wool and a bottle from her haversack and said briskly, "Hands, please."

The first man held out his hands. Smith saw them torn and bloody.

He said, "They tore down the wire with their *hands?*"

Taggart glanced sidewise at him and said dryly, "They've been faced by wire before."

Smith looked at them and at the men beyond them, faces stacked in rows as the tiers of bunks climbed the sides of the hold, their eyes watching him. Soldiers. There was nothing apparently unusual about them, except that coming from Salonika they were not dressed in drill shorts and shirts like Allenby's army. They wore thick khaki serge uniforms, trousers bound around with puttees below the knee and down to cover the tops of the ammunition boots. Their tunics were discarded but they still wore their heavy collarless, khaki wool shirts. And they were unusually, eerily quiet. There was no talking, no whistling, no whisper exchanged in the background and Smith knew why from the way they watched him: he was a stranger among them. Taggart and Adeline Brett were accepted, a part, but he was alien. They watched him in a silence that enabled him to hear the voices of the men far above him on deck, even to tell from those voices that the tow was being passed from *Blackbird*.

He asked Taggart, in a voice so low only the other could hear, "Who are these men? Why are they here?"

Taggart glanced at Smith, for a moment seemingly surprised by the question and asked cynically, "You mean, you care why?"

Smith said softly, savagely, "I saw Jutland and other actions before and since, a sight more than four hundred men killed and a lot of them were men I knew and liked. Always it's the best. We're sacrificing the cream of a generation and it sickens me. Now answer my question!"

The cynicism was wiped from Taggart's face. He said, "It's the bloody waste that frightens me." He looked straight at Smith then said slowly, "When you've served with men for a long time – but I don't need to tell you. I'd do anything for them but in fact I can do damn little. Of course you care. My apologies."

"Not needed." Smith thought Taggart was a good soldier and a good man, an instinctive judgment. But Taggart hesitated now, as if uncertain where to begin.

"We were ordered to attack—" He stopped and shook his head and after a moment started again. "It goes back before Salonika. In Flanders some regiments were so badly cut up they virtually ceased to exist, so sometimes they used the survivors to form composite battalions. *This* was a composite battalion, formed from men of a dozen different regiments. Survivors. From Flanders they sent it – us – to Gallipolli and at the end of that they took us across to Salonika." He paused, then amended, "I took them across to Salonika. Our old colonel was killed in Gallipolli and so I was the only officer surviving from the original battalion. We went to Gallipolli with a strength of eight hundred and thirty-four all ranks and we left for Salonika with six hundred and two."

The girl Adeline Brett had a bowl of water now and was swabbing at the torn hands of one of the men. He stood patiently, meekly, as she lectured him: "You should have more sense! All of you! Going mad like that! I can look after myself." Smith believed it. Even so, she looked very small and very young.

Some of the men looked as young. One seemed little more than a boy but there was a bitterness about his young face, the corners of the mouth drawn down, and a cold, flat stare to his averted eyes. Smith noticed him because he sat a little apart from the others, despite the crowding in the hold.

Taggart said, "In Salonika we soon got a new colonel. We didn't see much of him but even then it was too much. I ran the battalion. I'd come to it in 'fifteen when they started it, one of the original survivors, so it really was my battalion. Then we were in position on the Vardar river in Salonika and we were ordered to attack to straighten a salient in the line. It was hopeless, but we went in all the same. We were out on our own, assaulting prepared positions and under cross-fire from machine guns. The attack failed. We went in with nearly six hundred effectives and we came out with four hundred. They pulled us out of the line and in the back area the colonel came up from the rear where he'd been doing God knows what and called a conference of all officers. They assembled at an old farmhouse and the colonel rode up and told them to wait there while he spoke to the men. They were bivouacked a half-mile away and he rode down, called them out on parade and sat on his horse in front of them. He was so drunk he had to use both hands to hold on. He cursed and shouted at them and told them the attack had failed because they'd hidden in holes in the ground and not pressed it home. He called them cowards. And they stood there, what was left of them, dog-tired, some of them near asleep on their feet."

Taggart stopped, his gaze distant now, looking far beyond the confines of the hold. He said. "We don't leave men in the field, nor weapons if we can save them. We'd brought back thirty or forty rifles and pistols belonging to dead and wounded and the men had been told to bring them on to the next parade to hand them in. So. The colonel called them cowards. And someone used one of those pistols to shoot him."

Smith had been watching the young man who sat alone, the only one who did not stare at the stranger. But now his gaze snapped back to Taggart, shocked. "You mean – dead?"

Taggart said sardonically, "Three shots in the chest at close range. They knocked him back off the horse and he was dead before he hit the ground." And as Smith still stared, "That's why they are all aboard this ship."

Smith asked, "All? But surely only one man—"

"Fired the shot." Taggart nodded. "Right. But nobody would admit he saw it. The weapon belonged to a dead man and there was no record of who carried it on to that parade.

That's why the whole battalion was put aboard the *Morning Star* and sent to Cyprus. But the people there didn't want four hundred men who had been involved in mutiny and that is why they are still aboard and bound now for Port Said. The army doesn't know what the hell to do with them." The cynical smile was back on Taggart's face but Smith watched him and thought he was not as hard as he pretended; he cared about these men. He was a year or two younger than Smith, but in the gloom of the hold the lines in his face caught shadows that deepened them.

Smith said, "The officers were at a farmhouse half a mile away?" Taggart nodded, stood with eyes on Smith's face and waiting the next question. Smith asked it. "Then how do you know what happened?"

Taggart's face was expressionless. "I was there, the only officer present because I had a horse and I'd followed the colonel. That's why I'm here now: I didn't see who shot the colonel, either. I'm as much a prisoner as my men."

It was very quiet in the hold when Taggart finished speaking. Smith could hear their breathing, feel the eyes of all of them on him. Now he knew the reason for Taggart's wariness, their watchfulness; they kept a secret to themselves and from the world.

"Commander Smith!" The hail came from Brand, leaning over the hatch. "The ship's master is here, sir, Captain Jeavons."

Smith answered, "I'm coming!"

"So am I," Taggart said grimly. "I want to talk to him."

And Adeline Brett's voice came softly but clearly. "You find it uncomfortable down here, Commander?"

She turned towards him and Smith thought she might be quite a pretty girl if she was not in that mannish get-up. He said, "I've known better places."

"The first couple of days are the worst." She too was watching him now. He wondered what it must be like to spend two days in this prison. She went on, "You are in command. Something must be done for these men."

She was pushing Smith and he did not like it. He replied

shortly, "As you say, I command. And I will decide what needs to be done." He turned away from her and started to climb the ladder but her parting glance had told him she was not impressed.

He climbed out of the hold and picked his way through the barbed wire trampled on the deck. A party of four marines wearing leather gloves were starting to unroll a coil of barbed wire, sizing up the gap, working out how to repair it. Smith growled at them, "Belay that." They halted in the work and glanced at Brand. He looked puzzled, but nodded.

Buckley waited anxiously beyond the wire. As Smith climbed the last rungs, he had seen the big seaman like a shadow above the open hatch but drifting away as Smith came up. Behind Buckley were the half-dozen seamen from the cutter, hefting their rifles and peering curiously at the wire, in a muttering group around the two injured marines.

Smith rasped at them, "Into the cutter!"

The ship's master stood just clear of the shadows under the bridge. He was stocky, broad, the beginnings of a paunch pushing out the front of his old reefer jacket. He might have been fifty, no more, but he looked an elderly man, his wide shoulders sagging. He held out his hand. "Jeavons, sir. Master." And before Smith had released the hand: "*Bloody* business! Thank God you turned up, sir. They sent us away from Salonika with an old destroyer for escort but a U-boat sank her the first night out. Come morning and we got a wireless. They said there was no escort available and we had to crack on at full speed. We were doin' that already but the old *Star* can't better twelve knots. Then the bloody engines broke down and there was reports of a U-boat in the area, and us lying stopped with that murdering gang below forward and the cargo we've got aft. If a torpedo hit that lot—" He ran out of breath and mopped at his sweating face with a handkerchief.

Smith was sorry for him, believed he saw here just one more man worn down by three years of war. Like Pearce? But there was a U-boat out somewhere in the darkness, the hawser had been taken aboard from *Blackbird* and soon she would be ready to take the tramp in tow. He asked only two questions.

"What is this cargo aft?"

"What's left of what we brought out from England. They unloaded the two forward holds at Malta to fit them for the prisoners but the rest is still consigned to Port Said. Those two after holds are crammed with ammunition, high explosive."

"And what's wrong with your engines?"

Jeavons shrugged, indicating plainly that he left the engines to his engineer. "Just steamed too far too fast. The chief said he could get them going again by tomorrow but God only knows what might happen before then. Suppose a torpedo took us —"

"I see your point." Smith cut him off. He thought of the U-boat lurking somewhere close by. "We're taking you in tow and will escort you to Port Said. Send a signal to *Dauntless*, please, to take me off."

Jeavons turned to another elderly officer at his elbow. "Do that, George." George hurried stiffly away and Jeavons went on, "Will you leave a good-sized party aboard, sir? More marines?"

"No, I will not." Smith put that one down decisively. "We'll be escorting you and there's no question of Major Taggart's men trying to take over this ship."

Jeavons burst out, "You weren't on the bridge when they crashed through that wire! You didn't see their faces! They get on my nerves. All the way from Salonika and never a sound out of them, just faces at the hatch watching you! Gives me the bloody creeps!"

Taggart said, hard-voiced, "I'll answer for them. From now on I'll sleep in the hold. But I want to talk to you about the attack on Miss Brett by one of your crew —"

Smith stamped on that, too. "It can wait till we reach port." He turned on Captain Brand. "I want those men out on deck for the rest of the night. Rearrange your wire if you like and post every man you've got as sentries but those men come on deck and stay there."

Brand said hesitantly, "I was given written orders, sir, and they were explicit —"

"No doubt. And you had to carry them out." But Smith

added, "Now I am the senior officer present and in the light of
the conditions I'm giving you fresh orders."

"Thank you, sir." Brand sounded grateful and relieved. "I
don't like this job."

Jeavons grumbled, "You're taking a lot on yourself, Commander."

Smith said pointedly, "Your ship, for one thing. Now I'm
going back to mine." He strode to the rail. *Blackbird* was
ready to tow and *Dauntless* closing on the *Morning Star*.

Taggart appeared beside Smith and said simply, "Thank
you."

Smith shrugged. "The least I could do. They've had a bad
time."

Taggart said wryly, "You don't know the half of it. All their
food is out of tins and has to be cooked in the ship's galley that
was only designed to feed the crew by the ship's cook and he's
only capable of feeding the crew. So it's starvation rations and a
mostly cold mess when they get it."

The cutter was waiting alongside. Smith held out his hand.
"Good night, Major Taggart."

Taggart hesitated, still guarded, but gripped the hand.

Then the flash lit the northern horizon so that their heads
whipped around to stare. Someone on deck said hoarsely,
"God Almighty!"

The flash died away and the sound of the explosion came
rumbling across the sea. Smith said softly, "There's a convoy
out there." He dropped down the ladder to the cutter. Now
they knew where the U-boat was at work. He could understand
Jeavons's overstrung nerves with that cargo of explosives. In
July the *Elaby* had been torpedoed seventy miles south-east of
Malta. She was loaded with munitions, three thousand tons of
T.N.T., and ships a mile away had their bridge windows
blown in by the blast.

Midshipman Bright swung the head of the cutter to point at
Dauntless where she lay stopped less than a cable's length
away and the men bent to the oars, heaving the cutter across
the swell. Once aboard *Dauntless* Smith went to the bridge.
The cruiser was already under way and when he looked across

at *Blackbird* and *Morning Star* he saw the tow tauten as the carrier's screws threshed and both ships moved ahead.

Smith glanced at his watch and realised he had only been aboard *Morning Star* for ten minutes. How must it have been for the men of Taggart's battalion trapped in the hold all those hours she lay disabled, and all the long hours since *Morning Star* sailed from Salonika? They had got away with it, though some poor devils had not. That thumping explosion to the north. . . .

Ackroyd said, "Bit of a mystery ship, sir?"

She was. Smith wondered about the four hundred men aboard *Morning Star*, all that was left of a battalion of nearly nine hundred, and about Taggart. He must know the danger of his involvement in the plot, for plot it was, that could not be denied. An unknown number of men were lying to shield a murder and Major Taggart was a party to it. At the end of the day he would be lucky to be cashiered and dismissed, was more likely to end up behind bars and that was a tragedy because he was a good man.

Smith only said, "Tell you about it later." This was neither the time nor the place. "We'll be rid of her at Port Said." And he would be glad of that.

Lieutenant Cherrett, the signals officer, came hurrying up from the wireless office aft with a signal he had decoded. It was from Braddock: 'Make all speed Port Said. Report estimated time of arrival."

Smith dictated his answer to Cherrett, then prowled out to the wing of the bridge. He could have sat in the high chair bolted to the deck just behind the bridge screen but Braddock had demanded: "Make all speed." Why the sudden urgency when Braddock knew Smith was headed for Port Said anyway? Braddock must also know of the attacked convoy, yet *Dauntless* was not to go to its assistance. What had changed in a few brief hours? Smith was uneasy now and his apprehension kept him shifting restlessly about the bridge as the last of the light faded from the western horizon and night closed around the ships, hurrying as best they could.

3

A Killing Machine

The three ships anchored in the outer harbour of Port Said before the dawn, a light from the shore stuttering instructions and signals as they stole in over the still water. The signal yeoman read them. "'Admiral's coming off now, sir . . . accompanied by General Finlayson.'" And: "That one's for *Morning Star*. 'Stand by to receive engineering party to assist with engines'." And "For *Blackbird*. 'Stand by to receive Short'." That would be the replacement for the seaplane they had lost.

Lieutenant Ackroyd said, as the yeoman read on, signal after signal, "That looks like the admiral's picket-boat now, sir."

It did. A steam pinnace was pushing out from the basin where lay Braddock's armed yacht, *Phoebe*, which he used as his base afloat when running up and down the coast. Smith ordered, "Rig the accommodation ladder. I'll see them in my cabin aft."

The signals were still flickering out: times to be ready for ammunition and supply lighters, water tenders, the oiler for *Dauntless* and the coaling lighters for *Blackbird* and *Morning Star*.

Ackroyd said grimly, "They're in a hurry."

Smith nodded. The authorities were. The men aboard *Dauntless* or *Blackbird* had hoped for and expected leave ashore, but those hopes were to be dashed.

The yeoman was still reading but with a rising note of disbelief in his voice. "'Reference your report of ammunition expended in two weeks to date. This far in excess of expenditure of previous four months. Please state reason.'"

Ackroyd glowered at the yeoman as if he had sent the signal himself. "What the hell?"

Smith grinned at the first lieutenant's annoyance. But as the signal was addressed to Smith and as he and his operations of the past fortnight were responsible for it, he ordered, "Make: 'Found there was a war on.'"

The laughter followed him as he dropped down the ladders from the bridge to fo'c'sle and then to the upper deck. He strode aft, past the parties gathering to receive the oiler, the fenders being slung over the side, the engine-room ratings coming up with spanners, hammers and other gear. Another party was rigging the accommodation ladder on the starboard quarter, close by where the marine sentry stood guard at the door of Smith's main cabin in the superstructure. The ladder was rigged just in time for the admiral's pinnace, swinging around the stern of *Dauntless* and slipping in alongside.

Braddock was first up the ladder, nearly seventy but climbing steadily, not stiffly. He was broad, solid, black-bearded, almost always stern and now grim. Smith saw that look and knew there was trouble.

General Finlayson followed Braddock. Smith had met him once at his headquarters in Deir el Belah where he commanded the army on the coast. He was a Scot, stocky, with a face burned brick-red by the sun, tough and competent, a fitting commander for an army that had fought hard and won. He did not like Smith, who sensed it. And Braddock had told him: "Because you're too unorthodox. But he accepts men on results; he's accepted the Australians. So don't you worry."

Smith remembered this as he met Finlayson's cold stare, was certain the general had not yet changed his opinion of him.

Behind Finlayson came one more officer, a lieutenant-colonel of a line regiment, a man of Smith's height, wiry, lean and brown.

Smith led them to his after cabin and saw them seated. This main cabin of his was V-shaped, as the superstructure tapered towards the stern but it widened to better than twenty feet. It was really a suite: a sleeping cabin and bathroom opened from it. There was a dining table, sideboard, desk, cupboards, several armchairs. Smith never saw it while at sea. The scuttles were closed now and, though whirring ventilators circulated the air, it was stuffy in the cabin; all of them sweated.

Braddock said, "Saw your wireless reports. You've been busy."

"Yes, sir," answered Smith.

Braddock only nodded approvingly but that was enough. He set high standards. Now he glanced at Finlayson.

The general took his cue. "You know that Allenby has a tough nut to crack, that he faces an army of equal or greater size, defending entrenched and fortified positions. You may know also that we and the Turks have committed every man we can to the Gaza-Beersheba front; there can be no question of reinforcement by either side."

He glanced questioningly at Smith, who nodded. He knew the scales were finely balanced.

Finlayson went on, "We've received a report from London but it came out of Germany. God knows how, but it's rated as authentic. The Germans trained their crack Asia Corps at Neuhammer in Silesia. Now they've trained another similar force. It's of brigade strength, some five thousand men and is not to be spread out through the Turkish armies simply to give technical stiffening. It is a unit that will function as a unit, with its own guns and a very high proportion of machine guns. They are all highly-trained, crack troops and because of that and their high fire-power you can treble their numbers when you assess them as a fighting force. The Germans call them the Afrika Legion."

Finlayson paused. Smith waited, knowing what was coming, feeling the sweat itch on his face. Finlayson said, "The Afrika Legion is on its way, headed for the Gaza-Beersheba line."

Smith looked now at Braddock. Finlayson had given the explanation but the admiral would give Smith his orders.

Braddock said simply, "Find it. The Afrika Legion is coming from Germany by rail, and will pass through Syria and

Palestine the same way. You must find it. If – when – it arrives in this theatre of the war, we must know."

Smith was on the point of saying, "We'll try." But he did not. No marks would be awarded for effort. The Afrika Legion was a killing machine. It could turn the potential victory into a stalemate if not a defeat, the campaign into a long, bloody war of attrition like France and Flanders and the Dardanelles. He said, "Yes, sir."

Braddock asked, "No questions?"

"No, sir."

Braddock grunted, stirred uneasily in the chair, then went on. "Colonel Edwards, here, will also be looking for the Legion. He can pass among the Arabs, done it before. You'll put him ashore south of Jaffa tomorrow night. That will fit in with your other task of escorting *Morning Star* to Deir el Belah. Take her there and then go on and land Edwards. If her engines aren't repaired in time, tow her again."

Finlayson said grimly, "*Morning Star* is another of my responsibilities."

Smith glanced at Edwards. The lieutenant-colonel was sprawled in his armchair. He had a hooked nose that only gave added strength to his handsome face. There was a rakish air about him of high self-confidence and his dark eyes stared piercingly. Smith disliked him on sight.

"I'll find the Legion if it's there," Edwards said arrogantly. "Just have to grease a few palms, maybe cut a throat or two but I'll find it."

Finlayson snapped, "I want information, not senseless killing!"

Edwards smiled. "All part of the game, sir."

"It's not a *game*!"

"I'm sorry, sir," said Edwards but he neither sounded nor appeared contrite. "It's a war. But it's a war behind the lines, too, so if the odd throat gets cut you can't be surprised."

Finlayson eyed him with open distaste but then a knock came at the door and it opened to show Lieutenant Ackroyd, cap under arm and face without expression as he looked at Smith. "Sorry to interrupt, sir, but there's a boat alongside from *Morning Star*. Her master and a young lady have come aboard. She says her name is Miss Adeline Brett and that the general will know of her. She insists on speaking to him, sir."

Smith's lips tightened. That damned girl! He glanced at Finlayson.

The soldier said evenly, "I've heard of the young lady. How does she know of me? But I can spare a few minutes."

Smith nodded at Ackroyd who turned and beckoned, stood aside and announced in his flat Yorkshire accent, "Captain Jeavons and Miss Brett."

They entered the cabin, the girl leading the way, dressed in clean white shirt and drill trousers. Jeavons came behind her, snatching off his cap to show sparse grey hair and peering about him uneasily.

Finlayson, standing, indicated his chair. "Miss Brett. I am General Finlayson."

Adeline Brett sat in the chair stiffly upright, hands on its arms, and said as stiffly, "I believe you hold the responsibility for the ordering of the *Morning Star*."

Finlayson nodded. "That is correct. But how did you—?"

The girl broke in impatiently, "When a general comes out here before dawn it's a reasonable assumption that he has authority. I watched you come aboard through glasses."

"I see," Finlayson said dryly. He nodded towards Smith and the others. "This is Commander Smith's ship and his cabin, but if you wish to speak privately I'm sure he will—"

"That isn't necessary." The girl shook her blonde head. "I'm glad Commander Smith is present because he will be able to verify some of the things I have to say about the conditions aboard *Morning Star*. May I go on?" And when Finlayson nodded she told him about those conditions, the heat, the crowding, the barbed wire and the bad food. She paused to glance at Smith for confirmation. When he nodded impassively she finished, "Those men are held prisoner although no charge has been brought against a single one of them. They were turned away from Cyprus. Now we understand the ship is ordered to sail again, to some place called Deir el Belah. While we're talking those men are locked below in the holds. You might have noticed a certain stuffiness in this cabin. You should try five minutes in that hold!" She was leaning forward now, hands gripping the arms of the chair, voice lifted in anger.

Finlayson was leaning back against the table, his face showing only patience. He asked, "And what do you want of me?"

"That you give the order to bring them ashore, get them off that damned ship!"

Finlayson shook his head, answered quietly but positively. "No. I am aware of the facts of the case, such as are known and I'm sure you are aware of them. Those men were embarked on *Morning Star* under orders and I am bound by those orders. Until they are countermanded or new circumstances alter the case, then the battalion stays aboard *Morning Star*."

Adeline Brett took a breath. "Very well. Then there *are* some other facts of which you may *not* be aware. My father—"

Finlayson pushed away from the table. He did not raise his voice but there was an edge of anger to it as he broke in, "I know about your father and your uncle, *and* their friends, *and* their influence in Parliament and the press. I know you got aboard that ship by threatening to use what influence you and they possess at home but that weighs nothing with me. This job of mine brings difficult decisions but people like you make some of them easier. I will not be blackmailed. I have always tried to do my duty without fear or favour."

There was a moment of silence. Only the ventilators hummed as if the ship were breathing around them while the soldier glared at the girl who now sat white faced.

Then Finlayson said flatly, "Good-day to you, Miss Brett." And that was final, dismissal.

She stood up and went to the door and Smith moved quietly to open it. As she passed him he said softly, "Wait." He did not know if she heard him. He turned and found Edwards at his back.

The colonel lounged past him to the door and drawled, "I'll just get a breath of air." But as he went out his eyes were looking for the girl hungrily.

Smith turned reluctantly back to the cabin. Behind him

Jeavons was saying nervously, "None of that was my idea, but it's right that I want to put those men and the rest o' the cargo ashore. See, sir, I know my agents will have another waiting for me at Tangier in no more than a week."

Finlayson said, "You have my sympathy, captain. But the agents acting on behalf of your owners are contracted to deliver that cargo, and that includes the battalion, at a place to be stipulated. There was no time clause. That contract means that the *Morning Star* is under orders as much as any ship of war, virtually hired by the Admiralty."

Braddock nodded.

Jeavons looked from one to the other, then said heavily, "Very well. But you'll give me your word that you'll take off these men as soon as possible? Because as I told Commander Smith only last night, they get on my nerves. They're that quiet and the way they watch you . . ."

Finlayson said, "You have my word." Jeavons put on his cap and left.

Finlayson shifted in his seat and muttered, "That damned Edwards – drink and women! Whenever he gets to Cairo it's one damned woman after another."

His gaze fell on Smith and he was momentarily embarrassed and looked away. Then he cleared his throat and turned his cold eye on Smith again. "You endorsed those comments made by Miss Brett regarding the conditions aboard *Morning Star*. Maybe you think I'm being unnecessarily severe? That I could turn a blind eye to my orders? Remember this: one of those men shot and killed his commanding officer and some of them, if not all, know who fired the shots. Yet every one has denied knowledge and that under oath. Some or all were therefore involved in mutiny under arms, if not in the face of the enemy then certainly on active service." Finlayson jabbed a stubby finger at Smith. "Remember this, too: There was mutiny in the French army this summer. Now I don't believe *this* army will mutiny, not any part of it. But suppose we put Taggart's battalion ashore here, even under guard, and the questions were asked: Why are they held? What have they done? How many are guilty? How many are innocent and why are *they* held? I don't want this army asking those questions, doubting, looking over its shoulder because that could be fatal. It has come too far, suffered too much and I won't have its sacrifices wasted. I have to choose between the army and the battalion and I've chosen. Clear?"

"Yes, sir." Smith paused but would not let it go. "This battalion, sir. Can I ask for something?"

Finlayson said, exasperated, "Good God! Another one?"

Smith said, "Sir, when I went aboard *Morning Star* I countermanded some of the orders given to Captain Brand."

"You did, eh?" Finlayson scowled at Braddock, who in turn scowled at Smith.

Who pressed on doggedly, "It seemed to me the conditions aboard that ship were unfit for animals, let alone men."

Finlayson's lips tightened but Smith persisted. "When I boarded *Morning Star* it was because the men had broken out of the hold despite the wire and the marines. What really held them back and what holds them now is their discipline and the presence of the one officer with them, Major Taggart. There's no reason they should be kept in the hold, nor that the food should be so bad."

And he argued, until Finlayson looked at him thoughtfully and nodded assent and Smith said, "Sir, if the orders could be given before *Morning Star* sailed—"

Finlayson waved him into silence and said dryly, "I heard you don't waste time. I'm going ashore now and I'll have my aide see to it."

"Thank you, sir. Er – would you care for a drink?"

Finlayson said, "Thanks, I think you owe me one."

As he and Braddock were savouring neat Scotch Smith remembered Edwards and the girl and excused himself.

Out on the deck there was disciplined commotion among the oiling parties as the oiler came alongside. The ammunition lighter would arrive as soon as the oiler cleared. Jeavons waited disconsolately at the head of the accommodation ladder under the small light there, but Smith had to search for Adeline Brett, finally spotting her in the darker shadow of the superstructure and almost hidden by Edwards.

He was leaning over her but as Smith stepped up the girl laughed and Edwards eased away. His teeth showed in a smile as he said to her, "Another time."

"Possibly," she answered, "but very unlikely."

Edwards countered easily. "All things are possible."

Then Bright appeared on the run, halted before Edwards and panted, "First Lieutenant sent me to show you your cabin, sir. Your bag's gone below."

Edwards said acidly, "There was a bottle or two in that bag. I trust your heavy-handed sailor didn't break them. But lead on, little admiral." He followed Bright forward.

Adeline Brett faced Smith boldly, Edwards was dismissed from her mind. "I suppose you think that was a dirty trick? The way I tried to bully Finlayson?"

Smith answered, "It wasn't bullying. It was attempted blackmail and it was a dirty trick."

"I'm not sorry. I did it for the battalion."

"The end justifying the means?"

"Any means." She waited but when Smith did not answer she pressed him, "Well?"

He said, "The other day I had to order a seaplane to search for a train. They found the train but the seaplane was shot down. The pilot and observer we got back unharmed but suppose they had been killed? What should I write to their next-of-kin? So sorry, but the end . . .?"

She peered up at him. "You had to send them, of course, even knowing there was a risk."

"Yes."

"Then surely that was a case of the end—"

Smith said harshly, "I just mistrust the – the catch phrase. In war one man's means can mean another man's bloody end."

Adeline Brett was silent for a moment. "I agree with you." Then she smiled lop-sidedly, "I also agree with me, but then I'm a woman."

Smith stared down at her and thought he would not disagree with that.

Her eyes fell and she said quietly, "You asked me to wait."

He had forgotten but now he cleared his throat and said,

"The general has been thinking it over. The battalion will be allowed on deck once *Morning Star* is clear of the harbour and he's arranging for fresh food to be sent aboard and one or two other things." Then as she stared at him he said hurriedly, "Here they come . . . you'd better get away. Jeavons looks to be ready."

Braddock stood at the door of the cabin, peering about him. Smith took the girl's arm and handed her over to the master of the *Morning Star*, saw them both started down the ladder. Her voice came up to him, quiet but clear, "Thank you."

Braddock appeared at Smith's elbow. "Where's Edwards?"

"Gone to his cabin, sir."

Braddock muttered, "Extraordinary coincidence."

"Sir?"

Braddock shrugged. "I – know something of his background . . ." He paused then growled, "But I can't speak of that. All I can tell you is that the bloody man's a show-off. All that casual talk of cutting throats is said for effect but it's also true. He's a killer. Finlayson detests him because he's a long way from your conventional army officer."

Smith thought that Finlayson did not like *him* either, because he too came with a reputation of being unorthodox. Did Finlayson lump the pair of them together, he and Edwards? He did not like the thought of that.

But Braddock was rumbling on. "He's a brigand. Before the war he was some sort of trader all around these parts. I don't know what his trading was but he certainly didn't learn to use that knife in the British army."

Smith asked, "Knife?"

Braddock grunted. "You'll see. I've seen him in his Arab get-up." But now Finlayson waited at the head of the accommodation ladder and Braddock went on quickly, "Two bits of news for you: you'll be getting some help when the balloon goes up. There's an old French battleship coming from Malta: *Maroc*. She's slow but she mounts four 12-inch guns and she'll be under your orders. The other thing is that we've heard the three German ships in the Sea of Marmara have been exercising but they're back in port now." That was *Goeben*,

Breslau and the big cruiser *Walküre*, which had run through the Dardanelles to seek sanctuary with Turkey early in the war. "Three of them locked in there. Thank God. Still, it must be hard. . . . The Germans have some fine seamen."

"Yes, sir. Particularly in the U-boats."

Braddock cocked an eye at him. "You know that's damned near heresy? That they're supposed to be treacherous and cowardly?"

Smith grinned at him, knowing his man now. "Yes, sir."

Braddock turned towards the ladder, but paused to say seriously, "You've got to find this bloody Afrika Legion if it comes. We've got to know. It could scupper the whole campaign."

"I know."

Braddock nodded, strode to the ladder and went down after Finlayson.

The day came, the oiler cast off and was replaced by the ammunition lighter. The men of *Dauntless* and *Blackbird* toiled on, the latter coaling ship from a lighter alongside. At Smith's orders Ackroyd had sent a large party over from *Dauntless* to help with the back-breaking, filthy job of coaling ship. They had to break into the hard-packed coal in the lighter, shovel it into sacks to be swung up by the derricks, ten sacks to a strop, and then poured into *Blackbird*'s bunkers. The ship lay almost hidden in a cloud of coaldust that drifted on the wind.

Ackroyd said from the heart, watching *Dauntless*'s hands go to work at cleaning ship as the ammunition lighter eased away, "Thank God we burn oil." Like most of them, he'd had his share of coaling ship.

Smith had been busy with the chart, had made his plans, and now sent for Pearce and the Gang from *Blackbird*. The Gang were the four flying crews, an exclusive little club who messed together aboard *Blackbird* and went ashore together.

They climbed the accommodation ladder and saluted. The four pilots were Cole, Bennett, Kirby and Rogers, all Flight Lieutenants of the Royal Naval Air Service. And the observers, three of them lieutenants but volunteers from the army: big Hamilton of the Artillery, Wilson of the Norfolks, and Burns, fourth generation of family that had served in the India Army, from the Rajputs. Last was a small midshipman called Maitland.

Another lighter was towed alongside *Blackbird* by a steam tug and she carried on her deck a Short seaplane, wings folded back along the fuselage.

Ackroyd said with distaste, "What is *that*? And who painted it? Joseph?"

Pearce, pale and weary, answered shortly, "I suppose she is a bit gaudy."

Ackroyd muttered, "*Bloody* funny colour."

Smith thought 'bloody' was right; the fabric of the wings and fuselage was mottled red to pale pink, as if someone had tried to wash it clean of blood with only limited success.

Pearce explained, "She's a rebuild job. I went ashore to sign for her and it was still dark. They told me she'd been badly shot up and they've put her together again. Still needs work done on her engine but I said we'd do it; couldn't wait. I can only suppose some colouring got into the stuff the riggers slapped on her. The chaps I took ashore with me spotted some initials painted just below the cockpit. You can just see them through the dope: D.L.L.R. So they've christened her Delilah."

Ackroyd led Pearce and the fliers into the main cabin. Smith paused for a minute and watched as the Short was hoisted aboard *Blackbird*. If the plane had had to be rebuilt he wondered grimly what had happened to the pilot with the initials D.L.L.R. He turned and entered the cabin as Pearce said, voice high and impatient, "I know you don't believe me and I don't give a damn! There's a day not far off when there will be aircraft with an accurate bomb-sight and big enough, fast enough to sink capital ships! I'm telling you—"

He broke off as Smith entered the cabin. Chris was scowling, running fingers through his hair. Smith watched him and wondered. Sink capital ships? The rest of the Gang looked embarrassed at what they thought were Pearce's wild flights of fantasy, but Smith was not so sure. He grinned at the pilot.

"But for the moment, Chris? If you attacked a capital ship in a Short?"

The Gang chuckled and Flight Lieutenant Cole said "Pray, for one thing."

Pearce shrugged. "To hit a ship under way you'd have to sit a Short on the funnel and you'd be shot to bits trying it. Unless—" He stopped.

Smith prompted, "Unless—?"

But Pearce would not be drawn. "You'd have to be lucky."

He had been about to say something else but Ackroyd's dour Yorkshire eyes were on him.

Smith let it go. "Sit down, gentlemen, please." He told them about the Afrika Legion, and the task set *Dauntless* and *Blackbird*. "But particularly you. If the Afrika Legion comes then we – you – must find it." Though if they failed, Smith would have to answer for it. He looked at the Gang, ordinary young men of assorted sizes, from the big and beefy Hamilton to the diminutive Maitland, but all with serious, selfconscious expressions now. So he grinned at them. "Well, don't look so worried, for God's sake! You're only going to fly. I'm not asking you to do any real work like the rest of us aboard these ships."

That sent them back to their ship in a more cheerful mood but Smith knew the task he was setting them and its dangers, and that he would have to answer for them too, if only to himself.

He went to the bridge and Henderson said, "That was bad luck." And when Smith looked at him questioningly: "When they were hoisting that Short aboard *Blackbird* it swung and knocked one of the hands from the lighter into the harbour. Poor chap drowned."

Smith shook his head. It was a reminder that even in peaceful pursuits men died from a moment's inattention. He himself had watched the Short hoisted in and had not seen the accident. The man had slipped unnoticed out of life. He hoped Pearce was collecting the evidence. Inevitably there would have to be a court of enquiry.

Morning Star signalled that her engines were ready to take her to sea and the party of engineers climbed down into their boat alongside her and headed for the shore. *Blackbird* completed with coal and bombs, the lighter was towed away and the bloody Delilah was wheeled into the hangar and out of sight. A bare few hours after entering Port Said Smith led his little squadron to sea again. As he stood on the bridge of *Dauntless* he was grimly aware that the mood of confidence was gone, the anticipated victory now in jeopardy. They had to find the Afrika Legion.

He walked out to the starboard wing of the bridge as *Dauntless* turned on to the northerly course that would take her to Deir el Belah and beyond, to Edwards' landing south of Jaffa. Astern of her, and ahead of *Blackbird*, steamed the S.S. *Morning Star* with her cargo of ammunition and the silent, watching, waiting men of Taggart's battalion. He wondered which might prove the more explosive.

4

The Search

In the blazing heat of the afternoon of that day, the 25th October, *Morning Star* plodded into the anchorage at Deir el Belah. Smith watched from the bridge of *Dauntless* as the tramp passed inside the anti-submarine nets that formed the anchorage while *Dauntless* and *Blackbird* steamed on, altering course a few points to port so that they headed seawards as if bound for Cyprus. That was for the benefit of the Turks watching from Gaza.

There were many ashore at Deir el Belah who watched *Dauntless* slip by close enough inshore for them to see the clean lines of her. One was Sapper Charlie Golightly of the Royal Engineers. He was the driver of an engine that puffed up and down between Kantara on the Suez Canal and the railhead at Deir el Belah, twelve hours each way, hauling a train of open trucks. He brought supplies and reinforcements up from Kantara and took down wounded and leave men. The engine and its train stood in a siding now, close by the big sand-dunes that lined the shore, while a score of yards away Charlie reclined in a deckchair under the shade of a clump of palms. In that shade he was sweating only slightly. Short, moon-faced, bald and fifty, plump and fond of his beer, only the heat and his work prevented that plumpness running to obesity. He was well-dressed in tailored khaki drill, well-fed and comfortable. He sucked at a cigar and a glass of cold beer stood in easy reach by his chair.

Albert had brought him the beer, chilled in the box of ice Charlie had taken aboard at Kantara. Albert had also cooked the meal and was now washing the dishes. He was an Egyptian boy of fifteen or so with a wide smile who was Charlie's fireman when he drove the train, his cook and servant when he was at ease. Charlie had named the boy Albert. "Never mind what your Ma called you. Now you're with me you'll have a Christian 'andle. You do as I tell you an' we'll get on all right. If things had worked out different I might ha' had a son o' your age now." The probability was that Charlie did have a son or daughter of that age and several more in ascending and descending order of seniority. Somewhere.

Now, through a gap in the dunes, he watched *Dauntless* pass.

Albert sat back on his heels, wiped wet hands on a rag and smiled up at Charlie. "Fine ship."

"Fine ship?" Golightly sucked on the cigar. "Ah! Ships and women. Either one'll get you into deep water. Steer clear of them both, except when you has to – if you see what I mean."

Albert said seriously, "Like the French woman in Port Said."

Charlie nodded. "A feller needs a bit o' home comfort after the day's work."

That made him thoughtful. The day's work? It was time he gave some thought to it. He clasped his hands under his round, hard little belly and pondered logistics. Militarily speaking, Sapper Golightly's only concern with logistics was driving his train, but his present interest was not military. Charlie was in his thirty-second year of service, his thirty-fourth if you counted his time as a bandboy, and in all that time he had neither sought nor been offered promotion. He was without ambition but for many years now he had thought of the future and made provision for his old age. From a succession of stores and depots and while transporting supplies between them he had taken his toll. He would have his pension, of course, and the rents from half-a-dozen little houses he had bought in Bermondsey over the years. But what he yearned for, home and income both, was a pub. In 1914 it had been almost within his grasp and Charlie was ready to call it a day, but the army was not; there is no discharge in a war. So he decided to make the profitable best of a bad job.

So – logistics? His gaze rested on his tent in which were stacked souvenirs of the war at the front, from Turkish helmets to spurs, water-bottles and swords, bayonets and pistols. From there his gaze drifted to the engine with its tender piled high with coal. There was a false bottom to the tender that could be loaded from underneath. In Port Said there were plenty of buyers for souvenirs and from Port Said he brought back scotch, purchased remarkably cheaply because it was stolen, to trade for more souvenirs. He was making his profit but he knew that soon the army would move forward, the trip from the front would lengthen in distance and time and thus reduce his turnover. He was thinking that the answer might be to concentrate on the smaller souvenirs that fetched a higher price, like the pistols . . .

Lieutenant William Jackson of the Australian Light Horse looked up from the letter he was writing, and also watched *Dauntless* steam past Deir el Belah. He was a long-armed, long-legged six-foot folded on to an ammunition box, writing pad on his knee. He was not wearing the badges of his rank nor anything else, except a pair of cotton drawers and the Australian wide-brimmed slouch hat tipped forward to shade his eyes. He was burned nearly black by the sun and he needed a shave. He glanced at his watch, remembering that his troop was detailed for a working party and bawled, "Troopsarn't Latimer! Get 'em out on parade!"

From the tents around him came cursing, obscenities, grousing. No one appeared but a voice bellowed, outraged, "What the flamin' hell are you at, Jacka? We've done enough this week! To hell with it!"

Jackson took no notice. It was always the same so he always called them ten minutes before he wanted them. He stared at the palms and the glint of sunlight on the little lake they surrounded. Water. The horses, called Walers because most of them came from New South Wales, had gone mad when they finally fought their way out of the desert of Sinai and found Palestine and grass. The army had been told that in this coming battle they would have to go for twenty-four hours or more without water. Well, they were used to that after Sinai. Getting used to it had not been funny.

He returned to the letter, writing neatly, quickly. At home before the war he had worked on his father's sheep station and had grown up on horseback. The Australians were all natural horsemen. He finished the letter: "Your loving son, Bill".

Men were emerging from the tents now. Some were in riding-breeches, others in shorts. Most wore leggings and others made do with puttees. All were in sleeveless flannel shirts or singlets. When they had first come out of Sinai and supplies had caught up with them, they drew what new clothing there was, but unending patrols and skirmishes had set them back again. Jackson himself owned a tattered tunic and was lucky because many officers did not. Some of the men were clean-shaven but most were as black-jowled as he was. But every man had his rifle, bayonet and bandolier of ammunition, all his equipment and all of it clean and serviceable. And there was nothing wrong with the Walers, the troopers saw to that.

Jackson dragged on his breeches and reached for his boots, thinking that the troop had lost a couple of horses in the last stunt, a savage tussle with a patrol of Turkish cavalry. No remounts had come up but there was an English Yeomanry Regiment a mile down the road. When it got dark he could take some of the boys down there . . .

A clear night and the sky filled with stars. Smith came on to the bridge of *Dauntless* as she thrust steadily through a smooth sea, heading for the coast of Palestine south of Jaffa at an easy ten knots. That enemy coast lay five miles ahead of them, the long, low line of it hidden by the night. *Blackbird* kept station a cable's length astern. The two ships had steamed out of sight of the land and only turned to close it when the sun set.

Henderson emerged from the chartroom and said, "Twenty minutes, sir."

Smith nodded then asked, "Has Colonel Edwards been told?"

Ackroyd, who had the watch, said sourly, "I sent young

Bright to wake him ten minutes ago. He told Bright to go to
hell."

Ackroyd had extended the hospitality of the wardroom to
Edwards but he had not taken it up. Instead he sat with his
boots up on the bunk in the little cabin they gave him, the
curtain drawn back so that any who passed saw him steadily
making his way through the bottle of whisky that stood at his
elbow with a glass and a jug of water. He did not use much
water and stared up at the deckhead, lips pursed in an inaud-
ible whistle. By noon the bottle had been empty and he slept.

Now Ackroyd muttered, "He's a rum chap. Saw me looking
at the bottle and said: 'Won't get another chance for a while,
old boy.'" It was only a moderate imitation; Ackroyd's Yorkshire accent could not cope with the Home Counties drawl of
the colonel but he had got the huge confidence right. He said,
"But whatever he's got on his conscience, it doesn't trouble
him. He sleeps like a baby."

Smith wished he had Edwards's facility. He had tried to
sleep in his little sea-cabin abaft the bridge and failed miserably, had lain with his eyes wide open and thought about the
Afrika Legion, seeing with his mind's eye the trains packed
with the tough, élite soldiers hurrying towards Palestine.

He asked, "Is Jameson ready?" Lieutenant Jameson was a
boxer, a tough middleweight, quick and cool. More impor-
tantly he was a good officer, a fine seaman and was to command
an armed party in the cutter to set Edwards ashore.

"Yes, sir."

"I'm going along."

Ackroyd hesitated a moment, not liking the idea, then said
reluctantly, "Aye, aye, sir."

"You know what to do. Patrol till we return but if something goes badly wrong and we don't come off again then you
report to the admiral and carry on with the search for the
Legion as ordered. No rescue attempts."

"Aye, aye, sir." Ackroyd did not like that, either, but saw the
sense of it. If one armed party was taken then the coast would
be alerted and any rescue attempt would be suicidal.

Smith said, "I'm going for a word with Edwards." He turned

61

and went to his sea-cabin at the back of the bridge, took the Webley revolver from the drawer in the desk and belted it around his waist. He left the bridge, made his way aft and climbed down the ladder to the wardroom flat, then walked along to the cabin they had lent to Edwards. The curtain was drawn across the doorway now and Smith called, "Colonel Edwards?"

"Who is it?"

"Commander Smith."

"I'm changing. Come in."

Smith entered and drew the curtain behind him. Edwards stood by the desk, shirtless, tunic in hand. He scowled at Smith but that was only an edge of temper. Smith had seen many a drunk and, whisky or no, Edwards was stone-cold sober. He asked, "Getting close?"

"Less than twenty minutes." Smith did not like soldiers who were enjoying the hospitality of his ship to swear at his junior officers as Edwards had done at Bright, but this was not the time to make the point. Edwards was about to embark on a dangerous mission. Instead he said, "We'll put you ashore where you indicated. If there's anything else we can do—?" He let the question hang.

Edwards shook his head. "I've got all I want. But you can put my case ashore next time you're in Port Said. There'll be my uniform, boots and other kit in it." He tucked a silver cigarette case into the pocket of the tunic, dipped his hand into the suitcase and held up a full bottle of whisky. "And this. So tell your chaps to go easy will you?"

He caught Smith's deliberately neutral stare and laughed hoarsely. "You fight your war, Commander, and I'll fight mine. I suppose Finlayson told you about me. I'm a temporary gentleman, not Finlayson's style at all. Before the war I got a banker's draft from home once a quarter so long as I stayed out here. There'd been some trouble with a girl or two so I was thrown out. The draft was just enough to exist on, so I started dealing in any damned thing that would turn a few quid and let a man live decently. But after the war it'll be different. I've got friends among the Arabs and they'll be grateful to anybody who helps them kick out the Turks. I'll be somebody around here. That's what my war is about." He pointed a finger. "And the women? Look, when I get out of that bloody desert I look for a woman. I need a woman. I risk my neck every minute I'm out there so I think I'm entitled to all I can get. Money. Influence. And women." He paused, then: "So?"

But Smith only said, "You've got about ten minutes." He pushed through the curtain and climbed to the upper-deck.

He waited by the rail with Jameson and the cutter's crew, all armed with pistols. Buckley was among them – Smith had not ordered Buckley to come so he'd taken it on himself. Jameson had probably accepted that where his captain went, so also went the big leading hand.

Dauntless was swinging gently to port, turning her starboard side to the distant coast that Smith now thought he could see as a low shadow against the night sky. Turning also to make a lee for the cutter though there was little wind. The way was coming off her; she was stopping. The shore was in darkness but to the north-east there were lights and they marked the old Arab port of Jaffa, the town on its little hill. And beyond them . . .

Intrigued, Smith lifted the glasses that hung on his chest, found the lights and beyond them another that moved steadily, like a slowly descending star, towards the lights of the town. He realised what it was; the train from Lydda running down the last long gentle slope from the crest of the hill above the little township of Tel Aviv. So now that they'd had enough of being shelled and bombed on the daylight runs they were running at night. Probably that last bombing raid of Pearce and himself had been the final straw. He grinned briefly, finding satisfaction in that, but then the grin faded. It was a different game now. There was the Afrika Legion.

Someone among the crew of the cutter sucked in a startled breath, then muttered, "Blimey! Thought it was a ghost!" Edwards came to them out of the gloom, feet silent on the deck, wrapped in white robes from head to foot. He halted by

Smith, who now saw the belt around his waist, the knife, in its sheath, thrust through it. Edwards saw the glance and drew the knife, hefted it casually. It was long and curved, wicked looking. Edwards's teeth showed and his eyes glittered below the headdress as he said "The only friend I trust."

Smith said shortly, "Put it away and don't fool about."

Edwards chuckled, but he obeyed.

Dauntless was stopped and the cutter swung out, lowered. Jameson had had a net thrown over the side and the crew climbed down it and into the boat, Edwards following them easily and Smith went last. He settled in the stern sheets beside Jameson with Edwards alongside him and the cutter got under way. So did *Dauntless*, her grey steel hull sliding past and away as the cutter headed for the shore, and astern of *Dauntless* went *Blackbird* with her great, looming hangar.

The crew of the cutter rowed steadily, knowing they had a two-mile pull to the shore. As they closed it Smith asked, "This is the place?"

Edwards nodded, "Good enough. Anywhere along here."

Smith knew the coast was not defended here, only lightly patrolled by the Turks, and knew why. There was nothing inland but sand-dunes for five or ten miles, nothing to defend. But he used his glasses as they crept in, searching the shore to try to detect any signs of movement, a patrol. He could see none. It was a rock-bound coast but there were gaps and Jameson picked one and steered for it. The cutter slipped through the neck of oily swirling water between the rocks with their breaking foam. The beach ahead was deserted. Smith could see Buckley crouched in the bow, tensed to jump and Edwards was leaning forward, ready to go.

Smith asked, "Suppose you meet someone in the dunes?"

Edwards did not look at him, watched the shore over the bending and straightening backs of the cutter's crew, but he said casually, "His throat or mine. And I'll bet it's his."

The cutter grounded, Buckley leapt over the side into the surf and held the bow as Edwards picked his way light-footed between the men at the oars. He jumped ashore and walked quickly up the beach towards the dunes without pausing or looking back. He reached the dunes and his pale, drifting figure was lost to sight. Smith ordered, "Shove off."

They turned the cutter and headed back out to sea. Smith thought Braddock was right: Edwards was a brigand, a loud-mouth, a cut-throat. He was also a very brave man. Did it matter that this was only to further his own ambition, not taking risks for his country nor the Arabs but for himself? 'Money, influence, women . . .'

Smith shifted uneasily, admitting to himself his own ambition to succeed in his career – and hadn't he risked that career more than once because of a woman?

But he and Edwards were not two of a kind, he was sure of that.

Before dawn the ships were off Haifa, back on patrol, and *Blackbird* began launching the three serviceable Shorts in the first grey light, the start of a long day for the Gang. They flew reconnaissance patrols through all the hours of daylight as the ships steamed northward, the Shorts striking inland to Lydda, swinging north up to the big Turkish camp at El Afuleh, then westward down to Haifa and still following the railway. When a returning seaplane was sighted, another flew off to take up the hunt before the first came down on the sea. Further north they flew through the pass in the screening mountains of Lebanon, flying low to observe, never more than five hundred feet above the ground so that riflemen on the upper slopes were firing down at them.

When they came to the junction at Homs they flew north and south alternately, up and down the line of the railway, searching.

After the sun had set the ships hurried northward through the night and the next dawn found them off the Gulf of Alexandretta.

The Gulf was twenty miles wide and ran inland for thirty. Smith watched its northern Turkish shore lift slowly out of the sea as *Dauntless* steamed northward across the mouth of the Gulf. They were three hundred miles north of Deir el Belah and Cyprus lay seventy miles south-west.

The line of the railway ran north from Lebanon, inland of the Amanus mountains, and then swung around the head of the Gulf. There had been much argument in the first months of the war with Turkey that if the Allies had landed in the Gulf they could have struck inland to cut the Baghdad railway and sever Turkey from her armies in Mesopotamia and Palestine. Smith thought it would not have been easy and the Dardanelles failure had showed that. In any event, the attempt had not been made and the chance was gone for ever. A landing was still talked about, but neither the ships nor the men could be found so that was an end of it.

Henderson, the navigator, said, "The chart shows minefields right across the mouth of the Gulf with only one probable cleared channel along the northern shore and about a mile out. And the Turks have coastal batteries on that shore."

Smith nodded; he had seen the chart and the guns in the Turkish batteries commanded that channel.

Once through the new Bagcha tunnel the railway turned westward along the northern shore of the Gulf and so to the town of Adana. That was the northern limit of Smith's search because north of Adana the railway ran up into the Taurus mountains and inland, beyond the range of the Shorts. The line was broad gauge up to and through Adana but at the mountains it ceased. The Turks and Germans were building tunnels through the Taurus chain to link with the broadgauge track from Constantinople on the other side but these were unfinished. So there was a gap between the end of the line from Constantinople and the start of it again south of the mountains. The connection was made by a metre-gauge line and road transport.

Smith was curious to see Adana, so he flew in one of the Shorts with Mike Cole, lieutenant of the Royal Naval Air Service, taking the place of Cole's usual observer, Lieutenant Hamilton of the Field Artillery. The big, red-headed gunner officer and the short and wiry Cole were a pair of jokers, always laughing together, inseparable, except for now, when Smith turfed Hamilton out of the Short and left him standing disgruntled on the deck of *Blackbird*.

Cole had flown this one before and warned Smith before they took off, "There's a sort of downdraught because of the cup formed by the mountains right round the Gulf, so it'll be a bit bumpy."

When the Short hit the bumps it dropped like a stone for fifty or sixty feet. All the way up to Adana it wallowed and made heavy weather of the flight so Cole's whole attention was given up to flying the aircraft and it was left to Smith to look for any sign of the Afrika Legion. They flew over Adana less than a thousand feet above the ground. There was a train at the station and the platform crowded with troops, but all were Turks. Cole banked the Short and headed eastward, following the track along the northern shore of the Gulf and only turning away when it ran into the Bagcha tunnel that carried it through the Amanus mountains.

He was a tired man when he set down the Short in the lee of *Blackbird* and taxi-ied alongside after three hours of hard flying.

As Smith reached over him to hook on to the derrick, Cole shouted, "Not a shot fired at us all the way! But if they'd thrown up the kitchen sink we wouldn't have noticed! Those bumps!" Then, "Any luck, sir?"

Smith shouted back, "No!"

So the reports continued as the two ships steamed south again and the Shorts flew their searches. Traffic on the railway was normal. In the late forenoon *Blackbird* signalled that the replacement Short the fitters and riggers had christened Delilah was ready for a test flight. Smith looked across, saw Flight Lieutenant Bennett in its cockpit and Hamilton climbing into the observer's seat.

Ackroyd said, "Going along for the ride. Or maybe Bennett wants ballast aboard."

Smith smiled. "Hamilton will provide plenty of that." The lieutenant of artillery bulked large as he stood in the cockpit. He sat down.

Smith remembered that Chris Pearce had not flown for two days now. He wondered if it was time yet to lift the embargo . . .

Blackbird's speed was falling away, the Short was hooked on, lifted by the derrick. At that moment Hamilton suddenly and inexplicably stood erect again, just as the derrick swung. He wavered, arms flailing, then toppled over the side and fell to the deck beneath. He was right under the Short where it dangled from the derrick.

Bennett waved, Smith saw his mouth open, shouting an order and the evolution continued. It was the right thing to do – others would cope with Hamilton. As the Short swung out over the sea and was lowered, men aboard *Blackbird* rushed towards the inert figure on the deck.

Smith snapped, "Pass the word for the surgeon!"

The engine of the Short burst into life and Delilah, the mottled pink and red of her like a flame running across the sea, took off.

Merryweather, the surgeon, a burly young man who played rugby for his county till the war came, charged up the ladder and on to the bridge.

Smith told him of Hamilton's fall. "Will you need to go aboard?"

Merryweather asked, "Can I have a word with Maginnis?"

Smith nodded and told the signalman: "Make to *Blackbird*: 'Am coming alongside. Surgeon to speak to S.B.A.'" And ordered, "Starboard five. Revolutions for ten knots."

Pearce was on the bridge of the carrier as *Dauntless* closed to within a score of yards and Maginnis came onto the wing of *Blackbird*'s bridge. He was the Sick Berth Attendant aboard *Blackbird*; she carried no doctor. He was Glaswegian and an unlikely nurse. Broad and squat, long-armed and with huge hands, he looked more like a gorilla. The bridge megaphone in one hand dangled almost at his knee. He was without his cap, having come straight from the sick bay, and his hair showed black and close-cropped like a skull cap on his bullet head.

Merryweather spoke through the trumpet. "What's his condition?"

Maginnis's deep growl came over the sea, "Ach: He banged his heid but the skulls a'richt. He's got a bump like an egg,

68

that's a'. Concussion, mebbe. Ah'm keeping him in his bunk wi' some tea an' aspirin.''

Merryweather answered, "Very good. Let me know if there's any change.''

"Aye, aye, sir.''

So Hamilton was all right. Smith was relieved but then he bellowed through cupped hands, "What the hell did he think he was doing, standing up as she was hoisted out?''

Maginnis shrugged heavy shoulders. "He disnae ken, sir. Canna remember daein' it. Didnae believe it when first we telt him.''

It was an accident, but a stupid, unnecessary accident.

Maginnis, as if trying to explain away the wilfulness of a child, called, "He's only a soljer, ye ken.''

Dauntless took station ahead of *Blackbird* again and Bennett flew Delilah around and around the ships for an hour as they steamed southward. When he finally set the Short down and was back aboard *Blackbird* Pearce signalled: "Aircraft excellent. Needs only minor adjustments before operational. Estimated available four hours.''

Smith grunted, "Acknowledge.'' Then: "No!'' That was not enough. "Make: 'Well done. We need your painted lady.''' No harm in patting Pearce's back and thereby those of the mechanics and riggers who had laboured long hours to get Delilah into the air. Bennett flew it again later and this time reported Delilah ready for operations.

All the time the other three Shorts had been circulating, always two of them in the air, one taking off as another was recovered. The reports came in with each recovery, signalled to Smith in *Dauntless*, where he read them and pored over the map, compared, looked for omissions, for gaps in the patrol pattern. He found only those that were physically out of the range of the Shorts or screened by the mountains of Lebanon. But the Afrika Legion must be moving. If it had been passing through one of those patches of dead ground as the Shorts made their northward sweep the Legion would be out of it and in the open for the southerly search. He was certain they had not yet arrived, or he would be when the final reports come in to complete the pattern. He was also certain as to his next move. When the Legion did come they would be held up at the bottleneck north of Adana. There they would be slowed for a time to a snail's pace on the metre-gauge line and the road connection. There he would find them.

So in the early evening of the day he told Ackroyd, "We'll fly one more patrol down to Lydda and Jaffa and if that draws a blank we'll head north for Alexandretta at twenty knots."

Cole was the pilot and now Wilson of the Norfolks went as his observer. The Short was Delilah. They took off when the two ships were twenty miles north of Haifa and there was something over two hours of daylight remaining. Their mission was to fly down the coast to Haifa and from there follow the railway up to Afuleh, then south over Tul Keram and on to Lydda. From there they would return and seek out the ships at their projected position at that time.

So it worked out.

Smith was on the bridge at the estimated time of the Short's return. A few minutes' delay would not have caused nail biting. By nature of the task and the Short itself, flight timings were elastic. But there was no delay. Right on time a look-out reported, "Aircraft bearing Red three-oh!"

At that distance it was no more than just an aircraft, unidentifiable, but as ships and aircraft closed the gap at eighty knots it was seen to be a Short and then that it was Delilah.

Smith told the Signal Yeoman, "Make to *Blackbird*: 'Prepare to recover seaplane. Captain coming aboard.'"

He wanted to hear Wilson's report in person, even though he was so certain they would have drawn a blank that the course north to Alexandretta was already laid off.

So as *Blackbird* swung out of her station astern and stopped to make a lee for the Short, so *Dauntless* slowed, stopped, lowered the gig and Smith went down into it. Its crew pulled across to *Blackbird*, and Smith watched Delilah turning into the wind to come down on the sea. With a part of his mind he was thinking that Pearce still had plenty of aviation fuel in ranked drums in the hangar, and the store of bombs beneath it was almost complete. Bombing raids alone would not stop the Legion though – the Fokkers of the Asia Corps would shoot the Shorts out of the sky, and anyway—

There was something wrong.

As the gig came up astern of *Blackbird* the Short was down and taxi-ing, engine snarling. Wilson should have been on his feet and ready to grab at the heaving line on the derrick purchase but he sat slumped in the cockpit, head lolling. The boom of the derrick was swung inboard again. A seaman snatched at the line that dangled from the purchase, whipped it around him under his arm, grabbed at the hook and was swung out from *Blackbird*'s deck to hang above the Short. The steam winch chuntered and the seaman went down on the end of the wire, balanced briefly on the cockpit coaming by the pilot, then hauled down the block of the purchase and hooked on. The seaplane's engine died, the winch hammered and Delilah was hoisted, swung inboard.

The gig ran in along side *Blackbird*. Smith hooked fingers on the ladder and climbed aboard. The Short rested on its trolley. Now that he stood only yards away from it he could see the rents torn in the fuselage around the observer's cockpit. Cole was down on the deck, Pearce holding him by the arm and shouting orders at the men milling around the Short. Chris looked no better for his rest from flying, was still nervy, tired. He turned, saw Smith and led Cole over to him. They moved to stand right in the stern, out of the way of the men working around the Short.

Cole had pulled off the leather helmet and goggles. His hair was sweat-matted to his head and he blinked at Smith.

Who asked shortly, "What happened?"

Cole swallowed. "We didn't see the Afrika Legion or anything like it. Flew in up to Afuleh then down the line, circled around Lydda, headed for Jaffa and home, only saw the one train all the time. Then a Fokker dived on us. You know how it is, sir. They've got that bit more speed, manoeuvrability and can pick their shots. This chap must have been new, thank God. He tore round and round but never got his sights on us. Wilson gave him a few bursts from the Lewis and that kept him off. In the end he just threw up the sponge, fired one burst at long range and flew away. Just that one burst, but it got Wilson and cut him all to pieces below the waist. They'll have a hell of a job cleaning that cockpit—"

Smith cut in harshly, "What about the train?"

"The train?" Cole shoved fingers through his hair. "That was just north of Lydda. We dropped the bombs, missed, but one burst ahead and that was enough to make them stop and everybody got out of the train. The second time we buzzed down low, right over them and I saw them clearly. They were Turks, no doubt of it. They fired at us with rifles but never came near. Then that bloody Fokker." He shook his head.

Pearce asked, "What about Delilah?"

Cole brightened a little. "Marvellous. Still hard work, like all these Shorts, but she's the pick of our bunch and no mistake." They began to talk the technicalities of flying and Smith recognised it as a deliberate manoeuvre on Pearce's part to take Cole's mind off Wilson, if only briefly.

Smith looked over the pilot's shoulder. Surgeon Merry-weather was there. Smith had not seen him arrive from *Dauntless* but he had come quickly and was now up on one side of the observer's cockpit, Maginnis on the other. Merry-weather climbed down after a moment and stood on the deck, shoulders hunched. He turned and caught Smith's eye, shook his head wearily.

So it was Wilson's dead body Maginnis and the others were extricating from the cockpit. Smith watched the group of seamen, riggers and mechanics as they worked gently, voices hushed. Wilson had been seconded from the Norfolks as an observer, a volunteer, son of a farming family. Smith had talked with him several times. Wilson had known the Norfolk village where Smith lived as a boy. A likeable young man, shy but with an engaging smile and an eagerness to fly. He had been so enthusiastic, wanted to become a pilot.

Smith's gaze swung back to Cole standing weary and dejected before him. "It wasn't your fault, just bad luck," he said quietly. And to Pearce, scowling angrily at Delilah, "I think Mike has earned a drink, Chris."

"Aye, aye, sir." Pearce recovered himself, took Cole by the arm and led him away. "Come on, Mike."

Smith watched them walk forward and out of his sight, following the way the others had taken Wilson's body. The hands now folded back the wings of Delilah and began pushing the seaplane on its trolley into the gloom of the hangar. Right by the entrance stood the drum of fuel they had used for the Shorts, and Smith frowned at that. But he heard voices, glanced over the side and saw the whaler that had brought Merryweather, and the gig still waiting for himself. It was time he got back to his ship. Where was Merryweather? Gone forward with Wilson's body?

He faced forward. Suddenly Delilah twisted on the trolley, one wing nudging the drum of fuel and sending it toppling, crashing to roll on the deck. At that same instant a flame flickered at the tail of the Short and there came a yell of "Fire!"

Smith ran at the drum that rolled slowly back and forth with the gentle motion of the ship, a pool of petrol spreading beneath it. Two of the fitters came running. They all arrived at the drum together, Smith gasping, "Over the side!" He remembered the gig and the whaler but mercifully they lay the other side of *Blackbird*. They shoved at the drum and as it rolled Smith saw the fracture from which the petrol leaked, leaving a dribbling trail. He was aware of the potentially explosive fuel under his hands, of the other drums in the hangar, the bomb store beneath. They came to the side, and his feet slipped in the petrol on the deck, he sprawled and rolled out of the way of the other two, had his hands on the deck and his feet under him as the drum teetered on the edge. Flames whipped past him in the petrol trail across the deck and licked at the drum as the fitters heaved it over.

The explosion was muffled but the yellow flame of it lifted high above the side. Then it was gone. He was climbing to his feet again and felt a hand on his arm, saw Pearce helping him up, and jerked out, "The fire—"

"Out, sir."

Smith pointed at the two fitters sprawled at the side, went to them with Pearce, and swallowed. The flame had burned both men. As Pearce retched, Merryweather appeared with Maginnis at his heels. The surgeon took one look and sucked in his breath.

Smith dragged Pearce aside and demanded "What are the orders regarding ready-use fuel?"

Pearce blinked and a nerve twitched in his cheek, "Orders, sir? I – I don't think—"

"How long had that drum stood about, half-full and open?"

"I – don't know, sir. I didn't notice."

Smith rubbed at his face, tried to damp down his anger. "You didn't notice? You've given no standing orders regarding ready-use fuel? What the *hell's* wrong with you, Chris?"

Pearce had been shaken but now the shutter came down, his face went blank. "There's nothing wrong, sir."

Smith said softly, savagely, "For God's sake, Chris! There are two men lying there between life and death because of *bloody stupidity!*"

Merryweather moved across to Smith. "I'll have to get them aboard *Dauntless*."

Smith nodded and told Pearce, "Signal *Dauntless* to come alongside and take off two serious cases of burning."

Pearce left, running. Merryweather and the gorilla-like Maginnis were kneeling over the fitters. Smith walked into the hangar and found the men in there sprinkling sand about the deck. There was little sign that there had been a fire at all, just a smoke-blackened streak on the deck disappearing under the sand. And Delilah? Surely the fire had started in Delilah? He saw another rigger stooped under the fuselage and went to crouch beside him, asked, "This is where it started?"

The rigger glanced at him. "Yes, sir. I was at the tail and saw it start, just a little flame. I was up to it and had it out in seconds but by then it had caught on the petrol that splashed across the deck." He shoved back his cap and scratched at his head. "Can't make it out. Looks as if a bullet passed through here—" He poked a finger in the hole in the slender wooden spar, the fabric burned from it. He said doubtfully, "Might have been a tracer, but for the wood to smoulder all that time—" He shook his head. "I just can't credit it. Never known nothing like it."

They straightened together and Smith said, "The Short – what caused it to swing?"

"Damned if I know *that*, either, sir. She was coming in just like normal, like we run them in all the time. I'd swear the wheels of the trolley didn't snag or jam. She just – swung."

There would be a court of enquiry, of course. First the drowned man, and now this. Smith walked away from the head-shaking rigger, out of the hangar and on to the deck. A steward had come, carrying an armful of clean, white sheets. Smith watched as Merryweather and Maginnis carefully wrapped the two burned men, then Merryweather turned to his bag, took out a hypodermic and injected both of them. As he turned back to the bag he saw Smith and said, "At the moment they're both unconscious and in shock. Those jabs will stave off the pain when it comes, for a while."

Smith asked, "What's your opinion?"

The surgeon came close and said bitterly, "What a bloody day! First Hamilton nearly kills himself, then Wilson and now—" He rubbed at his face and sighed, "Not much of a chance aboard this ship or *Dauntless*, but if we can get them to Deir el Belah there's a big forward hospital and I know for a fact that the burns men there are top class, known them for years. And the hospital is almost empty at the moment."

Smith knew why the big hospital was empty. It was waiting for the attack on the Gaza-Beersheba line.

The sun was down and the night closing around them. *Dauntless* came alongside, her crew lowering fenders and the two ships were briefly secured while the burned men, lashed to stretchers, were swung over by a derrick to a waiting party that hurried them below to the sick bay.

Smith climbed to the bridge. He was certain Adana was the place to look for the Afrika Legion. His task was to find the Legion and if he delayed now, went south to Deir el Belah and so missed them, then he would be called to account.

The two ships eased apart and Henderson asked, "Course, sir?"

Smith hesitated, then said, "Steer one-nine-oh. Revolutions for twenty knots. Pass that to *Blackbird*. And I want a course for Deir el Belah."

"Aye, aye, sir!"

Dauntless slid away from *Blackbird*, starting to work up to twenty knots and every second on this course took him further from Alexandretta and Adana. He had been certain he should go racing north but he had been wrong before and anyway he could not let those men die.

"*Blackbird* acknowledges, sir." That was the signal yeoman. Smith had seen the light flickering from the carrier taking station astern, a shadow of a ship in the night. Doubt was racking him now.

5

A Quiet Little Run up the Coast

Dauntless and *Blackbird* made the passage to Deir el Belah in just four hours. A signal wirelessed ahead requesting permission to transfer two badly-burned men to the hospital, was rapidly answered in the affirmative. The ships raced through the night, passed Gaza, the town unseen but the opposing armies marked by the flicker and flame of the guns, and so came to Deir el Belah.

Smith conned *Dauntless* as she closed the darkened anchorage, a rectangle of sea enclosed by anti-submarine nets on three sides, the shore forming the fourth. A drifter patrolled at the opening in the nets, a lamp aboard her flashed the challenge and the signal yeoman answered from the bridge. *Dauntless* slipped past the drifter and through the gap in the buoyed nets.

Deir el Belah was no port but an Arab village and an oasis. In the anchorage ships discharged their cargoes into lighters and surf-boats to be carried ashore and a small army of men of the Egyptian Labour Corps worked at this. There was a ship discharging in the anchorage now, a lighter alongside her and winches hammering as the derricks swung, both ship and lighter alive with the figures of men labouring under the big lamps. The lighter was one of four at Deir el Belah that were engined and had first been used for landing troops in the Dardanelles. They were no more than big, shallow boxes with a ramp that came out over the bow and an engine right aft.

Morning Star lay at the far end of the anchorage, almost lost in the outer darkness beyond the lights of the discharging ship, but there was a guard-boat, a motor-launch, puttering around her.

Dauntless steamed gently on past the two M-class monitors, each with its single 6-inch gun, like a pointing finger, and there lay *Phoebe*, Braddock's armed yacht. Smith saw faces on *Phoebe* and the monitors, the ship and the lighter, turned towards *Dauntless*. He knew the picture she made as she slipped over the water of this man-made lagoon and was proud of her. She was his and a beauty.

The thought came: if a guard-boat patrolled around *Morning Star* then Taggart's battalion was still aboard her – and Adeline Brett? There was a blur of white moving on the deck of *Morning Star* that might be—

He ordered, "Stop both!" *Dauntless* came to anchor. The land prickled with a thousand lights, the fires of the army, but one stuttered at *Dauntless* a succession of signals: an oiler waited for *Dauntless*, a coaling lighter for *Blackbird*, and Braddock wanted to see Smith at army headquarters.

Smith told Ackroyd, "We sail in two hours. Pass that to *Blackbird*." He had to go back to the search, to Alexandretta. And here came a boat, a big, white-painted launch with a red cross on her side. He said, "Tell the doctor they've come for his patients." He dropped down the ladders and hurried aft to his main cabin where he stripped, shaved and dressed in fresh white drill. He returned to the deck in time to see the second of the burned men lowered on a stretcher into the white launch alongside.

Merryweather was there and turned a worried face to Smith. "I'd like to go to the hospital with them, sir."

Smith nodded. "You've got two hours." He added gently, "Cheer up, Doc. No man could have done more than you, I'm sure of that, and if they have a chance it's due to you." But the burly young surgeon refused to be consoled.

Smith went down into the motor-boat that lay astern of the launch. As the boat headed for the shore he thought that soon another boat would come off to take Wilson's body from *Blackbird*. He would be buried in the morning and not by strangers, though *Dauntless* and *Blackbird* would be at sea by then. There were two battalions of the Norfolks here, Wilson's regiment.

He landed at the temporary jetty, walked rapidly along its echoing planks and up through the gap in the dunes that lined the shore. He passed a train on a siding, the engine hissing softly as steam escaped somewhere, and took the dusty palm-fringed road towards army headquarters.

Charlie Golightly, in the shadow of the engine, glanced absently at the white-uniformed figure striding up the road, then turned back to business and Albert. "You say this feller was goin' round asking questions about scotch, had anybody seen any and where'd it come from?"

Albert nodded vigorously. "Corporal say a big man. Captain Jeffreys." He repeated the name carefully, syllable by syllable as the corporal had taught him. "Corporal say this man from Pip Emma."

"Provost Marshal," muttered Charlie. He did not like the sound of it. "We'll give things a rest for a bit."

Albert nodded knowingly, "Big fighting soon."

Charlie said shortly, "Bugger the fighting. That's the army's business." He was only concerned with his own. "It's this Jeffreys feller I don't fancy." He hesitated, weighing odds and not wanting to take a loss on a transaction. He decided, "There's one more lot o' scotch at Port Said already paid for. We'll fetch that, then pack it in."

Smith strode up the road that now ran between ranked tents, fires burning before them, their light glinting on the water of a small lake in among the palms. He had come this way in the light of day past crowded horse-lines and these tents had swarmed with men cleaning arms and equipment, currying horses. Now the horse-lines were deserted. A few men moved among the small fires, keeping them burning, but the tents were empty. He was not surprised, knew the men had moved eastward and the tents and fires were there only to fool any Turk watching from Gaza.

*   *   *

Lieutenant Bill Jackson, standing tall in the darkness, watched Smith pass and thought that must be the captain of the cruiser. He remembered the talk of her raiding the length of the coast and of her hell-raising commander. There was a driving energy in the way he hastened up the road.

A big trooper slouched up to the fire nearest Jackson, scowled at it morosely and spat into it. Jackson rasped, "You're supposed to keep it going, Jasper, not put it out!"

Without turning the trooper grumbled, "Aw, give it a rest, Jacka. We're all sick o' this flamin' job." He threw wood on the fire and slouched away, hands in the pockets of his patched breeches. Jackson grinned sympathetically. These men of his were a handful when out of the line as now. In Port Said they were worse than a handful and they weren't allowed in Cairo at all. They had thrown a piano through a window in the course of one fight. There were men from sheep stations but also from many other jobs and backgrounds such as teachers and lawyers, including men who read poetry and one who wrote it. Their only uniformity was their toughness and soldiering skill and up here at the front they were the best, the very best, Jackson was certain.

And they would be in the attack. Jackson's grin faded. They would be moved up at the last minute and he thought maybe they were too good because when the attack came they would be right at the bloody front.

The village of Deir el Belah was a huddle of little grass-thatched houses and Finlayson's headquarters lay north of it, in a tent the size of a large bungalow. It stood at the centre of the mesh of roads built by the army who had named them Dover Street, Oxford Street, the Strand – there was even a Marine View. In all the way from the shore Smith had met only the two men, but now that emptiness was behind him and he walked through a crowded, tented town. He had to wait for a convoy of camels to pass before he could cross to the H.Q. They rocked by under mountainous loads roped on to the big Buladi saddles, with their high cross-trees sticking up front and rear, 350 pounds to a load that included two *fanatis*, galvanised iron tanks of fresh water. They plodded past at their flat-footed two to three miles an hour and passed on into the night, heading eastward. In the day the roads and tracks carried traffic north up to Gaza but now they were crowded with column after column of camels, mules, horses and chugging lorries all moving eastward while night hid them from the Turks.

An aide led him through an ante-room in the huge tent where a dozen clerks hammered at typewriters by the yellow light of paraffin lamps. Beyond was a room with a desk and a wide table spread with maps. Finlayson and Braddock straightened from stooping over the maps and Braddock said, "All right, Smith. Come on over here." And as Smith crossed to the table: "How are those two men?"

"They have a chance, sir."

"Bad luck, that."

"Yes, sir." Two men he knew and liked, respected for their skills and the men they were, might die. But Braddock knew that and how Smith felt. There was nothing more to say.

Finlayson said, "We've studied all your wireless reports and so have my Intelligence staff. Anything to add?"

Smith hesitated, marshalling his thoughts, then said, "From Adana down to Gaza is roughly three hundred miles as the crow flies but the railway is about five hundred miles long because of the way it winds about. There are stretches the Shorts can't reach but they have twice flown over the accessible areas – and that means most of the line from Adana down to Lydda – and seen nothing. This isn't France or Germany where there are railway systems like spiders' webs. There's only the one track which runs down from Adana to the Gaza-Beersheba line with only a spur off here and there to Haifa, Jaffa and so on."

He paused and saw Finlayson shift impatiently. So he went on. "I know you are aware of this, sir. I only repeat it because it is relevant to my conclusion." And when Finlayson nodded Smith went on, "Five thousand men on that railway means a dozen trains at least and they would be seen, if not on the first search then certainly during the second. They might have been passing through one of those patches of dead ground we couldn't reach but the second search would have caught them in the open. They wouldn't be hanging about in that dead ground because Kressenstein won't let the Legion rest. He'll ram it down to the Gaza-Beersheba line as fast as he can because the summer is ending and he knows General Allenby's attack must come soon." He paused then finished positively, "At this moment therefore I don't believe the Afrika Legion has cleared Turkey."

Finlayson was nodding and smiling now. "I told you my staff studied your reports. They reached the same conclusion but they went a stage further. The Turks and Germans have supply problems already because they are desperately short of rolling stock on that railway. If they want to maintain their rate of supply to the front line, then they can't turn over a dozen trains to the Legion. They'll have to bring it down piecemeal and that means it will be too late."

Smith did not like that reasoning and said uneasily, "With respect, sir, I'm not too sure. Maybe the Germans have thought of a way around that one."

Finlayson's fingers drummed testily on the map. "You bring us good news then try to put a dampener on it."

Smith remembered Finlayson's distrust of unconventional officers and that with Edwards he was classed as such in Finlayson's book. "Only giving my opinion, sir."

Finlayson grunted, glanced at Braddock. "I'd like the search to go on. When they do arrive, we want to know."

Braddock nodded and Smith said, "I propose to sail north immediately and patrol off the Gulf of Alexandretta. I believe the break in the line at the Taurus mountains will slow them up and that's where we'll find them."

They discussed it for a few minutes, leaning over the map and then Braddock agreed. Smith asked, "Any word from Edwards, sir?"

Finlayson shook his iron-grey head. "Nothing. I'm not surprised because clearly the Legion isn't there to be found." He stretched wearily. Under the yellow light he looked older, tired, but he seemed less tense than when Smith had entered.

As if summing up he said, "The date for the attack is confirmed, final. The build-up is exactly on time and Allenby will have the advantage of surprise on the day that he must have, that he has worked for. Only one German aircraft got over our lines in recent weeks and a Bristol Fighter of the Flying Corps shot it down. About two weeks ago a certain staff officer got lost in the desert and rode out into no-man's-land. A patrol of Turkish cavalry saw him and shot at him so he ran for it, but he dropped his briefcase. The Turks found it covered in blood and stuffed with marked maps from a staff meeting – maps that showed a plan for an attack on Gaza." Finlayson chuckled softly. "It worked. The Turks have reinforced Gaza." His smile faded and he finished, "We need a victory. Badly. Allenby has been told to provide one and God willing, this time we shall have it."

As far as Finlayson was concerned, it was obviously the end of the interview, but Smith asked, "What about *Morning Star*, sir?"

Finlayson said bitterly. "I could have done without her and that damned battalion! A team of investigating officers came up from Cairo and spent a day aboard her. They said the men talked, when they talked at all, like a lot of bloody parrots! They found out nothing. After the attack, when the army has moved on, I'll have them brought ashore and interrogated again because a man has been murdered and regardless of the rights and wrongs in the case, the murderer must be found and tried. Justice must be done." He sighed, then said dryly, "Meanwhile, I've had all your suggestions acted on. Go and see for yourself if you don't believe me."

The motor-boat headed for *Morning Star*, passing close under *Blackbird*'s stern and Smith smelt the lingering stench of the fire, borne on the breeze from the black cavern of the hangar. *Blackbird* was coaling and Smith saw men from *Dauntless* working aboard her.

The launch patrolling around *Morning Star* turned to intercept the motor-boat. The Lewis gun mounted forward in the launch was manned and as she came alongside the lieutenant commanding her called across the gap, "What boat is that?"

Smith stepped to the side where he could be seen and answered, "*Dauntless*. Commander Smith." And: "What are your orders?"

The lieutenant called, "To keep everyone away except those on my list."

"What list is that?"

"The admiral gave it to me but it came from General Finlayson. Your name is on it, sir."

"Is it a long list?"

"Ten names, sir."

The launch swung away and Smith thought that Finlayson meant to keep the battalion isolated and that came as no surprise. But Smith's name was on the list of those authorised to board and that did surprise him. Had Finlayson assumed that Smith would return to ask about the men aboard *Morning Star*? Or had Braddock guessed that Smith would be unhappy about the situation and would return to it when opportunity offered?

But the boat was swinging around under the stern of *Morning Star*. The pink-faced midshipman at her helm looked down his nose at the grime on the ladder the tramp had rigged. Smith climbed it nevertheless, found one of Captain Brand's marines on guard at the head of it and asked him, "Major Taggart?"

The marine peered, recognised him and said, "The major's forrard, sir."

Smith walked past the superstructure and found that the entire deck forward of the bridge was now a large cage of barbed wire, in a fence across the deck and erected along the sides. There was a door in the wire where a marine sentry stood guard and Smith could see another sentry on the fo'c'sle. The deck inside the cage was covered with the bodies of sleeping men but one man saw Smith and rose. He picked his way through the others to the wire and the sentry let him through. In the dim light Smith saw that Taggart's left eye was puffy and cut at the side.

Taggart said, "They've shipped extra stoves, army cooks and fresh food, so we're eating much better. We've got drill uniforms in place of the serge and we're allowed on deck day and night. I'm very grateful."

Smith muttered something, embarrassed. Over Taggart's shoulder he saw that one other man was awake, sat with his head propped against the bulwark, staring unseeing across the deck of the *Morning Star*. Smith thought he recognised him. Hadn't he been the only man in the hold not to watch Smith that first night? To change the subject he nodded towards the man, and asked Taggart, "Who's that?"

Taggart answered casually, "Garrett. He's a bit young. I use him as a runner so as to keep my eye on him." He went on quickly, taking Smith's arm, "Come on, we'll go where we can talk."

They passed the superstructure and crossed the deck away from the marine sentry at the head of the ladder. A rectangular, tarpaulin-covered shape was lashed to the deck. Smith glanced at it curiously and Taggart explained, "Adeline's wagon for carrying her supplies or wounded. There's a harness but most of the time we haven't had a horse or mule so we've man-hauled it. That's easy enough, it's light and well-sprung." They halted, leaned on the bulwark and looked out over the anchorage to where *Dauntless* lay, *Blackbird* astern of her. For a time they were silent then Taggart said, "Good-looking ship."

Smith said simply, "She's beautiful." Then, remembering Taggart's swollen eye, he turned and asked casually, "Any trouble?"

But Taggart shook his head. "The feller that tried to grab Adeline, Captain Jeavons put him ashore in Port Said. We've had no more trouble."

So the eye was unexplained. Smith looked past him.

"They are a remarkably disciplined body of men." That didn't say a part of what he meant. "I mean—" He searched for words.

Taggart glanced sideways at him. "I think I know what you mean. They hold together, fight together. But they're not a herd of regimented cattle. They've learned and they think. Loyal to King and Country and all that and damn this talk of mutiny, but above all they are loyal to themselves because they're infantrymen and they've soldiered together a long time. They are the best."

Smith remembered the faces in the hold and he had seen strain and in that one man, Garrett, a cold hardness, but in none of them either viciousness or fear. He thought over what Taggart had just told him and it confirmed and clarified the unformed impression he had gained, that in a unit under Taggart the men of his battalion would be a force to reckon with in the field. But that would not happen because no matter what the outcome, whether the murderer among them was found or not, the battalion would never fight again as a unit. It would be held in the rear and sooner or later split up, scattered across the battlefields of Africa and Europe.

Taggart's gaze slid past Smith and he went on hurriedly, "Sorry if Adeline gave you the rough edge of her tongue the other night. She feels for the men and she's a grand girl when you get to know her."

Smith said dryly, "I'll give her the benefit of the doubt."

"Do it now."

Smith turned and saw Adeline Brett coming towards them, soft-footed in canvas shoes, a dressing gown wrapped around her slim figure, her hair tousled. She stopped before them, pushed at the blonde curls with one hand and said, "A boat came alongside and woke me. I couldn't get off to sleep again." She looked at Smith. "Was that you?"

He nodded. "Sorry."

She shrugged that aside. "I doze a lot in the day now because I haven't much to do. Except when somebody organises a boxing tournament, takes on the battalion champion and gets his block knocked off."

Taggart touched his swollen eye and said defensively, "I slipped."

The girl smiled. "Three times." Then she became serious and asked Smith, "I thought I saw wounded taken ashore?"

He answered heavily, "Two, and an observer was killed."

Taggart said, understanding, "Sick?"

Smith nodded. "I'm bloody sick."

Taggart caught the girl's eye on him and he asked Smith abruptly, "You're off soon?"

Smith looked across to *Blackbird* and saw the coaling lighter being towed away. "Very soon."

"I'll see you again, maybe." Taggart walked forward and left Smith and the girl alone.

She said, "I want to thank you."

"It's been said already." Smith was gazing after Taggart. "He's in trouble up to his neck. He knows who did it and when the truth finally comes out they'll know he lied to shield the man and they won't be easy on him. He's an officer and can give no excuse." His eyes came down to the girl. "Do you know?"

"I wasn't there when the colonel was shot."

"That's not what I asked. Do you know who did it?"

She answered angrily, "The colonel was a drunken fool! John Taggart had seen the position they were to attack and told him it was hopeless. The colonel hadn't even seen it but he still told the general that his battalion would take it! He was safely behind the line when the attack went in and he didn't even see the wounded come back, but *I* saw them!" She shuddered.

Smith waited then pressed her again. Because Finlayson was right and this secret was a poison. Taggart would suffer for it, and many others. "Do you know who did it?"

Adeline hesitated, then: "I – have a suspicion but it's no more than that. I wouldn't tell anyone." That was final.

He said, "I have to go." She walked with him to the head of the ladder, guarded by a marine sentry. He paused awkwardly. "As Taggart said, 'See you again.'"

She smiled but with lips tight-pressed and he wondered if she was laughing at him. But she asked, "What's your name?"

"David."

She set her hands on his shoulders, put up her face and kissed him. "Thank you, David." She walked away. The marine sentry stared blankly out into the night as Smith glared at him, then turned and descended the ladder. The marine grinned.

The motor-boat crept in alongside *Dauntless* and Smith forgot the battalion, Taggart and Adeline Brett. The launch from the shore was hooked on to the foot of the ladder and it had brought Merryweather back to the ship, but Braddock was also aboard it. As the boats rubbed together and Merryweather climbed up to the deck of *Dauntless* Braddock leaned over the side of the launch and growled, "They've just brought in an Arab with a message from Edwards. Another throat-cutter by the looks of him but the word from Edwards is that there's a supply dump by the railway at Lydda and a company of Germans are guarding it. Know anything about it?"

Smith shook his head and explained, "There's an anti-aircraft battery just south of Lydda so we give it a wide berth. Shorts are a gift to Archie."

Braddock grunted. "Don't know if it means anything." Then: "How did you get on with that feller, Edwards? What did you make of him?"

You did not beat about the bush with Braddock so Smith answered baldly, "I think he's totally selfish, ruthless, very brave."

Braddock nodded and said wryly, "A gallant blackguard. Or black sheep, because he comes of a good family . . ." He stopped there and straightened. "You still think this Afrika Legion might arrive in time to ruin everything?"

"Yes, sir."

Braddock muttered, "I hope to God you're wrong."

The launch headed away and Smith climbed aboard *Dauntless*. He had his orders, both ships had completed with fuel and the search would go on as long as they could keep the sea. When the Afrika Legion came, either this detour to Deir el Belah would have done no harm and they would find it at Adana – or a court martial would break Smith.

Before the sun rose, when the first light was a pink edging to the Hills of Judaea, *Dauntless* led *Blackbird* out of the anchorage as quietly as they had come and headed for the Gulf of Alexandretta.

*   *   *

Telegraphist Lofty Williams curled his long frame to lean his head in at the door of the galley blinking after the glare of the afternoon sun. "Wotcher, Cookie. Any chance of a wet?"

Leading Cook Matthews, sweating rivers in the heat of the galley, jerked his head at the stove and the big kettle of tea that stewed there. "Help yourself." He watched as Lofty produced the two pint mugs from behind his back like a conjuror performing some sleight of hand and poured tea the colour of gravy into the cups, added sugar and a spoonful of condensed milk. Matthews asked, "What's goin' on, then?"

Lofty eyed the tea. "Looks a drop o' good."

"It is. Cooks only, that is."

Lofty sipped and swore as he burnt his tongue. "What's goin' on? Nothing much, mate. Just another fast run up the coast by the looks of it. Them flyers in *Blackbird*'ll be busy tomorrow but that's about all. Not like them first two weeks when the ol' man was trying to shoot everything that showed itself ashore."

Matthews nodded. "We've got a fire-eater there. I've heard one or two tales about him. Quiet feller, but—"

"Ah! But! Still waters, mate." Then Lofty added thoughtfully, "He's been quieter than ever since we started this trip. I was talking to that Buckley, you know, the big killick as came with him and acts as his dog-robber. He says the Skipper's too quiet an' that means he's got one o' his feelings . . ."

Matthews peered at him suspiciously. "What? You mean like second sight?"

"Naw! Second sight my—! Just that he puts two and two together and smells a rat a lot faster than the rest of them. At least, that's what Buckley reckons and he knows him."

"So?"

Lofty shrugged. "So nothing. Except that the balloon'll be going up ashore pretty soon when the army attacks and maybe Smith knows when that will be. We'll be busy then. But now? Nothing. Just a quiet little run up the coast."

He walked aft, easily adjusting to the motion of *Dauntless* so that he did not spill a drop from either of the mugs he carried even when climbing down the ladders to the lower deck. At the wireless office he edged in through the thick pall of tobacco smoke from the pipe of Leading Telegraphist Bailey, who sat slouched in one chair with his feet propped up on another and the headphones pushed comfortably down so the earpieces rested against his jaw.

Bailey took the pipe from his mouth, glanced up at the clock and said, "Blimey, you're early. Are we sinking?"

"They haven't told me."

"If it happens they probably won't."

"Just thought I'd get a wet before I started." Lofty was to take over the watch from Bailey at four. It was now five minutes to. He offered a mug and asked, "Anything goin' on?"

Bailey shook his head and sipped at the tea. "Routine."

"Just what I was telling Cookie. A quiet little run—"

He stopped as Bailey's feet slammed down from their resting place on the chair and he shoved the mug aside, reached out to the Morse key and rattled off a brief acknowledgment. Someone was calling *Dauntless*. His hand moved from the key, picked up the sharpened pencil and he began to print neatly in blocks on the signal pad. Lofty leaned over his shoulder, watching the letters as Bailey set them down one by one.

The signal was in code.

Lofty nipped out of the office, ambled aft past the warrant officer's mess and halted at the first cabin he came to. The curtain that served instead of a door was drawn back and Lieutenant Cherrett, the signals officer lay on his bunk, a magazine open on his chest, snoring gently. Lofty reached in, shook Cherrett's foot and as he grunted and opened sleepy eyes, said, "Beg pardon, sir. Signal coming in. Coded."

Cherrett grumbled, "Probably some highly-secret request for the number of teetotallers on board." But he got up quickly and went to the wireless office, sat down with the signal and the books and started de-coding.

Minutes later he was racing forward along the upper deck and taking the ladders to the bridge in long, leaping strides. To Ackroyd, who had the watch, he panted, "Captain?"

Ackroyd jerked his head towards the sea-cabin. "In there. What's the rush?"

Cherrett threw at him: "*Walküre*'s out!"

6

Dawn Rendezvous

Why?

Smith was snatching some much-needed but uneasy sleep on the narrow bunk in the sea-cabin when Cherrett brought the signal. After the initial moment of shock that question came first to his mind. Why had *Walküre* broken out? What was her intention?

The signal advanced no theories. *Walküre* was known to have sailed the previous night, evading her watchers and passing through the Dardanelles under cover of darkness. Her course and destination, her present position, were unknown. *Dauntless* and *Blackbird* were to proceed to a rendezvous just west of Cyprus, where they would be joined by the old French battleship *Maroc* and her two escorts at first light. They would then sweep westward. Smith would command – and that was welcome confirmation of what Braddock had told him three days before at Port Said.

He went into the chartroom with Henderson the navigator, laid off the new course and worked out their time of arrival at the rendezvous. Twelve hours of steaming at *Blackbird*'s best speed of twenty knots would see them there at dawn to meet *Maroc*. Their dash to the Gulf of Alexandretta would have to wait. Dangerous as the Afrika Legion was, a German warship at large in the Mediterranean constituted an even greater threat.

He returned to the bridge and Ackroyd said, "Reckon we're in for a blow and there'll be a sea running before tonight."

Smith thought he was right and it was bad news. He wanted *Blackbird* in the searching line as another pair of eyes, an extension of that line, with her Shorts to increase the range of the search enormously. If bad weather prevented them flying then the area of search would be only that seen by the spread line of ships.

Henderson said, "*Walküre's* a funny sort of ship. With twelve 8.2-inch guns, and fifteen thousand tons, she's too big for a cruiser. Yet at the same time she's too small for a battle cruiser or a battleship."

Ackroyd shrugged square shoulders and said with heavy humour, "A pocket-sized battleship."

That brought grins to the faces on the bridge and Henderson said, "Some pocket."

Ackroyd mused, "Wonder what she's up to? Out after the convoys?"

It was a possibility. Smith said, "Maybe."

"A raid on Port Said?"

There were people who had worried in case *Goeben* and *Breslau* and *Walküre* broke out and tried to block the Suez Canal. Smith was sceptical of the practicability of that and shook his head. Guessing was a waste of time when they knew only that *Walküre* was loose somewhere in the Mediterranean. They had to know more.

It was night again and the two ships were racing through a rising sea when Cherrett came running again with a signal. *Walküre* had been sighted in the dusk west of Crete and her course was due west. Now it made sense of a sort and Ackroyd said tentatively, "The Adriatic?"

Smith nodded. It was possible for *Walküre* to fight her way into the Adriatic and join the Austrian fleet lying at Pola, where it had lain since the start of the war doing almost nothing. That might be the idea, for her captain to persuade the Austrians to engage in active operations with himself to give them adventurous leadership. The Allies had trouble enough in the Mediterranean trying to counter the U-boat threat, Braddock had made that clear. If the Adriatic boiled up it would stretch still further the naval reserves that were already strained to breaking point.

But the signal came as an anti-climax. Their orders were

unchanged so Smith's little squadron, once assembled at the rendezvous, would sweep westward – but now only to close the stabledoor, become ultimately part of a screen of ships in case *Walküre* was forced back and tried to return to the Aegean.

Smith went to his bunk and tried to sleep but only dozed restlessly, waking often in the night, and he was up before the dawn and standing again behind the bridge screen.

Ackroyd had the watch and greeted Smith. "'Morning, sir. Only one signal an hour or so back from *Maroc*, confirming she'll be at the rendezvous on time but she's had to send back one of her escorts with engine trouble. She's carrying on with the other one. That's S.C. 101, American submarine-chaser."

Smith nodded and took the mug of scalding hot, bitter coffee that Buckley brought him. The American submarine-chasers were new to the Mediterranean as they were new to the war. They had only crossed the Atlantic in the last summer months and were little more than a big motor-launch, a hundred feet long with a single 3-inch gun forward, a Y-gun aft for lobbing depth charges over the side and a speed of only some seventeen knots. He asked, "What about us?"

Henderson came out of the charthouse, long fingers wrapped around a mug of cocoa. "We'll be on station in another fifteen minutes, sir."

"That's right on time."

"Yes, sir."

"Very good." And *Maroc* had done well. Like the elderly British battleships employed in the Mediterranean, she was slow and the powers that be had set her a tall order when they sent her to keep this rendezvous on time.

The Afrika Legion . . . He should have been close to the Gulf of Alexandretta by now and instead he was two hundred miles off and getting further away with every second. But maybe the Intelligence officers with Finlayson were right, that the Legion would be too late now, anyway. He shifted restlessly, took a turn across the bridge, sipped the coffee as he prowled and *Dauntless* crashed on through the big oily seas, the spray from her bow like rain on his face. Astern of *Dauntless* came *Blackbird*. She was a good seaboat and was plugging on well but Smith was still uneasy, continually looking over his shoulder, actually or mentally, at the carrier because he could not trust her young captain, Chris Pearce.

He swore under his breath, finished the coffee and balanced the mug on the shelf below the screen. It would be light soon. By the time the sun was up he should have his little squadron together and shaking out into a long line sweeping westward.

Ackroyd asked, "Any sign of *Maroc?*"

Dauntless and *Blackbird* were about on station now, as near as dead reckoning could make it, and reduced to fifteen knots. The sun was close under the rim of the sea astern and the visibility was lengthening with every second, although there was an early morning mist and the lowering clouds seemed to fur the edges of everything.

Smith thought absently, the Afrika Legion giving him no peace, that Kressenstein would know the attack on the Gaza-Beersheba line must come soon. He would not be content for the Legion to dribble down to him as trains became available—

The port look-out called, "There she is, sir! *Maroc!* Thirty on the bow!"

Smith set his glasses to his eyes and saw her coming out of the mist about three miles away, that mist cloaking her and blurring the outline, but her size could not be hidden. The twin funnels, the turrets, the tripod mast like that of *Dauntless* but bigger—

Ackroyd said, "Make the challenge, Yeoman."

"*No!*" Smith shouted it. "*Hard astarboard! All guns load!*"

Ackroyd stood open-mouthed and pandemonium broke loose as Smith jabbed his finger on the button and the klaxons blared through *Dauntless*. The ship emerging in that half-light from the thin mist was as big a warship as *Maroc* but there the resemblance ended. *Maroc* had three funnels and no tripod mast. This was *Walküre* and now the long guns in those turrets fired.

Dauntless was coming around, heeling in the turn. Smith saw the crew of her forward 6-inch gun skidding on the tilting fore deck as they strove to load the gun and bring it into action.

He remembered the seaplane-carrier astern, whirled and saw her still coming on, holding her course. Pearce *must* have seen *Walküre* firing and *Dauntless* turning wildly away. Was he slavishly waiting an order to turn? He rapped at the Signal Yeoman, "Make to *Blackbird*: 'Turn sixteen points. Take evasive action. Enemy bears three miles west.'"

And no more than three miles. That salvo she fired would be falling—

The salvo plunged into the sea in a straight, spread line a cable's length from *Dauntless*'s starboard quarter.

The bugles were blaring and the deck was alive with racing men. The signal yeoman reported, "*Blackbird* acknowledges, sir." He added, "An' she's turning!"

It was high time. "Very good. Wireless to C. in C. Eastern Med and all H.M. ships: 'Am in action *Walküre*. My position—' get that from the pilot – 'enemy course and speed due east fifteen knots.'"

Ackroyd had gone to take command of damage control. Lieutenant Jameson said, "Guns requests—"

Smith snapped, "Yes, dammit! All guns commence!"

Seconds later the two after 6-inch guns fired together and the vibration shook loose the mugs under the screen and sent them rolling across the bridge. The after guns because *Dauntless* had turned and as Smith had ordered, "Full ahead both! Starboard ten!" was tearing away from the big German cruiser. He was out on the starboard wing of the bridge now, looking for *Walküre* and seeing her guns firing. Her outline was blurring again through the gauzy draperies of the mist and the rapidly widening distance between the two ships. And Smith thought the distance must not spin out too far as he looked for the fall of that salvo and cast a hasty glance around at *Blackbird*. She made a fine target for *Walküre*'s shells with that haystack of a hangar, her load of petrol for the Shorts and the bombs below her deck.

Pearce should have turned sooner. If *Walküre* hit her—

The shock threw him into Henderson, sent the pair of them slamming into the screen and the sea fell across their shoulders and almost drove them to their knees. Smith wiped water from his face and pushed away from the screen and Henderson. The salvo had burst to port and close alongside, hurled sea water aboard in tons and heeled *Dauntless* over but she was running on an even keel again now.

"Port ten!"

"Port ten, sir!"

He snapped at Jameson, "Damage reports?"

"Nothing yet, sir."

The after 6-inch guns fired as one and Smith fumbled for the glasses hanging against his chest, lifted them, searched for *Walküre*. He saw her stern on, insubstantial as the mist itself on that blurred horizon and the range had opened, he heard that confirmed by the range-taker, the ranges repeated on the bridge: " . . . ten thousand . . ." *Walküre*'s guns fired and they were her after turrets that were firing now. She and *Dauntless* were on widely diverging courses, *Walküre* still headed east while *Dauntless* ran away to the south. Soon they would be out of range of those big guns in the enemy cruiser but then she would be out of sight also.

He could not let that happen. He had found *Walküre*, or stumbled on her. He dared not lose her again. He wondered briefly at her presence here, could make no sense of it but that speculation could wait. He swung around and saw that *Dauntless* as she worked up speed had overhauled *Blackbird*, was close on her.

A salvo howled overhead and burst off the port bow, well clear of *Dauntless* but straddling *Blackbird*. Deafened he heard only distantly Jameson's bellow, "They've dropped one on *Blackbird*!"

Smoke was pouring from the carrier's deck forward of the bridge on the starboard side and trailing from a hole just above the water line. The plunging shell had penetrated the deck and smashed on out of *Blackbird*'s side.

Smith ordered, "Port ten!"

"Port ten, sir! . . . Ten of port wheel on, sir!"

The cruiser's knife-edge stem swept around through a semi-circle until Smith said, "Meet her . . . steady. Steer two-oh degrees."

He stared out over the forward 6-inch gun, over the bow at *Walküre*, seen now clearly, now blurred but dead ahead. He heard somebody cheer on the deck below. Did they think he was steaming to attack the huge cruiser? That would be madness because *Dauntless* would stand no chance in a stand-up fight against that heavily-gunned, heavily-armoured ship. That was not a job for *Dauntless*, not the purpose she was built for, and if *Dauntless* was damaged and her speed reduced she could lose *Walküre*. But if he had to keep her in sight he would have to stay within range of those big guns, and now, additionally, he had to draw their fire to give *Blackbird* a chance.

He told the signal yeoman, "Wireless to C. in C. and H.M. ships: 'Maintaining contact with enemy. Enemy's course east, speed—'" He hesitated.

Jameson suggested, "Think she's working up to about twenty knots, sir. Hard to tell, but she's making more smoke and she looks—"

"I agree." Smith finished: "'—speed twenty knots.'"

He watched *Walküre* through the glasses, the lenses shivering in his hands and shaking the image as the forward 6-inch gun fired, losing sight of her as the smoke swirled back across the bridge. He found her again as Jameson said, "She's fired again."

"Starboard ten," Smith ordered, to take *Dauntless* out of the path of that salvo hurtling towards her. "Meet her . . . steer that."

Henderson said, "I think that round of ours fell short, sir."

Smith grunted assent. *Walküre* was still in range of the 6-inch, just, but the range-taker up on the fore-bridge would be having trouble reading ranges, the twin images in the lenses of the range-finder blurred by the mist, and the smoke that *Walküre* was pouring out now. She was definitely making a run for it.

Walküre's latest salvo fell abeam of *Dauntless*, hurling up huge spouts of water. Smith snatched a glance at them, well clear, about three cable's lengths away.

Jameson said, "Damn! Lost her!"

Smith peered at the mist on the horizon, a low, grey ribbon, and somewhere behind it was *Walküre*. He swept the glasses along the ribbon but saw nothing, could not even see her smoke now. He swore softly under his breath but made himself ask casually, "What's our speed?"

Henderson answered, "Twenty-two knots, sir."

"Good enough." Still carefully casual. *Walküre*'s best speed was about twenty-five knots but she had not worked up to that yet, nor would she for some time, so she would not get away from *Dauntless*. Provided she did not change course. He managed to maintain his cool tone when he said, "There she is."

The mist had thinned or *Walküre* had pushed out of it. But there she was, now broadside on and her guns firing.

The 6-inch gun forward slammed again. The crew of it were having a bad time with *Dauntless* steaming at this speed and in this sea, the bow wave coming inboard to wash around them where they fought the gun, breaking over them in sheets of spray.

". . . ten thousand . . ."

Jameson said, "Range is closing, sir!"

Walküre's salvo burst to starboard and a good cable's length astern of *Dauntless*. And *Walküre* disappeared.

This time Jameson swore. "What the hell does her skipper do for an encore? Pull rabbits out of a hat?"

Smith managed to laugh though it was far from funny. In seconds the big cruiser had done her vanishing trick again. The sea and that hazy horizon were unchanged but *Walküre* had gone as if she had sunk beneath the waves. He picked up the train of thought interrupted when she last appeared: She would not get away provided she did not change her course and leave Smith blundering about in the mist while she raced away in a different direction. That raised the question: where was she bound for, anyway? When *Dauntless* had come on her *Walküre* was headed eastward and that course could take her to Cyprus. What for? To bombard the shore and whatever shipping she might find? Or had she intended a change of course soon that would send her tearing down towards Port Said and the convoys?

99

Smith shifted restlessly. Where *was* she? Only the empty sea and that fringing mist lay ahead of *Dauntless*. The sun was up now, but still very low so Smith had to squint against it, a watery sun but sparking lights from the sea. How long since they saw her? Five minutes? Ten? If she had doubled back on her track and headed westward she could have made three miles by now and in another ten minutes be hull-down over the horizon and lost to him when the mist lifted. It should have lifted by now!

Suppose that he, Smith was in command of *Walküre*, pursued by a shadowing cruiser he could not escape and suddenly the mist came between . . .?

He said quietly, not needing to shout because there was an uneasy silence on the bridge, all of them aware of the danger of losing *Walküre*, "Starboard ten."

"Starboard ten . . . Ten of starboard wheel on, sir!"

"Meet her. Steer that."

"—Course eight-five degrees, sir!"

Now *Dauntless* was heading eastward and that had been *Walküre*'s course when last sighted. Smith glanced out over the starboard quarter and could just make out *Blackbird*, tiny under her smoke and the light of a signal lamp flickering from her. She was far enough from *Walküre* to be safe and maybe *Dauntless* was, now that she was steaming on a course parallel to that of *Walküre*. Approximately parallel; the gap between the ships might be closing or opening. Smith saw Jameson watching him worriedly, wondering at his captain's change of course. Smith stepped out to the port wing of the bridge and leaned on the screen beside the look-out, who said, "I think this mist's coming apart, sir."

It was; the sun was sucking it up so now they had glimpses through gaps in it of a clear-edged, empty horizon. Around them the mist still gave a false horizon of only three or four miles, sometimes less where it lay thickest.

The look-out bawled in Smith's ear, *"Port quarter! Christ!"*

Smith whipped around, saw *Walküre* for an instant vaguely, then only too clear as she burst out of the mist almost astern of *Dauntless* and steaming straight for her. He shouted, "Starboard ten!" As *Dauntless* heeled to that order he thought she had nearly caught them, had turned back to port in a wide circle that would have brought her out of the mist right on top of *Dauntless* if Smith had not ordered that last change of course.

The bridge gratings bucked under his feet, flame towered from a hit aft and blast threw the port look-out into Smith, sent both of them staggering. Smith pushed away, saw the smoke boiling up right aft and streaming out astern on the wind. *Walküre*'s captain *had* succeeded, had sprung the trap.

Smith swallowed. The ship's heeling turn meant he could no longer see *Walküre* from where he stood. He plunged back across the bridge to the starboard wing, felt the air and the deck shiver and heard the *slam!* of a 6-inch gun firing from aft. So one at least of the two after guns was still in action. He waited for the other to fire but it did not. He could not see the damage in the stern for the smoke there but he could see *Walküre* only too well. She had been headed straight for *Dauntless* when she first came out of the mist but now she was turning to starboard to fire broadsides and at a range of barely three miles.

He ordered "Port ten," to send *Dauntless* swerving away from those big guns. The 6-inch aft fired again and at the same instant the salvo from *Walküre* howled into bracket the ship, heeling her over, hurling spray to hang against the sun so they steamed through a jewelled curtain that stank like the pit. *Dauntless* thrust through, seemed to shake herself free of it and was in the open sea again.

A report came up from Ackroyd that the aftermost 6-inch gun was dismounted, so the gun still in action was that mounted on the superstructure and almost over Smith's main cabin. The wrecked gun was right over the wardroom, the snug comfort of which would be a scene of bloody chaos.

In the mad minutes that followed *Dauntless* swerved and ran for her life, the surviving 6-inch gun aft slamming away and the salvoes from *Walküre* howling in. She almost bracketed *Dauntless* again and twice the salvoes fell terrifyingly close alongside so the men below deck heard them like hammer-blows on the thin steel shell of the cruiser. She survived, but

Smith knew she could not hope to survive much longer, that one of those salvoes must land on her soon. The range was opening but she was still well within reach of those 8-inch guns and the mist that had hidden *Walküre* would no longer save *Dauntless*. The sun was wiping it away from the surface of the sea like steam wiped from a mirror with a stroke of the hand. The sea glittered, though still flecked with white horses that the wind drove in spray, and opened out around them to a wide, clear horizon. Visibility for gunnery was excellent now and *Walküre* bulked huge under her black trail of funnel smoke.

"Ship bearing green nine-oh!" That yell came from the starboard look-out.

Smith lifted his glasses and saw the ship hull-up on the horizon. The look-out went on: "That's *Maroc*, sir! I'm sure of it – saw her in Malta many a time."

It was the French battleship but closer and running something like a mile ahead of *Maroc* was a much smaller vessel. Smith thought that would be the American Sub-chaser, S.C. 101, the battleship's solitary escort. Doubtless she had gone scouting ahead when they heard the gunfire and mist still shrouded the sea, her captain making the most of the two- or three-knot advantage in speed that his little craft had over *Maroc*.

Smith said, "Yeoman! Make to *Maroc*: 'Enemy bears north-west four miles'."

The searchlight on the platform above the bridge clattered its shutter, blinking out the signal but before it was done Smith saw it was superfluous. And Jameson said, "*Walküre's* shifted her fire, sir! She's firing on *Maroc*!"

Maroc was already turning, presenting her side to the enemy. A column of water-spouts rose short of her and as she steamed clear flame winked from the turrets fore and aft in her. Smith swung the glasses, searching for *Walküre*, found her shivering in the lenses then still as he held them on her. *Walküre* was turning.

He ordered, "Port ten!"

"Ten of port wheel on, sir!"

Walküre had turned eastward again. She had held *Dauntless* almost in her grip but now she faced *Maroc* with her four 12-inch guns she dared not fight on. The balance had tipped the other way and now the odds were loaded against *Walküre*. Smith wondered how her captain must feel, first of all to have got this far unseen, only for *Dauntless* to blunder on to him? And then to turn under cover of the mist and almost catch the cruiser at point-blank range, but not quite. Smith appreciated that manoeuvre, its cunning and quick execution, the use of the mist to achieve surprise, and knew that only his own order to turn had saved *Dauntless* . . . "Meet her. Steer oh-six-oh." And: "Revolutions for fifteen knots."

"Course is oh-six-oh, sir!"

Now *Dauntless* was following *Walküre* but sedately, the range opening between them as *Walküre* pulled away. Her after-turrets still fired at *Maroc* and the French battleship had turned in pursuit, was returning the fire. It was a long-range duel between the big ships even to start with and it became still longer as the range opened. Both ships achieved some near-misses and aboard *Dauntless* they watched and hoped that *Maroc* would not be hit but would hit *Walküre*. The first wish was granted but not the other.

The sub-chaser had fallen back to patrol abeam of *Maroc* and one salvo from *Walküre* fell around the cockle-shell craft. Smith held his breath then saw her pushing out of the smoke and spray. He said, "Make to the chaser: '*Walküre* flying Turkish colours. Understand U.S.A. not at war with Turkey'."

Inside a minute the signal yeoman gave him the answer. "From the chaser, sir: 'Submit your last signal should be addressed to *Walküre*.'"

Smith laughed with the rest of them on the bridge. Whoever commanded the chaser had a cool head and a sense of humour. He asked, "Who is her captain?"

Henderson had already checked the list. "Lieutenant Petersen. That's with an 'e', s-e-n, sir." Smith nodded and Henderson added, "Suppose he's Norwegian by origin."

If he imagined a tall blond Viking, he was wrong.

*   *   *

103

Harry Petersen was dark and blue-chinned, short and broad. An ex-mate, he had been commissioned to command a sub-marine-chaser when the United States came into the war. He stood in the cramped wheelhouse of his little command now and scowled at the smoke that marked *Walküre*, hull-down over the horizon. She was no longer firing and *Maroc*'s guns fell silent, the long barrels lowering gently from their high elevation of maximum range.

Young Ensign Cleeve on the deck below turned to look up at Petersen, whom he worshipped, and laughed. "Well, it sure was exciting while it lasted. Goodbye *Walküre*."

Petersen took the stubby pipe from his mouth, tamped down the smouldering tobacco with a horny forefinger and clamped his teeth around the stem again, sucked thought-fully. "We might see her again."

It was a procession now, *Dauntless* shadowing *Walküre* while *Maroc* and the chaser tried vainly to keep up. *Blackbird* was there, too, but three or four miles astern of *Dauntless* and hardly faster than the French battleship now. Petersen knew only one ship could keep up with *Walküre* and that was *Dauntless*. So he muttered, "Watch yourself," and he was talking to the slim light cruiser, because *Walküre* would not tamely submit to being shadowed.

Ackroyd, filthy with soot and grime, came briefly to the bridge to report to Smith in person. "Fire's out, sir. The shell didn't penetrate, exploded on impact but the gun and its crew are a total loss."

He did not go into details and Smith could imagine the scene of carnage around the 6-inch gun after a direct hit from one of those big shells. But it might have been worse. Suppose that shell had torn through the bare inch of steel that was all that armoured the deck and exploded below, leaving *Dauntless* a crippled hulk? Suppose an entire salvo—

He tried to black out the pictures from his mind because he had seen them all too often in reality during recent actions. And the loss of the gun crew was bad enough; he had known the men personally, as he knew every man aboard *Dauntless* and *Blackbird*. In the ear-ringing silence after the guns' firing he experienced the too-familiar reaction. The excitement, the detached concentration that gripped him when in action, these were past now and the coldness crept in on him.

Jameson said, "*Blackbird* reports she's making water but her pumps are coping and she's making repairs, can steam fifteen knots."

Smith nodded. *Blackbird* was three or four miles astern. Again he was uneasy about Pearce. Why had the man been so slow to react? He jammed his hands into his pockets, clenched tight out of sight. He saw Buckley at the back of the bridge, caught his knowing look before the big man could wipe it from his face and told him, deliberately casual: "See if you can get us some tea, please."

He swung up into his chair behind the bridge screen. "Resume normal working." This would be a long shadowing operation, he was certain. "But tell the masthead look-outs they're to report if *Walküre* makes any change in course or speed." That was only a reminder to keep the look-outs on their toes; they would report changes anyway. He could see *Walküre*, just a speck under her smoke, safely out of range, but from the look-out platform high above the bridge they would see her better. She was far enough ahead so he ordered an increase in speed. "Revolutions for twenty knots." There would be changes of course and speed, he was certain of that. *Dauntless* with her advantage of speed could comfortably shadow *Walküre* like this indefinitely, but her captain had already shown he would not just accept that. They had to watch *Walküre*.

Through the morning the shadowing went on as *Walküre* ran eastward at around twenty knots. To the south lay Cyprus and to the north Turkey but both of them were hidden below the rim of the sea and the two ships ran down the middle of the hundred-mile-wide channel that lay between. First *Maroc* and the chaser were dropped, slipping down below the horizon. *Blackbird*, making better than her hoped-for fifteen knots was still steadily left astern, became only a smudge of smoke and then that too was gone. There was only *Dauntless* and *Walküre* tearing through the big seas. But soon the weather moderated, the wind easing, the sea falling away to a long swell and *Blackbird* wirelessed that she had worked up to twenty knots.

It was close to noon when the report came down from the masthead: "Enemy turning south."

Smith saw her turn to starboard and she continued to turn until she was roaring back along her own wake. He ordered, "Starboard ten!"

Dauntless came around to show her stern to *Walküre* and for minutes the ships raced westward with the long gap still between them. Then *Walküre* turned once more, headed eastward again and *Dauntless* copied her neatly, the two ships almost turning together as if manoeuvring under a common command.

The pursuit went on. The sun was overhead now, glittering on the sea so it hurt the eyes. The German ship was tiny with distance and blurred by smoke and heat shimmer that made it tremble in the lenses of the glasses. Smith felt relaxed, able to smile easily and there was a moment of wry humour when Cherrett brought a wireless signal and Smith read it.

He said, "It seems that report of *Walküre* being sighted off Crete was a mistake. It turned out to be *Agamemnon*." She was a British pre-Dreadnought battleship.

Ackroyd snorted, "She don't look anything like *Walküre*!"

Smith said straight-faced, "Maybe we saw *Walküre* a bit closer than they did."

Ackroyd said into the laughter, "Too bloody true! This is close enough for me."

But much later the bridge was quiet when Henderson emerged from the chartroom to say, "She could turn any time now, sir."

He meant that *Walküre* had steamed past Cyprus and now could turn south towards Deir el Belah, Port Said and the convoy routes. They watched Smith because that would call for a decision from him. The night would cloak *Walküre* long before she reached any of those destinations and he dared not lose her thus. But he had anticipated this moment and only nodded acknowledgment of Henderson's words and said, "She won't turn. She's headed for Alexandretta."

There was silence on the bridge, then Ackroyd asked, "What would she want there?"

Smith shook his head. He didn't know. There was nothing at Alexandretta for *Walküre*. A scattering of small shipping lay at the head of the Gulf by the port itself, one of them the big German freighter, *Friedrichsburg*, and she had swung to her anchor there since the start of the war in 1914. He said, "She was headed eastward when we ran into her. If she was bound for Port Said or the convoy routes, why should she go north-about around Cyprus?"

Ackroyd hazarded, "Maybe she was intending an attack on Cyprus and changed her mind when we turned up with *Maroc*."

Smith did not believe it. *Walküre* had not broken out just to bombard the island. But what *was* she up to?

Walküre held on to the eastward and when the coast of Turkey was sighted off the port bow it was certain she was bound for Alexandretta. Ackroyd and Henderson looked at Smith, still sitting easily in the chair, and exchanged glances of puzzled respect behind his back. Midshipman Bright eyed his captain as if he had foreseen *Walküre*'s destination by second sight. She finally altered course but only to edge in towards the coast and Ackroyd said, "She's holding close to the northern shore." That was the Gulf of Alexandretta before them now, twenty miles wide. Thinking of the minefields Ackroyd added, "Of course."

Smith nodded and ordered, "Revolutions for ten knots."

Walküre was on a course to take her through the gap in the Turkish minefields that closed the mouth of the Gulf, hard by the northern shore, running under the protecting muzzles of the batteries there. Smith got down from the chair, stretched and leaned his arms on the screen to set the glasses to his eyes again. He watched the big cruiser haul away as *Dauntless* reduced speed, to shrink and finally disappear into the distance of the Gulf. It was twenty-five miles from the mouth to the head of it where lay the small port of Alexandretta itself.

He lowered the glasses and rubbed at his eyes. "Starboard five." *Dauntless* started on a steady patrol across the entrance to the cleared channel. *Walküre*'s captain knew his way through those minefields but Smith did not. Besides, he was not going to fight Ackroyd's 'pocket-sized battleship' anywhere, let alone in the constricted waters of the Gulf. That would be suicide.

Ackroyd said, "Well, she's safe now." He scowled into the Gulf.

Smith answered grimly, "We'll see about that. Where's *Blackbird*?"

"Twenty miles astern of us. She should be up in an hour or so."

It was an hour before *Blackbird* heaved up over the horizon under a pall of smoke as her stokers laboured at the furnaces to keep her engines pounding. Meanwhile the signals had gone out telling the Allied navies that *Walküre* was trapped in the Gulf of Alexandretta and *Dauntless* held the door. Smith watched *Blackbird* come on with the huge hole torn in her hull just above the waterline. It was well for her that the sea had moderated at noon. In the heavy weather of the morning she had shipped water through that hole despite the hastily-rigged patch clapped on it. She could make her twenty knots only in fine weather and that was not good enough in a consort for a fast light cruiser like *Dauntless*. That hole had to be mended soon and he must have another talk with Pearce, who must pull himself together or—

He put Pearce from his mind, turned instead to what he had to do now. He knew *Blackbird* had plenty of bombs left. So they would try . . .

He ordered, "Make to *Blackbird*: 'Prepare to launch two seaplanes.'"

Smith wanted to see *Walküre*, where she lay, whether she was anchored or still shifting about the Gulf. He needed the information for the future and the near future at that, because something would have to be done about *Walküre*; she could not be left as a threat, another German warship constantly to be guarded.

Another point: only twenty-four hours before *Dauntless* and *Blackbird* had been on a mission that would have brought them to this Gulf anyway. The Afrika Legion. That mission had been postponed but not abandoned.

"*Blackbird* acknowledges, sir." That was Ackroyd.

"Tell Pearce that one of them is to reconnoitre the railway from Adana to the Bagcha tunnel. I'll fly in the other up the gulf as observer and we'll carry bombs."

He walked out to the wing of the bridge as the signal was hoisted, broke out. He did not need the glasses to see that one seaplane had already been pushed out of the hangar on its trolley; *Blackbird* was close now.

Ackroyd appeared at his shoulder. "Wireless from *Maroc*, sir." He handed the flimsy to Smith. *Maroc* estimated her arrival at the Gulf at 1900 hours. Ackroyd added cheerfully, "That'll turn the key in the lock."

That it would. *Maroc* might be slow but *Walküre*'s captain would not be bold or mad enough to steam out into the fire from the old French battleship's 12-inch guns.

Ackroyd said, "Surely *Walküre* must have known she'd be bottled up in here. Or did she hope to get this far without being spotted?"

Smith pointed out, "She nearly did."

Ackroyd blinked as he took it in, that if *Dauntless* had been an hour later at the rendezvous she would have steamed west in accordance with her orders because *Walküre* would already have passed and been on her way eastward to Alexandretta. A scouting aircraft from Cyprus might have found her, but only might.

Smith handed the flimsy back to Ackroyd. "Call away my boat."

The gig headed for *Blackbird*. She was stopped now, one seaplane in the water, tethered by lines and boomed off from the ship's side by the long poles. He could see the four sixty-five-pound bombs slung horizontally under the fuselage.

That was his. "Pull for the Short."

The gig's head shifted around. Looking between the men who tugged at the oars, Smith could see Flight Lieutenant Rogers in the plane's pilot's cockpit. He was a thin gangling young man, known to his brother fliers as 'Captain Webb', named after the famous Channel swimmer, because Rogers had only too often crashed in the sea and had himself to swim for it. Beyond him, aboard *Blackbird*, a second seaplane had been wheeled out of the hangar and was now hoisted from its trolley, pilot and observer already aboard. Delilah. He recognised Hamilton back from the sick bay, sitting in the observer's cockpit, then he dragged on his helmet and his thatch of red hair was hidden. Cole was the pilot. Of course. Delilah was his darling and he and Hamilton were a team.

"Oars!" The gig slipped up to the Short and bow grabbed for and caught a strut, hauled the gig in alongside a boxy float, the sea breaking over it.

Smith stepped across the thwarts and over the side of the gig with a steadying hand clutching the strut. Rogers reached down a long arm from the pilot's cockpit, a flying helmet in the outstretched hand and Smith snatched it, slung his cap into the boat and waved it away, yelling, "Lose that and I'll stop your grog for the rest o' the war!" He saw them laughing as he hauled himself up into the cockpit and the gig sheered away.

He had to lift the map and sketchpad from the seat. The Lewis banged at the back of his head and he shoved it away as he plumped down into the cockpit. Rogers reached up and slipped the toggle release when Smith had settled himself in. The Short's Maori engine fired, climbed from its growling tickover to a snarl and then a thunder as they ran across the sea. The vibration eased to a thrumming, the flying spray was gone, they were airborne and climbing, tilting on one wing as Rogers turned the Short and headed her for the Gulf of Alexandretta.

Rogers kept climbing, a slow climb, as the lumbering Short hauled slowly up into the blue and the Gulf opened out before them. All three sides of the long box of the Gulf were backed by mountains, to east and south the shore was thickly wooded and to the north clothed in brush. Smith glanced out to his left and behind and saw Delilah, a barely-moving speck inching towards the crags and Adana. Then he turned his attention ahead.

They were half way up the Gulf now and right ahead was the little town of Payas with its old castle and the sun catching a dome and a minaret. Down in the right-hand corner of the Gulf was the port of Alexandretta but the tiny harbour there was unimportant. Smith's chart aboard *Dauntless* had showed thirty fathoms all up the Gulf except for close inshore so *Walküre* had plenty of room to manoeuvre and anchor . . .

There she was! He leaned forward and thumped Rogers's shoulder, pointed and Rogers nodded. *Walküre* lay near the head of the Gulf at anchor, smoke only wisping from her two funnels, and close by her lay the big freighter *Friedrichsburg*, which had been trapped here from the early days of the war. The picture of still ships on a glassy blue surface tilted on its side as Rogers banked the Short and turned towards *Walküre*. He was not wasting any time. They had climbed to a thousand feet or so and circling about would only lose them what little element of surprise, if any, was on their side.

The nose of the Short dipped as Rogers put her into a shallow dive. Smith rose in his seat to see the better, braced against the wind that tore at him, searching *Walküre* for signs of damage. He thought he saw where she might have been hit forward, between the fore-turret and the stem, but he could not be sure till they were closer.

He could guess at the feelings of the German captain and his crew, hounded into this dead-end and knowing the enemy were gathering outside. Smith had bitter experience of that earlier in the year when he commanded the cruiser *Thunder* in the Pacific. The German captain was a bold man to have got this far. He would need all his boldness.

They were close! The Short's dive steepened and her speed mounted. Smith could make out the details of *Walküre* now, the big-gun turrets, one forward, one aft and two either side of the centre-line – and *Dauntless had* hit her forward! – the 5.9s and 3.4s, those last with barrels at high elevation pointing up at the Short.

Smith gulped, eyes still scurrying over the ship that grew bigger beneath him with every second, seeking more signs of damage, finding none but seeing instead the flames winking from the guns along her deck. He clung on to the cockpit coaming as Rogers threw the Short heavily about the sky in an attempt to put off the gunners, the lumbering seaplane cavorting clumsily, a duck trying to imitate a wasp. Shells were bursting around them now and tossing the Short about. The Lewis jammed into Smith's back, painfully reminding him that it was there and he turned and cocked it, stretched to aim it down over the side of the cockpit, squeezed the trigger as the Short pulled out of the dive. *Walküre* still lay far beneath them but they would never get closer in the face of that gunfire.

He did not see whether he hit anything or anybody but he felt the jerk as Rogers let go the bombs. Smith swore as he saw them fall, one to starboard and two to port of *Walküre*. Three near-misses, but misses all the same. Three. It only proved Pearce had been right because *Walküre* was anchored and still they could not hit her. He had said, "Sit the Short on the funnel" – but the gunfire made that impossible. But only three? Where was the fourth?

Walküre was sliding swiftly away astern of them now, her guns still hammering away, chasing the Short. Smith leaned out, peered down and saw the fourth bomb still hanging below the fuselage, looked up and saw Rogers bent to one side as he worked at the toggle release, flying one-handed. The engine was hiccoughing and Smith saw oil flying on the wind. Right ahead of them was the big freighter; Rogers was easing the Short around and they were going to pass close above her stern. Smith felt the lurch, tried to bring the sight of the Lewis on to the bridge of the *Friedrichsburg*, the lurch putting him off so he fired the Lewis at the sky but he saw the bomb burst, right on the water line of the *Friedrichsburg* and under her stern. He saw the chunk of steel plate spinning skyward and turned to slap a hand at Rogers' back and yell at him. *That* was a hit.

Rogers glanced over his shoulder, gave a quick excited grin then turned back to his flying. Smith dropped down in his seat and shoved the Lewis away from the back of his neck. They had not hit *Walküre* but he was not disappointed; it had been too much to hope for. They *had* hit the freighter and that was a pointed reminder to her that she was still in a war and not safe here. He had seen *Walküre* at anchor and knew now that she was not coming out for a while and in a few hours *Maroc* would be up. As for attacking her . . .

He stopped making plans. The engine of the Short was still coughing and Rogers had gained little height, if any, since they had rid themselves of the two-hundred-and-sixty pounds of bombs. Now Smith became aware that there were great holes torn in the fuselage and they were only four or five hundred feet above the waters of the Gulf. It stretched out before him to an empty horizon. To his left the Amanus mountains lifted clearly visible because the Short was nearer to that shore but the Taurus range to the right, on the other side of the Gulf, was hazy in the far distance.

He looked behind him and saw *Walküre* and the freighter, the latter marked by a tendril of smoke, but both of them tiny now. He thought they must still have close on twenty miles to fly to reach the open sea, *Dauntless* and *Blackbird*. The Short's maximum speed was around eighty knots but they weren't making that or anywhere near it. He remembered that when they took off the wind had been out of the north so that was a crosswind for them now, better than dead foul but no help. He looked over the side of the cockpit and down at the white etching of the wave crests beneath him, the Short's shadow, cast sharp by the sun, sliding over them. They were making fifty, possibly sixty knots but no more than that. So they had to stay in the air for twenty minutes.

He realised that his neck hurt, and his head at the back, where they had caught the Lewis. At some time he had skinned his knuckles and he sucked them where they bled. The Turks had launches patrolling the Gulf, none of them in sight at the moment but if the Short came down in the Gulf it would mean a prison camp for Rogers and himself. Twenty minutes . . .

*   *   *

Dauntless and *Blackbird* were in sight now to the north-west, hull up on the horizon. *Maroc* and the chaser had still not arrived. He shouted at Rogers, pointed, and the pilot nodded and heeled the Short into a gentle, banking turn towards the ships. In minutes Smith could see they were steaming south from the north headland at the mouth of the Gulf, patrolling. Now the Short's engine died. In the silence, with only the wind's sighing through the wires strung between the two planes, Smith heard Rogers say clearly, "Hell and damnation!" He eased the nose of the Short down so it glided towards the sea which was not far below. Smith squinted at the ships. *Blackbird* steamed astern of *Dauntless* but the gap between them was widening. Had the cruiser cracked on speed or—? No. *Blackbird* was stopping and now Smith could see the reason: the seaplane coming down out of the north. That was Cole and his pal Hamilton in Delilah. But what were they doing here? They were supposed to be flying a reconnaissance from Adana all the way to the Bagcha tunnel and that was a round trip of close on two hundred miles, about three hours.

Rogers shouted, "Hang on!"

They were slipping just above the surface of the sea now, Rogers turning the Short just a point, right into the wind, straightening her, keeping her nose down, flying her. The floats touched so gently as to raise only a feather of spray but the Short kept on sinking so that briefly the spray rose. But then they were slowing, stopping. They were down but not yet home and dry. The seaplane bobbed and swung on the choppy sea as the wind pushed at it and the Short had a lot for the wind to push at. Rogers was using the rudder in an attempt to keep the Short into the wind but not succeeding. Smith stood up to see over his head: *Dauntless* was big and rapidly growing bigger, cracking on speed now with her stern tucked down and a big white bow-wave. Slender and graceful, despite the stains and scars of battle, he thought for the hundredth time what a beauty she was and how lucky he was. In a few minutes she would be up with them.

The Short lurched under him and he lost his balance and sat down with a bump. The big boxy floats, riddled with bullet holes, had filled with water and sunk so the fuselage collapsed on the sea. The tail of the Short went under as the wind pushed her astern and now she was being blown back with her propeller stuck up in the air and her tail in the sea. Rogers shoved up out of his seat to sit on the fuselage, blaspheming steadily and pulling off his shoes. "Can't do anything with her, sir. Not now. She's going to sink in a minute."

He was right. The wind blew the Short sideways and the weight of the engine and the water-filled floats dragged down the wings and fuselage inside a few minutes. In that time *Dauntless* came up, stopped and lowered a boat. It picked up Smith and Rogers as they paddled around with their shoes hung around their necks but the Short had gone.

As they sat in the sternsheets of the boat Smith said ironically, "I suppose this swimming home is standard procedure for you."

'Captain Webb' Rogers took it philosophically, "Oh well, sir. It could have been a lot worse."

Smith agreed. "If you hadn't got us this far we would be prisoners."

"Not only that, sir. There were an awful lot of holes in her where lumps of shell went through. They might easily have gone through us."

Smith remembered Cole talking about Wilson, the lieutenant of the Norfolks who was killed while flying as his observer over Lydda, " . . . cut him to pieces below the waist."

Smith swallowed sickly.

But why had Cole returned in Delilah now?

The boat was alongside *Dauntless* and he climbed the ladder and thrust his shoes into the first pair of hands he saw. "Give them to Buckley and tell him I want another pair and some clothes." And to Rogers: "Come on."

Rogers followed as he climbed the ladders to the bridge where Ackroyd waited, face serious. Smith dripped water as he peeled off his shirt. Someone handed towels to him and Rogers but Smith was asking Ackroyd, "Why did Cole return early?"

"They were hit, sir." He paused, then went on, "Hamilton's

dead. Cole is hurt pretty badly. They're sending him over to us for the surgeon to handle."

Smith was still for a second then went on mechanically rubbing at his face with the towel. First Wilson, now Hamilton. The big lieutenant of artillery had seemed indestructible, even after his fall, bursting with life. He and Cole had been closer than brothers. Now Hamilton was dead and Cole was hurt.

"There's some good news, sir." That was Ackroyd. Smith lowered the towel to rub his chest and saw Ackroyd was smiling now. "Signals, sir."

Smith leafed through the signals and saw the reason for that smile. The armoured cruiser *Attack* would arrive in thirty-six hours. Another French battleship, a new one, *Océan*, was tearing up from Malta and would arrive soon after *Attack*. A transport was to be sent from the Adriatic carrying four M.A.S. boats, the Italian torpedo-boats with electric motors for silent night attack, ideal for slipping into the Gulf over the minefields and slamming torpedoes into *Walküre*. Smith looked up and grinned. Ackroyd said, "One way or the other we've got her."

Smith agreed but now *Blackbird* ranged alongside, the way coming off both ships. *Blackbird* was stopped. *Dauntless*'s propellors thrashed astern, then stopped as she nudged in gently against the seaplane carrier. The lines flew over and the ships were briefly lashed together. *Blackbird*'s winch clattered and the stretcher with the blanket-wrapped Cole was swung up on the derrick and swayed over to the deck of *Dauntless*.

Smith rubbed at his loins with the towel wrapped around his waist. He said, "Mr. Bright."

The midshipman answered quickly, "Sir?"

"Ask the surgeon if I can talk to Mr. Cole as soon as convenient." He wanted to see Cole, wanted to know what had happened to him and Hamilton.

"Aye, aye, sir!" Bright dashed away.

Rogers, naked as the day he was born and rubbing at his hair with a towel, stood out on the wing of the bridge and carried on a shouted conversation with Pearce in *Blackbird*. Smith heard 'Delilah' mentioned. Buckley came with clothes draped over one arm as Rogers turned his head, and said, "They've sent Hamilton's map and notebook over with Cole, sir. And it seems Cole wants to talk to you."

At that moment a seaman brought a canvas-wrapped bundle to the bridge. "Come over with the pilot, sir. For you."

Smith nodded at Buckley. "Open it."

He grabbed his clothes from Buckley and dropped them on the deck, picked out the shirt and pulled it on. He carried on dressing as Buckley took out a big clasp knife, cut the twine lashed around the sailcloth-covered packet and unwrapped it. It held a map clipped to a board and a sketchblock of plain, unruled paper. Buckley held them out for inspection and Smith stooped over them as he tucked shirt into trousers.

This was Hamilton's map, Hamilton's notepad.

Both of them were spotted with blood. The pad had a hasty sketch in the corner, the back of a head in a flying helmet, shoulders humped up grotesquely each side, obviously meant to be Cole. Then the notes in Hamilton's bold, scrawled hand. Of Archie, the anti-aircraft battery on the northern shore of the Gulf, the bouncy crossing "Up and down like a see-saw". Then: "Beautiful, incredibly beautiful, the sunlight on the mountains and the ravines so deep and dark." And then: "Adana station: the scrawl became bigger: "Germans at Adana! More than a company! Five hundred! Flat cars with guns. Caught them napping! Not a shot fired and I could count the buttons on their shirts! Good old Cole. Good old Delilah!"

That was the last entry.

Smith slowly folded the map and put the notepad carefully inside it. He looked up to see Rogers and Ackroyd staring at him. Rogers asked, "Something wrong, sir?"

"They found the Afrika Legion."

Ackroyd burst out, "That's bloody marvellous!" Then as he saw Smith's set face, "Isn't it, sir?"

Smith did not answer him but said to Rogers, now dressed in shirt and trousers lent by Jameson, "Let's go and see Cole."

*   *   *

He lay in a cot in the sick bay, his face as white as the sheet tucked up around him. Merryweather came to meet Smith and Rogers at the door and said, "He wants to talk to you."

Smith stared past him at Cole. "I need to hear him. Is it – is he all right?"

Merryweather said bitterly, "There's nothing I or anyone else can do for him. I can't understand how he's still alive."

Smith heard the catch of Rogers' breath. Merryweather stood aside and Smith moved forward to kneel by the cot. Cole's head turned, eyes looking for him.

Smith said softly, "Hello, old son."

Cole whispered, "Hamilton? How is he?"

"He'll be all right," Smith lied.

"Good." Cole smiled. "I was worried about him."

He was silent, then Smith prompted, because he had to ask, "What happened?"

Cole whispered, "Got over Adana. Hell of a trip – you know what it's like – up and down like you were in a bloody great lift – and the wind. But Delilah took it like a bird. She's a beauty! And Adana. Train there. Lot of Germans. Hundreds!"

Hamilton's pad had said five hundred.

". . . Afrika Legion. Must be. Guns. Got right down low, buzzed them. Not a shot fired at us. Then – Archie, I suppose. Don't remember anything. Found I was still flying or Delilah was flying herself. Couldn't see Hamilton or hear him. Don't remember much about the rest. Saw *Blackbird*. Kept dozing off but got down. Delilah got us down. Good old Delilah. Is she all right?" He peered anxiously at Rogers.

Who nodded. "They got her aboard. A few holes, that's all."

"Great." Cole was silent, eyes closed.

Smith waited, watching the pilot. He felt a touch on his arm, turned his head and saw the surgeon point at the door where Midshipman Bright waited. Smith glanced back at Cole but the surgeon was bent over him, one hand moving in a gesture of dismissal. Smith and Rogers rose and left the sick bay.

Bright said, "Sorry to interrupt, sir, but the first lieutenant said to fetch you at once. There's a local boat alongside and that Arab chap has come aboard, the one we put ashore south of Jaffa."

Smith stared at him, remembering Edwards saying arrogantly, "I'll find the Legion for you, if it's there. Just have to grease a few palms, maybe cut a throat or two but I'll find it." Edwards about to leap into the surf on an enemy shore: "His throat or mine. And I bet it's his!"

"Where is he?"

"In his cabin, sir, the one he had before. He said a friend had brought him. He asked if his kit was still aboard and then if he could use the cabin. An' he said he wanted to talk to you so the first lieutenant said he could have the cabin and you would see him all in good time, sir, when you were ready."

Smith's lips twitched as he pictured Ackroyd telling the colonel that and enjoying it. He said, "Very good," dismissing Bright. He wanted to hear what Edwards had to say.

Rogers said unhappily, his mind on Cole, "I'd like to get back to *Blackbird*, sir."

Smith asked, thinking ahead, "What's the state of aircraft? How many available? Two?"

"Yes, sir. The captain—" that was Pearce, captain of *Blackbird*, "—said Delilah wouldn't be ready to fly for a few hours but the other two are on stand-by."

The gig took Rogers back to *Blackbird* and Smith strode aft to the wardroom flat and Edwards's cabin. The soldier sat on the bunk in his white robes, his open suitcase beside him and his tunic across his knees. He looked thinner, his cheeks sunken and he was dirty as if the dust was ingrained into his skin. He had pulled off the head-dress and his hair was matted. A bottle of whisky stood on the desk and he held a glass in one hand while he rummaged in the pocket of his tunic with the other. He pulled out his cigarette case as Smith entered and a photograph came out of the pocket with it and fell to the deck at Smith's feet.

Edwards said, "Blast!"

Smith stooped and picked up the photograph, rose slowly. It showed the head and bare shoulders of a young woman, a half-smile on her full lips that the camera had frozen in open invitation. He asked neutrally, "Friend of yours?"

Edwards stuck a cigarette in his mouth, took the photograph, glanced at it and grinned. "Livvy? Not exactly a friend, old boy. More a sort of tenant. When I met her in Cairo she was living in some scruffy married quarter – too many service wives around watching her for her liking. I've got a flat I only use when I can get to Cairo and that's not often enough, so I let her have it. Her husband doesn't get to Cairo much either, so it works out very well." He gulped at the whisky and sighed appreciation. "Don't know what her husband does or where he is and I don't care. Livvy's a nice little piece, though now she's hinting at a divorce and giving me those 'what-about-it' looks. To hell with that. As soon as I turned my back she'd be after somebody else. I know I'm not the first by a long sight. She's notorious."

He tossed the photograph carelessly on to the desk, dismissing the subject, and showed his teeth in an exultant grin. "I want you to send a wireless signal to Finlayson. I've found the Afrika Legion."

"So have we." Smith held out Hamilton's map and pad, saw the grin wiped from Edwards's face. "We've located some of them, a half-battalion or so at Adana but we don't know whether that's an advance guard, rear-party or what. We'll send your signal, of course. It's just as well we are here to send it." That was said casually but he knew the message had got home, that but for *Dauntless* and her wireless it would have taken Edwards a week or more to reach Finlayson with his information. But then Smith said honestly, "Congratulations. It was a tremendous piece of work. You're an extraordinary man."

Edwards nodded complacently, accepting the compliment. "I'll make damn sure I get the credit for it, too. Takes me another step along the way, old boy, because it'll count for something when the war's over. It's like money in the bank." He sucked whisky and muttered, "I was lucky to get out at all. I was coming down from Adana when I saw the ships and I found an old pal to bring me out in his boat." He squinted up at Smith. "You don't seem overjoyed by *your* success."

Smith said flatly, "I'm not. For one thing, it cost the lives of two good men." There was another reason, a spectre that had haunted him since he began the search for the Afrika Legion, but he asked, "What did you find?"

Edwards reached for the bottle and filled his glass. "I first got word of them at Lydda where they have a dump of supplies waiting for them. Did that report of mine get through?" And when Smith nodded Edwards went on, "Another thing I found out at Lydda: they don't run trains down to Jaffa during the day any more. Instead it leaves Lydda well after dark and gets back just before it's light. But that's just information; I can't see any connection with the Legion." Smith already knew why the train ran at night; the Turks had had enough of being shelled and bombed on their daytime runs. Edwards said, "From Lydda I worked up to Aleppo and then round the Gulf to Adana, by train all the way, riding and hiding how I could, greasing palms. I saw some of the Legion pass through Adana – that was the rear-guard your chaps saw. I also found a railway clerk at Adana I'd used before and he's been working with and for the German Asia Corps. He didn't want to tell me anything because they'd sworn him to secrecy and as good as told him they'd shoot him if he talked. I told him I'd give him away if he *didn't* talk and that coupled with a big bribe opened his mouth."

He gulped whisky, coughed, glanced at the photograph on the desk and drawled "Ye-es. Livvy old girl, I'm for Cairo after this. I need a rest, a bed and a bottle and you-know-what." He looked up at Smith "But Livvy has to go before long. That other girl, Adeline, was it? Where is she now?"

Smith said, expressionless, "Get on with it."

Edwards gave his hoarse laugh. "Sorry. Not stepping on your toes am I, old boy?" But when Smith neither spoke nor blinked he shrugged and went on. "The Legion's in a hurry and travelling fast and light. Supplies are waiting for them, so they've been able to cut down on the trains. It's something like five or six hundred miles from Adana down to the front but everything is being cleared from the railway to let them through. Kressenstein insisted on that." Smith listened, apprehension growing. He had said Kressenstein would ram the Legion south as quick as he could.

Edwards said, "They'll pick up their supplies and ammunition at Lydda early on the 31st and arrive at Beersheba by midday. That's in two days' time."

Smith stared at him. Edwards did not know how bad his news was. He knew it *was* bad, that Allenby's attack would take place soon and that the Legion's presence might endanger the success of that attack. But because he was sent behind the lines he had not been told of the details of Allenby's plan of attack. Smith knew them all too well.

Edwards explained, "They're to relieve the Turkish garrison at Beersheba so that the Turks can be sent down to reinforce Gaza."

So the Turks and Germans still believed the main attack would fall on Gaza, they were still using the fine road the German engineers had built to stiffen the defences there. As Allenby meant them to, as the ruse of the staff officer, supposedly wounded, fleeing in panic and losing his briefcase had encouraged them to. Beersheba was the real key to Allenby's plan of attack, his entire campaign. He was not going to accept a challenge to a bloody assault on the 'impregnable' Gaza-Beersheba line. The attack on Gaza would be a feint while the real attack would be made at Beersheba, to take it and roll up the 'impregnable' line from that flank. The plan called for surprise and Allenby would clearly have achieved that. It also demanded that the desert fighters take Beersheba before the end of the first day, before it could be reinforced, and before the attackers had to withdraw for more water. That was essential. And that first day was October 31st.

Smith said thickly, "I'll send a signal."

Edwards stared at his face and said, "It's worse than I thought?"

Smith said, "I'll explain. Wait for me."

As he walked along to the wireless office he thought it could not be worse. Allenby's army could take Beersheba on the 31st but not by midday; the ground to be covered and the defences made that impossible. And before midday the Afrika

Legion would be at Beersheba, five thousand picked men, heavily armed with machine-guns and field artillery and highly trained. They would treble or quadruple the fire-power of the defences of Beersheba, the fortress on the left of the line.

And the spectre that had haunted Smith since he began his search now stood at his shoulder. Right from the start he had asked himself the question he dared not voice: When they found the Afrika Legion – what could they do about it?

He still had no answer.

Telegraphist Lofty Williams, emerging from the wireless office stood back to let his captain pass, saw Smith stare right through him, saw his face drawn and pale and heard him whisper bitterly, *"Oh, Christ!"*

7

"They'll Bury Me There – And I Won't Be The Only One!"

Smith went aboard *Blackbird* and saw Pearce in his cabin.

"Why didn't you turn when *Dauntless* did, when *Walküre* opened fire? Were you waiting for an order from me?"

Pearce stared down at his desk. "No, sir."

"I'd hope not. I expect you to show some initiative in a situation like that. So?"

Pearce looked up and said honestly, "I just couldn't seem to think for a moment." He had stared dumbly at the scene before him as the look-outs shouted and his first lieutenant pointed at *Walküre*, her guns flaming.

Smith asked, "Have you any excuse?" But there could be no excuse. "Any reason?" He let his gaze drift to the photograph on the desk, suddenly aware of Edwards aboard *Dauntless* who had that same photograph of Olivia Pearce, Chris's wife and Edwards's 'sort of tenant'.

Pearce's eyes followed his to the photograph, glanced quickly at Smith then away. He shook his head. "No excuse, sir."

Smith said, watching him, "Colonel Edwards came off in a boat an hour ago."

Pearce was astonished but that was his only reaction. "The one who acts as an Arab? How on earth did he wangle that?"

"Some old pal he met." Smith decided that Pearce did not know about Edwards but was clearly worried about his wife and would not admit it. "You can't go on like this, Chris. I'll give you leave as soon as I can." That, though, would present problems; Pearce was far and away the best man for his job –

124

when he was up to it. There was no one else so qualified. "Meanwhile I want to see an improvement. If I can help in any way, just ask."

The offer was there. Pearce could unburden himself if he cared to, but he only said, "Thank you, sir."

So Smith had to leave it at that. Instead he told Pearce about the Afrika Legion. "I sent a signal to Braddock and he replied ordering us back to army H.Q. in Deir el Belah as soon as *Maroc* comes up to take over here. I intend to leave Ackroyd in command and fly back, taking Edwards with me."

Pearce brightened, was on familiar ground here. "It's a hell of a long flight, sir, and all of it over the sea or enemy territory. If you have to come down—" he shrugged. "But the Shorts can do it. They've got the endurance and this northerly wind helps. It'll be right on the tail and a good eight knots."

The two Shorts charged heavily across the sea, butting into the wind coming out of the north and lifted off, banked gently and headed southward. Smith sat behind Kirby in one of them while Beckett flew the other with Edwards as passenger. Smith watched his little command become toy ships on the wrinkled surface of the sea as they fell astern. *Maroc* and the chaser should arrive soon, and then they could start for Deir el Belah.

It was a long flight and his thoughts were not pleasant company. He had almost missed the Afrika Legion because he had not sailed north to Alexandretta forty-eight hours before but instead had run to Deir el Belah with the two men burned in the fire aboard *Blackbird*. He had let sentiment affect his judgment when his duty was plain and if the Legion had slipped south unseen, it would have been his fault. No matter that Finlayson and Braddock had thought the Legion would be too late – he himself had not believed it. Edwards had found the Afrika Legion but had not been able to pass his warning until *Dauntless* with her wireless came to the Gulf of Alexandretta, where she should have been long before. It had been up to Smith and he had almost failed them all, simply because he had not shown the cold, callous objectivity es-

sential to a commander in time of war. His concern over two
men he knew might have set at risk the lives of thousands
committed to the attack on the Gaza-Beersheba line. He had
come to Palestine believing this to be a time of crisis in his
career, make or break, and he might have been broken, had
survived only by luck. And what if he had to face the same
choice again? What would he decide? He did not know.

Night fell early in the flight and they flew in darkness but
the wind did not fail them, nor did the Shorts. They made a
landfall at Jaffa, banking to pass low over the little harbour
tucked in tight under the town on its hill.

Kirby pointed, head turned and shouting, " . . . Boats!"

Smith saw the harbour was crammed with small craft,
dhows or surf-boats as far as he could see in the night. He
wondered if the Turks intended to try to supply the Gaza-
Beersheba line by this kind of small, coastwise traffic. If so
they were being wildly optimistic. *Dauntless* had already
shown how vulnerable such traffic was. So—? He shrugged off
that question; he had enough to be going on with.

The Shorts droned on down the coast past Gaza, marked by
the gun-flashes pricking the night, and came to Deir el Belah.
A line of buoyed lights had been laid across the anchorage for
them and the Shorts turned into wind, its direction shown by
the wisping smoke from the funnels of the ships anchored
there, and one after the other slid down to settle on the sea. A
decked-over lighter took the seaplanes aboard and set Smith
and Edwards ashore.

Dauntless turned to lead *Blackbird* south. Astern of them, off
the Gulf of Alexandretta, the French battleship *Maroc* patrolled across the channel that was like the narrow neck opening into the bottle of the Gulf beyond. *Maroc* steamed at a
sedate ten knots while the little submarine-chaser No. 101
scurried fussily around her. *Maroc* was old and slow but she
commanded the narrow channel with her 12-inch guns.
Walküre was a ship in a bottle and *Maroc* the fat cork jammed
in its neck.

Smith and Edwards, the naval officer and the colonel still in his flowing Arab robes, walked up through the gap in the dunes. In the darkness a locomotive slowly *clunk-clunked* along the siding, halted with a hiss of steam and a squealing of brakes and the trucks behind banged together like a ragged salvo of artillery. Smith saw the sapper on the footplate as he passed, the round moon-face shining with sweat. They trudged rapidly up the road, both of them weary, forcing their stiff legs to stretch out. The wind out of the north set the palm fronds waving and clashing above their heads and brought to their ears the thunder of the guns before Gaza. In the night muzzle-flashes flickered against the dark sky.

An aide met them at Finlayson's headquarters and ushered them hurriedly through the ante-room into the tent where Smith had seen Finlayson and Braddock before. They stood over the map now as if they had never moved. They were not alone: a lieutenant of Australian Light Horse stood tall by the table, and Jeavons, master of the *Morning Star* waited a little apart. He looked easier in his mind now, straight and spruce and he had a smile for Smith. Major John Taggart was there also. He nodded, still wary in the presence of the others.

A haggard Finlayson performed the introductions. The Australian was a Lieutenant Jackson. Smith nodded. He did not know the man but he knew of the Light Horse and Jackson looked a good sample, lean and hard. Finlayson got down to business, outlined for all of them the background of the Afrika Legion, then: "The Legion is on its way to reinforce Beersheba and will pick up supplies and ammunition at Lydda on the morning of the 31st. The Flying Corps are going to try a bombing raid but they say the guns south of Lydda station will keep them high and it will be difficult to hit the dump, let alone destroy it. The chances of cutting the railway line are negligible." He rubbed at tired eyes and looked at the officers grouped round the map. "The Legion must be stopped. There is only one place it might be done and that is at Lydda. A force must strike inland to destroy the dump and demolish the track."

In the silence Smith heard the beating of moths against the

lamp and their wings sent shadows fluttering across the map. He said, already disliking the idea, "A landing?"

"A raid," Finlayson corrected him. "We haven't the ships, the men, or the time to mount a conventional landing." He looked at Edwards. "You were put ashore south of Jaffa and I understand the coast isn't defended. Could you guide a small force through the dunes and on to Lydda, a night landing and a night march?"

Edwards hesitated, then: "I could. But it's heavy going for troops in the sand, they wouldn't better two miles an hour and it's all of ten miles from the nearest point."

Finlayson brushed that aside impatiently. "We know that! I'm talking of mounted men, a single troop of horse. We know from aerial reconnaissance and your own reports that there are guardhouses spaced along the road from Jaffa to Er Ramle which lies across your route to Lydda. The Turks also have a regiment in reserve camped on that road. Therefore, while you passed through as an Arab, a troop of horse could not. Correct?"

Edwards nodded, licking his lips.

Finlayson went on: "There is a Turkish garrison camped outside and just south of Jaffa and another regiment five miles north – that's about a mile north of the Auja river." His finger moved deliberately across the map, marking them. "There's a ford at the mouth of the river where the depth is only three feet, and there is only one machine-gun post. Major Taggart's battalion will land there in daylight after a preliminary bombardment by *Dauntless* on the evening of the 30th, that's tomorrow, and establish a bridgehead, acting in all respects as if preparing the way for a full-scale landing on the next day. There are four motorised lighters fit for this work. Three of these will land Major Taggart's battalion at the mouth of the Auja."

He looked up. "The Turks have feared a landing north of Gaza to turn the line there and have guarded against it. While this will be a lot further north, they will certainly react with all the force available. That will pull in the regiment from north of the Auja, the garrison at Jaffa, *and* the regiment on the

affa-Er Ramle road. The way will then be clear for Mr.
ackson's troop which will land south of Jaffa in the remaining
notorised lighter. They must reach the railway and the dump
before first light and at least demolish the track – and if possible destroy the dump."

He paused, gazed round at them and asked quietly, "Ques-
ions? Colonel Edwards?"

Smith glanced sideways at Edwards and saw sweat on his
face, though the night was chill. Edwards said, "There's a
chance. There'll be some odds and ends of Turkish troops left
about but we should be able to cut our way through. The
dump—" He hesitated, then said, "It's guarded by a company
of Germans and they're not rear-echelon troops. They'll
fight . . ." His voice trailed away.

Finlayson said bitingly, "I asked for questions, not a recital
of obstacles to be surmounted. This raid must be attempted."
His eyes shifted round the room. "Mr. Jackson?"

The tall Australian shrugged. "We'll give it a go."

Finlayson said grimly, "You'll have to. Taggart?"

Major Taggart asked, "Has anyone got a better idea?" He
waited but no one spoke. He said, "I know what you want,
sir."

Finlayson rubbed at his forehead with the tips of his fingers
as if trying to rub out the lines etched there. "Thank you,
gentlemen. I can think of no alternative. The chances of success are small but so long as they exist we must make the
attempt. I will give you your orders in writing." He looked
straight at Taggart. "Will your men obey orders?"

Taggart answered coldly, "Yes, sir."

Finlayson said, "Arms will be sent out to the *Morning Star*
tomorrow morning but ammunition will be carried aboard the
lighters. The battalion will sail in the *Morning Star* and will
not transfer to the lighters till the moment of landing and will
land at your orders or those of Commander Smith," now he
stared at Smith and said deliberately, "who will use whatever
force is necessary to impose discipline and enforce the landing."

Taggart said angrily, "That won't be necessary."

"I trust not. But the landing must be made."

There was silence for a moment as the threat, or the warning hung in the air. Now Smith knew the reason for the change in Finlayson. Ordering men into action was a heavy enough responsibility but this—! Finlayson had weighed the possible gain to Allenby's whole army against the lives of Jackson, Taggart and their men and had the guts to give the order. He was already paying for it, had aged ten years.

Now he asked, "Captain Jeavons? You're happy with this – ah – *unusual* extension of your contract?"

The master of the *Morning Star* asked in his turn, "I'll take my orders from Commander Smith?"

Finlayson nodded. "He will command the operation."

"That's good enough for me. I've heard a lot about the Commander." Then Jeavons said bluntly, "Those lads of Major Taggart's, they're all right when you get to know them. There's still a wall they keep around themselves, if you see what I mean, but I can't hardly credit that they're hiding a murderer—"

"That will do!" Finlayson cut him short and looked sharply at Jackson who had shown no surprise. "Keep that to yourself."

Jackson drawled, "It's a bit late, sir."

"What have you heard?"

"About this battalion? Rumours."

"Stop them."

"Yes, sir."

Finlayson forced a smile. "Captain Jeavons has been a frequent visitor at these headquarters. I think everyone in Deir el Belah knows he has a cargo waiting for him at Tangier. In forty-eight hours, Captain, you will be on your way. You have my word on it."

"Thank you, sir." Then Jeavons added, "That ammunition in the after holds should be unloaded now."

"That it should." Finlayson threw at an aide, "See to that as soon as it's light."

Jeavons took his leave and the rest of them got down to detailed planning but it was an uneasy cooperation. Smith was not an insensitive man and became immediately aware of the hostility or mistrust that separated the three soldiers, Jackson, Taggart and Edwards. Taggart was guarded and Jackson spoke hardly at all but his dislike of Edwards showed clearly. Edwards's description of the defences that would face Jackson and Taggart was detailed; he traced the route for the Australians and quoted the distance of every stage, the guns and men in every position. The man was an expert, had observed everything, forgotten nothing. But he spoke mechanically, reciting a well-learned lesson while his mind was clearly elsewhere. Smith wondered what he was scheming.

They worked under the yellow light of the lanterns while the aides came and went. Each time the flap of the tent opened it let in a swirl of red dust, and all the while came the muffled tramping of the convoys of horses, camels and trucks that churned up the dust as they headed eastward through the night, towards Beersheba.

Jeavons walked down to the shore and as he came abreast of the locomotive in the siding he saw a small coal fire burning in a brazier with a kettle hissing atop of it. Charlie Golightly stood by the fire and called, "Evening, Captain! Fancy a nightcap? Mug o' toddy?"

It was not the first such invitation. Charlie knew Jeavons captained the *Morning Star* and so made a point of getting to know him because a ship, *if* she called regularly and *if* Charlie could get aboard her to seek out a kindred spirit, could bring him in more contraband.

Jeavons shook his head. "I have to go back to the ship."

"Sailing?"

"Tomorrow."

"Where are you bound?"

Jeavons hesitated, then: "Tangier."

"Ah!" There went Charlie's hope of an alternative supply route. But it had been a tiny hope and he accepted the disappointment philosophically. "Well, pleasant v'yage, Cap'n."

Jeavons said bleakly, "Thank you. Good night." He passed on and left Charlie waiting by the fire. Albert was out on business and overdue. It was another ten minutes before he trotted out of the darkness.

Charlie grumbled, "Where the 'ell have you been?" He took the sack that Albert carried over one skinny shoulder and peered inside.

Albert said breathlessly, "Good business. Two pistols. But then man come and I hide. Come back—" He sketched a wide half-circle in the air, showing his roundabout route.

Charlie said worriedly, "Same feller? Asking about the whisky?"

Albert nodded definitely. "I saw him. Big man. Big nose."

Charlie muttered, "We've got a dozen bottles left but I'll not risk selling them here. We'll take 'em back to Port Said and keep them as stock-in-trade."

He would give it a rest. There was no point in stretching your luck and he didn't like the sound of this feller with the big nose going around asking questions. What was his name? Jeffreys. Captain Jeffreys of the Provost Marshal's staff.

When the conference broke up an aide said he had tents for Edwards and Smith. Edwards took up the offer and curtly ordered the aide to find him a bottle of whisky. He was a changed man, the arrogance and the mocking grin were gone. Now he stalked away, silent, sombre, withdrawn.

Smith went to the *Morning Star* with Taggart to be met by Adeline Brett as they climbed aboard, her dressing gown wrapped around her.

"David! That *was* you in the first seaplane?" He nodded and thought she seemed briefly pleased to see him, but then she turned to Taggart. "What did Finlayson say? Is he moving the men ashore?"

Taggart said wryly, "In a manner of speaking." He glanced around at the marine sentry at the head of the ladder.

Adeline caught that glance and said quickly, "Come into my cabin."

She curled into the one big easy chair and the two men sat on the lower bunk. Smith leaned back against the bulkhead, his cap hooked on one knee. Taggart started to tell Adeline Brett of the Afrika Legion, the plans made and the task set the battalion. His voice was quiet and Smith closed his eyes as he listened and the words ran together to form a murmur of sound that lulled him.

Adeline Brett's whisper came, "It'll be nothing short of murder putting those men ashore!"

He struggled to open his eyes and saw her white-faced.

Taggart said, "There's no help for it, Adeline. There's too much at stake and this has to be tried by somebody. If it wasn't Jackson's troopers and the battalion then they'd have to send somebody else to make the attempt. But we're here."

Smith saw her eyes turn to him, pleading. "David? Isn't there some other way?"

He had to answer, "No," and prayed that Taggart would not mention that Smith was to drive the battalion ashore by force if necessary.

Adeline Brett lowered her face into her hands. Smith closed his eyes and his cap slipped to the deck. Taggart's voice murmured on . . .

Adeline Brett feared for the pair of them as she listened to Taggart trying to reassure her and failing because he could not lie to her. She feared for all those who would be thrown ashore. Taggart ran out of words, was silent. She raised her face to look at him and the young commander sprawled limply, half-sitting, half-lying across the bunk.

Taggart followed the direction of her glance and said softly, "I gather he's only snatched what sleep he could when he could in the last few days."

The girl said, "Then let him sleep here." And when Taggart hesitated, "You're not worried about my reputation, John? I've been the only woman aboard this ship for days and the only woman with the battalion for months. No one will talk and I wouldn't care if they did."

So he lifted Smith's legs on to the bunk, pulled off his shoes and the girl spread the blanket over him. Taggart went out to lie on the deck among his men and she climbed to the upper bunk but could not sleep, and lay thinking of the man in the bunk below.

*   *   *

"David!" He woke muzzily, hearing her softly calling his name, just able to see in the faint moonlight from the open scuttle that she knelt by his bunk. He realised he was propped up on one arm, the other thrust out defensively and she held that outstretched hand.

He asked, "What's the matter?" His voice was thick and slurred. He wondered where he was, then remembered. He should not be here with this girl.

"You cried out." Her face was close, her eyes wide. The blonde curls were tousled but he thought she was beautiful.

He said, "I must have been dreaming."

"What about?"

Smith shook his head. "I can't remember." But he knew he had been afraid.

She rose to sit on the bunk at his side. His tension eased. He could hear her breathing, the catch in it. He reached out and for a moment she held back but then he drew her to him, felt the warmth of her body through the thin stuff of her night-dress. He forgot the morrow and his precious career, the crowded ship enclosing them.

Later he did not care, for himself. He thought that for her sake, for appearances, he should rise and dress and go out to sleep on the deck. But she lay close on him, his arms about her, and he slept.

Maroc cruised off the Gulf of Alexandretta with the U.S. Submarine-Chaser No. 101 as the sun climbed above the Amanus mountains and struck sparks from the waters of the Gulf. Harry Petersen sat in a deckchair by the wheelhouse of the chaser, the chair's canvas stretched under his weight, his pipe between his teeth and one big hand wrapped around a mug of coffee. Eyes squinted against the sun, he watched the R.E.8 reconnaissance plane flying back from the head of the Gulf.

Young Ensign Cleeve came on deck, yawning and rubbing at his eyes, peered sharply up at the aircraft then saw Petersen relaxed and asked, "British, sir?"

Petersen nodded. "Dawn reconnaissance from Cyprus. Went in 'bout a half-hour ago."

The biplane closed the ships, circled lazily and a signal lamp blinked from the observer's cockpit. The chaser's signalman read: "*Walküre* . . . at . . . anchor . . . no . . . steam . . . *Friedrichsburg* . . . staging aft . . . making repairs . . . see . . . you . . . tonight." He lifted his lamp and flickered an acknowledgment. Another lamp on *Maroc's* bridge winked up at the R.E.8 and it turned and headed westward.

Cleeve said glumly, "It doesn't look as though she's coming out." He glanced across at *Maroc*, at the long barrels of her twelve-inch guns and added, "Don't know as I blame them."

Petersen chewed on the pipe and thought the captain of *Walküre* must know that time was running out for his ship, daily the blockading force would grow stronger and he must eventually be attacked. *Walküre* was no longer in the Sea of Marmara with the tortuous channels of the Dardanelles and the batteries and patrolling gunboats to protect her. Here she was vulnerable. But she had not broken out of the Dardanelles just for an airing. What the *hell* was she doing here?

Smith woke with the sunlight streaming through the scuttle to light the cabin. For a moment he was lost then remembered where he was, threw back the blanket and stood up. Adeline Brett's dressing gown lay on the upper bunk but the bunk was made up. He dressed and splashed water on his face from the basin in the corner, stepped over the coaming and out of the cabin. The marine sentry at the head of the ladder had been changed, of course. This one glanced quickly at Smith then faced his front, face inscrutable under the round, flat cap. Smith returned his salute and growled, "Good morning!".

The deck aft swarmed with men of the Egyptian Labour Force working at unloading the ammunition from the after holds and stowing it in surf-boats alongside. Forward—

He walked forward and halted under the bridge at Adeline Brett's shoulder. She turned and they smiled at each other but there was a shyness between them now and she quickly turned to watching Taggart. He sat on the bulwark, legs dangling,

talking to the men of the battalion who squatted around him
on the deck and the hatch-covers. Only the R.S.M., wiry and
Welsh and leather-faced stood ram-rod erect, stick under his
arm.

Taggart was saying: ". . . so that's what we're going to do
and why. As soon as the chaps working aft have finished, we'l
be drawing arms." He paused. The men sat very still and
watched him grim-faced. He said, "I'm not calling for volun
teers. As the R.S.M. says, 'When I wants volunteers I'll detai
them.'" That got a smile. "Any questions?"

In the silence Smith noticed a number of faces he recog
nised because he was getting to know these men. The
youngster, Garrett, who always stood apart with that cold
bitter stare—

A carroty-haired corporal at the front said flatly, "No ques
tions, sir, but to me it looks a right bastard."

There was a long growl of agreement with a deep savage
undertone of anger. Smith had wondered whether this bat
talion might prove more explosive than the ammunition aft
now had no doubt that only Taggart had prevented that ex
plosion.

Taggart nodded. "It is." He waited, looked around. "N
more? Then carry on."

The R.S.M. snapped to attention and bawled, "Eyes front!"
The men scrambled to their feet and Taggart returned th
R.S.M.'s salute. Smith stared at the faces, the eyes on Taggart
and knew that these men would follow him. They would g
ashore sweating with fear and praying the soldier's prayer
"Not in the face or the guts, O Lord!" But they would follov
Taggart.

He walked past Smith and Adeline Brett with a set expres
sion. As he passed he said hoarsely, "Couldn't blame them i
they shot *me*!"

Smith took his leave of Adeline Brett awkwardly, but gently
After a hurried breakfast in the saloon of the *Morning Star* h
went ashore in a boat loaded with ammunition from the afte
holds. It had to pass the scrutiny of the guard-boat that sti
kept watch on the ship, though now only searching boat

leaving the tramp, while others coming off from the shore were not stopped. A lighter was beached close by the jetty, its ramp coming out over its blunt bow like a hump-back bridge. Smith halted on the hump and stared down into the lighter: it was all one big hold, a hundred feet long and twenty wide, with an oil engine aft. A score of carpenters worked in the hold, hammering and sawing, setting up stalls to take the horses and hold them safe during the sea passage. Jackson moved among them and Smith went down to him, eyeing the work and testing the strength of it. He said, "It looks all right."

Jackson pushed back the slouch hat and rubbed sweat from his brow with the back of his hand. "It looks right to me." Then he added bitterly, "The only thing about this caper that does."

Smith thought that Jackson was a good soldier and as he gave orders so he would take them. Now he told Smith straight, "I wouldn't trust that bastard Edwards an inch but I've got to and he's been on the bottle all night. I've got a good bunch o' blokes and I don't fancy risking any one of 'em. But there's a few thousand Anzacs an' Tommies waiting in front of Beersheba tonight so if it's possible to blow that dump and track then we will. I just wish there was another way."

Smith answered from the heart, "So do I."

He spent the rest of the morning in a rapid stalking of the beach and the camp at Deir el Belah, urging and hastening the work of unloading the *Morning Star*, the shipping of arms for the battalion and the conversion of Jackson's lighter. He had another brief conference with Braddock and Finlayson, going over the same ground and liking it even less. The sweat turned the red dust that hung on the air into a paste on his face. Only at the end did he find a few minutes to go to the hospital. He did not see either of the injured fitters but their doctor told him, "They're over the worst. The burns are extensive and severe but we can mend them. It will be a long business but fortunately their faces weren't touched, nor their sight affected. In a month or so we'll move them to Cairo and eventually we'll ship them home. They know that and it's cheered them no end." Then as Smith was leaving: "You did well to bring them in so soon. We got them only just in time."

That was some comfort.

It was noon when *Dauntless* led *Blackbird* in through the gap in the anti-submarine nets and work ceased on the *Morning Star* and the lighter ashore. On the single monitor left in the anchorage (her twin was at sea and pounding Gaza) the men stood back from cleaning the 6-inch gun. All eyes in the anchorage and ashore turned to watch the two ships enter the harbour.

The 6-inch gun right aft in *Dauntless* was a drooping, twisted wreck, the deck torn and buckled around it and the two remaining guns were blackened with muzzle flashes. *Blackbird*'s side wore a crude patch like some huge poultice slapped on her and the funnels of both ships leaked smoke from scores of holes punched by splinters. They were a battered pair but Smith was proud of them.

A launch took him out to his ship and the pipes shrilled as he climbed aboard. Buckley, standing in the waist saw Smith's grim face and thought, "Christ Almighty! What now?"

Smith told Ackroyd, "We sail as soon as possible." So *Dauntless* disembarked her wounded over one side while the ammunition was taken aboard on the other. There was a brief hiatus when the bugles sounded the 'Still' and the dead, Cole among them, were lowered into the lighter alongside, the ship's company standing at attention. Then the bugles blared again and the work went on.

Part of that work was embarking sacks of mail for the ship's company. The corporal issued it while the hands still worked, thrusting the letters into their pockets to be read later and in peace.

It was some time afterwards that Smith went aboard *Blackbird*, his cutter slipping alongside her unnoticed while her first lieutenant was engrossed in rigging a staging to examine the patch on her side. Smith brushed aside his apologies. "Ceremony can wait. Where's your captain?"

"In his cabin, sir."

The door of Pearce's cabin stood ajar. Smith tapped, pushed his head around it and saw Chris Pearce seated behind his desk. An oil bottle and cleaning rod lay before him and Pearce was loading a Webley pistol but he dropped it into a drawer and stood up as Smith entered.

Smith told him about the planned operation. "I want *Blackbird* repaired and fully seaworthy by tomorrow. The admiral has promised any assistance you want." He paused, watching Pearce and asked, "You think you can do it?"

Pearce had changed and Smith wondered if it was for the better. If anything he was more gaunt and hollow-eyed than ever, but the nervous edginess had gone. His face was still, and there was a cold hardness about him that reminded Smith of Garrett, the young soldier in Taggart's battalion.

Pearce answered, "Yes, sir." He was silent a moment, then: 'I kept something back the other day when you asked if I was worried about anything. I was. I hadn't heard from Livvy, – that's my wife, sir."

Smith nodded, thought, "Oh, Christ!"

Pearce said, "On top of that, for a long time I had – suspicions. Then about three weeks ago, the day we sailed on this lot, I got a letter from a so-called friend in Cairo . . . and they weren't just suspicions any longer. Since then I've been waiting for us to get back to Port Said so I could get some leave and go to see her. But there's a letter from her today that saves me the trouble. She wants a divorce. There's this bloody soldier—" He stopped there.

Smith said quietly, "I'm sorry, Chris. I'd like to give you leave but—"

Pearce was shaking his head. "I told you, her letter makes it clear that would be a waste of time."

Smith went on, "We need your knowledge and experience with the Shorts, Chris."

Pearce asked, "Permission to fly, sir?"

"Not that, Chris." Now least of all times.

Pearce nodded, accepting it with his new-found calm. After weeks of torment the blow had fallen. He was too calm by far

139

and Smith didn't like it, made a guess and said baldly, "She told you who this soldier is."

Pearce didn't even blink. "She identified him very clearly, name, rank and that he's in Intelligence. He's Edwards, that imitation bloody Arab."

"What's the pistol for?"

"Just cleaning it, sir." He met Smith's gaze frankly, too frankly, a man with his mind made up.

Smith said deliberately, "I'll need you and I'll need him You'll get that into your head and give me your word that you won't try something stupid. Or I put you ashore under guard Do I have it?"

Pearce said quietly, "I won't do anything stupid, sir. Livvy was everything in the world to me, my life, and he's wrecked it. But I'm not going to hang for Edwards."

"You're not answering my question!"

"Accidents happen, sir, and it is wartime."

"Don't be a fool, Chris!" Smith told himself this was just wild talk on Pearce's part, men did not murder – but Edward did. The thought stopped him dead. He stared at Pearce realising he meant what he said and would act on it. Like Edwards. Pearce was not insane, he met Smith's eyes calmly He could send Pearce ashore and report to Braddock – but the admiral would not believe it, nobody would. Smith did.

Pearce said, "I know you need us both and so long as you do – you have my word, sir."

Smith reasoned with him, raged at him – and accomplished nothing. Pearce was cold and correct and again pledged his word to Smith – for now. Smith had to accept the situation because he needed both Edwards *and* Pearce. His only consolation was that Pearce could do nothing for a time – at least not until this operation was over and then it would be up to Smith to act quickly.

He returned to his ship and plunged into his work but with one more worry to plague him. First, Jackson and Edwards a arm's-length from each other and now Pearce coldly plotting murder. As if the operation itself was not bad enough.

The operation haunted him.

In the afternoon *Blackbird* took aboard her two Shorts from the decked-over lighter that then went to the shore to have her deck ripped from her because she was to sail with *Dauntless*. Smith, watching the shore, saw Jackson's lighter with its ramp on the beach and the Australians leading the reluctant horses aboard. There were thirty-eight of them, though Jackson's troop only numbered thirty-five with Edwards. Two horses would be carrying explosive charges for demolition and Jackson had demanded a spare in case one went lame or was injured before it got ashore. Finlayson had said, "I'll see you get it, if only to stop you stealing it."

Jackson had not batted an eyelid.

The red dust haze hung over the land and north, towards Gaza, the guns pounded as if ticking the seconds away.

Sapper Charlie Golightly did not see the ships because his back was to the sea and he was watching the officer from the Provost Marshal's staff. Charlie lay in the grove of palms hard by the siding and Jeffreys, Charlie knew it had to be Captain Jeffreys, stood a score of yards away, by Charlie's engine. The captain was tall and long-nosed with cold eyes. There had been a hanging judge called Jeffreys and Charlie was certain this was a direct descendant and any man the captain caught out in a crime would pay the maximum penalty.

Jeffreys hefted a bottle of the whisky Charlie had smuggled up from Port Said and was asking Albert where Sapper Golightly could be found. Two burly military policemen flanked Jeffreys and now a third crawled out from under the tender and spoke briefly to the captain. Albert smiled and looked everywhere but at the grove of palms where Charlie lay and sweated, then pointed up the road towards the main camp but Jeffreys did not believe him, Charlie could see it in his hard face.

He knew he could not stay in the palms. He could not stay in the army either or in Palestine, because Jeffreys would hunt him down and Charlie was too old to go to prison. He shuddered at the thought and the fat money-belt under his shirt dug into him. His business here was finished, his pension had gone down the drain and the sooner he moved on the better. So he eased back until the trunks of the palms hid him from the group by the engine and he could climb on to shaky legs and hurry through the grove. He stopped at its edge and peered out at the *Morning Star*. He had meant it when he told Albert to steer clear of ships; Charlie did not like them. But the tramp was due to sail for Tangier this very day.

Men of the Egyptian Labour Corps swarmed by the shore, unloading the boats as they came in from the *Morning Star*. A few soldiers moved among them overseeing the unloading but Charlie did not know any of them. He started down through the gap in the dunes, wanting desperately to look back but knowing that was the last thing he must do. If Jeffreys saw a man with his head turned as he hurried away . . . He reached the beach and shoved through the throng, his eyes flickering from boat to boat till he saw one almost empty and pushed towards it. He clambered aboard as they ran it out, pushed past the rowers and sat by the man at the steering oar. Nobody took any notice.

When the boat ran alongside the *Morning Star* he climbed the dangling ladder with his heart in his mouth and set foot aboard the ship.

" 'Ere! What are you up to?"

The challenge shook Charlie but then he turned and saw the owner of the voice: Sapper Barney Cockcroft. He was another old soldier with a crime-sheet as long as his arm but it would have been as long as his leg as well if Charlie hadn't got him off numerous hooks by guile, perjury and bribery. So Charlie looked him in the eye and said, "You never seen me, Barney, no more'n anybody else did. Like I done for you afore now.'

Barney returned his stare then closed one eye and turned his back. Seconds later Charlie was wheezing down steep and narrow iron ladders. In five minutes he was in a small, dark little room with one grimy scuttle that let in a ray of sunlight and gave him a view of the anchorage. Drums of red lead and white spirit stacked around him showed this was the paint store and he sat down on one drum, slowly relaxed. From what he had seen of this old bucket nobody did much painting so he was safe here for the time being. And later? He would cross that bridge when he came to it. He patted the money belt and thought about Tangier.

It was almost time. The last of the ammunition was coming aboard, *Morning Star* and the four lighters had all signalled that they were ready to proceed. Smith, in the only good suit of white drill left to him, waited on the torn quarterdeck of *Dauntless* with Taggart, Jackson and Edwards, all of them watching the launch coming off from the shore bearing Finlayson and Braddock. Ackroyd stood behind Smith. They were a silent group. The three soldiers were to sail aboard *Dauntless* where they could discuss final details with Smith.

Edwards broke the silence. "The old bastard isn't going to change his mind and call it off." His eyes were slitted and the whisky smell hung around him.

Taggart answered shortly, "He can't."

Finlayson had already sent a terse signal: the Royal Flying Corps had raided Lydda but the guns kept them high and they paid a savage price in machines and men – for nothing. The dump and the railway were still intact.

Edwards laughed with some of the old arrogance but there was bitterness in it. "I started this war with the intention of being a rich man at the end of it. I've made some useful friends among the Arabs. I told them I'd pledged my life to the defeat of the Turks so they could set up their Arab state. That wasn't just talk. I wasn't about to go back to being a sort of second rate commercial traveller up and down this coast but I was going to keep my end of the bargain. I pledged my life but I didn't mean to give it, just *lend* it till Johnny Turk was finished. Now I'm going to be kept to my word. As soon as Finlayson came out with his bloody plan I knew I was going to die in this country." He looked at Smith. "Bloody luck. Maybe your albatross has something to do with it."

Smith stared at him, not understanding. "My – what?"

"That Delilah, the bad-luck seaplane." And as Smith still stared: "I heard some of your men talking about it."

Ackroyd broke in, eyes fixed on the approaching launch. "I

haven't heard the talk myself, sir, but I understand it's been going around."

"What has?"

"Well, Delilah was a rebuild job, had already been shot to bits once. She drowned a man at Port Said as soon as we got her. Then Hamilton fell out of her. Wilson was killed. Two fitters were caught in the fire that started in her. Then Hamilton again and Cole. Maybe she's bad luck." He stopped with Smith's eye on him.

Smith could not believe it. These were skilled technicians manning modern fighting ships and aircraft, not ancient mariners with tarry pigtails. He said irascibly, "I'll see the first man you catch spreading that tale."

There was an uneasy silence.

Jackson eyed Edwards and asked laconically, "Reckon you'll be sober when we go ashore?"

Edwards leered at him. "Stone cold, old boy." The leer slipped away and he muttered, "Stone cold. I mean it. They'll bury me there and I won't be the only one—"

Jackson said contemptuously, "Aw, shut up! You make me bloody sick."

Taggart eyed him coldly, "You'd better keep your mouth shut as well, Mr. Jackson."

Edwards mumbled, "Damned colonial cowboy."

Jackson looked them over. "A right caper this is goin' to be. Out of all the millions in the British army I draw you two. One slobbering drunk and another with a mob that shot their C.O."

Edwards fumbled at the knife in his belt.

Smith pushed in among them, shoved Taggart back and with the heel of his hand cut Edwards's hand from the knife. He snapped, "That's enough from all of you."

"That was rank insubordination!" Taggart was pale with fury.

Jackson said calmly, "What are you going to do? Bust me and send me home?"

Smith shook his head. "No. This operation goes ahead, be sure of that. You all have your orders. I have mine and I'll carry them out."

He turned his back on them, sick at heart as the launch hooked on to the foot of the ladder. Finlayson and Braddock climbed to the deck, saluted as the pipes shrilled and the marine guard presented arms. Their visit would of necessity be brief; the ammunition lighter was casting off and it was time to sail. Finlayson must have sensed the tension in the group, looked watchfully into their faces as he shook their hands, spoke with each of them in turn. Smith thought the general probably put that tension down to the impending operation. He was only partly right.

Smith did not have time to dwell on it though. Braddock took his arm and drew him aside out of earshot. "Did you receive any mail?"

"Yes, sir. It came off and was distributed to the men a couple of hours ago."

"I meant personally, yourself."

"No, sir."

"You will." Braddock hesitated a moment and Smith wondered what the admiral was working up to. Were they giving Smith another command? But they would not take him away from *Dauntless* now, could not—

Braddock said, "I must be brief. Anyway, there's little to tell. Just the same, I think you'll find it more than enough. I knew your grandfather for many years—"

"My *grandfather?*" Smith stared stupidly. He knew no family but Reuben Smith and his wife Hannah. He had wanted to find out about himself but they had been unwilling to answer his questions, and once they were dead he had not known where to start.

Braddock repeated firmly, "Your grandfather. We were never friends but I served under him when he commanded a squadron. He told me all this because he'd heard I'd spoken up for you once or twice. I'll say now I did that because of my faith in you. No other reason. His wife was dead, but they'd had a son and daughter. The son was lost at Jutland. Just over thirty years ago the daughter ran away with a man a deal older than herself, a wild character who was cashiered from the army. He had no profession or prospects and little money and he was already married, though his wife had left him years before. He and the girl skipped to the continent and wound up in Italy, living cheap on what money he had left."

Braddock paused then said gruffly, "It seems he was good to her, loved her. Anyway, he had an idea for a new type of grenade and he was working on this with some Italian chap, hoping to get a contract from the army, but there was an accident one day and the pair of them were killed. The girl was left alone, near penniless – and pregnant. She wrote to her father for help, for the sake of the child, and he went to bring her home for the same reason. But he hadn't forgiven her. Reuben Smith went along as his servant and Hannah Smith because she was a midwife. They took passage in a tramp from Italy and the child was born when they were two days out. But the mother died and was buried at sea."

Smith guessed what was coming now, could not believe it. But Braddock would not lie nor be mistaken.

Braddock nodded, watching him, and continued, "The entry in the ship's log showed the child's parents as Reuben and Hannah Smith. Lord knows how that was wangled, maybe the ship's master was an old friend or there was bribery, or both. But it was done. The Smiths took you to Norfolk."

Smith was trying to take it in. The 'wild man', his father; that phrase had been used of himself. His impetuous mother, the rigidly stubborn grandfather – all traits he admitted in himself.

Braddock said, "He did the best he could for you, according to his lights. He wouldn't bring further disgrace on his daughter's name or the family by acknowledging you, but there was always enough money to send you to school, the word in the right place to have you accepted as a cadet in the navy. He was doing his duty – as he saw it."

Smith said quietly, bitterly, "Jesus *Christ*! Only his *duty*? Wasn't she his daughter, his flesh and blood?"

"It was thirty years ago. Attitudes have changed since then, not much, but a little. When I last saw him he was a dying man. His doctor was there and we witnessed his will. He showed it to me. He left the estate, the house and the land to you."

Smith said, "Wait." Braddock was going too fast for him. "You mean – now?"

Braddock nodded slowly, "I've just heard that he died a month ago. You inherit the estate and the name." He told Smith the name and it was a famous one in their profession. Braddock said, "It's not unknown for a child like that to be put out to another, poorer family. It happened then and still does."

Smith knew that, was struggling to accept that after all these years of wondering . . .

Braddock sounded a warning note. "I must tell you that your inheritance will not come easily. There's not a shred of evidence to support the story I've just told you except that it is set out in the old man's will. And that will includes a small annuity left to the only other surviving relative, a distant cousin. He hasn't the family name but, knowing the man, he will contest the will. Your grandfather was something of a recluse and an eccentric in his last years. I think the will may be contested on the grounds of his sanity and while I'm sure you'll win, I think you should know that it won't be plain sailing."

Sailing – Smith saw the ammunition lighter being towed away. Finlayson waited at the head of the ladder, heads were turned towards Braddock and himself, Ackroyd glanced surreptitiously at his watch.

Braddock took a letter from his pocket and handed it to Smith, saying, "A personal message from me, not official, but not to be opened until this operation is finished. Understood?"

Smith tucked it into the pocket of his tunic and followed the admiral to the ladder. Braddock became official. "Two things: complete wireless silence, of course, from the moment you sail. And you command this operation but you will *not* go ashore! That is an order. Understood?"

It was said clearly: Ackroyd and all of them heard it. Smith could only answer, "Aye, aye, sir."

The salutes were exchanged, the pipes shrilled, the marine guard presented arms and Braddock and Finlayson went down into the launch. It curved away across the anchorage, side-party and guard fell out and Smith strode forward to the bridge. Minutes later *Dauntless* was under way and leading the little squadron of *Morning Star* and the four lighters towed by the tramp out through the opening in the nets. There was a scattering of cheers from the deck of *Blackbird*, taken up by the men of the monitor and the soldiers thronging the dunes to watch the ships depart. The crew of *Dauntless* were cheering and Jackson's troopers in the lighter, in between cursing the horses to hold still. The men of the battalion, spread around the decks of the tramp now that she was stripped of her barbed wire, cheered as loud as any. Smith saw Taggart and Jackson on the deck below him but yards apart. They did not cheer.

Ackroyd grinned. "Quite a send-off!"

Smith did not smile. Braddock's order: – you will not go ashore! – had rammed home that in his opinion they were gambling enough already. Smith said quietly, certainly, "It won't work."

Ackroyd glanced across at him, had hardly heard the words. He temporised, "It's a gamble but—"

"It's a hell of a gamble, not just a hundred or a thousand-to-one against."

"We-ll—" Ackroyd dragged the word, not wanting to voice his own suspicions about the plan, not wanting them confirmed, either. He, like Taggart and Jackson, preferred to hope.

Smith swung to face him. The weight of responsibility had passed from Finlayson to him because he had to land those men who cheered now, and that weight showed in his face.

His voice was savage. "That supply dump has two defences. One is the company of infantry guarding it and the other is the ten miles of country between it and the coast. Taggart's diversionary attack should clear the way, but at the same time it will destroy any element of surprise. With a landing that close, the guard on the dump will be alerted and they'll *stay* alert. They won't stand meekly by while Jackson blows up the railway and if he tries to attack the dump he'll be taking on odds of three to one. He knows it. So do Taggart and Edwards. They know also that we can put Jackson and Taggart and all their men ashore but we'll never get one of them off again because the Turks will bring up guns that will make it impossible."

He paused. Ackroyd seemed as dour as ever but Smith felt sick.

He finished flatly, "There is only one sure way of stopping the Afrika Legion and that is to strike the railway and the dump with overwhelming force and total surprise, in some way the Germans and Turks could never imagine, never guard against."

He turned away to face forward, staring blindly out over the bow at the sunlit sea. Impossible. It was a bitter pill to swallow, that he was committed to this and could neither avert it nor save something from the slaughter. There must be a way to rescue some of them. *Must* be.

The ships steamed southward as if headed for Port Said until Gaza and Deir el Belah had slipped below the horizon. Then they turned and headed northward out of sight of the land.

Charlie Golightly had fallen into a doze, snored gently with his mouth open until cramp woke him and he rose stiffly from the drum of red lead to rub at an aching behind. It was some minutes before it stole into his consciousness that something had changed in the crowded little store, and minutes more before he identified it: the ray of sunlight no longer pierced the grime on the scuttle to point a slim finger of light at the deck. He stepped to the scuttle and peered out, up at the sky. The sun was low on the other side of the ship; the shadow of the tramp on the sea showed that. The sun had not passed over the ship because it had been past its zenith when Charlie came aboard, was already started on its long descent to the west. So – Charlie sucked in his breath – the *Morning Star* had turned and was headed northward where lay Palestine, Syria, Turkey – all in the hands of the enemy. Cyprus? No better to Charlie because the long-nosed Jeffreys would sniff him out there. But Jeavons had said he was bound for Tangier . . .

Charlie had always intended to disclose his presence, nurtured no fond hope of being able to hide without food or water all the long way to Tangier. He decided this was as good a time as any.

Smith shifted about the bridge, huddled into himself. He knew it would be impossible to take off any of the landing force but still he sought a way. He visualised the two landing places, imagining how they would be. First the River Auja, with German and Turkish batteries pouring a murderous crossfire down on the beaches. Then saw again the shore where they had landed Edwards, the sea sliding oily through the gaps in the rock-bound coastline, the distant lights of Jaffa and one light like a descending star that was the train from Lydda . . .

He halted in his restless pacing across the bridge, his thoughts racing and the plan forming, then stepped to the engine-room voice pipe and spoke to the engineer commander: "Chief, I want you to find a volunteer for me . . ."

When he finished he turned back to the bridge to find Henderson, who had the watch, eyeing him curiously. But then the yeoman said, "Signal from *Morning Star*, sir." He read it as the lamp blinked from the bridge of the tramp astern of *Dauntless*.

Smith listened absently, his mind busy with details now, all the pieces of the plan dovetailing into place. Then a phrase caught his attention and jerked his head around, but he waited till the yeoman finished and Henderson ordered, "Acknowledge."

Then Smith said, "Read that again."

Henderson grinned and read: "'Stowaway. Sapper Golightly, C. Engine-driver, Royal Engineers. States ordered to Tangier to find availability railway sleepers and lines but orders mislaid. Request instructions.'" Henderson was laughing now. "Never heard such a lot of balls! Cheeky blighter, whoever he is."

Smith grinned at him, excitement restoring his good humour. "Make to *Morning Star*: 'Heave to. Sending boat for stowaway.'"

Charlie Golightly clambered aboard to be met by the master-at-arms who took him forward and up to the bridge at the double, barking at him, "Where's your cap?"

"Lorst it." Charlie stumbled on the ladder.

The master-at-arms caught him by his belt and rammed him up the ladder by brute force. "You'll lose a sight more than that if you say one wrong word up 'ere. Our bloke eats wrong 'uns. Get *hup!*"

He obeyed Henderson's pointing finger and thrust Charlie into the sea-cabin at the back of the bridge, bellowed, "Sapper Golightly, sir!" and closed the door behind Charlie.

Who for one gut-sinking moment thought he was in a cell. Then his gaze skidded off the encroaching, sweating steel walls and focused on the officer seated at the desk. He was a slight, wiry figure, thin-faced and his naval cap had left the fair hair pressed close to his skull. He smiled and Charlie was briefly relieved.

Smith saw a round, open face devoid of all guile, the natural camouflage of a regular soldier with thirty years of undetected crime behind him and thirty years of beer now showing in a belly in front of him. He saw no viciousness. Smith said, "I've heard your story and that you're an engine-driver." He paused, waiting.

Charlie answered quickly, "Yessir! Drove 'em all over for the army for the last twenty year. All kinds. If steam makes it go then I will. So on account of me being an expert an' my experience an' that, they asked me to go to Tangier to see what . . ." His voice faded. The thin face before him had stopped smiling and Charlie remembered the warning of the master-at-arms and thought it no exaggeration as he looked into the cold eyes.

Smith said, "I think I can promise you no more than a reprimand. But first you've got to tell me the truth."

Charlie swallowed and told him the most favourable version of the truth he could contrive, then waited and sweated.

Smith grinned to himself, his suspicions of Charlie confirmed. "No doubt the provost marshal takes a serious view of your crime. But I'm going to ask you to do something for me, and if you agree, I'll do my best for you and I'm certain you'll get away with a ticking-off. If you don't agree then I must send you back to Deir el Belah at the first opportunity to be dealt with. That is my duty. Understood?"

Charlie jumped in eagerly, "I'm your man, sir!"

"Wait till you hear what you have to do," Smith answered dryly, then told him.

Some minutes later the master-at-arms took a thoughtful Charlie Golightly below to find him a place on the already crowded mess-deck. The engineer commander reported that he had found two likely volunteers but Smith answered, "Thanks, Chief, but I've found my man." Then he told Henderson, "Pass the word for Major Taggart, Colonel Edwards and Lieutenant Jackson. And the first lieutenant." Because Ackroyd must be in on this.

He went to his sea-cabin, threw off his one good suit and pulled on another, old but serviceable. So he was workmanlike when they found him in the charthouse with the large-scale map of Southern Palestine spread before him. He waited until they were all present and then said abruptly, "I'm changing the plan." He told them what he intended and watching their faces saw his excitement take alight in them.

Oddly enough it was Edwards, his drunken depression forgotten, who spoke for all of them. "It's still a hell of a gamble but this way at least there's a fighting chance."

Smith looked at each of them in turn. "We sink or swim together in this. No more back-biting." And when they nodded stiffly he told Taggart, "Tell Mr. Jackson about the battalion. What really happened."

Taggart grumbled obstinately, "He thinks he knows."

"I don't give a damn what he thinks! Tell him the truth as you told me!" Smith's patience was cracking and it showed in the edge of his voice.

Taggart swallowed his pride and curtly recounted the story of the colonel's shooting. They heard him out in silence, then

Jackson rubbed at his jaw and said wryly, "They still sound a funny mob to me, but at least they had their reasons."

Taggart snapped, "That's right! And I'll tell you this: they've been caged too long, they're ready to fight *anybody* and God help any man in their way!"

So now instead of mistrust there was a guarded truce between Taggart and Jackson. Smith thought bitterly that it was better than nothing and he blamed neither. He looked at Edwards, who said, "You can rely on me to carry out my orders." All his huge confidence and arrogance had returned.

Smith wondered at the change in him, but then Ackroyd said doubtfully, "Will the general agree to this change, sir? It's – an unusual plan."

"It has to be and I'm not asking him." And as Ackroyd scowled worriedly at the enormity of this, Smith said, "Wireless silence, remember?"

Taggart chuckled softly. "Not so much turning the blind eye, more: 'none so dumb as he who will not speak.'"

Smith said grimly, "You and your battalion know something of that." He glanced at his watch. "There's a lot to do." A whole new set of orders to be drafted and when that was done Taggart and Jackson must be returned to their men to brief them on the changed plan. Every man had to know exactly what he had to do and that applied to the ship's company of *Dauntless*, too.

They set to, working against the clock and Smith knew every flying second brought them nearer to committal. Once he paused, his thoughts harking back to *Walküre*, blockaded in the Gulf of Alexandretta. Sooner or later she would have to be winkled out or sunk and he wished that job was his instead of this attack. Then he concentrated once more on his planning for now on his own account he had taken into his hands the lives of the four hundred men to be landed and the thousands who waited before Beersheba.

8

The Raid

There was a chill dampness to the night and the sky was overcast. Smith sat at the helm of the cutter with Edwards on one side of him and Lieutenant Jameson on the other. Edwards still wore his robes and carried the villainous knife. Three of Captain Brand's marines were crowded into the sternsheets but Brand himself crouched in the bow along with Buckley.

Ackroyd had pointed out, "With respect, sir, the admiral's order was that you were not to go ashore."

Smith had answered solemnly, "In that operation. This is a different plan." It was Smith's plan and he was going ashore.

The coast loomed like a black frieze of dunes against the dark with the thick silver line of the surf underlining it. That line was broken some three hundred yards to Smith's left where lay the mouth of the Auja river. No day attack this, as Finlayson had ordered. And no feint either. To his right and about four miles away, Jaffa lifted a ragged silhouette on its hill. Then it was lost to sight behind a headland and the cutter ran into the surf, bucked and pitched as it rode it, then crashed in on the beach. That crashing landing half-threw Buckley over the bow, Brand with him. Smith made them out, standing in water to their knees and grabbing at the bow, then with the sea above their waists as it crashed in again and they hauled on the bow of the boat.

Smith called, "Oars!" Whispering was pointless in this thundering surf. The oars came in and he saw the seamen rowing bow go over the side to add their muscle to hauling the boat in. Smith shoved Edwards forward after the marines and

154

lambered over the thwarts behind him as the rest of the
cutter's crew plunged into the sea to wade in, hauling at the
boat. Edwards was in the bow and jumped. Smith followed
him into the surf, turned to give a hand with the boat but saw it
being run up on the shore. Edwards slipped like a shadow
across the beach, Brand and his three marines following him,
Brand with pistol in hand, the marines with rifles at the trail.
Smith brought up the rear with Buckley panting at his
shoulder.

Their boots began to slip in the soft sand; they were into the
dunes. Edwards turned to his left and headed towards the
mouth of the river. Smith was up with the marines now,
passing them, his breath coming fast. Edwards lunged to his
right and reached one hand down to the sand. Smith saw him
lift up the loop of telephone wire and the flash of the knife.
Edwards tossed aside the severed wire and moved on. Now the
machine-gun post was cut off from Jaffa, and from the Turkish
regiment hardly more than a mile away to the north.

Edwards was crouching, moving cautiously now, edging
away from the sea and further into the dunes. The sea's pounding became muffled and their own panting breathing could be
heard. Edwards swung left towards the sea again and, as Smith
turned to follow, he caught a glimpse of the river close to his
right. The Turkish machine-gun post must be . . .

Edwards halted, went down on one knee and flapped a hand,
signalling, "Down". Smith knelt beside him, Brand and his
marines up close, faces blank with tension. Edwards pointed
at the rise of the dune ahead of them, curled the finger over, his
meaning clear: just over the crest. Smith and Brand nodded.
Brand gestured and the marines spread out, hefting their
rifles. Smith had told them: "No shooting. Use the butt if you
must but no shooting without my order." Smith found he had
his pistol in his hand and checked again that the safety catch
was set: no shooting.

Edwards crawled forward, knife in hand, and the line of
them went with him and only a yard behind. He went down on
elbows and knees to inch up to the crest of the dune, edged his
head above it, was still, then without turning beckoned with

the knife. They all edged up to the crest. Smith saw the surf
the beach, and then, as his head still lifted, he saw the Turks in
their machine-gun nest below him. They were just below the
crest in a semi-circular earthwork built of timbers and sand
the rear of it open. There were three of them. Two lay wrapped
in blankets or greatcoats, just bundles, and one stood by the
machine-gun that pointed out to sea, his arms folded on the
front of the breastwork, head on his arms. He seemed asleep
on his feet and Smith was not surprised. After scores of night
spent peering at a black and empty sea with the surf's regular
pounding, it was no wonder the man dozed. And it was
blessing.

Smith's eyes lifted briefly, peering out to sea. The lighter
should be there. He could not see them but he *ought* not to see
them; they should not be that close but lying off, waiting.

There was no reason for him to wait. He scrambled forward
over the crest and at his movement they were all up and over
then plunging down into the nest. There was no work for the
rifle-butts, nor for that wickedly long knife and Smith was glad
of that. The two huddled Turks were buried under Brand
and his marines. Buckley fell on the one who stood by the
machine-gun and yanked him away from it and down, slamming him on to his back with one of Buckley's big hand
across his mouth. Smith pointed his pistol an inch from the
wide and horrified eyes and Edwards hissed something. The
Turk lay still, eyes flicking frantically from the pistol to the
knife, the whites showing.

Smith took a breath and tried to keep his voice steady. "Good
enough. They're all yours, Mr. Brand." He left Brand to secure
the prisoners and threw at Buckley, "Bring up Mr. Jameson
and the cutter's crew."

Buckley vaulted out of the nest and ran off along the beach
Smith dragged the torch from his pocket, pointed it out to sea
and flashed the dot-dash of the A. And again. He waited
staring out to sea. Brand came to stand beside him, breathing
heavily and he said with satisfaction, "All secure, sir."

"Very good." Smith still stared out to sea but he said ra-
idly, "They'll probably telephone this post from inland during

he night and when they don't get an answer they'll certainly
end out a party to check along the wire. So when the rest of
our marines come ashore, send a good N.C.O. and some men
back along the line to lay an ambush for them."

"I know the man to send," answered Brand.

But Smith was hurrying on, "Colonel Edwards will show
you the ford. Take two of your men and set up a defensive
screen as I ordered."

Edwards leaned on the earthwork, but now he stirred impatiently. "Come on! Where are the boats?"

Smith snapped, "I told them to lie off. No point in their
being seen before *we* got ashore. Now get *on!*"

Edwards's head jerked round at the rasp in Smith's voice,
then he shoved away from the earthwork and scrambled out of
it, ran off into the darkness and headed for the river, Brand and
two marines doubling after him. The third marine dropped to
one knee just below the crest of the dunes, butt of his rifle
grounded and peered inland keeping watch. There might be
wandering Turks.

Smith stared into the darkness. Was there a square shape?
And a silver flashing out there that would be a bow wave?
Suddenly there they were, ugly and unwieldly like floating
boxes butting in towards the river's mouth. One, two – four of
them!

There came a sound of scrambling to his left and he spun to
face it, pistol lifting, then a voice gasped, "*Dauntless!*" And on
the heels of the password Buckley ran out of the darkness and
behind him came Jameson and the cutter's crew.

Smith said, "Come on!" He swung out of the machine-gun
nest and trotted along the edge of the dunes, then turned into
the river's mouth. He ran along the bank, heading inland for
some fifty yards and there he halted. A track led down through
the dunes to the water's edge. Edwards waited there, peering
out to sea. Smith tried to control his breathing. "Where's
Brand?"

Edwards pointed up the bank of the river that rose gently to
about twenty feet. Smith ran up the slope, made out the figure
of Brand kneeling below the crest and dropped on one knee

beside him. Brand glanced at him and said softly, "All quiet sir. I've one man *there*, the other *there*." He pointed to left and right.

Smith peered but could not see them. He and Brand knelt on the track where it climbed the bank from the ford. From there it ran level for two or three hundred yards, then lifted again to a crest of dunes. There was no sound, nor movement. He realised Jameson now crouched at his shoulder, and said, "Take your orders from Captain Brand."

Jameson nodded; he already knew that and that he and his men were to form part of the defensive screen in case of a Turkish patrol coming this way. Smith told Brand, "Get up to that crest now. The lighters are coming in." He ran down the bank again to stand beside Edwards who held a masked torch, its glow pointing seaward. They waited by the ford as the lighters came on, in line ahead as they ran into the mouth of the river steering by that pinprick of light from the torch held by Edwards. Smith looked for the motor-boat from *Dauntless* and saw it by the far shore. The first lighter was thrusting in steadily, easily now in this sheltered water, and Smith could hear the putter of its engine. A low, flat, black shape with just a creaming of a bow wave. A shift of the wind brought the smell of horses to Smith's seaman's nostrils. He wondered how Jackson and his troop of hard-swearing horsemen had coped with their mounts on the long run from Deir el Belah.

He flashed the 'A' again and the engine of the lighter stopped, thrashed briefly astern, stopped again. She slid on gently with the way left on her, and grounded on the ford. There was a trampling and clattering aboard her. Smith saw a horse's head lifted briefly above the bulwark and a voice came clearly, "*Hold* still, yer flamin' cow—!"

The ramp was coming down and Smith waded out on to the ford towards it. Buckley loomed beside him and Smith said, "Tell Captain Brand the Australians are coming ashore." Buckley splashed away and Smith waded on, the river nearly up to his waist now, but he could feel firm sand under his feet.

He came to the lighter as the ramp hit the water and drenched him in spray. He wiped with one hand at his face, saw a man, tall, slouch-hatted, striding over the hump in the ramp and then down into the waters of the ford. He was half-turned to heave on the reins of the horse that followed him gingerly. Smith recognised Jackson and waved with the pistol, pointed, shouted, "Head for Edwards! On the bank! See him?" Edwards in his robes was a pale blur.

Jackson answered laconically, "I see him." He waded towards the shore. The horse bucked and kicked as it plunged into the river but Jackson cursed, hauled it on, and as it became surer of its footing it followed him more easily. A trooper towing his horse was following Jackson over the ramp and another came after him. The second lighter slid in close alongside the first and grounded with a *thump!* Smith waded on past it, was drenched again as its ramp crashed down and Taggart ran over it to jump into the water.

Taggart carried a rifle across his chest. He grinned at Smith, a flash of teeth in the darkness, and headed for the bank. Smith pushed on, seeing the third lighter and beyond it the fourth, creeping in. And there against the far bank lay *Dauntless*'s motor-boat.

Smith splashed out on to the bank and was met by Lieutenant Griffiths, the gunnery observer. He was out-of-breath but he reported with satisfaction, "Our marines are deployed at the top o' the bank, sir. Sergeant Harriman's up there. The whole country seems quiet but the Vickers is set up with a good field o' fire." He added, "We slipped in ahead o' the lighters like you said, sir. Kept as close in to the bank as we dared."

Smith nodded and used his torch, shielded inside his hand, to glance quickly at his watch. They were two or three minutes ahead of time but he might need all of that and more.

He re-traced his wading passage across the ford and this time he had to push his way among the men of Taggart's battalion who streamed towards the shore in a stumbling, breathless, hurrying mob. They stared straight ahead and Smith had to fight his way through them. And silently they moved, he never heard a word.

All four lighters were aground now. When the water fell to

his knees he managed to run, awkwardly, lifting his feet high like a prancing horse. He thought briefly that he must look a fool but he didn't care if it got him ashore the quicker.

The bank swarmed with men. Their boots whispered, scuffing, trampling in the sand, and there was an overtone of hoarse whispering, "Ack Company here!" "Beer Company here!" "Charlie Company—" He ran past them and came on the Australians where the solid block of them stood holding their horses' heads. Edwards stood by Jackson, and he held the reins of two horses.

Smith asked, "Ready?"

"Yes." Then Jackson added, "—sir."

Smith took a breath. Now for it. He said to Edwards, "Hold the thing still." Smith had ridden horses but knew he was no horseman, nor ever wanted to be. But Edwards held the horse's head, Smith found a stirrup and clawed himself up into the saddle, gathering the reins. There was a guffaw in the Australian ranks, cut short as Jackson said, "Shut it, Jasper!"

Edwards mounted with the ease of practice and Buckley said, "Sir?"

Smith stared down at Buckley, remembering him too late. "There isn't a horse." Smith was astride the only spare.

But Jackson said, "Jasper Beaver! You put this sailor up behind you! Mount!"

The troopers mounted as one and the voice of Jasper Beaver complained, "Aw, Christ! Come on, Buckley, chum. The ol' neddy ain't going to like this but he'll stick it."

Smith saw Buckley hauled up behind the big trooper but then Edwards was spurring his horse at the bank. Jackson swung alongside and his hand shot out to grab at Smith's reins so they went up the bank together with Smith clinging on for dear life.

Up. And over. Smith was bouncing along, Jackson on one side of him, Edwards on the other. The track was faint, only just discernible in the darkness but following the line of the river as it curved to run south and then turned eastward again. There Edwards reined in and said, "One man." The track joined another that ran due south and this was broader, clearly seen.

Jackson said, "Phil!" And a man wheeled out of the ranks to wait at the junction to guide the foot-soldiers coming on behind as the rest of the troop turned on to the main track and rode on to the south.

The track was climbing gently now but the horsemen were hurrying, Edwards leading at a fast canter, a muffled thrumming of hooves in the sand, squeak of leather and jingling of harness. Smith risked a glance behind him and saw the troop closed up tight behind, hastening, eager. And beyond them was the black glint of the river with the white of the surf at its mouth.

He faced forward. They passed a hump of ground rising on their right hand and briefly the track descended before lifting again. Now he could see the ground falling away on either hand, to his left to the plain, to his right down to the sea.

Dauntless was out there, somewhere.

There was a village ahead, a scattering of houses closed and dark on both sides of the track: Summeil. They dashed through it. Stealth was pointless; the villagers could tell no one of what they heard, if they *knew* what they heard. And anyway, stealth was impossible.

Smith's legs and rump were sore. The track was climbing again now and they came on a road that was the Jaffa–Tul Karam road but deserted in the night and they crossed it without pause, leaving another trooper to mark the way. To the left and a quarter mile away lay the houses of the village of Sarona, dark and silent, but the troop hurried southward, rode on up a long, gentle rise until they came to the crest, lifted over it and trotted down on the other side for two hundred yards. There they halted. They had ridden some three miles.

Smith slid off the horse and shoved the reins at the nearest trooper. He was done with it and thought the horse might be almost as glad as himself. He hobbled stiffly forward, rubbing his thighs, to stand by Edwards and saw Buckley coming up, walking as gingerly as himself. So somebody else was in the same boat. He grinned at Buckley. "Enjoy yourself?"

Buckley was not amused, answered shortly, "No, sir. Me arse feels as if its up between me ears."

So Buckley was all right. But Smith was looking around. He had been able to afford that moment of humour, just, because the railway track was empty. It ran away down to his right, twin lines of dull silver in the night, towards the distant black hump of Jaffa. Further round to his right he could make out the black, square-cut shapes of houses, slightly below him and about a quarter-mile away. That was the little Jewish township of Tel Aviv but now it was deserted. The Turks, believing rightly that the Jews sympathised with the British, had threatened to deport them. So the Jews had evacuated it, left a ghost town in the desert. He wondered if the war dragged on for years whether the little town would go back to desert? To be dug over by some archaeologist a thousand years from now?

But that was only with a part of his mind. The orange groves grew close and thick on the other side of the railway track. Here on this rise was the point where the line coming up from Jaffa swung in a curve to run away downhill to his left and towards Lydda.

The Australians had dismounted, one man from each section of four holding the horses, the others gathering behind Jackson, who ordered, "Flankers out." Troopers broke away from the group and trotted off, two up the line and two down it, and were lost in the darkness. Jackson pointed and the horse-holders led their Walers across the railway track and into the orange groves.

Smith called, "Follow me!" He ran down the track towards Lydda for a hundred yards, Jackson and his troop at his heels, gasping and swearing as they stumbled in the darkness. Smith halted and panted, "One of these. *That* one!"

Two troopers crossed the track, axes glinting in their hands and a moment later the blades *chunked* into the orange tree. Another trooper shrugged a coil of rope from his shoulder and made one end fast around the tree, while the others paid out the length of it and took up the slack as he stepped back. The furious chopping sounded loud in the stillness. The Australians threw their weight on the rope and the tree creaked and swayed.

Smith ran back up the track to where Buckley waited, halted beside him and stared down towards Jaffa. From *Dauntless* he had seen the pinprick glow of the train go down into the town – but what if it did not return? He swallowed and rubbed at the sweat on his face. The desert troops would be moving up to mount the attack on Beersheba and if he failed there would be slaughter.

Somewhere a jackal howled. From far to the south came the mutter of the guns before Gaza and their flashes lit the sky. But there was another light, closer and moving, a tiny pulsing red glow that crept up the hill from Jaffa towards Smith. Thank God.

There was a crash away to his left and he ran back to where Jackson and his men were hauling the felled tree from the grove to lie across the rails. Smith gasped, "The train's coming! Where's that trooper—" Then saw the man on hands and knees close to where the tree lay, emptying out his haversack, pushing the contents into a heap, scraping a match. The yellow flame caught the paraffin-soaked rags and the fire blazed for a second, then sank to a steady burning. Three of the troopers lay down beside the little fire, their rifles under them.

Smith glanced around, saw only Jackson and Edwards facing him across the track; the other troopers had vanished. Jackson lifted a hand, then he and Edwards retreated out of the fire-light. Smith backed away from it, pulled the Webley from its holster and sank down in the outer darkness. A trooper was bellied-down only a yard away, smelling of horse and tobacco, holding his rifle in front of him in his right hand, his left spread flat on the sand.

Smith's gaze went back to the little fire that just lit the tree and the sprawled figures of the seemingly sleeping men in their tattered, unrecognisable uniforms. Then his head jerked around. The pulsing glow was in sight, the train rounding the long curve where the track bent around the orange groves. It moved slowly after the long haul up from Jaffa, smoke from its chimney lifting against the sky as it trundled down towards him, a black mass taking shape out of the darkness and with brakes squealing now. It was close enough for him to see the driver leaning out from the footplate, outlined against the glow of the firebox.

The train ground to a halt right above him with its buffers only feet from the felled tree. The driver bawled, outraged, and jumped down, advanced into the firelight where one of the prone figures stirred sleepily. The driver stopped short, peering and Smith shoved himself up shouting, "Now!" He ran at the footplate, conscious of the trooper beside him, of the three figures jerking upright like puppets yanked up on the one string, their rifles pointing. He jumped at the steps leading up to the footplate, grabbed at the handle and pulled himself aboard. There was a soldier, a Turk, swinging the slung rifle from his shoulder and backing away across the footplate in the face of the Webley. Smith snarled at him, "Keep still!" The man still fumbled at the rifle, the engine's fireman peering over his shoulder, eyes wide, mouth gaping. Then Edwards appeared from the other side of the engine, materialising like a ghost in his white robes. He shoved the fireman aside, laid the blade of the knife across the soldier's throat and tore the rifle from his slackened fingers as he stood rigid under the cold pressure of the flat of the knife. Jackson came crowding in after Edwards, grabbed first the fireman, then the soldier and bundled them off the footplate to the little knot of troopers waiting for them by the track.

Smith thought: "Not a shot fired so far." The rest of the train? He jumped down and started back past the tender, shouting, "Douse that fire!" He glanced around and saw a trooper kicking sand over the flames.

As the darkness closed in Buckley came trotting up from the rear of the train. "Right y'are, sir! Eight trucks and not a soul aboard. Only these two at the front are loaded."

Smith halted and took stock. They had the train without raising an alarm; that was one more step along the way. Eight trucks. He had expected eight, based his plans on that figure because every reconnaissance that had seen this train had reported eight trucks or more. It was just enough. He would have tried with less if he'd had to, simply because he'd had to, but was relieved there were eight.

Jackson appeared on the top of the wood-stacked tender and leapt across to the first truck and balanced on its load. Troopers climbed up to join him and started hurling sacks and crates over the side into the orange grove. Smith called up, "They've got to be out of sight!"

A voice answered impatiently, "Aw, we know that, for Christ's sake."

Smith grinned and set out on a rapid tour of the position, Buckley hurrying at his heels. He checked the flankers at either end and found the country silent, empty. He passed along the edge of the grove where the cargo from the train was disappearing into the lanes between the trees, the prisoners lay under guard and the Walers stood patiently with the horseholders. He rounded the front of the train and found the track clear, the tree dragged away into the grove. Jackson and his gang were working on the second truck. Smith called up, "Quick as you can! I'm going to look for Taggart!"

Jackson lifted a hand in acknowledgment. Smith turned and ran up the slope to the crest, stood there peering back along the trail they had followed from the Auja river. It was too soon for Taggart but – something moved out there in the darkness below him. There was a rhythmic whispering that might have been wind in trees but there was no wind, nor trees on this crest and the whispering came steady but rapid. A snake coiled up the hill towards him, thick and black, hurrying, and as it came on out of the night it grew legs. The whispering was the scuff of boots in sand and the laboured breathing of Taggart's battalion.

Smith ran down to meet them and fell in by Taggart who marched at their head, stepping out at a rapid pace, head thrust forward and thumb hooked in the sling of the rifle over his shoulder. Garrett, his runner, came behind him like a shadow. The two Australian troopers left behind as markers now rode out on the flank.

Smith told them, "Ride over the crest and report to Mr.

Jackson. Tell him we're coming." He looked at Taggart and asked, "What about the men?"

"They're all right," Taggart jerked out between panting.

"Any stragglers?"

"We don't – have – stragglers."

Smith could not believe it. The men had been cooped up aboard the *Morning Star* for days, and it had been a killing march: Taggart must have doubled them for some of the way. And the men who carried rifles were the lucky ones; others humped Vickers machine-guns or deadweight boxes of ammunition.

He halted on the crest to watch them go by. In the darkness he could see little, though he stood in close to the ranks that flicked past him, peering into faces. He recognised a lot of them now and Taggart's battalion was a live thing, not a mass of uniformed numbers. All of the faces were like Taggart's, drawn and sweat-slicked, mouths gaping as they panted, eyes wide and fixed on the back of the man in front. He saw why there had been no stragglers. Here and there was a man who carried two rifles, and there were pairs of men who supported another shambling along head-down between them. But nobody halted the column, nobody interrupted that quick pace set by Taggart at their head.

And at the side of the column moved the sergeants and warrant officers, hurrying up the length of their respective companies, "Keep closed up! Keep the step an' keep closed up! Not far now! *Close up!*" Repeated again and again until they reached the head of the company, waited for it to pass them and all the time keeping up the chant: "Close up! Close up!" And when the tail passed them, hurrying forward again: "Keep closed up! Keep the step!"

There were no stragglers but there should have been. Smith watched the last company come up to the crest and called, "Well done!" Some eyes slid his way, blank, then blinking with recognition. That was all.

And at the tail of the column, last of all, came the battalion's medical orderlies towing their little cart with its stretchers and cases, Merryweather the surgeon at their head and—

Smith burst out incredulously, "What are you dong here?"

Adeline Brett did not check her pace any more than the soldiers ahead of her, but she wiped at a tendril of hair that clung to her sweating brow and answered, "I should think it was obvious. The men have their duty – I have mine."

Smith strode along beside her and glared across at Merryweather. "Are you out of your mind?"

Merryweather said defensively, "Not my fault, sir. I didn't find her till I was aboard the lighter. Too late then."

"You could have stopped her landing!"

"No, I couldn't sir. Somehow she was ashore before me."

They were over the crest and marching rapidly down on the train. Smith could see the battalion already lining out along it, a confused mass of figures in the dark, spreading out and thinning.

Adeline Brett said quickly, her breath returning on this last downhill stretch, "You have duties to attend to, Commander. It was not my intention to distract you from them. We'll go along as best we can, help when we can and when we can't we'll keep out of the way. If you'd only stop thinking of me as a woman, I would present no problem."

Smith grabbed her arm, pulled her out of the column and halted. Stop thinking of her as a woman? That was not only difficult, it was impossible. He said, "I don't want you involved in – I don't want—" He could not put it into words.

She said softly, "I know what to expect, David. I've seen dead and wounded before, too often."

He knew that. But here she was not behind the lines, would have only the doubtful protection of a Red Cross flag. He stared at her, the short fair hair tousled, the eyes that looked steadily back at him. Let her go on with the rest to what surely awaited them? It was unthinkable, but . . . He looked beyond her to the men of her battalion who were clambering into trucks now, looked ahead to the morrow's dawning, when these men would need Merryweather and he would have his hands full. He said, "I'm very glad you've come. Take care, that's all."

It was her turn to stare, bewildered at the sudden change in him.

He saw a short, plump figure easing out of the tail of the little cart to stand on fat legs. Adeline Brett followed his gaze and explained, "We had to put him in there. He couldn't keep up. He's just not built for marching."

Smith said, "I don't care how he got here as long as he does the job." He called to the muscle-easing, groaning figure, "Come on!" Then he turned and ran and Charlie Golightly waddled after him.

He found Taggart striding along the edge of the track marshalling his men into the trucks. Smith said, "Three companies, no more. Anyone who had to be carried—"

Taggart turned to grin at him. "The N.C.O.'s are sorting them out. Three companies to go. The rest stay here with Jackson."

Smith said, "Quick as you can. Let me know when you're ready. Come up to the cab and ride with me, or—"

"I'll come to the cab now but I'll ride with the men."

Smith nodded. He had thought that would be Taggart's decision. It would have been his. He ran towards the head of the train and in the glow that seeped out round the edges of the firebox door he saw Charlie Golightly on the footplate of the engine looking round gloomily. Smith clambered aboard. Buckley hovered in the background, or as much in the background as he could be in that restricted space. Edwards leaned on the far side of the cab.

Golightly said, "Right bloody lot this is. They run it by praying and bugger-all else by the look of it."

Smith frowned, "Can you drive it?"

"Well, understand, sir, it's not like what I've been used to and an engineer like me, I'm used to a proper way o' going about things and—"

Smith broke in, exasperated, "*Can you make the bloody thing go?*"

Charlie Golightly tried to step back from that icy glare but found Buckley behind him. Aboard *Dauntless* Smith had said, "You don't have to come. I'm not giving you an order. I've engineers aboard this ship who will make that engine run somehow. You just might be able to do it a little quicker. You can come with me and I'll do all I can for you. Or you can go in the cells now and take your chance back at Deir el Belah."

Prison had seemed chillingly close to Charlie just then and Smith wasn't asking him to fight, only to drive an engine. Charlie could do that, was confident he could drive any engine but he doubted if he would come out of prison alive.

Now he stood on the footplate and wondered if he would come out of this alive. Prison now seemed solid and safe by comparison, but it was a long way off and the Germans and Turks stood between it and him. His life depended on this young naval officer and the breathless, hurrying men about him. Charlie said huskily, "I c'n drive it all right. It's just been a bit neglected, like."

Taggart appeared by the cab. "Ready."

Smith answered, "Right." He turned on Charlie Golightly. "Full ahead."

Charlie wound off the brake, rammed the reverse lever to forward and eased over the regulator handle. The engine wheezed, chuffed rapidly, jerked with a rattling of couplings, then eased forward.

They were moving.

Smith shoved past Charlie Golightly to lean out over the side of the cab and look back. He saw the figures of Jackson and his troopers, slouch-hatted, lined out along the side of the orange groves. Somewhere in the orange groves were a hundred or more of Taggart's battalion and Adeline Brett's cart, but the rest, three hundred of them, were packed into the trucks behind him. He could see them standing, heads and shoulders above the sides of the trucks, but only by the pale blur of their faces. There were no distinguishable figures, just blocks of humanity that lurched as one as the train moved forward. And Adeline Brett was somewhere among them.

He swung back into the cab to see Charlie Golightly peering out of a round window over the footplate. Smith called to him, "Can't we go faster than this?"

Golightly sniffed and rubbed at his nose with a fat hand. "I should say so, as soon as we gets down on the flat. But I don't want her to run away on this hill 'cause this officer 'ere—" he jerked his head at Edwards, '—he tells me there's a bend at the bottom. After that I'll let her out for what she's worth and Gawd 'elp us all."

Smith leaned out again and peered ahead down the slope. The train rocked as it swung around a right-hand curve, straightened out, steadied, and chuffed on. It swung again, to the left this time and Edwards shouted, "That's it! Should be a straight run from here!"

Smith turned and saw Golightly's hand grope back and find the regulating lever as he peered out of his window at the track running into the darkness ahead. He eased the lever over and the train's panting breathing quickened until it was hammering along with the wood smoke from the chimney pouring back even more thickly over the roof of the cab.

Golightly turned his head for a second to yell at Buckley, "Chuck some wood on!"

Buckley staggered across the footplate as it rocked with the speed, clawed down an armful of logs from the tender, kicked open the firebox door with his boot and fed the logs into the flames within. The red glow lit them all, Buckley sweating as he threw in the logs, Edwards hawk-faced and eyes glittering, Charlie Golightly's round face turned to keep an eye on how Buckley fed the furnace, professionally watchful.

Buckley slammed the door and for seconds they were all blind. When Smith's night vision returned he saw they were rushing past more orange groves. The little old engine was giving all she had, screwed out of her by Golightly, and probably running faster than she had in twenty years. Not even Jackson's horsemen could have stayed with her now. Smith enjoyed a brief moment of exhilaration, then was jerked back to reality as Edwards shouted, "Beit Dejan!" And pointed.

Smith peered past him and saw the cluster of houses away to the right of the track. He asked, "How far now?"

"Half way. Another ten minutes at this rate, if that!"

Ten minutes or less. Ten minutes in which mentally to

skim over the plan again to see if he had forgotten anything –
but he could not anticipate *every* possibility. Plan as he might,
an operation like this was dependant on luck, necessity its sole
justification. Smith was gambling with the lives of three hundred men but only because he had to. The lives of thousands
hung on the outcome. Not for the first time that night he was
afraid, swallowed his fear, or tried to.

Suppose they were too late, that somehow the Afrika Legion
had already passed through, the supply dump was stripped
bare and the whole reckless adventure nothing but a waste of
lives? And Allenby's attack was stalled after all?

He tried to shake off the haunting possibility but failed. The
Legion was pressing on as fast as it could, which was very fast.
Only by sea could it have moved faster with all its equipment
and supplies – the thought raised in him a suspicion that he
had overlooked something, that was eluding him – something obvious.

"We're getting close!" That was Edwards.

Smith said, "Slow down!" He peered past the length of the
engine and ahead along the track. He knew what he was
looking for, a little bridge. The speed of the train was falling
away.

He heard Golightly say, "Keep clear o' that brake 'andle, Mr.
Buckley, if you please. I might want it any time now."

And Edwards said, "Here it is! Stop her!"

The stone parapet of the bridge came up out of the darkness,
flicked past, was gone. Now the brake was winding on, beginning to bite. And Charlie Golightly knew his job: the wheels
did not lock and there was no grinding nor showering of
sparks. The train slid smoothly to a halt with just the barest of
jerks as it came to rest in a sighing of steam.

But Smith still thought they must have been seen. The
smoke and sparks from the engine's chimney would have
marked them and while the train was expected at Lydda station, lying a mile south of the town itself, it was not expected
to stop here. Soon the sentries at the dump and the station
would start to wonder and shout for their non-coms. He dared
not waste a second.

He dropped down from the cab, Edwards and Buckley leaping after him and stared out across the dark countryside. A half-mile away to his left and north were the scattered lights of Lydda but there was another light closer and to the south-east, so he did not need Edwards's pointing finger.

Edwards said, "The dump. A quarter-mile away, no more, and fairly open country as I said."

Just ahead of the hissing engine the track curved to run south. In half-a-mile it joined the main line and Smith could see the junction with his mind's eye, as he had seen it on the map and Edwards had described it, though now the night covered it. The station lay there. The two lines, the main and the spur from Jaffa, made a V as they ran down to the junction. The wood and the dump it hid lay in the top of that V.

Smith turned to find Taggart at his shoulder, face calm but eyes staring at the lights. Beyond him the men poured in a cataract of shadows over the sides of the trucks and again there was that whispering: "Ack comp'ny here!" . . . "Beer comp'ny here!" Figures came running out of the night, slipping and stumbling in the darkness on the uneven going. They halted in a semi-circle behind Taggart, the warrant officers and sergeants of the battalion.

Taggart turned on them. "Ack company cross the line there—" his finger stabbed, "—deploy and move up on the right of the dump *now*. Charlie company deploy and move up on the left *now*. I'll lead Beer company in the centre and we'll give you five minutes start to work around the sides, then I'll head straight for the light." His finger pointed at the solitary light marking the dump. "No firing till we're fired on, then rapid and *get in*! Flare men in the rear of Beer company with Sergeant Carmichael and the demolition party." He paused, went on: "Ten rounds rapid, then we'll do the work with the bayonet." He paused again, then finished, "This won't be like Salonika. This is to show *them*." His head jerked at those far, far behind him, Finlayson, the generals, the whole military machine that had locked him and his men away in the hold of the *Morning Star*. "Carry on!"

The group dissolved, the men trotting back to their companies and Taggart glanced at Smith. "Those are all the orders they need. They know what they're doing."

Buckley murmured at Smith's shoulder, "That Arab feller, sir."

Smith turned and saw Edwards in his robes drifting spectral through the deeper shadow by the engine. "Colonel Edwards!" Smith strode over to him. "You'll come with me."

Edwards said flatly, "Not on your life. My orders were to guide the attacking force to the dump and I've done that. I agreed your plan gave a fighting chance of taking the dump but getting out again is another matter. When your attack goes in you'll raise the countryside and even if the Turks are a bit slow coming out of Jaffa, that regiment north of the Auja will have a bit more time and they'll come down like the hammers of hell. I'm an Intelligence officer, I'd be no help as just one more rifleman and I'm too valuable to risk in that kind of scrap." He finished cynically, "Don't worry about me. I'll make my own way home from here and I wish you the best of luck."

Smith thought that Edwards must have seen his chance when he had disclosed his plan back aboard *Dauntless*, and had made his own plans to slip away before the attack on the dump. That was the reason for his sudden change from depression to his old cock-sureness. Smith said softly, "I told you that we sank or swam together in this and that means right to the end. No one walks out. And besides, we may need you on the way back." He glanced at Taggart. "I want him guarded."

Taggart nodded, turned and saw Garrett at his heels. For a moment Taggart hesitated, then jerked his head at the rifleman. Garrett stepped forward and Smith ordered, "Put this officer in the front truck along with the Vickers and its crew. You can all keep an eye on him."

Edwards exploded, "Don't be bloody ridiculous! Surely you can see the sense—"

Smith finished, "If he tries to escape, shoot him."

Edwards glared but Garrett's rifle was trained on his chest and Garrett said, "Into the truck – sir." There was unmistakable menace in the words; Garrett would shoot.

Taggart said quietly, "I'd advise you to do as he says."

Edwards muttered under his breath but recognised that menace, swung away and climbed into the truck, followed by Garrett.

Smith looked up at Golightly where he stood on the footplate. "So far you've done all I asked. Now stay where you are and be ready to go. There are twenty men and two machineguns with you."

Golightly stared uneasily about him into the darkness, cleared his throat and said, "I won't leave her, sir."

Smith turned away, his anger with Edwards subsiding. The man was neither a fool nor a coward, simply cold-bloodedly selfish – prepared to take any risk that furthered his ambitions but not one step beyond. Objectively Smith could appreciate his argument but equally he could not let one man walk away. And he might indeed need Edwards yet.

For a moment the night was quiet, the men of B company still . . . and in that silence the thought came from nowhere: was it coincidence that *Walküre* broke out as the Afrika Legion headed for Beersheba? But what could be her purpose? Now, admittedly, she was a prisoner in the Gulf of Alexandretta, but would her captain, a man with the skill and daring to break out of the Dardanelles, accept that? But what could he do—?

The silence and the train of thought were broken as the long line of B company moved forward and he followed them, Buckley at his side. Taggart was a moving blur ahead of his men, the last of a thousand randomly thrown together when the battalion was formed but made by him into a unified fighting machine, with a heart and inner loyalty of its own. He had said they had been caged too long and were ready to fight anybody. Now they were isolated in a hostile country but as they marched steadily forward Smith could sense the power in them. He had wondered whether they might prove more explosive than the massive cargo of ammunition in the after holds of the *Morning Star*. If so, then that explosion was close now.

Great clumps of cactus made gaps in the long line, they caught in Smith's clothes and tore his skin but the line washed around each clump as it came and formed again. A blacker edge of darkness rose against the sky as they advanced. That was the wood, a hundred yards across and hiding the dump. Edwards had said the Germans had strung barbed wire between the trees and hung it with empty tins, not as a defence but to keep thieves out. The battalion would have to get through it.

Somewhere out to right and left were A and C companies that had moved off before B so as to strike at the sides, surrounding the dump, while B company struck in the centre. There was no steady tramp of boots, the step deliberately broken so there was a continual rustling as the boots scuffed the sand.

The wood was close; he could make out branches of trees traced against the dark. Off to the right a German voice called, uncertain, then after a moment's pause called again and this time louder, a definite challenge. The line was trotting now and Smith went with them, the dust rising around him. Flame spat briefly away to the right and was answered by a ragged volley. Taggart's command lifted in a bellow: "Get in! Get in!"

The line was ragged now because the men were running and the faster ones got ahead of the others. They were close to the wood and above the pounding of the booted feet Smith heard shouting from inside the belt of trees that suddenly overshadowed him. The line halted, the men kneeling before him. The wire was a web between the trees and the tins bounced and jangled together as the kneeling men thrust rifles through the wire and rifle-fire exploded around the wood, the bolts worked furiously in 'ten rounds rapid'. Others with gloved hands and cutters were snatching at the wire, cutting, the strands parting with a dull *thwang* and trailing. The men around him and right down the line were bawling madly, "In! In! In!" The bayonets were coming out, long streaks of silver snapping on to the muzzles of the rifles. Grenades exploded. Away to the left a machine-gun hammered and tracer sailed through the darkness.

Taggart was right forward against the wire, his face turned back to Smith and mouth opening and closing as he shouted. Smith could not hear a word above the din but the men passed it back to him and he threw it on: "Sergeant Carmichael! Flares!"

"Sir!"

Taggart lurched forward, tripped, staggered then recovered. Smith lost sight of him as the men came up off their knees and poured through the gap cut in the wire in a yelling, cursing flood. Smith went with them, swung right when the flood split on a square bulk that was no building but crates stacked under a camouflage netting hung on poles to form a roof. Deeper darkness covered him and the men around him but there were phantom figures ahead. A single shot was fired, the flash blinding them all, then a flare burst overhead, brilliant blue-white and smoking. Smith saw the men of the German guard, half-dressed and bare-headed as they had run from their tents, saw them only for the blink of an eye then Taggart's men were on them.

The supply dump was ranked piles of crates and sacks and tin containers, all in among the trees and under the sagging roofs of camouflage nets. He moved in a narrow lane that ran through the dump, stumbling over the bodies of men, other panting, running men on either side of him. There was firing all around the dump, a continuous harsh rattle of musketry and now and again the thump of a grenade and the smell of it caught at the throat. Inside the confines of the wood, in the narrow lanes was bedlam. The battalion was not shouting now – there was a different accent to the yelling all about him. The Germans were fighting as always. They had been surprised in the night, finding their attackers upon them and not knowing who those attackers were nor whence they came, but still they fought. The flares burnt, the bayonets flickered. Smith, feeling remote, an onlooker, saw more than most and he only retained a memory of charging, clashing figures, of men fighting hand to hand, even wrestling on the earth. Of a man charging huge out of the darkness, bayonet uplifted like a sword and Buckley stepping in to beat him down with the butt of the rifle. Taggart turning to face Smith, lifting his rifle and firing, it seemed, directly at him but in fact at the Unteroffizier coming up behind him. He fell on Smith and Taggart and

Buckley dragged him out from under the German's dead-weight.

Running on under the spectral light of the flares. A blank-eyed private of the battalion crouching in the way, long bayonet pointed at Smith, who croaked, "*Dauntless!*" The bayonet swung away and ahead were trees with barbed wire dangling. This was the far perimeter of the dump and he had passed through to it. He stood in the wreckage of the guards' bivouac, the canvas of the tents trampled underfoot.

He realised it was over. The firing had ceased and voices called all about him but the accents were Cockney or Yorkshire, Welsh or Glasgow Scots. Taggart showed at Smith's side and said huskily, "Well, we've done it."

They had taken the dump and were astride the railway line to Gaza and Beersheba.

9

Dawn Patrols

The changed Pearce had demanded and got from Admiral Braddock two hundred Egyptian labourers to shift the coal and stores in *Blackbird* from starboard to port, listing the ship so that the shell-hole in the hull was clear of the water. Blacksmiths and engineers from the army worked with *Blackbird*'s crew, ripping a plate from her deck and fitting it as another unsightly but more seaworthy patch on her side. They took aboard fuel for the Shorts and bombs that Pearce begged from the Royal Flying Corps. They wondered what drove him. He kept them all hard at it because Smith had said, "I'll need you." The flying personnel he sent ashore with orders to sleep and they too obeyed him. Even little Maitland's excitement surrendered to the accumulated fatigue of weeks and he slept like the dead in the tent the army gave him.

Pearce brought them off an hour before dawn and *Blackbird* sailed in the night, heading north at full speed. She only slowed to bring the three remaining Shorts out of the hangar and launch them. At first light their wings were spread and they were hoisted out. Kirby was the first pilot away with Burns of the Rajputs as his observer. Then Rogers and Maitland in *Delilah* and last was Beckett with one of the riggers called Phillips, chosen from a dozen volunteers, in the rear cockpit as his observer. With barely a minute between them and heavy with bombs they laboured across the sea and lifted slowly, climbing and heading north. Pearce had told them: "Reconnoitre the railway and the dump at Lydda and note any damage. Then look for *Dauntless* off the mouth of the Auja river."

*   *   *

Lieutenant Harry Petersen was in the little wheelhouse of the submarine-chaser, sleeping in the old deckchair wedged into one corner, with his feet propped up on the screen and his cap tipped forward over his eyes. When the hand gently shook his shoulder he came awake, tipped back the cap and squinted up into the round young face of Ensign Cleeve, who said softly, "Starting to get light, sir."

Petersen pushed up out of the deckchair, stretching and yawning as he stepped up beside the quartermaster at the wheel to peer at the compass. He saw their course was north-west by north, looked up and narrowed his eyes to penetrate the darkness. There was just a hint of grey in that darkness now. Cleeve said, "*Maroc* three cables on the starboard bow, sir."

Petersen grunted, made out the shadowy bulk of the old French battleship as she plodded steadily across the mouth of the Gulf six hundred yards to starboard and ahead of the chaser, saw her against the lighter sky of the eastern horizon. Somewhere beyond that horizon the sun was lifting behind the Amanus mountains and soon its rays would be sweeping over the Gulf and out across the sea. It would be lighter already far up the Gulf where *Walküre* and the freighter lay. The R.E.8 sent out from Cyprus on patrol the previous evening had flown low over *Maroc* and the chaser as it came out from the Gulf, signal lamp flickering as it reported that *Walküre* showed no sign of getting up steam, no sign of fires at all, and the freighter still had the staging hung over her stern, there were still divers working. The R.E.8 had finished, "See you tomorrow. Good night!" And buzzed away home to the westward.

Cleeve asked, "Do you think we'll see some action today, sir?"

Petersen thought about it. That new French battleship, *Océan*, coming up from Malta might be here by noon, and the cruiser *Attack* would certainly arrive before the day was out but they would be just another bolt on the door. Really they were all waiting for the transport to turn up with the M.A.S. boats that were able to slip into the Gulf and over the mine-fields with their electric motors. *Walküre* would defend herself of course, but even if she was successful she'd know her time was limited. Then she might come out and make a fight of it.

He said slowly, "Not today. And when she does come out we'll only be looking on." He explained with weary patience to the puzzled and disappointed Cleeve, "Because this bucket hasn't even got a torpedo. She's anti-submarine, remember? Besides, *Walküre* is flying Turkish colours and is technically a Turkish warship and the U.S. isn't at war with Turkey. So we'll have to sit back and watch because that'll be somebody else's ball-game." He finished, "But anyhow, you'll have a grandstand seat when that comes off in a day or two." Then he asked, "Anything from *Maroc?*"

"No, sir."

Petersen growled. "I don't like getting all my information second-hand and in some Frenchman's American." The chaser's wireless was only a tactical set for manoeuvring, its range barely five miles.

The light was growing now and Petersen could make out details of *Maroc*'s rigging, see her as a three-dimensional ship and not a shadow cut out of the greater darkness of the night. The sea was calm and quiet now, there was no wind and hardly a ripple on the surface of the black water except for those from *Maroc*'s bow and the white water at her stern . . .

"*Torpedo running across the bow to starboard!*" The port look-out yelled, pointing out into the dark.

Petersen lunged forward to glare out over the bow, eyes frantically searching the sea as he shouted, "Action stations! Submarine!" and hit the button of the hooter that blared through the little ship. That was when he saw the line of foam drawn across the sea ahead of the chaser and running towards *Maroc*. He bawled at the crew of the 3-inch gun on the fore-deck. "Fire!" He pointed out to port. "At any damn thing!"

They'd have hell's own job to hit a U-boat even if they saw it out there, but that wasn't the point. The gun would draw the eyes of *Maroc*'s look-outs so they might see the torpedo's track. But Petersen had a sick feeling that even if they did it would be too late now for *Maroc* to do anything about it. He snapped at the quartermaster, "Hard over left rudder!" And to the rating at the telegraph: "Full ahead!" As the chaser's head came around he swung out of the wheelhouse to hang from one hand clamped on the doorframe as his eyes searched back along the torpedo's track, seeking its point of origin.

He ordered, "Meet her! Steer that!" He could see no periscope, no U-boat, just a point on the black sea where the line of bubbles had begun and somewhere there lay the submarine that fired the torpedo. He saw young Cleeve dashing aft to the Y-gun, so called because it was shaped like a Y, its arms able to throw a depth-charge out on either side of the chaser.

They were coming to the beginning of the torpedo track and he turned to bawl at Cleeve, "Fire!" The depth-charges shot up and out over the side to plummet into the sea as another slid over the stern. The crew of the Y-gun were re-loading as Petersen told the quartermaster, "Hard right rudder!" The chaser's head started to swing, he was watching for the explosion of the depth-charges, saw the sea erupt.

The flash came to starboard of them, from *Maroc*, a leaping, soaring flame that lit the sea and reached high into the sky, that seared the eye. Blast snatched the cap from Petersen's head and punched him in the chest, almost tore him from his hold on the doorframe.

Then the sound of the explosion came, not so much a sound as a blow to the ears. As the flame had blinded them so the explosion deafened. But vision returned so that Petersen could see *Maroc* burning in half-a-dozen places along her hull – but there were two hulls now. The middle had been blasted out of the battleship as her magazines blew up and now her bow and stern stuck up separately and ever more steeply from the sea as they burned and sank. The stern went down with a rush even as Petersen watched, horrified.

He ran his hand through his hair and ordered hoarsely, "Midships!" Because the chaser had turned and was tearing down to pass over the place where the U-boat was, or must have been. Water still boiled where the three depth-charges had exploded but there was no debris, nothing. He turned to see Cleeve at the Y-gun on the fantail, his mouth gaping as he stared at the destruction of *Maroc*. Petersen yelled at him, "Fire! Damn you, Mr. Cleeve! *Fire!*"

The Y-gun lobbed the depth charges wide over the stern of the chaser. They exploded, hurling water at the sky and Petersen looked for a trace of oil, of the U-boat but there was nothing. He swung back to stare again at *Maroc* and this time the blast from her plucked him loose from his hold on the doorframe and sent him sprawling across the deck. The four men crewing the 3-inch gun forward joined him in a heap, one of them with his nose bleeding from that blast. The flash had been even brighter than before, their ears rang. The chaser swerved as the pressure thrust at her and the quartermaster was thrown across the wheelhouse, then clawed his way back to the wheel. The bow, all that was left of *Maroc* had blown up, disintegrated and disappeared in that one monstrous, flaming explosion. The sea was empty and dark again now and the chaser the only ship on it.

But not alone.

Petersen was well aware of that as he climbed to the wheel-house again. Somewhere below the surface lay the submarine that had sunk *Maroc* without leaving a solitary survivor – he knew no man could have survived those terrible explosions. He had dropped six depth-charges without result. He was on a cold trail now, with the U-boat creeping further away with every second. He had an ever-increasing and already huge area of sea to search and no matter how many depth-charges he dropped now, his chances of a hit were tiny and shrinking steadily.

Only one tactic remained. He ordered quietly, "Hard left rudder!"

The chaser's head came around until she was headed out to sea and her stern to the growing light over the waters of the Gulf and he looked at the compass and said, "Steer due west." So they ran away from the Gulf and the light until, at Petersen's order, speed was reduced to a near walking pace of five knots when they were a mile to the westward of the sunken *Maroc*, and then turned again to steer due east. He was speaking very quietly now and all of the boat was hushed as the look-outs stood silent with the glasses to their eyes. The chaser crept back across the sea towards the Gulf with her engines barely ticking over and only a ripple at her bow.

Petersen said, "Keep a good look-out all around." He thought this was a long shot and a manoeuvre that could only work, if it worked at all, just the once. The light was growing fast and flooding out across the sea from the Gulf of Alexandretta. In minutes it would be all around them, but it was not around them yet. The chaser crept in over a still-dark sea: the night was behind her and she was showing no blaze of white at bow or stern. And she was not a big boat, hardly better than a motor-launch and low in the water, surely hidden by the darkness.

He sensed someone beside him and turned to see Cleeve standing by the wheelhouse steps. Cleeve asked softly, almost whispering as the hush aboard subdued his voice as it subdued all of them. "D'ye think the bastard's still there, sir?"

Petersen said, "Maybe." It was no better a chance than that. He went on, "He knows he hit the bull's-eye because he felt those explosions but without looking he doesn't know whether he's sunk her or not. He hasn't heard a depth-charge for better than ten minutes so maybe he'll think we've gone home, or gone to assist if the battleship is still afloat or to look for survivors. So it might be worth coming up for just one quick look. There might be another sinking in it if we've stopped to pick men out of the sea."

Cleeve said, "I see." He licked his lips and started, "Sir—"

Petersen continued, "Of course, he might have worked all this out and then gone a stage further and be out there to port or starboard now, lying stopped and waiting for us to come on to a bearing so he can fire his fish."

Young Cleeve swallowed. "Yes, sir."

"Which is why I ordered a good look-out kept all round, though I shouldn't have to, even with a bunch of soldiers like these."

The quartermaster grinned faintly and Cleeve returned his grin behind Petersen's back. "No, sir."

Petersen said, glasses set to his eyes and still now, "Port

five . . . steady." And: "She's dead ahead an' a half-mile away." He heard Cleeve scampering aft to his post at the Y-gun, watched through the glasses the slender, stick-like periscope standing out of the sea with the smallest feather of white water at its base as the submarine moved slowly ahead, the chaser trailing it. He asked casually, "Got it?"

The voice of the layer on the 3-inch gun came back across the quiet deck: "Right." He waited for the order to fire but Petersen did not give it. The chaser slipped on slowly, still at that creeping five knots, and the gunlayer with the periscope of the U-boat big and clear and steady in his sights was certain she must see them.

But Petersen knew differently. The periscope stood against the growing light while the chaser was still out in the darkness with the night behind her. So he waited as the look-outs stood rigidly with their glasses all trained on the periscope now, as Ensign Cleeve chewed at his lip and the gunlayer sweated and swore under his breath as he carefully inched around the wheel that laid the gun, bringing down the barrel as the range steadily shortened, keeping the sight laid on that white feather of water where the periscope cut the sea.

Then Petersen snapped, "Fire!" And: "Full ahead!"

The layer and the engineer were both ready. The gun slammed and the shell fell just short of the periscope or hit it, Petersen saw the water kicked up and hiding the periscope. When the water fell the sea was empty but the gun was loaded again, fired. The chaser was working up speed now and almost on top of the U-boat. Cleeve shrieked at his crew and once more the Y-gun hurled depth-charges over the side, another dropped over the stern and as they exploded Petersen set the chaser turning, lining her up to run in again.

That was when the U-boat came wallowing to the surface off the starboard beam, her bow down, stern high and listing over so her bottom nearly showed. The 3-inch fired before Petersen's order, slamming a shell into the black hull. Petersen threw at the quartermaster, "Hard right rudder!" He wanted to circle around the U-boat in easy range of the chaser's 3-inch gun and machine-guns. He told the men who manned them, "Lay on the conning-tower and fire as soon as anybody shows." Because the U-boat carried forward of the conning-tower a bigger gun than the 3-inch and she could not be allowed to use it to make a gunfight of this.

The 3-inch was punching holes in the steel skin of the submarine and she listed further so he could see into the conning-tower as it lay over towards him. A man crouched in the hatch with the cover held open above his head and Petersen was not the only one who saw that. The machine-guns chattered and the hatch-cover slammed down. Then the 3-inch took its cue from the machine-guns, shifted its point of aim to the conning-tower and shells burst on and around the hatch, penetrating the side of the tower, exploding in there.

The submarine was still listing, the hatch under water now and sinking further. The conning-tower disappeared as she capsized and lay there briefly, bottom up, as the 3-inch fired into her again and again, until she slid below the surface for the last time with the oil running from her like blood from a wound, a death wound. When she had gone and there was only the oilstain to show where she had been, only then did the gun cease firing. Its crew stood around grinning a little foolishly and a little uncertainly. They had not sunk a U-boat before, not many people had so they did not have a precedent to guide them as to behaviour. And Petersen was no help because he was not smiling, not looking particularly pleased that his command had sunk a U-boat. Men had died. That they were Germans no longer seemed to matter.

He ordered, "Secure that gun. Steer east-north-east. We'll look for any survivors from *Maroc*."

They were as certain as he that it was a fruitless quest but it was undertaken for the record and in case of a miracle. So the crew of the gun turned to quietly and there was no celebration aboard the U.S. Submarine-Chaser No. 101, which had just sunk her first submarine and so gloriously justified her existence. She ran down on the patch of flotsam that spread across the surface of the sea and marked the grave of *Maroc*.

The chaser crept into that patch of floating debris and her crew lined the sides of her and searched among the litter for signs of human life. They found none, though they patiently quartered the area, creeping back and forth across it until there could be no question of anything being missed. Finally Petersen accepted that he would have to abandon the search; there was no point in going on.

He looked up from the surface of the sea as the look-out at his elbow pointed and said huskily, "Jesus, Cap'n! On the bow!"

Petersen squinted out on the bearing that was due east as the chaser crept along with her bow towards the Gulf of Alexandretta. He was staring into the first rays of the sun showing over the Amanus mountains and sending shafts of light sparking blindingly up from the sea. He heard Cleeve say at his side, "Sir, I can't see anything out there. We've—"

Petersen cut him off. "You were hoping to see some action. It looks like you'll get your bellyfull."

It was Cleeve's turn to strain his eyes into the rising sun. And then he breathed, "Oh, my God!"

Still far distant but menacing, sharp and black in silhouette against the light, *Walküre* came thrusting out of the Gulf.

10

The Legion

The dump was theirs but this was still only a beginning.

Taggart was bellowing, "Sarn't Major! Ack and Beer companies man the perimeter! M-g's at the corners! Even numbers face *out* and odd numbers face *in*! Charlie company sweep through from north to south – and I want outposts! Commanders of Number One sections to me!"

They came at a run and Taggart gave his orders. Then, as the sections scattered to take up their outpost positions outside the dump, Taggart turned on Smith and explained, "Odd numbers to face in to pick up any birds flushed by the beaters of Charlie comp'ny. There might be one or two hiding under the netting." His tone was calm but his eyes glared. He looked across at the little group of prisoners and wounded under guard and the wild glare died away. He said quietly, "Poor bastards. But they were the lucky ones." His gaze returned to Smith. "We were lucky. Hardly lost a man. Incredible, and all down to surprise. By God, we owe you something, Finlayson owes you . . ." He rubbed at his face and walked away.

Smith found his pistol was empty. When had he fired it? He could not remember. The barrel was sticky wet and he wiped it on a dangling loop of camouflage net, re-loading with fumbling fingers as he strode behind Taggart to the northern perimeter of the dump. Charlie company were falling in there, chivvied by the non-coms who stalked up and down the line.

Men of A company were bellied down under the trees on the northern perimeter. Taggart halted there, Smith stood beside him and they stared out to the north and the east. To their right the railway track ran down from the north and it was deserted, but for a dozen kneeling figures about two hundred yards away. Smith could make them out in the growing light.

Taggart said, "Carmichael's demolition gang."

Smith nodded. Sergeant Carmichael was a quick bow-legged Scot. He and his gang carried ten big packs. Smith had seen those packs loaded with the charges, coils of slow and fast fuses and a handful of Number 8 detonators like cartridge cases without bullets.

Taggart said, "Carmichael knows what he's doing. He was a shot-firer in a pit in Scotland before the war and he's done a lot of demolition work with the Engineers."

Further round to the right and lying north-east of them were the lights marking the town of Lydda and there were more of them than before. Just the other side of Lydda was a Turkish garrison and it would be wide-awake now after the firing at the dump. Smith looked over his shoulder, over the shadowed alleys of the dump and the prowling figures of Charlie company sweeping through them to where the outer darkness of the last of the night hid the station. That was only a quarter-mile from where he stood and there would be troops there, if only a guarding platoon. Then three miles further south lay Er Ramle where there was the German anti-aircraft battery and the Turks had cavalry.

Taggart read Smith's mind: "We haven't got long." He shrugged inside his stained and ripped tunic. "It's turned bloody cold."

The day was coming. There was a thin line of orange light along the Hills of Judaea where they lifted out of the plain in the east but it had a murky, dirty tinge to it. The summer had gone and the rains were on their way. Smith's eyes came down and focused on the lights, yellow in the approaching dawn, that marked Lydda. "Where are the outposts?"

Taggart pointed towards the town. "Straight out a couple of hundred yards there's a corporal and two men. Others out on either side and in rear."

Smith moved towards a gap in the wire. "I'll walk out that way." Taggart was the soldier and this was his business. Smith was wasting Taggart's time standing here.

Taggart said, only half-jokingly, "Don't get lost out there. And remember the password when you come back. We're in the middle of enemy country. We can't challenge twice."

Smith answered, "I'll remember." He picked his way through the flattened wire and started to walk towards the lights. He found Buckley was dogging him as always and grinned to himself. Voices called behind him in the dump but they grew fainter as he walked out. The day was coming on them quickly now. With every stride he took the visibility lengthened, the scattered clumps of cactus could no longer be taken for men, their own lumpy, spined outlines were now clear. He could see the railway lines not only where they lay just a hundred yards away on his right hand, but stretching straight and dull-silver, running away to the north.

"Who goes there?" The challenge came sharp from a cluster of cactus below a slight rise in the ground.

Smith answered, "*Dauntless!*"

"Advance an' be recognised!"

Smith walked on and a khaki figure rose up from among the cactus ahead of him. The soldier said, "Hullo, sir. Having a look round?" He jerked his head, indicating the rise. "Corporal's up top, sir."

"Thank you." Smith passed through the cactus and climbed the low lift in the ground in three long strides to halt when he could see over the crest. The corporal lay before him, peering over the crest. Another private lay a couple of yards away. Both of them had rifles tucked into their shoulders so they peered out over the pointing barrels.

The corporal turned his head to take in Smith with one quick glance then faced forward again, but not before Smith caught a glimpse of a face covered in a paste of sweat and dust and a fringe of carroty hair poking out from under the pushed-back cap. Smith remembered him. At Taggart's briefing aboard *Morning Star* he had said: "It looks a right bastard."

It still did. They weren't out of it yet by a long chalk.

Smith waited silently with the two soldiers as the day grew upon them, until they could see Lydda as a crowding of white houses. Carmichael's demolition gang still worked close by, spaced along the railway track at intervals of twenty or thirty yards. Carmichael's voice came to him, the accent clear though Smith could not make out the words. A minute later the Scotsman trotted back towards the dump on his bowed legs, his team behind him.

On the other side of the railway a road ran north and south, from the station past the dump and on northward to the town . . .

The corporal said huskily, "They're just coming out, sir. On the road this side o' the town. See 'em?"

"Yes."

Tiny, ant-like figures were moving out of Lydda, a marching column, and was that a horse at their head? But then his attention was distracted and he cocked his head, listening.

The corporal told the private. "Joe, you nip back and tell the Major—"

Smith said, "Wait." And when the corporal turned to stare at him; "Can you hear a train?"

Now they all heard it, like distant, panting breath. The corporal muttered, "Strewth!" And then, "Anything been said about water, sir?"

Smith saw the tunics of the two soldiers were black with sweat down their backs. They had been out here alone and could easily have sneaked a drink but they had not. Discipline. He said, "Take a mouthful, no more." He unslung his own bottle and let the water wash cool around his mouth before he swallowed. It was water from *Dauntless* and briefly he wondered if he would see her again.

He turned as rifle-fire spattered briefly, distantly behind him, from the other side of the dump, to the south of it. That would be a curious patrol from the station. A Vickers rattled and the rifle-fire ceased. He told Buckley, "Go and relieve that sentry. Watch our rear." In case of a Turkish patrol edging around the dump. "And send him up here."

The man came up at the double and dropped down beside the corporal. In the silence that followed they heard the train more loudly, closer. And—

"Here she comes." That was the corporal.

Smith licked his lips, his mouth already dry again. He could have emptied the bottle but it was slung on his hip. The train was coming, had passed the town and the body of marching men. It would arrive in less than a minute. He ordered, "At the train. Six hundred yards. Ten rounds rapid."

The three rifles cracked as one but then stuttered as the faster shot got ahead of the others. The smoke wisped from the barrels and Smith smelt it sharp on the morning air. He saw the train slowing and said, "Five hundred!" There was a pause in the firing as the soldiers thumbed at the back-sights. The train stopped and there were men jumping down from the wagons. At five hundred yards and in this poor, leaden light, they were not so much men as moving dots but you could see the colour of their uniforms. He could not be sure . . .

But the corporal said, "Christ! They're Jerries!" And fired.

Smith stared at the men who were running towards him now and deploying into line as they ran. Here and there a section halted as one to kneel and fire, then rise again as one and run on. They had been hurriedly thrown into action but were moving like a well-oiled machine. Crack troops. These were the men Smith had sought. This was part of the Afrika Legion.

There was a ripping in the air overhead and ricochets bumbled and whirred. Smith knew that soldiers breathing heavily from running would make poor marksmen but he found he was instinctively crouching, lowering his head so he could just see over the crest. The corporal was re-loading, thumbing the rounds into the breech and closing the bolt as the clip fell away, firing.

Men had fallen out there, bodies lying on the plain between the clumps of cactus, but the line came on and there was another behind it and a file running up the railway track to outflank the British outpost. Smith glanced behind him over the two hundred yards of ground, sprinkled with the inevitable cactus, that lay between them and Taggart's command in the dump, and saw a man standing in the gap in the wire and waving furiously. Taggart? Smith faced forward and found the line nearer, the file on the track coming up on his right. Had he hung on too long? Almost.

Blast whipped a hot breath past his face then the thump of an explosion slammed against his ears like a blow from an open hand. He spun around and saw the cloud of smoke and up-thrown earth, the twisted rails and the crater in the railway track. Even as he watched there was another explosion. Another. They came again and again, marching regularly back towards the dump along the line of the railway and every one left a crater, splintered sleepers and twisted lines. The first fruits of Carmichael's work. The railway to Gaza and Beersheba was severed for two hundred yards.

He shouted, "Cease fire! Retire! At the double!"

The corporal got off one last shot then pushed back from the rise and bounced to his feet. He yelled, "You 'eard the officer! Leg it, lads, an' keep your heads down!"

Smith followed them out through the cactus, Buckley appeared alongside, and they were all out in the open and running for the dump. It was a long two hundred yards. The wire came slowly up towards Smith as the sand dragged at his boots, his legs felt like lead and there was a pain in his chest. He was aware that the machine-guns, the Vickers mounted at each end of the wood facing him, were firing now and loaded with tracer that slid out lazily, pale sparks in the light of day. Rifles blazed and he could see the heads of the men lying behind them, their hands working the bolts as the dump came up at him, until he stumbled through the gap in the wire and threw himself down.

He lay still a moment, winded, then pushed up on to his knees. Taggart squatted on his heels behind the riflemen, elbows rested on his knees with the rifle dangling from one hand. He stared out through the wire intently but spared a glance for Smith. "All right?" He had to shout it above the rattle of musketry and the hammering of the two Vickers. Smith lifted a hand. Taggart faced forward again but he went on: "Carmichael has reported he's just about ready and I think it's time we left. We've got a tiger by the tail here. We've slowed 'em but they're still coming on." He glanced at Smith again, "Your Afrika Legion."

Smith crouched beside him, staring out at the open ground.

The long line of men was gone, only a figure lay very still here and there, but rifle-fire winked from where the survivors had found what cover there was in a fold of the ground or behind a hummock of sand. One of the Vickers fell silent for a moment and a German seized his chance, rose up and scurried forward a dozen yards to throw himself down again out of sight. Smith's head turned, eyes seeking the line of the railway. Firing came from that direction too, and almost abreast of the dump.

Taggart said, "That's right. They're working down that flank. They're north, south and east of us. There's only our way out left open and it's time we took it." He raised a whistle to his lips and blew one long blast. Both Vickers ceased firing and a moment later Smith saw their crews rise from their positions and trot back through the dump, humping the guns and their tripods, and ammunition boxes. Taggart's whistle shrilled again and the firing ceased in the line before him. Rifles still snapped in the open ground like fire crackers but Taggart's men were on their feet and scurrying back through the dump with rifles at the high port across their chests. Taggart turned on Smith and Buckley. "Come on!" The three of them ran after the soldiers, pounding down a lane between the net-draped heaps of sacked and crated supplies, the dust swirling around them as it was kicked up by the boots.

Smith almost fell over a man sprawled full length with his head and shoulders under the netting. He paused, Buckley hovering impatiently, just long enough to see the prone figure was Carmichael, saw him cut six inches off the end of a short length of black safety fuse, carefully push a matchhead into the end of the fuse and rub the matchbox over it. The matchhead spurted flame and Carmichael tucked the fuse away under the netting and dragged a crate in front of it.

Smith ran on. They emerged from the lane, filed through gaps in the wire and were out of the wood and trotting across the open ground with its scattered clumps of cactus. A hundred yards out they came on a straggling, well-spaced line where a platoon of the battalion lay, rifles covering the dump, a Vickers mounted at each end. The other soldiers kept running, streaming through the line and going on, headed for the train.

Smith and his two companions halted. Behind them Carmichael and his demolition gang were filtering through the trees and breaking into the open ground. They no longer carried the big packs. As they came on, more smoke wisped above the trees to add to that from the fires which had smouldered since the dump was taken. It thickened to drift on the breeze over the dump. Carmichael halted, panting before Taggart, who asked, "All right?"

"Aye, sir, fine."

"What's that smoke?"

"They had a lot o' coal oil, hundreds o' gallons. We splashed some about and set it alight." Carmichael took a breath. "I set the charges in the ammo mysel'. We've less than two minutes now. I think we should get out o' it."

Taggart watched the other men trotting towards the train. The groups of running soldiers were stringing out into a long line, the non-coms gesturing with sweeping gestures of their arms. One half of the line halted and went to ground with a Vickers at its centre but the rest of the line ran on.

Taggart answered Carmichael, "Too bloody true. When that lot goes up—" His whistle pierced the din again and they ran until they came on the flank of the second line, flopped down behind a low dune and stared over the top of it. They could see men of the Afrika Legion scurrying in the dump now.

The ground lifted beneath them as a flash leapt up in front of them from the dump. The crash of the explosion drowned the firing, smoke and debris soared, seemed to climb for ever and the dust boiled out towards them, rolled over them in a choking cloud. Smith dragged out his handkerchief and covered his mouth and nose. Through that fog of dust he saw Taggart climbing to his feet and heard his yell: "On your feet and fall back! Pass it on!" His whistle shrilled. "Fall back! Pass it on!"

Figures moved through the swirl of red dust that was billowing away, settling. The dump came into view as a smoking ruin of littered wreckage and trees felled like matchsticks, only stumps left standing. There were fires burning, pillars of yellow flame that belched black smoke to roll down like the dust. No one moved, no one lived in that seared area of ground. But somewhere beyond it was more of the Afrika Legion and its reaction would be swift. Smith stood up and with Buckley followed Taggart as he headed for the train on the run. The job was done. The Afrika Legion would be too late at Beersheba and now was without supplies and ammunition, crippled as a fighting force.

Now the battalion, and Smith, had to get out if they could.

The battalion were all running ahead of him but stiffly, tiredly, two ragged lines of them carrying their wounded, and the further line was almost to the train. Two trucks in the centre flew Red Cross flags from short poles. Smith thought he could see the blonde head of Adeline Brett showing above the side of one of them. A Vickers was mounted in the first truck and the last.

The first line of men were climbing aboard the trucks now. Taggart was up with the second, urging them on and Smith came up at his shoulder and panted, "Get 'em aboard, Major. Quick as you can."

Taggart grinned at him. "You don't need to tell me!" He reached out to shake Smith's shoulder. "It worked like a charm! Up to now we can't have more than a couple of dozen wounded. As I said, it's a miracle!"

A shell fell to the left of the train, two hundred yards away and short, hurling up rocks and dust and making a small crater. Taggart swore. "There's a mortar somewhere in the trees!"

Smith swore in his turn and headed towards the engine. The crew of the Vickers in the front truck were manhandling the gun around but suddenly, as another mortar shell landed close by, two of them collapsed. The gun fell back into the truck and Edwards rose inside it, wrestling with Garrett. A rifle was between them and it fired into the sky. Then Garrett slipped from sight and Edwards leapt over the side of the truck to the ground, rifle in one hand. He crouched there, lifting the rifle to his shoulder.

Smith halted and aimed the Webley though it was a long shot for a pistol and he was no marksman. "Drop it!" But Edwards only worked the bolt and Smith saw death glaring madly out of Edwards's eyes. Then a rifle cracked at his side and Edwards pitched over backwards into the dust.

Taggart panted, "It was him or us!" Smith knew that. The colonel's arrogance and self-seeking had made him a killer, might have made a murderer out of Pearce – and brought him to this.

Edwards was dead when they went to him and they left him where he lay, the red dust blowing over him. Taggart bellowed to a group of his men who came running and climbed into the truck. They passed down one of the Vickers' crew who was alive, though wounded, and Garrett. Across Garrett's belly a red stain was spreading. He looked up at Taggart grey-faced, and said bitterly, "When the machine-gunners got hit I took me eye off him for a second. Bastard had a knife."

"Never mind." Taggart raised his voice, "Get them into the ambulance truck!" One of the men tending Garrett glanced up and shook his head. The young soldier's eyes were wide open, staring sightlessly at the sky.

Smith stood by the footplate. Charlie Golightly crouched in a corner with the shovel held up before his face. He stared at Smith and his fat cheeks wobbled as he shouted, "They're in among the trees an' right close!"

Smith could see them in the wood two hundred yards or so on the far side of the engine, figures flitting in the striped shade under the spread branches, kneeling and firing. Probably a force from Lydda station south of the dump. There might be ten or a hundred, he could not tell. A mortar shell landed, dangerously close, spattering the engine with stones. He glared at Golightly. *"Get on your feet!"*

He looked back along the train, saw the last men clambering into the open trucks, Taggart standing by the track with his rifle dangling loosely from one hand, head turning as he urged the men aboard while others gave covering fire. He saw Smith and waved, grinned. Smith swung back to Golightly. Smith's glare and his order had dragged Charlie to his feet though he still hunched as if expecting a shot to strike him, as well he might because the riflemen in the trees were firing rapidly and some were advancing in short rushes, halting to fire and run on across the open ground. Smith said, "Drive it away!"

He ran forward down the train to the first truck flying a Red Cross flag, leapt up to hang on the side and peered in. The wounded were laid on its floor and as always the sight of them was a shock, the blood, the filth and the pain. Adeline Brett moved among them and Smith shouted, "Keep your heads down!" He saw her turn, startled, then he dropped to the ground as the train jerked forward.

The engine rolled down on Smith and Buckley where they stood alone. Buckley tried to step aside but Smith snarled at him, "Get *on!*" He shoved Buckley at the ladder, shoved him again so he sprawled forward on the footplate, himself grabbed at the handrail, missed, grabbed again and this time seized hold. He ran alongside the train for three long, leaping strides then jumped for the ladder, found it with one foot, swung wildly off-balance but then threw himself in after Buckley.

There was a hand on the rail on the far side of the footplate. Then a head showed and another hand, this one pointing a pistol. Smith stared across at the dark face with its bar of black moustache and the eyes that glared into his. Golightly stood in the centre of the footplate, one hand on the regulating lever and the other gripping the shovel. Now he swung the shovel and the flat of its blade blotted out the face, the hand slipped from the rail and the pistol fired but the bullet only kicked splinters from the wood piled at the rear of the footplate. The Turk disappeared but the echo of the shot still rang in Smith's ears.

He climbed to his feet shakily, moved cautiously to the side of the footplate and looked back along the track. The dump still built its tower of smoke, the top of it leaning southward and spreading on the wind. There were men coming around the dump into the open ground and others swarming from the wood and on the track now. All of them small with distance and shrinking as the engine pulled away from them, working up speed, the train ahead rocking and swaying as it ran across the plain. The enemy had been on the point of capturing the train and they had escaped only by seconds. But they still had a long way to go. Yet for this little breathing space he was just glad to be alive, to have survived.

The sun would be well above the Hills of Judaea now but it was hidden. They ran beneath low-hanging grey cloud and the wind of their passage was cold on his body and he shivered from that.And from reaction. They roared past the village of Beit Dejan that Edwards had said was the half-way mark and a Turkish patrol appeared from among the little houses to fire at the train, but harmlessly. Golightly laughed with a flush of false courage, feeling safe and at home on his leaping, racing footplate. But that firing was bad news for Smith because it meant that word had gone ahead of them and the Turks at Jaffa would be waiting.

Golightly shouted, "Stoke 'er Mr. Buckley, if you please."

Buckley swung open the door and fed logs into the furnace. Ahead the track lifted to the crest of the hill where they had captured the train and there they would leave it. Smith wiped the sweat from his hands on his jacket, took out the Webley and checked the load, shoved it back in the holster. Buckley hauled the pull-through with its oiled scrap of four-by-two cloth through the barrel of his Lee-Enfield, took a clip from the bandolier slung over one shoulder and loaded the rifle. Golightly watched these preparations and was quiet.

They were slowing now, the engine puffing short-windedly as it pulled up the gradient. Smith leaned out at the side of the footplate to peer forward past the swaying trucks. A man stood by the track, tall, rifle held at the small of the butt, barrel resting on his shoulder, the slouch hat tipped forward. He held up one hand and Smith said harshly, "Stop her!"

As the train clanked to a halt he jumped down and ran forward. Taggart dropped from the train and Smith threw at him, "Get them out and moving!" and ran on.

Jackson asked, "Any luck?"

Smith nodded breathlessly, "The track and the dump."

Jackson whistled softly and his gaze went past Smith to

where the battalion poured from the train and lifted down their wounded. "I owe Taggart an apology."

He turned and walked long-striding with Smith hurrying at his side towards the point of the wood where the track curved round to go down into Jaffa. "Just before it got light I occupied the crest."

Smith saw up on the crest the heads and rifles of those men of the battalion left behind. Jackson halted at the point of the wood. Dust hung above the road out of Jaffa and under the dust was a fast-marching column of infantry, an officer on horseback at their head. Smith had seen their like coming up from Lydda. He hadn't liked them then and he didn't like them now. They were four or five hundred yards away, abreast of the deserted township of Tel Aviv. Jackson said laconically, "Somebody passed the word."

Smith remembered the Turks who had fired on the train at Beit Dejan. He turned to look back at the train where the men milled about, still lifting down the wounded, few of them but more than enough to fill Adeline Brett's little cart, dragged from its hiding place in the orange groves. He could see her blonde head and the big figure of Merryweather. Some of the wounded would have to be carried.

He said, "We can't stop to fight. Once we stop we're finished. And the wounded – we need time because of them. We've got to get out quick, no long rearguard actions. But we need time. . . ." He knew what he was asking.

So did Jackson but he said only, "All right."

He strode into the grove past a big trooper who asked, "What's goin' on, Jacka?"

"Mounted action, that's what," Jackson tossed at him. "Get your horse."

The horse-holders brought up the Walers, troopers snatching at the reins and swinging up into the saddles. One of them held a horse for Smith, who was not expecting that, hesitated but saw no help for it and let another impatient trooper boost him up into the saddle. He caught a glimpse of Buckley's face, worried, disbelieving and exasperated all at once. Then he grabbed at the reins and held on as his mount went with the others. Somewhere ahead of him in the jostling throng of shifting, stamping horses Jackson shouted, "Remember, you jokers, it isn't a flamin' steeplechase!"

One of them grumbled, "Aw, give it a rest, Jacka. You *told* us once!"

"Come on, then!"

The horses plunged forward, the troopers whooping and yelling, and Smith went with them, out of the shade of the orange grove, leaping the railway track, and before them lay the long, gentle fall of the hill to Tel Aviv. Jackson was in the lead, horse stretching out into a gallop and the ragged line of ragged troopers tore howling after him. Smith was caught up in their madness. He may have howled like the rest of them but he did not know, though afterwards he was hoarse. The rest of the world slipped away so the little troop of horsemen seemed to gallop down a funnel leading them to the centre of the blue-grey enemy column and nothing else existed. The Turks were firing, he could see the muzzle-flashes of their rifles, but the rush of the wind in his ears blotted out the reports and he only heard the whistling rip as the bullets sped past.

A man dropped his rifle, collapsed on the neck of his Waler but clung on. A horse plunged forward on its knees and rolled, throwing its rider over its head to sprawl in the dust. The column of Turks floated up towards Smith and now he could make out faces under the caps, staring eyes, fingers jerking at the bolts of rifles, all glimpsed across a shrinking strip of sand that the charging Walers gobbled up in seconds. And the charge struck home.

There was no bone-jarring impact, just a moment of slipping about precariously in the saddle as he reined in one-handed and snapped the trigger of the Webley at faces looming out of the fog of dust churned up by the hooves of the horses that circled and pranced. The Australians wheeled, followed Jackson's lead and charged in again on the column, the troopers firing the rifles one-handed, slashing with the barrel, clubbing with the butt.

The Webley was empty. The Waler surged under him, rode

down a man who shrieked as he went under the hooves. Smith swung with the Webley at the face of another and he spun away . . . He was alone. For a second he faced back up the hill and saw fallen horses, a trooper on foot wandering with his hands pressed to his head, the men from the train heading up towards the crest and the road to the Auja. Then his horse wheeled, galloped on of its own accord, nearly throwing him. He managed to pull it to a halt and the beast stood trembling under him, both of them running with sweat.

Before him lay the plain where the Turks had stood. Some of them lay there still, marking the line they had held, while beyond them the rest ran madly for the shelter of the houses of Tel Aviv, Jackson and his troopers hunting them, firing, clubbing. There was no sign of the mounted Turkish officer as his shattered command reeled into the streets of Tel Aviv, disappearing among the houses.

Jackson's voice bellowed, the words lost but the horsemen turned and trotted back to him. Smith realised slowly and with disbelief that he had been in a cavalry charge. It was ridiculous and he was a fool – he was a seaman and not even a half-way competent horseman. These were the real thing, the men riding towards him now with Jackson at their head, dirty and ragged in their weird miscellany of uniforms that was not uniform at all, some of them with laughter showing the teeth in the brown faces, others silent and witdrawn. He thought all of them incredible. Already it was being said that this Anzac mounted force was the greatest cavalry in the history of the world. Smith believed it.

He turned his horse and urged it back up the hill. Jackson and his troopers had cleared the way for the rest of them; there was no Turkish force to be engaged in a rear-guard action: the fugitives in Tel Aviv would not be rallied for hours. But now they faced the long march back to the Auja. Smith was as weary as all of them were weary, but there could be no rest. Now it was a race. All surprise was gone and Edwards had said the Turkish regiment north of the Auja would come down like the hammers of hell. Edwards . . . the memory of his mad face still haunted Smith.

*　　　*　　　*

He marched with Taggart at the head of the column, Buckley two paces behind him. The Australians rode as front and rear-guards and flankers and inside that screen the battalion marched, boots pounding, foot-slogging on. Adeline Brett's cart was pulled along in the centre of the column, crammed with wounded but there were others who walked or limped along with a man propping each side.

They were heading up the long lift to the distant ridge, beyond which lay the Auja river and the sea. Smith turned his head to peer back at the column, a rippling carpet of bobbing caps, cropped heads and the muzzles of slung rifles under the cloud of red dust. He looked past them over the village of Summeil in the hollow to the road where it fell down from the crest that hid Tel Aviv. For a moment he thought he saw a bird but then it turned and he made out the biplane wings, the floats and the big radiator like a basket planted right in front of the pilot. It was a Short.

Another swung over the crest behind it and the pair of them came charging along the column, roared low overhead and circled, the noise of engines hammering at his ears. Both Shorts carried bombs slung in the racks under their bellies and one was unmistakably the bloody Delilah with little Maitland waving excitedly from the rear cockpit. Smith was glad that Peace had not let him down but he wondered where the third Short was? The two straightened out and tore away ahead of the column. Smith saw them turning again in the distance, dropping below the ridge ahead and so out of sight. In the silence after the engines' clamour he heard the distant crump of the bombs. Minutes later, above the shuffling tramp of the boots, there came the rattle of rifle and machine-gun fire and it was heavy. He had lost his race, the Turks had come down from the north to slam the door shut in his face.

He swallowed and ran forward as the familiar shrieking of a falling salvo of shells ripped the air. Lieutenant Jameson stood on the crest ahead and Smith laboured up to him and stopped, chest heaving. Before him the ground fell away to the river that lay under swirling, drifting smoke. Through it he saw the lighters running in to beach at the ford, the motor-boat over by the far bank and on the ridge beyond it and on a level with Smith the sprawled figures of marines, rifles at their shoulders. He could not see over the ridge but heard the bursting shells of the salvo beyond it, saw the smoke lifting in the middle distance and he whirled to peer out to sea. *Dauntless* patrolled scarcely a mile off-shore and the salvo came from her. A light flickered rapidly just below the ridge and that was the signaller relaying to *Dauntless* Griffiths's orders for the shoot. He was up there on the ridge putting to use the expertise he had displayed in the Dardanelles, bringing down the fire from *Dauntless* to lay a protective curtain ahead of the little party of marines.

Jameson was saying, "The Turks came out of Jaffa in the night to look for the break in the telephone wire but there were only a couple of signallers and we grabbed them before they knew what was going on. But a patrol came down the coast from the north at first light and Brand took his marines across to the other side when the firing started."

Smith saw this crest was a line of defence held only by the men of the cutter's crew strung out along it. He said, "Watch me. I'll give you the sign and you get out quick."

"Aye, aye, sir," answered Jameson and asked, "What success, sir?"

Smith told him and the cutter's crew cheered.

The column came up. Smith knew they had only minutes because there was a full regiment of the Turks and, despite the guns of *Dauntless*, they would slip around that thin line of marines and then only Jameson's men would stand between them and the river and the lighters. He shouted to the battalion R.S.M., trying to keep his voice tight and controlled but it croaked in his ears, "Get 'em aboard anyhow, but as soon as you can!"

"Sir!"

Smith stood on the crest with Taggart and watched the battalion pass, boots plodding wearily, eyes staring through the mask of red dust that coated them all. You could not order these men to double, it was a miracle they kept up the pace.

Adeline Brett's little wagon came up, dragged by a dozen

men, the girl striding stiffly alongside, Charlie Golightly hobbling behind her. Now the rear-guard of Jackson and a file of troopers came up. All the time the shells from *Dauntless* howled in and burst, while the two Shorts trundled desperately low on the far side of the river and a mile or so away, their bombs all gone but the Lewis guns chattering.

Smith left Jameson's men to hold the rear, went down with Jackson and Taggart, hurrying after the column that trailed along the track beside the river, and waded the ford crowded with exhausted men stumbling and splashing out to the lighters and scrambling aboard. He went on, found Brand, the marine captain, with Griffiths and his signaller lying at the top of the ridge and knelt beside them. Taggart and Jackson flanked him, crouched at his shoulder and behind them down the slope stood Buckley.

Griffiths rubbed a hand over cracked, dry lips and shouted above the rifle-fire, "They can't cross the open ground but that scrub is swarming with them!" Beyond the ridge was a stretch of sandy plain but three hundred yards away it ended in rolling scrub and cactus. Griffiths said, "I've brought fire from *Dauntless* and swept it but they're still there and working around to the right. Some of them are in that wood—" The salvo rushed overhead and burst near a copse straggling back from the river and a quarter-mile away to the right. Griffiths went on, "*That* one. In a few minutes they'll be able to fire into the lighters and enfilade *us*. And the instant we cease firing to move out they'll be out of that scrub and up here."

A half-mile away the two Shorts came floating down to skim across the top of the scrub. Griffiths used his glasses and said, "Don't know who's leading but that's Delilah in the rear. They're firing the Lewises."

Smith muttered, "They're dangerously low . . ." He had told Pearce he needed them and they were giving all they had, chancing too much. There were machine-guns firing back at them, the lines of tracer sliding up, criss-crossing.

Griffiths said, "They've done it two or three times in the last few minutes."

"They'll do it once too—" Smith bit off the rest of it. The

leading Short had suddenly erupted in flames that streamed back along the fuselage. It tilted on one wing and slid away, down into the scrub. They did not hear the smash as it drove into the earth but the smoke rolled black across the plain. Delilah was climbing and turning away inland.

Smith swore under his breath. Soon Turkish machine-guns would be brought up and sited in the edge of the scrub facing him, which already sparked with rifle flashes along its length. He turned to peer back at the ford. "In a minute or two we'll be out of it." Two of the lighters were afloat and going stern-first towards the mouth of the river. The last horse was being hauled up the ramp of the third lighter, the last men stumbling up the ramp of the fourth close by the shore. He ordered Brand, "Take your marines now."

Brand shoved back from the crest, bawled at his men and led them down the slope at a run. As they splashed across the ford to the lighter Smith stepped down the ridge, until he could stand below it out of sight of the Turks. He pulled the handkerchief from his pocket and flagged it over his head, saw an answering wave from the far crest and then Jameson and the cutter's crew came spilling down towards the river.

He turned – and saw shells burst on the open beach in a close-packed line. As the dust blew away Griffiths said, "That's torn it. They've got a battery of field guns in action."

Smith rubbed at the dust and sweat mingled on his face. "Take your signaller out now."

He snatched a rifle and bandolier from the man and sprawled behind the crest, Jackson, Taggart and Buckley spaced out to his left. They opened fire, shooting rapidly into the scrub. The Turks had to believe the ridge was still held in strength long enough for Jameson and Brand to get their men into the boats.

The next shells came down just short of the ridge, raining sand and pebbles on the four of them huddled down over their rifles. Smith twisted round to peer through watering eyes at the ford. Brand's men were already away, and Jameson's men were shoving out the cutter, scrambling into it. Griffiths was at the tiller of the motor-boat. Smith shouted "Right! Let's go!"

He pushed back from the crest but Buckley said, "Sir!" And pointed. Smith's eyes followed the line of his outstretched finger and saw the far shore deserted except for Adeline Brett's abandoned wagon – and Adeline herself on her knees beside the wagon, bent over the body of a man.

Jackson said, "Why the hell doesn't she get out?"

Smith answered, knowing her, "She can't lift him and she won't leave him. The rest of you get down to Griffiths. I'll fetch her."

He ran down to the ford, waded across it and realised Taggart, Jackson and Buckley were with him. Jackson panted, "If she won't leave him, you'll need us."

They trotted on stiff and leaden legs to the wagon and now Smith saw it hid Charlie Golightly, sitting with legs sprawled and eyes closed, exhausted. The wounded man was the red-headed corporal, his tough face twisted in pain. Adeline Brett, knotting a field dressing around his leg, looked up at them. Her face was dirty as theirs, her hands filthy with blood and dust. She said hoarsely, "He'd crawled under the wagon so nobody saw him except Charlie and he came along to help me."

Smith thought Charlie was game but hardly able to help himself now, a sight too old for this. Jackson grabbed Charlie's arm, Taggart and Buckley lifted the corporal between them and Smith pulled Adeline to her feet. "They'll be firing down on us at any second!"

They started down to the ford, boots sliding in the soft sand, and waded out on to it. The motor-boat was under way, Griffiths sending it sidling down to them. The shells from *Dauntless* no longer howled overhead and Smith could hear the rasping breathing of Adeline and the rest of the party ahead of them. The sea washed up into their faces as the motor-boat slid down on them with hands reaching out to lift aboard the wounded corporal, grabbing at Smith and the others. He was last aboard and panted at Griffiths, "Get out!"

He saw Turks appear some three or four hundred yards away at the bend of the river but then the engine opened up and the boat surged seaward.

The shore lay far astern of them now and the motor-boat with the cutter in tow plugged out to sea. On the banks of the Auja river the Turks swarmed like ants. Smith sat with Major Taggart in the sternsheets beside Griffiths, Adeline Brett forward with the wounded corporal. The men lay about the cutter and motor-boat in slack exhaustion, uncaring of the rain that fell on their faces now. Ahead, under a grey sky, were *Dauntless*, *Morning Star* and the four lighters, while *Blackbird* was hurrying up from the south. Smith thought it was a ramshackle little armada, thrown together to attempt a desperate enterprise with a landing force of a handful of the world's finest mounted troops and an indomitable battalion of outcasts, but they had done the job.

He said to Taggart, "You must be proud of them."

Taggart nodded wearily. "I am. But they'll be split up after this." And when Smith looked the question at him: "Garrett is dead, so there's no more need for silence . . . It was he who shot the colonel back in Salonika – his brother had been killed in the last attack there and when the colonel started bawling about cowardice Garrett walked out in front of the battalion and fired three rounds as cool as you like, while the rest of us just gawped at him."

Taggart shook his head as if to shake off the memory. "I'd seen Garrett in action a few times. I suppose he was just a killer, and him and Edwards were a pair."

A killer? Smith remembered the cold menace as Garrett had ordered Edwards into the truck, a menace Edwards had recognised.

Taggart said, "The others protected him because they felt he did it for all of them – they were all guilty of wishing the colonel dead before he could be the death of every one of them. And me? Well, I didn't think Garrett deserved a firing squad. Not after what he'd been through." He shifted on his seat. "If we get out of this I'll make a full report to Finlayson and he can do what he likes."

He rose awkwardly and moved away forward. Smith felt only compassion. No outrage, and no surprise either . . . perhaps he had guessed the truth long before. Now he was weary to the bone, numb. He thought that later he would consider the risks he had so boldly taken and they would cost him sleep, but now he did not care. He held his arms folded tightly across his chest and watched the ships creep closer.

11

Walküre

Adeline Brett said, "I've had enough."

She had come aft. They were close to the ships now. She pushed at damp tendrils of hair that clung to her brow. Her hand was steady as she lowered it to stare at it, and clean; the sea had done that. She raised her head to look at the lighters and, knowing Smith was watching her tenderly and what he was thinking, she said, "There's plenty still to do – the wounded – and I'll do it. But afterwards—" She glanced sideways at him. "Garrett is dead."

Smith nodded. "I was there. And Taggart's just told me all about him. He's going to make a full report to Finlayson."

Adeline asked worriedly, "Will John get into trouble for hiding it all this time?"

Smith thought about it, watching Taggart and Jackson further forward in the boat, sitting shoulder to shoulder in companionable silence. He said with relief, "I think he'll get away with it. After his part in this action they'll hush up the business of the colonel. Garrett is dead and there's no point in trying a dead man." His gaze shifted to Charlie Golightly where he lay in the bow, his bulk limp and drained by exhaustion, plump cheeks sagging loosely. Charlie would get away with it, too, especially as Smith would recommend him for a decoration – the public did not like tarnished heroes so there would be no court martial for Charlie.

Tarnished heroes . . . Edwards. Smith would tell Braddock and Finlayson the truth but his report would say only that Colonel Edwards was killed during the attack on Lydda. Because Edwards had found the Legion and even more import-

209

antly, the exact date of its planned arrival in Beersheba. Also he had led the battalion to Lydda. If anyone played a crucial part in this operation and deserved a hero's laurels it was Edwards.

Adeline Brett went on, "They'll break up the battalion now and I won't go to another for a while. I have money in Cairo and I'll go there and rent a house or something. I'll see this war through to its end but just for now I'd like to live a little."

She paused, then said very quietly, "Could you come with me, please?"

The question was unexpected but he needed no time to think. *Dauntless* would undoubtedly go into the dockyard and he would get leave. "I'd like to. Yes."

Dauntless was looming, the way coming off her as she stopped to pick up her boats. Her crew were lining the side and cheering. Smith saw Ackroyd out on the wing of bridge, saw him take off his cap and wave it wildly, his Yorkshire stolidity cast aside.

Smith climbed to the bridge and leant against the screen with head on his folded arms. He was leg-weary, ached as if beaten all over and his eyes were rubbed red raw by the dust. The breeze was chill, the rain fell coldly. And still he felt young again, full of hope.

He raised his head as Ackroyd said delightedly, "Terrific, sir! Shall I send a signal to the admiral now?"

Smith answered huskily, "Just send: 'Attack complete success. Dump destroyed, railway cut and Legion halted. Few casualties. Force re-embarked'."

That was all Braddock and Finlayson wanted to know for the present. Braddock would have to be told, but not now, that Smith had flagrantly disobeyed orders and gambled on his own initiative – yet again. The old admiral's comments would be blistering but delay would temper them. Besides, the thing was done and successful.

Ackroyd passed the message, turned back, "I must say I was surprised as well as relieved, sir, when I saw the troops coming off, that there were so many. I'd thought the casualty rate would be much higher."

Smith knew Braddock and Finlayson also would be relieved. The raid could have been a bloody disaster. If the men had dawdled, hesitated, if they had not been so brave, so well drilled, well led. Taggart and Jackson. The Australians had got them in and got them out at the end, but it was Taggart's battalion that had actually done the job, had stopped the Afrika Legion in its tracks. While the Shorts and their crews, the guns of *Dauntless* and the parties ashore, all had played their part and he must make that clear in his report.

He realised he was staring vaguely out over the screen as his thoughts meandered and that Ackroyd was watching him curiously. What had Ackroyd said? Casualty rate? The casualty rate was a statistic and a phrase that Smith hated. Men were being lifted senseless from the lighters to be hustled below to the sick bays in *Dauntless* and *Blackbird*, while Ackroyd talked glibly of the casualty rate as if it was no more than figures or a list of names on a roll, yet Ackroyd was a humane man, concerned about his own men and their welfare. Smith wondered if he was himself overly sensitive. He remembered the faces of the wounded as they were dragged along the long, dusty track from Tel Aviv to the Auja river . . .

He said, "Maybe we were lucky." And: "Will someone fetch me a cup of coffee, please?"

He drank it standing on the bridge, telling himself not to be so *bloody* detached when everyone else was in such high spirits. They had steeled themselves to meet a disaster and now they were relieved and excited, jubilant. Buckley stood at the back of the bridge, teeth showing white in a face smeared with dust and streaked with sweat runnels, grinning widely. The signal yeoman had shoved a mug into his hand, Buckley was gulping from it and Smith could smell the rum from six feet away, which meant that stern disciplinarian the yeoman had been hoarding his tots and that was against regulations, but in this case at least in a good cause. Buckley had earned it.

The wide grin on the face of the big leading hand was infectious and Smith wondered why he remained depressed on this bridge with the open exuberance all around him. They were returning to Port Said and there would be leave then, the battalion would be breaking up as Adeline Brett had said, and she wanted him in Cairo. But still his jaded mind was uneasy, he felt there was something he had overlooked, that had clamoured for his attention during the raid but had been lost in the press of events . . .

Ackroyd said, "Here's a Short."

She came out from the coast as if she had flown along the line of the railway from Lydda to Jaffa, passing north of the town and right over Tel Aviv, losing height steadily as she flew out towards the group of ships lying under the rain. *Blackbird* was close now, turning to make a lee for the Short, and they could see the mottled red skin of her. Smith said, "Ask *Blackbird* who's in Delilah?"

A pause as they watched the Short, then the signal yeoman reported, "Rogers and Maitland, sir."

As she came closer Ackroyd said uneasily, "Is Captain Webb going to swim for it again? That engine sounds a bit funny to me. I'm no engineer but—" His voice drifted away but Smith knew what he meant. Smith was no engine fitter, either, but he had heard the Shorts fly off and return often enough these last weeks and the engine of Delilah had a different rhythm to it, there was a recurrent faltering. He thought the aircraft looked to be flying heavily, one wing-tip sagging and a misty vapour streaming back from the big, laundry basket of a radiator just forward of the pilot. He glanced quickly across at *Blackbird* and saw Pearce running across her bridge as the Short swung around the carrier, turning into the wind. The fitters and riggers in *Blackbird* were on the run, too, and there were men already over her side and balanced on her wide rubbing strake. The men in *Blackbird* knew there was something wrong.

Smith said, "Tell the motor-boat to stand by."

Delilah came down, flying into the wind with her starboard wing still tilted low but she straightened the instant before the big floats rubbed into the long, kicking waves. Rogers was slumped and head hanging now and Maitland's white face was turned desperately towards the cruiser as the Short ripped past her across the wave-tops and sent the spray flying. Then the floats dug in and the Short settled, sat back on the tail float and the engine died. She was out in the open rocking in the sea, the wind was pushing her and must soon overturn her but the motor-boat from *Dauntless* surged past the seaplane, swung in under Delilah's nose and stopped. A man leapt on to a float and made fast a line that paid out as Delilah drifted rapidly downwind. She was still upright and the man on the float lifted a hand, Smith saw his mouth open, shouting, and the motor-boat forged ahead. The line straightened and the Short followed the boat into *Blackbird*'s lee.

Ackroyd muttered, "That was lucky." He meant that the Short had not been blown away like a fallen leaf but Smith doubted the extent of Delilah's luck. They were hooking on the Short but at the same time they were lowering Rogers down into the motor-boat and young Maitland was climbing down after him.

Smith said, "I want to talk to Maitland."

They brought him to the bridge and he was pale and deliberately calm as he told Smith that following Pearce's orders the three Shorts had flown to Lydda. "But we passed too close to that German anti-aircraft battery just south of the station and they got Beckett. We saw them go down." He swallowed, "Anyway, Kirby and we pushed on – and the dump was burning like mad, sir! All the track was chewed up and there were two trains stopped on the line, but we couldn't see any sign of our chaps so we headed for the mouth of the Auja and that's when we saw you."

Smith nodded.

Maitland went on, "Well, we saw all the Turks coming down towards the river so we dropped the bombs and then made a few passes over them. That's when Kirby caught it. There was a lot of machine-gun fire."

Smith nodded again, remembering as he watched Maitland trying to keep his thoughts in order, his tongue from running away and stumbling.

"So we cleared off and saw you all get away. Then Rogers

shouted that we should have another look at Lydda. He said you'd want to know. So we did and the dump was still smoking and there were four trains stopped on the line, one behind the other and the place was swarming with Germans. We nipped over just once pretty low and there was no mistaking them – Germans."

Smith thought there might be ten or a dozen trains halted on the line north of Lydda by now, the Afrika Legion halted dead in its tracks. Maitland had stopped. Smith waited, then prompted him. "So?"

Maitland took a breath. "So we started back, following the railway to Jaffa. We were at about seven hundred feet but then the engine cut out. We glided down and it fired again when we were only a couple of miles from the coast but pretty low. There were some Turks by that little place Tel Aviv. They fired up at us, only with rifles but Rogers was hit and a shot went through the radiator." He stopped for a moment, then finished, "That was rotten bad luck, sir, being hit by chaps with rifles."

Smith saw Ackroyd standing behind Maitland and shaking his head. Smith said, "You did very well. I'll send you back to *Blackbird* and you're to get some sleep. That's an order."

"Aye, aye, sir." And: "How is Rogers, sir?" Smith hesitated and Maitland turned and saw Ackroyd's face and said miserably, "I see." He went down to the boat that waited to take him back to *Blackbird*.

Ackroyd said, "The surgeon can't understand how Rogers got the damned thing down. A signal from Pearce says it's shot to bits and he can't tell yet when it will be ready to fly again." He added bitterly, "But no matter what, it seems Delilah herself always gets back." Then he caught Smith's cold eye on him and looked away.

The wounded were hurriedly taken aboard *Dauntless* and *Blackbird* and Ackroyd reported that Adeline Brett was below assisting Merryweather. The two ships then patrolled around *Morning Star* and the lighters as the tramp finished embarking the men of the battalion. When she finally signalled that she was ready to proceed the weather had worsened with the rain driven on a wind gusting out of the north. The coast was still visible but clouds hung inland and their weeping was a grey curtain hiding the Hills of Judaea.

Smith went to his sea-cabin at the back of the bridge as the convoy got under way, leaving the bridge to Ackroyd. Now he could and should sleep, sat on the edge of the bunk, then saw his only good suit of white drill lying where he had thrown it when they sailed from Deir el Belah. Braddock had given him a letter and said he was heir to an estate and a name but that the inheritance would be contested. That meant in court like a trial, didn't it?

He had not consciously thought of this sudden revelation nor of its full implications all through the planning and execution of the raid on Lydda, but it must have been at the back of his mind. He was sure of that because now he knew for certain that he would not defend the will in court, would not have the whole story pawed over and his dead mother the target of gossip. Let her lie in peace. Whoever wanted the inheritance could have it. As David Cochrane Smith he had made his way and so he would go on.

He reached out to his tunic for the letter but froze as boots pounded on the ladder to the bridge, was on his feet as the door burst open. Cherrett, breathless from his run from the wireless office aft, thrust out the signal and panted, *"Walküre's* done it again! She's out!"

Smith snatched the signal, saw it was from Braddock and started to read, unaware that he was shouldering past Cherrett. "A reconnaissance plane from Cyprus . . ."

Walküre and the freighter *Friedrichsburg* were gone from the Gulf of Alexandretta. There was no sign of the battleship *Maroc* nor the U.S. Submarine-Chaser No. 101 except for some unidentifiable floating wreckage. Unidentifiable? Yes – if the reconnaissance aircraft was not a seaplane or the weather was bad they would only examine the wreckage from the air.

He read on: *Dauntless* and *Blackbird* were ordered north-westward to take up a position between the Gulf and Port Said.

The French battleship *Océan* and the cruiser *Attack*, both only hours from Alexandretta now, would swing south-westward once they cleared Cyprus.

Blindly he climbed the ladder to the bridge. He rubbed at his face and stared at the signal. He could not believe it. Four ships, two inside the Gulf and two outside had simply disappeared. How? When?

Clearly Braddock was sending Smith's force to act as a first line of defence for Port Said and the shipping lanes out of it. So it wasn't over. No Cairo, no leave, no Adeline. Not yet. Braddock was concerned with convoys, so vulnerable with only anti-submarine escorts of elderly destroyers and armed yachts. *Attack* and the French battleship were more than a match for *Walküre* but first they had to find her and she had too long a start on them. Even though she had the freighter with her and that ship's best speed was no more than fifteen knots. Why was the *Friedrichsburg* in company? She was not acting as a tender because she would slow down the big cruiser, so – was *Walküre* in fact an escort for the freighter?

Smith stared unseeingly past Ackroyd. During the raid on Lydda he had had the suspicion that he was overlooking something and it had eluded him, but now he had it. The Germans and Turks had difficulty in supplying their army, hauling everything down that long railway line from Constantinople. Smith had told Finlayson that the Germans might foresee a bottleneck in the supply line and find a way around it. And so they had. Load a big, fast freighter with all the stores and ammunition that would need fifty trains and weeks to move by rail, and send that ship on one swift passage to deliver her cargo to a port near the front-line troops in less than twenty-four hours. To Haifa where there was a rail link to the main line, or – on the flight south Kirby pointed out the surf-boats the Turks had gathered at Jaffa. *Friedrichsburg* could lie off the port while the boats unloaded her under the protection of *Walküre*'s guns. The railway would take her cargo to Lydda and thence to Beersheba and Gaza. The Afrika Legion would be re-supplied and many more besides, Turkish resistance would be strengthened and the campaign drawn out.

But *Walküre* had not broken out of the Dardanelles only to run the blockade with one ship's cargo. She would have another task . . .

He realised Ackroyd and Henderson waited before him and he was out on the bridge and did not remember leaving his cabin. Young Bright the midshipman stood further back, hands clasped behind him and watching Smith covertly out of the corner of his eye. Smith said, "Make to *Morning Star* and the lighters: 'Proceed to Deir el Belah independently.'" And as the signal lamp flickered: "Pilot! A course for Alexandretta!"

Henderson blinked then strode quickly to the chartroom. He had seen the signal, had laid off the course for the position ordered, had it scribbled ready on a scrap of paper – but now Smith wanted a course for Alexandretta. Why?

Ackroyd was asking himself that same question, uneasy.

But Smith ordered, "Starboard ten! Steer nor'-nor'-east. Revolutions for twenty knots. Pass that to *Blackbird*." *Dauntless* came around onto the new heading, marginally altered as Henderson came out of the chartroom with the exact course for Alexandretta – that was also the reciprocal of *Walküre's* course if she was bound for Jaffa. Smith told the signal yeoman, "Signal to Rear-Admiral Braddock: 'Submit . . .'"

He had to word it carefully because if you are only a commander suggesting to an admiral that you disagree with his orders then you must be tactful. If you are already acting in contravention of those orders on your own initiative then you must be very tactful and realise you are asking for trouble. Smith was only glad that the signal was to Braddock, who he thought would understand.

He waited for an answer, shifting about the bridge, as restless as his mind.

Braddock's reply only said, "Affirmative." Ackroyd looked relieved but not overjoyed. Smith had to prove himself right or take the consequences. Smith knew that, too, read the signal without change of expression, then returned to prowling about the bridge with his collar turned up against the rain and hands jammed in his pockets, trying to think ahead, forming some conclusions and not liking them.

He asked *Blackbird* when a seaplane would be ready to fly and was told repairs to Delilah, the sole remaining aircraft, would take a minimum of eight hours. He thought about that and then signalled curtly, "Complete in six hours."

The lamp aboard *Blackbird* flickered and the yeoman read, "*Blackbird* acknowledges, sir." Smith grunted. The riggers and fitters aboard the carrier would be working like beavers now. Smith glanced at his watch. Six hours would be just good enough. If he had guessed correctly then in six hours he might have found *Walküre* unaided but that was wildly optimistic. It was a large ocean and *Dauntless* could only see a narrow track of it. In six hours they would need the Short to search.

For half that time he lay in his sea-cabin staring red-eyed at the deckhead, until he could stand it no longer, went out to the bridge and sat in his high chair. He woke later to find Bright watching him and Smith thought that the boy would put his dozing down to imperturbable coolness when in fact he was just dog-tired. He found wry humour in that and laughed at himself. He was still smiling when he drifted into sleep again.

The commotion on the bridge woke him, jerking upright in the chair as Ackroyd said at his elbow, "'Top reports a ship right ahead of us, sir!"

Smith climbed down from the chair and leaned against the screen, looked at his watch – he had slept three hours – and growled, "Why did you let me sleep?"

"We've sighted nothing till now, sir." Ackroyd was undisturbed by Smith's censure and added frankly, "I thought you were due for some rest."

Smith grunted reluctant agreement; he felt better for his uneasy dozing in the chair.

Ackroyd muttered, "She's not making any smoke, sir."

Smith made no comment, Ackroyd's inference clear. *Walküre* was a coal-burning ship and would make smoke and plenty of it so the vessel ahead was not she. The first lieutenant was worried that Smith might have guessed wrongly and

Walküre had eluded them. Both had glasses to their eyes now, could see the dot on the horizon that was the ship but no more than that. Then the report came down from the fore-top: "She's bows-on but she could be that Yankee sub-chaser!"

No one spoke but a ripple of excitement ran through all of them on the bridge. Smith said, "Make the challenge."

The shutter on the searchlight clattered, then an answering light flickered on the horizon. The signal yeoman, telescope to his eye, called, "She's S.C.101, sir!"

Smith took a breath. Now for it. "Ask: 'Where is the enemy?'"

Again the light flickered and the signal yeoman read: "Enemy-bears—" The signalman stood at his elbow and wrote it down.

Ackroyd was grinning broadly, relieved "Good man, Petersen!" His grin slipped away as he saw his captain carefully expressionless, not showing his own relief as he reached out for the signal.

Smith read it, translating the terse sentences into a mental picture of the ships ahead of him. Petersen said *Walküre* lay ten miles astern of him and a point or two off the chaser's port quarter, her speed fourteen knots. That the freighter *Friedrichsburg* was keeping station astern of *Walküre* and smoke still indicated two ships.

Smith said, "Tell the Sparks: Wireless silence." And to the yeoman, "Make: 'Where is *Maroc*?'"

He was thinking quickly. *Walküre* would be leading *Friedrichsburg* because the Turks would have wirelessed that *Dauntless* was off Jaffa that morning. *Walküre*'s captain would therefore be expecting any trouble to come from ahead, would be ready to head it off from the freighter. He was not aware of the chaser because if he had been, he would not have tolerated her surveillance, would have caught and sunk her. The chaser was petrol-engined, not making any smoke to give her away and the look-outs in *Dauntless* could only see her now because she was close. The same applied to the look-outs in *Walküre*. A man in the crow's-nest at the chaser's masthead, however, had a bigger ship to look for in *Walküre* and her smoke to lead his eye.

Ackroyd said, "Sparks acknowledges wireless silence, sir."

Walküre was twenty miles away from *Dauntless* over the rim of the world, could not see her, nor would hear her as long as *Dauntless*'s wireless was silent.

The yeoman was spelling out the chaser's answers: "*Maroc* – torpedoed – by – U-boat – and – blew – up. U-boat – sunk—" There was a growl of appreciation on the bridge. "Submit—" Petersen submitted his opinion that *Walküre* had called up the U-boat and been ready with the freighter in the mouth of the Gulf, waiting for the submarine to clear the way.

Smith agreed.

"Make: 'Maintain observation of enemy but avoid action. Well done. Thank you.'" That was meagre payment for the chaser's part in this. She had somehow led the big cruiser and kept her in sight all through the day, despite a maximum speed of only seventeen knots so at best she'd had only a couple of knots in hand between her and annihilation. And Petersen's cooperation had been, strictly speaking, a breach of neutrality; his country was not at war with Turkey and *Walküre* was technically a Turkish warship because of the flag she flew. So Smith's curt 'Thank you' was the only official acknowledgment Petersen would ever get.

Smith went into the charthouse and peered at the crosses Henderson had pencilled neatly on the chart marking the positions of *Dauntless*, *S.C.101*, *Walküre* and *Friedrichsburg*. He dared not meet *Walküre* head-on because that would be suicide and would accomplish nothing. But she must be stopped. *Friedrichsburg* was a part of the German plan to break Allenby's attack. The Afrika Legion was stopped but the supplies crammed into the freighter's holds could be crucial to Turkish resistance as the campaign went on. These thoughts raced through his mind, and finally that the only cards he held were *Dauntless*'s advantage in speed, and surprise. That was little enough. It had saved him last time, but only just.

He pushed away from the chart and stepped out on to the

bridge. Ackroyd looked grimly expectant, young Bright was nervous and excited, Smith saw him swallow that nervousness as he swallowed his own, seeing them all waiting for him. He said, "Make to *Blackbird* . . ."

It was a long signal and he had to be careful in his phrasing of it. There must be no mistake. But he had recovered his faith in Pearce – and Chris knew Edwards was dead, could forget vengeance. The lamp flashed out to the carrier astern and from *Blackbird*'s bridge came a flicker of acknowledgment, then her stern swung to port as she turned and headed out to sea on a course almost due west. The chaser followed her.

Smith ordered, "Starboard ten! Steer Oh-four-oh! Full ahead!" And added: "General quarters!"

Ackroyd, expecting it, punched the button and the klaxons blared through the ship, calling her crew to their action stations. Then he left the bridge to take command of damage control.

Dauntless turned to starboard and settled on the new course that would take her to the coast, working up to her full speed now as *Blackbird* rapidly disappeared into the distance off the port quarter. In minutes the coast lifted higher, the mountains of Lebanon looming vague behind the curtain of rain but *Dauntless* held on until Smith ordered, "Port ten!"

He watched the ticking round of the compass needle as the ship's head swung. "Meet her! Steer three-five-oh." *Dauntless* ran northward close along the coast with the mountains standing to starboard while to port the horizon was blurred also with rain. Smith shivered, cold in the battle-stained light drill uniform. In the course of a day the summer had gone, the air was chill and the rain whipped in on the wind of the ship's passage and dripped from the signal halyards, dripped from the peaks of their caps on the bridge. All of them looked out on the port bow and beam now, glasses and telescopes trained out to sea. As were the loaded guns.

The report came down from the control-top. "Smoke Red three-oh!" The glasses and telescopes jerked around to seek on the bearing.

Jameson muttered, "I can just see something."

Smith grunted. There was a darker streak lying like a short pencil stroke along the grey line of the seaward horizon. From the height of the control-top the look-outs would see it better. *Dauntless* held on. She and the other ships out there were on opposite and parallel courses with the wide, grey sea between. As the distance between them shrank, as they came almost opposite each other the control-top reported: "Warship hull-down! Red eight-oh! Can just make out the topsides of her! But it's *Walküre*, sure enough!"

Henderson growled irritably, "What else? The chaser's had her in sight all day!"

The control-top was still reporting: ". . . smoke astern of her, a mile or more . . . It's that big freighter, *Friedrichsburg*, all right! Seen nothing else like her this side of Port Said!"

The lowering sun was hidden behind leaden clouds, what dirty light there was came from beyond the seaward horizon and the ships on that horizon stood against it, so from the control-top they could make out their silhouettes. From the bridge Smith could see only their smoke. From *Walküre* and *Friedrichsburg* they would see grey ocean and grey mountains and there was no light behind *Dauntless*. They might see her smoke but even that would be difficult against that background and in this visibility.

Now was the time. He ordered, "Port ten! . . . Steer two-four-oh!" There was a shifting on the bridge now, a scraping of feet and a clearing of throats, an easing and then a settling-down again as the ship's head came around to point at the smoke on the seaward horizon. Now they were committed. *Dauntless* was making twenty-nine knots and she was headed towards the enemy. Smith cocked an ear to the ranges continually repeated from the rangetaker: ". . . Eleven thousand . . ." They were ranging on to *Walküre*.

He said, "We'll engage *Friedrichsburg*."

Before that could be relayed to the gunnery officer in the control-top he was himself reporting; "Range to *Walküre* is opening! She's hauled out of line and she's headed out to sea, course about south-west!"

Smith heard his order to engage the freighter passed and

acknowledged from the control-top and Jameson said, '*Black-bird*, sir?"

Smith nodded. It should be *Blackbird* that *Walküre* was going after, over the horizon and fifteen miles to the south-west and towards the sinking sun. *Blackbird* and the tiny submarine-chaser.

Jameson muttered, "I hope Pearce is ready to run." Because if *Walküre* could see *Blackbird* even in this visibility she would not challenge. Why should she when she knew every ship in these waters was an enemy and she was expecting *Dauntless?* Once within range she would fire on any ship.

". . . Nine-five-oh-oh . . ."

The range to *Friedrichsburg* was below five miles now, and as *Dauntless* raced out to sea the big freighter steamed on, maintaining her course, passing distantly across the bow from starboard to port. Even from the bridge she was hull-up now, ten thousand tons of her and deep-laden, they could see her big derricks and the single funnel belching out smoke.

Jameson said, "They must all be blind aboard her, thank God!"

Smith thought she was close, should have seen *Dauntless* even though she was still four miles away and in bad light. But they were also astern of *Friedrichsburg*, off her port quarter, and all eyes in the freighter would be drawn in the opposite direction to where *Walküre* had gone to seek out the ship under the smoke to the south-west.

"*Walküre*'s opened fire!" That came from the control-top but on the bridge also they had seen those distant flashes out on the far horizon. *Walküre* was eight miles away with *Friedrichsburg* lying between.

A chorus of voices shouted, "She's turning!" They referred to the freighter, swinging out to starboard to run after *Walküre*. Some look-out had finally turned his gaze astern. But as if pointing up that belated sighting of the threat storming up on the freighter, the rangetaker chanted, "Seven thousand!"

They were close enough. Smith snapped, "Hard aport! Open fire!" And as *Dauntless* turned to head south on the course that had been *Friedrichsburg*'s, so the barrels of the guns trained out to starboard and fired, shaking the bridge. *Friedrichsburg* was showing her stern to them now and Smith saw the salvo fall to starboard of her but close alongside. The light was poor but the range short and *Friedrichsburg* a huge target. He thought briefly that the same could be said of *Blackbird* with that huge hangar built on her after end and she was under fire from *Walküre* now. The chaser he did not worry about. She was small, and could look after herself. But he hoped to God that his own attack on the freighter would soon bring *Walküre* hurrying back. That had been the plan. He did not want *Blackbird* and her crew on his conscience.

Dauntless fired again and Bright shouted excitedly, "Hit her!"

Water was hurled up close to the freighter but one shell burst inboard with a streaking flash and smearing, trailing smoke that sprouted flames. The guns were firing with the relentless rhythm of a trip-hammer, three rounds a minute from each gun and a good half scored – and this was not a towed target, some erection of timber and canvas to be taken back to the dockyard at the end of the day and patched up for use on the morrow. This was a ship with men in her and the 6-inch shells were bursting among them, crashing down through the thin decks to explode below, tearing out the heart of her.

At the end of a few minutes of that punishment she had three fires and smoke trailed from the length of her. Soon afterwards she swerved to port and her speed fell away. The range closed rapidly now. There had been no comment on the bridge of *Dauntless* since that first exclamation of: "Hit her!" They watched the murderous pounding in silence as *Dauntless*, slowing to ten knots, closed the freighter and Smith said, "Tell the torpedo-gunner to fire when he's ready."

Seconds later the two torpedoes leapt one after the other from the tubes amidships and their tracks streaked out towards the freighter. The range was down to three thousand yards and the 6-inch guns still hammered away.

Jameson said, "She hasn't struck."

Smith knew he could not take this ship prisoner, not with *Walküre* only a scant few miles away. *Friedrichsburg* had to be sunk. But he admired the courage of the German crew and was not enjoying this.

Nor were the others on the bridge. A grumbling mutter ran through them as Henderson said, "Christ! She's blown up!" They saw the debris of boats and hatch-covers flying into the sky and raining down while the ship listed further, settling. That was when the torpedoes struck her, breath-held seconds between the two muffled explosions. They rumbled dully across the sea as Smith turned his ship to pass close across the bow of the blazing freighter. Almost immediately she lay over still further and smoke and steam roared out of her. *Friedrichsburg* was finished and would sink in minutes.

He had stood with arms rested on the screen, watching stone-faced, but now he stirred. All through the action the other reports had come in, laconic: "*Walküre* firing . . ." "*Walküre* ceased firing." And now: "*Walküre* turning. Bears red-seven-five. Six miles." Smith walked out to the port wing of the bridge as *Dauntless* turned around the bow of *Friedrichsburg*. He peered through the glasses, searching for the big German cruiser and found her, a tiny blip on that grey horizon under her smoke. She was tearing back, too late, to the ship that she escorted, had thought safe astern of her as she steamed out to meet the threat from the south-west.

He watched her as he ordered, "Steer north-east by north! Full ahead both!" That was a course to take *Dauntless* running away from *Walküre*. "Make a signal to the admiral . . ." Now he could break wireless silence and report to Braddock.

Jameson said, "She's opened fire, sir."

Smith nodded. Huge shells were shrieking through the atmosphere towards *Dauntless*. But *Walküre*'s shooting would be largely based on guesswork. He himself could hardly see her, so from *Walküre Dauntless*, stern on and against the grey background of the coast, was hardly a target at all. He was not surprised when the salvo fell little off for line but a half-mile astern. *Walküre*'s guns had ample range to reach *Dauntless* but her rangetaker would be having trouble reading the distance.

Jameson said, "*Friedrichsburg* is going, sir!"

They could hardly see the big freighter now under the huge cloud of smoke that trailed from her across the sea, just the tilted masts and funnel of her and, as Smith watched, they slipped from sight. He made out two boats pulling clear of the smoke so some few souls had survived the hail of fire that *Dauntless* had poured into their luckless ship.

He shifted the glasses until *Walküre*'s smoke appeared and under it the ship, tiny in the distance. Another salvo from her plunged into the sea, still short by a quarter-mile or more. He watched her and wondered what her captain would do? Engage in a fruitless chase of *Dauntless*, that experience would have taught him he could not catch? Return to Alexandretta? But she would not have come this far solely to escort that one freighter, vital though her cargo might be.

He could not be sure, she was so small on the far horizon and the light was so bad, but—

"Control-top reports she's turning, sir." That was Jameson.

Smith answered, "Yes." He waited, as they were all waiting on the bridge to see what *Walküre* would do now.

"Control-top reports she's steering south-east, sir."

If *Walküre* could see those two life boats, though it was doubtful if she could, being much farther from them than *Dauntless*, she was not going to try to pick up the survivors. That was only to be expected because she would not dare to stop while *Dauntless* was in the vicinity. Smith knew now that she was headed for Gaza and Deir el Belah, the shipping anchored off Allenby's forward base and strung out all along the coast to Port Said. Destruction of that shipping would be a severe blow to Allenby's army and the sight of a big German cruiser running wild in waters they had come to expect the navy to control would be an unpleasant shock. And all the back area running up to Gaza was crowded with troops and *Walküre* would shell them, no doubt of it. Smith had a horrifying mental picture of those big 8-inch shells exploding in that packed, tented town.

He ordered, "Port ten!" And: "Steer two-oh-oh!" *Dauntless* swung steadily around, settled on the new course and was now chasing after *Walküre* at full speed, not to come up directly astern of her but headed a point or two to seaward. With *Blackbird* no longer as a decoy he did not relish being trapped between *Walküre* and the mountainous shore. *Blackbird* . . . he wondered briefly how Pearce had fared.

He said, "Tell them in the control-top that we mustn't lose her for an instant." It had to be said, though they would already know that *Dauntless* dared not lose *Walküre*. He dictated another signal to Braddock, reporting the survivors from the *Friedrichsburg* he'd had to leave behind, and giving *Walküre*'s course and speed now. "Submit . . ." He tersely set out what he believed were *Walküre*'s intentions. And then he told Jameson, "I want the men fed. One man from each detachment to go to the galley to draw for the rest. We've got something like half an hour, I think." Provided *Walküre* kept her course and he was coldly certain that she would.

There was an air of grim expectancy throughout the ship now. Lofty Williams the wireless telegraphist, found himself outside the galley alongside Buckley and said, "No orders come over the wireless but it looks like your bloke's going to have a go anyway." To the lower deck Smith was Buckley's bloke.

Buckley shrugged. "He's not one to hang about waiting for orders."

"How d'ye reckon our chances?"

Buckley looked up at him. Lofty, with his gangling length, was the only man aboard whom the big leading hand did have to look up to. Buckley said patiently, "You've seen this bloody big cruiser before, haven't you?"

"Cruiser! Jimmy-the-one calls her a pocket-sized battleship!" Ackroyd's description had stuck. "Bloody big pocket, if you ask me."

Buckley said, "Well, then?"

Lofty blinked down at him, thought it over, then said, "Ah! Well."

Buckley nodded. "That's right." Then he added, "But I'll

say this much: You'll have a better chance with Smith than with anybody else."

On the bridge Jameson said, "Signal from the admiral, sir."

Smith read it, brief and to the point: "Engage the enemy." So Braddock also had seen the danger and had the courage to send that signal, knowing it must mean the destruction of *Dauntless*. In a battle with *Walküre Dauntless* would be torn apart, sunk, but in that battle she might cripple *Walküre*, so impair her efficiency as a fighting ship that she would be forced to abandon her mission and run for shelter. It was a possibility, no more than that, but it had to be tried. *Dauntless* could not stand meekly by while *Walküre* roared down on Deir el Belah. And the relieving ships, *Attack* and the French cruiser *Océan*, would not come up in time.

With a part of his mind he had been listening to the reports that came down continually from the control-top and from the rangetaker. Now he asked, "What's her speed?"

Henderson answered, "The plot shows her making around fifteen knots."

But *Walküre* was capable of twenty-four knots, so why was she steaming comparatively easily now? Trouble with her engines? He walked out to the wing of the bridge and stared out at her where she steamed off the port bow. The ship was still just a speck on the horizon even seen through the glasses, but he watched her for a long time as they crept up on her. *Dauntless* was overhauling her, not at fourteen knots, the difference in their respective speeds, because *Dauntless* was still clawing her way out to sea, but *Walküre* was still edging steadily back along the port bow and would soon be abeam.

Jameson came to stand at his shoulder. "Strange that she hasn't fired, sir. We're within range of her."

"Just." Smith answered absently, mind probing at the problem, seeking the reason for *Walküre*'s behaviour. He said, "Too far for good shooting in this light."

"We can't reach her."

Not yet, thought Smith, but when they closed her . . . The answer came to him then. *Walküre*'s captain knew the only ship he had to deal with was *Dauntless* and that Smith dared not let him reach Deir el Belah without a fight, so he was waiting for *Dauntless* to try to close within range of her own 6-inch guns when she would make a sitting target for *Walküre*. He had to settle with *Dauntless* so he would do it now in the light of day, not risking a night action which was always chancy. And Smith dared not wait for the night. If he did and lost *Walküre* in the darkness then with the dawn she would come roaring in on Deir el Belah. *Dauntless* could be waiting to sacrifice herself then but it would be too late. *Walküre* had chosen the place and the time and Smith could do nothing but accept the challenge.

The crew of *Dauntless* had eaten though Smith had not, had refused the food, drunk only a cup of coffee. Now they were at their action stations and ready to fight. On *Walküre*'s terms? Smith rubbed at his face. He had to do something to shorten the odds against them, could not throw them senselessly into the path of destruction. He turned and saw Jameson staring at him and realised the man was waiting for an answer. He forced a smile and said, "Still, this pottering along at fifteen knots is a bit of luck for Pearce and that sub-chaser. At full speed she'd have been on top of them by now." Then, as he saw the smile and the words take some of the unease from Jameson's face, Smith added, "Pass the word for the men to rest at their action stations."

Jameson blinked. So they weren't going to attack yet? *Walküre* lay abeam and was slipping astern now. He had thought that once they came up with *Walküre* then Smith would carry out his orders, and launch *Dauntless* at the enemy. Why this delay? But Smith had turned away. Jameson answered, "Aye, aye, sir."

So they rested at the guns as *Dauntless* raced on at near thirty knots and they saw *Walküre* slide slowly down the port quarter until she was miles astern of them and still they kept on. They grumbled because of this stretching of their nerves when they had been keyed up for the attack and looked up at the bridge where Smith stood out on the wing. "What the 'ell is he *waiting* for?"

Smith was working out in his head a little problem in relative times and distances as he listened to the bearings and ranges monotonously repeated . . . "Red one-six-oh . . . twelve thousand . . ." "Red one-six-five." He had the answer now, turned and walked back to the centre of the bridge.

The bridge staff watched him come and Buckley, standing at the back of the bridge, saw the quick, restless stride and though, "Here we bloody go!"

Smith ordered, "Action stations! Make smoke!"

The wind was still out of the north-west. As their twin funnels began to belch out thick, oily smoke the wind's thrusting rolled it down across the sea astern to drift out eastward and southward. Soon it had drifted far enough to hide *Walküre* from them. *Dauntless* maintained her course and her speed as the trail lengthened and spread astern of her. Smith joked, "A little of that goes a long way." That only brought tight smiles from one or two on the bridge, all on edge now and trying not to show it. Smith saw this and supposed his own act did not fool them. Was it an act? No, the uneasiness, the tension had gone from him now, leaving only excitement.

He looked out at the smoke and thought that the first of it would be starting to thin on the wind. Five minutes had laid a screen better than two miles long between him and *Walküre* and now *Dauntless* could achieve some element of surprise. "Hard astarboard!" She came around to run back along her wake. "Steer that!" Now they were rushing down past the smoke that banked to starboard of them. Smith looked at his watch as the second hand ticked up to the twelve. A minute had passed.

"Starboard ten! Tell Guns to fire when he's ready!" *Dauntless* swerved into the smoke and it closed around them, hiding the sea alongside and the sky above. It caught at their throats and their eyes watered. But now *Dauntless* had straightened out and the smoke was thinning, becoming patchy so that they caught glimpses of grey sky. *Walküre* would be waiting for them but her guns would not be laid on *Dauntless* and ready to fire. They would have to lay on her when she appeared out of the smoke and that could be anywhere along its two mile length. That would give *Dauntless* some seconds of breathing space, all the surprise Smith could wring for her but it was better than none, better than simply steaming down into the muzzles of the waiting guns.

There was light ahead, patches of sea visible through the smoke and then only shreds of smoke lying on the sea and rolled by the wind.

Bright shouted, "Fine on the port bow!"

Walküre steamed barely four miles away but it was *Dauntless* that fired first with the only gun that would bear, the forward 6-inch bellowing out and its smoke whipping past the bridge. Smith ordered, "Starboard ten!" Then, as the ship came broadside on so that both forward and aft guns would bear, "Meet her! Steer that!" Both 6-inch guns fired – and twenty seconds later they fired again.

Jameson said excitedly, "Caught her on the hop!"

"Starboard ten!" Smith watched the enemy as *Dauntless* turned again and headed back towards the smoke. *Walküre* had finally got her guns trained around and he saw the ripple of flame down her side, the wisping of smoke as the salvo was hurled at him – also a yellow flash and a spurt of smoke in the stern of her.

He nodded as Jameson shouted, "That was a hit!" The 6-inch aft still fired as they rushed back into the smoke. *Walküre*'s salvo fell well astern in a close-packed line of water-spouts, then the gun fell silent as the smoke swirled around them, choking but nobody minded. The signal yeoman smiled wryly at young Bright who was laughing, excited, but all of them on the bridge were elated. Only Jameson said thoughtfully, "That salvo of theirs was well together." He did not add the unspoken rider: Suppose it had hit us?

"Port ten!" Smith's eyes were on his watch as *Dauntless* emerged on the seaward side of the smoke and turned to run south on her original course, still trailing smoke.

So for thirty seconds, then: "Port ten!" *Dauntless* plunged back into the smoke, tore through it and burst out into the open sea. *Walküre* had turned and was steering towards the long bank of smoke. This time both the 6-inch guns bore but there was a pause before they fired as the range had opened because of *Walküre*'s turn and *Dauntless* running south away from her so that the guns had further to train around and elevate. They still got off two salvoes before *Walküre* replied and by then *Dauntless* was already heeling in the turn, spray bursting in a continual fine curtain over the bow, wake boiling astern and the guns training around. They fired two more salvoes and the second scored, hitting *Walküre* amidships and right aft. As *Dauntless* rushed into the smoke the shells from *Walküre* plummeted close alongside in huge green towers of water topped dirty white.

They seemed to pass more quickly through the acrid pall, were out in the grey light of the dying day. Smith did not want the range opening further because that was to *Walküre*'s advantage. "Starboard ten!" He sent *Dauntless* running northward with the smoke lying to starboard, until he ordered again, "Starboard ten!"

They were becoming used to the dive into the smoke now, though it was not so thick here and dispersing on the wind, so their emergence into the open came sooner. *Walküre* had turned and was heading south again, so she had closed the range as *Dauntless* had done. She loomed so large that each of her turrets was distinguishable and Smith saw she still had a fire aft. As the 6-inch guns fired the ripple of *Walküre*'s salvo ran along her side. Smith waited for the guns to fire again and, as the shudder of them laid *Dauntless* over, he ordered, "Starboard ten! Steer two-six-oh!"

But as the stem began to swing the salvo from *Walküre* came in.

They did not hear it coming. There was only the shock of it, a glimpse of the sea lifting right under the bow and a camera-blink later a blinding light as the end shell of the salvo burst forward of the bridge. If her turn had been delayed for a second then *Dauntless* would have steamed under the whole salvo and probably that would have been the end of her. It was almost the end of Smith. He never lost consciousness, was clearly aware as he was lifted from his feet and hurled backwards. Though blinded by the flash, he felt the cushioning bodies behind and beneath him as he hit the back of the bridge and then the air was agonisingly driven out of him as someone crashed on to his chest. He was still for only a second as he whooped for breath, then shoved at the man on top of him, thrust him aside, saw it was Jameson, now sitting on the deck and lifting a hand that dripped blood. Smith climbed to his feet, lurched to the front of the bridge and fetched up against the screen.

He looked around him. The coxswain lay on the deck and was dead, there was no doubt of that, but the quartermaster, who had stood behind him, was now at the wheel and *Dauntless* was still turning in accordance with Smith's last order. Even as he watched she came on to the bearing and steadied on the new course that would take her back to the sheltering smoke. The quartermaster reported, "Course is two-six-oh, sir!"

There was not only the screening smoke ahead now. It poured also from the fore-deck where the 6-inch lay askew on its mounting, its crew scattered around it. A damage control party came running under the wing of the bridge, dragging at hoses, a bawling petty-officer at their head. Smith looked out to starboard and saw *Walküre* fire again as there came the shudder and slam of the gun firing aft, the only 6-inch left to them.

The smoke was looming. Smith told the quartermaster, "Keep her at that."

"Aye, aye, sir."

There were huge holes in the splinter mattresses around the bridge screen, torn by ragged lumps of steel as they smashed on across the bridge. But the heap of bodies at the back was pulling itself upright as one after the other the men crawled to their feet and staggered back to their posts. Buckley swearing in thick Geordie, Midshipman Bright blinking uncontrollably, Henderson hanging on to the frame of the chartroom door, pale but seemingly unhurt.

Ackroyd came on to the bridge and said hoarsely, "Forward 6-inch is a wreck. The fire is still burning but under control. How are things up here?"

Smith glanced around at the quartermaster at the wheel, at Henderson, Bright, Buckley. "We'll cope." He asked Jameson, "How's the hand?"

"I'll be all right, sir."

Then the smoke whipped around them but *Walküre* hit *Dauntless* again. It shook them on the bridge so they all staggered, and Smith stared past Ackroyd and saw the smoke soaring aft and the debris in it, the leaping flames. Almost immediately he felt the ship's speed fall away. He told Ackroyd flatly, "Let me have a report as soon as you can." And to Jameson, "Ask the chief as well." Jameson went to the engine-room voice pipe as Ackroyd slid down the ladder and ran aft.

Smith thought *Dauntless* could barely be making ten knots now as she limped away from the smoke that was shredding on the wind. He heard the shriek of *Walküre*'s next salvo and snapped his head around to see the shells fall close ahead off the starboard bow. He swore. This limping progress had saved them. But neither smoke nor poor visibility could hide *Dauntless* for long while the fire roared aft to mark her position for *Walküre*'s guns, a pillar of flame bent by the wind of passage. Only distance would save her now.

He began ordering changes of course to try to evade the German salvoes that fell with awful regularity every thirty seconds. For a time he could not see the enemy ship and the salvoes screamed down as if simply hurled from the sky. Then Bright shouted, "Enemy green one-oh-oh!"

Smith saw *Walküre* distantly off the starboard quarter and she was headed southward. No doubt her captain had deduced from the opening range that, although damaged and on fire, *Dauntless* was still running away from him, and thought he could not catch her. He would also have concluded that if she had broken off the action she was probably too badly damaged to continue it. He would not engage in a pursuit drawing him northward because he had easier meat waiting for him in the south at Gaza, Deir el Belah, and all along that coast. Smith watched *Walküre* bitterly, tasting defeat as she drew farther and farther away, still firing her after-turret so that *Dauntless* had to keep swerving and the howling, plummeting shells kept following her.

The chief's voice came metallic up the voice pipe from the engine-room. "It's a right mess down here, sir. To start with—"

Smith cut in, "Details later, chief, please. For now, what speed can you give us?"

"Maybe another couple of knots. It'll take a dockyard to—"

"I know nobody could do more than you, chief. My thanks to all of you."

Smith shut the cover on the voice pipe and wondered what it must be like for the chief, his engineers and stokers trapped far below deck when *Dauntless* was hit like that, expecting any moment that the sea would burst in on them or the engine-room become a flaming coffin.

Ackroyd reported over the voice pipe, "We took two hits aft, sir. Luckily neither holed us below the waterline but that's all the good news. The engine-room is a shambles and the 6-inch is wrecked. So are the gig and the motor-boat, the 3-inch and the searchlights mounted forrard of them. And the starboard torpedo tubes; the training and firing gear is all smashed to bits."

These reports from the chief and the damage control officers meant that though *Dauntless* survived as a ship she was written off as a threat to *Walküre*.

The shells continued to harass *Dauntless*, came close sometimes though *Walküre* herself disappeared, lost on the rim of that rain-blurred horizon. But finally the shells ceased screaming in and there were some minutes of blessed peace. The flames aft ebbed away, were gone and Ackroyd climbed on to the bridge, his face soot-blackened and his jacket burned down one sleeve. He reported huskily, "Fire's out, sir." He looked at Smith, that look asking, "What now?"

And what, Smith thought, of *Blackbird* and the sub-chaser, lying somewhere in *Walküre*'s path? His orders had been, once the Germans had been drawn away, for them to circle out of range. He could only pray that they had survived the first brief minutes of *Walküre*'s attack.

Make or Break

Dauntless was running northward. Smith ordered, "Port five! Steer one-six-five!"

"Five of port wheel on, sir! . . . Course one-six-five degrees!"

Dauntless edged around on to the course that set her in hopeless pursuit of *Walküre*. They would never catch her.

The bridge had been hurriedly swept and swabbed, the debris cleared away. But as he looked along the slim length of *Dauntless* it hurt him to see the wreck the battle had made of her. He saw Bright, a dirty dishevelled small figure, puff-eyed with weariness, and thought Adeline Brett would mother the boy if she was there and give Smith the edge of her tongue because of him. That set him grinning and he called, "Buckley! See if you can get us some coffee, please! I've still got the taste of that smoke in my mouth!"

His grin had an effect on them all and the bridge became a more cheerful place. He told himself that they should be cheerful for they had done all that men could. If anyone had failed it was himself. Now he must send a signal to Braddock telling him *Dauntless* was crippled and *Walküre* running loose, another repeating that to *Blackbird* and calling her to maintain radio silence and join him. And he must hope.

Dauntless crept southward as the signals stuttered out from the wireless office. Smith stood pressed against the torn screen, chin rested on his folded arms and his face impassive but his mind filled with black despair. He pictured the anchorage at Deir el Belah, *Morning Star* with the men of Taggart's battalion, Jackson's Australians in the lighters and the other ships that in a few hours would be penned there under the guns of *Walküre*. While *Dauntless* limped southward and he stood helpless on her bridge.

The report came down from the control-top high above the bridge: "Ship bearing red one-oh!"

Smith set the glasses to his eyes; every pair of glasses on the bridge was in use now. He searched on the bearing, thought—

Ackroyd said slowly, "I think – it's *Blackbird*, sir."

So did Smith. The square boxy shape, even seen dimly through the rain could not be *Walküre*, had to be the seaplane carrier. The look-out in the top confirmed it. "Ship is *Blackbird*, sir, and that sub-chaser is with her."

Thank God! Smith rubbed at his eyes and looked around to meet Ackroyd's stare, knew what he was thinking. Smith said, "Make to *Blackbird*: 'Where is the enemy?'" He waited while the searchlight's shutter clattered and *Dauntless* slowly closed the gap between her and *Blackbird*, saw the light blinking back her answer.

The signal yeoman reported, "Enemy not sighted, sir."

Ackroyd said softly, "*Hell!*"

It was no more than Smith had hoped for. The sea was huge and it was easy enough for two ships to pass without sighting each other. It was quiet on the bridge, they were waiting for Smith to make his decision, give his orders. He stared out across the sea, head turning as if looking for *Walküre* and so he was but only with his mind's eye. Some might think she had a dozen courses to choose from but Smith knew she was racing for Gaza and Deir el Belah.

He pushed away from the screen and shifted restlessly about the bridge, the others sliding unobtrusively out of his way. He saw Buckley watching him from the back of the bridge, worried. He always knew now when Buckley was worried about him, recognised that accusing scowl. *Blackbird* was close now, the little chaser keeping station astern of her. Petersen had done magnificently all the way through, but so had they all, every man. Now at the end there were just the three ships ploughing through a choppy sea under a weeping sky.

He swung on the signal yeoman. "Make to *Blackbird*: 'Is aircraft now available and pilot prepared to attempt reconnaissance?'"

The searchlight clattered and Ackroyd said doubtfully, "It's foul weather for flying."

Smith pushed past him into the charthouse and worked over the chart, laying off a course. He stood still and looked at it a long moment then went out on to the bridge. The signal-lamp was flashing aboard *Blackbird* and men were crowding around the hangar in her stern. The signal yeoman read: "Affirmative. Pilot and observer ready to fly."

Smith said shortly, "Belay that! Tell him to load one big bomb – and I'm going as observer."

For a moment there was silence except for the clatter of the lamp then Ackroyd said, "Sir—" But there he stopped.

Smith stared out at the sea, the long waves and the spume whipped from the tops of them on the wind, and wondered if a Short could get off in this weather. "Well?"

Ackroyd went on, "I don't want to question your decision, sir, but I don't think you should go."

"I want to see for myself." And he would send no one else on this flight.

"Maitland is a good observer, sir."

Smith said drily, "And I'm not?"

"I didn't mean that, but Maitland could do it."

"No." He was so bloody tired. He had scarcely slept since long before the raid on Lydda.

"Any attempt to take off in this sea will be risky, sir—" Smith shook his head and Ackroyd stepped closer, lowered his voice. "You've done enough, sir! Too much!"

Bright said, "They're bringing out Delilah." That caused on uneasy stir on the bridge. The plane's reputation had not been forgotten.

Smith ordered, "Call away my boat." He started towards the ladder but Ackroyd clutched at his arm and Smith swung around, startled.

Ackroyd held on. "That bloody thing has killed five men already that we know of and damned near killed a few more!

I'm not superstitious but there's something wrong about that Short. It's a bad luck—"

"*Balls!*" Smith pulled away and glowered at Ackroyd, saw him about to try again and Smith could not believe it, saw Buckley hovering and even more incredibly about to back up Ackroyd, Smith could read it in his face. "That's enough! Good God Almighty! I never heard anything like it! And on my bridge!" For a moment he glared at them and they stared back but woodenly now after his outburst. He rubbed at his face and told Ackroyd, "We'll fly a course of one-six-five degrees. Follow us and report to the admiral."

He ran down the ladder from the bridge, strode aft to where they were lowering the cutter and in the waist he saw Adeline Brett. She stood amid the wreckage, huddled into a bridge-coat someone had lent her, probably Merryweather, and it hung to her ankles. He halted and stared at her white face under the short curls that fluttered on the wind, into the wide eyes that watched him.

He remembered how he had held this girl in her cabin aboard *Morning Star*, but he could find nothing to say.

He turned away and went down into the cutter where Buckley sat in the sternsheets, the tiller under his arm. The sea threw them about as they made the crossing and he saw Buckley glancing sideways at him, knew he was thinking that the odds were against the Short getting off, that the wind and the sea would wreck it. As they ran alongside *Blackbird*, stopped to take Smith aboard, he saw the Short on its trolley outside the hangar. Its propeller was a spinning disc as the pilot warmed up the engine. A little crowd of riggers and fitters hung on to the Short to hold it down against the tearing wind, looking like black finger strokes on the red-washed skin of Delilah.

Smith climbed aboard and up to the observer's cockpit, seeing the single big bomb slung under the fuselage, a 264-pounder. He settled into the cockpit, pulling on the leather flying helmet and goggles he found on the seat and tossing his cap out to one of the fitters. The pilot stood up to hook the derrick purchase on to the ring on the centre section. It was

Pearce, of course, because the Gang was virtually destroyed. As this was the sole remaining aircraft, so Pearce was the only surviving pilot. Smith flew with him in Delilah or not at all.

Chris turned, his face drawn and the eyes dark in their sockets. He shouted, "Course, sir?"

Smith peered at him, the driven rain cold on his face. "Fly a mean course of one six-five degrees." That meant Pearce would search in dog-legs along that line. But they were not in the air yet. The faces of the men holding on to Delilah were strained and not only because of the physical exertion of stopping the wind from tearing her away, there was worry also. This was filthy weather to try to fly off a seaplane.

Pearce reached down and the engine cut out. Smith said into the silence, "You know what I want you to do."

Pearce only nodded, turned back and dropped into his seat. The winch hammered, the hands stood back from Delilah and she lifted from the deck, swung briefly and jerkily on the wind as the derrick swung out, then plummeted towards the waves.

As the floats smacked into the sea Pearce opened the cock on the bottle of compressed air and the Maori engine kicked over and fired. He yanked at the toggle and the derrick purchase snapped away, Delilah was free of the ship and pushing away from *Blackbird*'s side as the note of the engine rose. The seas were huge and the wings rocked under the thrusting wind, the floats at the wing-tips smashing into the sea. Pearce fought her into the wind with bursts of throttle and kept her there. Smith could see his face as his head turned, the concentration on it and the lips moving. He realised Chris was talking to the machine he held in his hands. Now he looked back at Smith and shouted, "Ready?" He grinned recklessly and was for a moment the old Chris Pearce that Smith had first known.

Smith shouted back, "Right!"

Pearce swung away and opened the throttle. Delilah hammered across the rutted surface of the sea, bucking and rocking as the spray burst up from the floats and flailed over the open cockpits. Through the water that streamed across his goggles Smith saw Pearce shoving forward the big wheel on the control column and felt the tail float lift off. Delilah tried to slide sideways and one wing dipped but Pearce yanked her into the wind once more, straightened her up. He hauled back on the big wheel, and she lifted off.

Smith hardly dared to believe it. Delilah tilted and soared as the wind shook her, the murderous sea close under them, but they were airborne and climbing. He thought that only Pearce could have done it; Chris was the best pilot of them all. He peered behind him and down at the ships falling away below, the boot-shaped *Blackbird* with the patch on her side marked by the raw new paint, *Dauntless* with her upper deck devastated, a ravaged beauty now.

He faced forward, reached down and turned the wheel that let the wireless aerial unreel and trail out below and astern. He switched on the set and tapped out on the Morse key "D-L-L-R . . .", until a signal-lamp acknowledged from *Dauntless*. The wireless could send but not receive. He switched off and reeled in the aerial.

Five minutes later they levelled off at a thousand feet, and when the ships were lost from sight astern Pearce started flying the dog-legs of the search.

He did not look at his watch because time meant nothing, the light everything and there was little of the day left. They should turn back soon if they were to find *Blackbird* again but he was still certain *Walküre* lay ahead of them, would not turn back while there was yet light. He had to find her, would find her along this course. His eyes were slitted, bleared behind the goggles as they strained to search the sea on either hand. He shifted in the cockpit, checked because for a moment he thought . . .

He stood up and leaned to one side to peer past the radiator, pushing up the goggles. He tapped Pearce's shoulder, pointed to a thicker patch of darkness in the murk ahead and Pearce nodded, eased the Short over a point or two and steadied it on the new course. Smith remained standing in the battering wind as the Short closed the smoke. If it *was* smoke? Delilah was losing height as Pearce brought her down. There was something . . . it was smoke . . . *and under it a ship!*

Pearce yelled, "*That's her!*"

Smith dropped back in his seat, switched on the wireless, unreeled the aerial furiously, then tapped out again and again *Walküre*'s position, course and speed as Pearce sent Delilah sliding down after the cruiser. Smith wondered if his signal was being received or whether they were out of range. He had no way of knowing. He reeled in the aerial as Pearce glanced back at him and nodded, tight-lipped.

Long ago the pilot had said you would have to be lucky to get near a ship like *Walküre*, but Smith knew Pearce had been keeping back some idea of his own. Now he eased forward the big wheel, Delilah's nose dipped and their dive steepened until Smith could see over Pearce and the upper wing to *Walküre* floating up towards them. They had been seen. The guns were flaming aboard the big cruiser and the Short lurched as a shell burst close, then steadied under Pearce's hands.

Walküre was big now and Smith saw she had been mauled by *Dauntless*, there was damage amidships and aft and one gun pointed askew. She was huge! She seemed to climb above them as Pearce hauled back on the wheel and Delilah pulled out of the dive with her floats skimming the surface of the sea. They were under the traverse of the worst of *Walküre*'s guns. Smoke streamed past them and it was smoke from *Walküre*'s funnels rolling down across the sea, half-hiding them for the final approach. But then they were through it, above it as Delilah climbed. She lurched again, side-slipped, then, for brief seconds only, was flying level and sweeping in through a torrent of fire, low over *Walküre*'s stern. Smith remembered Pearce's harsh dictum: "To hit a ship under way you'd have to sit the Short on the funnel!"

Pearce did it.

The smoke-belching funnels loomed like towers as Delilah bucked and dipped wildly in the heat-laden air they streamed. Smith saw Pearce yank on the toggle release, felt the lift as the bomb fell away and a second later they were past *Walküre*, tearing away ahead of her over open sea and he was twisted in his seat. He saw the after of the two funnels topple and the smoke jetting, the soaring wreckage, felt and heard the explosion. *Walküre* dwindled as the Short laboured away, her guns still firing. Delilah shook again and again, holes appeared in the fuselage and fabric streamed on the wind then tore away.

The Short was climbing slowly and turning in a shallow bank to port. *Walküre* was far behind them but Smith saw she still poured out smoke – and she was stopped. There was neither bow-wave nor wake and *Walküre* lay dead on the sea.

He thumped Pearce on the shoulder and bawled at him, "You *got* her, Chris!" Pearce looked round and his teeth showed in a grin but then he turned back to his flying and briefly his head sagged, jerked up again to peer ahead past the radiator. Smith shouted, "Chris! Are you all right?" Pearce nodded but he was lying, Smith could see the great holes torn in the Short around the pilot's cockpit. He shouted again, "Anything I can do?" This time Pearce shook his head and slowly Smith sat down. He wound out the aerial and switched on the wireless, tapped out that *Walküre* was hit and stopped and her position. That Delilah was returning. She droned on shot through and tattered, over a darkening sea.

He was first to see the light that wavered on the horizon like a beckoning finger. He leaned forward to point it out to Pearce who nodded, hands opening and closing more tightly on the big wheel. They flew towards the light and Smith made out through the rain and the darkness closing around them that it was a searchlight from *Dauntless*. *Blackbird* was alongside her and stopped to make a lee, her funnel smoke trailing downwind.

Pearce had shrunk down in his seat, struggled ineffectually to sit up but Smith grabbed his shoulders and hoisted him upright, held him there. Pearce's lips were moving again as he turned Delilah into the wind and brought her down until she skimmed the tops of the waves then rubbed the floats into them, set her down in a burst of spray. Smith's arms ached with holding Pearce as the pilot worked the throttle and the Short swerved erratically into *Blackbird*'s lee, turned too late and crumpled a wing against the ship's side, despite the seamen on the rubbing strake striving to boom her off. The engine cut out. Smith had to let go of Pearce to crawl past him and grab at the heaving line, haul down the block and hook on the Short. He turned then and sprawled across the fuselage as the Short was tossed on the sea, saw Pearce collapsed in the cockpit and reached down to lift his head.

Pearce said, "Good old Delilah."

Smith barely heard the whispered words, felt Pearce sag. The winch hammered but as the wire tautened the ring on the Short's centre-section tore loose, its retaining wires severed and trailing. Smith realised they must have been cut by shell-fire, also that with the engine dead and the Short not secured she would smash herself to pieces against *Blackbird*'s hull.

"Sir!"

He twisted his head around to the shout. The cutter was slipping in below him, bow reaching out to seize a float, Buckley at the tiller. Smith croaked, hoarse now, "Give me a hand here! Mr. Pearce is hit!"

Two of the cutter's crew clawed their way up to him and together they got Pearce down into the boat as the sea pounded Delilah on to the steel of the ship's side, tried to tear them from their hold on the breaking-up Short. Smith sat in the sternsheets and held the pilot as the cutter pulled back to *Dauntless* where Merryweather waited. But Chris Pearce died in Smith's arms in the cutter.

Smith went to the bridge and asked Ackroyd, "You received our signals?"

Ackroyd frowned. "Signals? Sparks only heard bits of one that said *Walküre* was stopped and you were on your way back."

So if the Short had been shot out of the sky as Pearce made his attack on the cruiser then her position would never have been reported and Smith would have vanished without trace. He looked across and saw the seamen busy aboard *Blackbird*, trying to get lines around the damaged Short, and ordered Ackroyd, "Tell them to belay that and sink her." Then he added, "We haven't time." That was as explanation and it was true. If there were many who would be glad to see the last of Delilah, they were wrong. The war, not Delilah, had killed

Chris Pearce. Delilah had found *Walküre* for them, in Pearce's hands had stopped her and then got them home. And Chris was dead . . .

He stirred uneasily, turned his back on Delilah as *Dauntless* got under way. It was true they could not waste a second let alone a half-hour rescuing one smashed seaplane – *Walküre* had been stopped but her engineers might get steam on her again. So *Dauntless* worked up to her pitiful twelve knots while *Blackbird* took up station to port and the little chaser to starboard. They went hunting *Walküre* in a creeping line.

Henderson, one eye on Smith propped against the bridge screen, said, "This is like shoving your head in the lion's mouth."

Ackroyd muttered, "You're a cheerful bastard!" But Henderson was right.

Dauntless rocked to a beam sea and the sluicing rain made worse the darkness of the night. Smith asked Jameson, "Torpedo gunner is ready?"

"Yes, sir."

"He fires on my order and not before. Tell him."

"Aye, aye, sir!"

Because they would only get one chance.

And it would come soon.

Walküre, if she were still stopped, was somewhere close ahead of them. She still had teeth, more than enough to deal with this puny force of ships. If he was to have any chance at all, Smith needed *Blackbird* and the chaser, but *Walküre* could destroy the carrier with one salvo and the chaser with a single big shell from her 8-inch guns. And *Dauntless* would get only one chance.

Smith rubbed sore and aching eyes, set the glasses to them again. He picked out the bulk of *Blackbird* under her smoke, then swept the glasses slowly through an arc across the bow of *Dauntless* and then on, seeking the chaser now. He only found her because he knew where to look. Low in the water as she was, only the broken water of her bow and the phosphorescence of her wake marked her.

Jameson said softly, "Hell of a game of blind-man's buff."

Apart from her labouring engines the ship was eerily quiet, as if every man aboard her held his breath, nerves strung tight by waiting through the dragging minutes, waiting for the flash out in the darkness and the shattering blow from the salvo that would follow if *Walküre* saw them first . . .

The flash and the crash came as one and snapped their heads around.

"Chaser, sir!" That was Bright reporting. But all of them had seen the flaming explosion to starboard.

Was she hit?

But a heartbeat later a star-shell burst ahead and to starboard. The chaser had not been hit but had fired her gun and the star-shell lit *Walküre*.

"Starboard ten!" Smith gave the order as he saw *Walküre* was still stopped and a scant mile away. *Dauntless* turned as the darkness rushed back to hide *Walküre* and he ordered, "Steady! . . . Steer that!"

The beams of searchlights poked out from *Walküre* and fingered jerkily across the surface of the sea until one of them found the chaser and the other beams closed on the little ship, lit her up. She was turning as she fired her little 3-inch again and a second star-shell burst above *Walküre* as the gun-flashes prickled along the big cruiser's side. The fall of those shells hid the chaser in huge towers of water and when they fell she was gone. Smith tore his eyes away from the beams where they lit a torn and empty sea and stared ahead of him over the bow at the source of those lights, at *Walküre*.

A gun cracked again to starboard and Jameson yelled, "The chaser ducked out of it! Bloody good, Petersen!"

The beams of light were searching frantically. Smith's orders to both the chaser and *Blackbird* had been to draw the fire to give *Dauntless* a chance to close. As things had turned out Petersen had drawn the short straw because *Walküre* lay at his end of the line, and now he was carrying out his orders. They were certain to kill him in minutes – Smith had known that when he gave the orders, and gave them anyway because he had to, because it was the only way he might win that one chance for *Dauntless*.

But *Walküre* was alive to the threat now. The night vision of all aboard her would be destroyed by the firing and the lights but the beams of the searchlights were swinging out to sweep all around her, not just seeking the chaser. And this was no textbook torpedo attack by a greyhound destroyer hurtling in at thirty-odd knots; this was one battered, frail light cruiser limping to destruction. But they were closing.

A beam flickered over *Dauntless* and on, wavered, returned and it lit them all on the bridge. Smith ordered, "Starboard ten!" *Walküre* lay only a half-mile distant and the turn would take *Dauntless* closer still before pulling away. The bow started to swing. Flashes licked out at them from *Walküre* and a second later hell broke loose on *Dauntless*.

She rocked and shook through her frame as the shells hit her, flame spurted and splinters whirred. The tripod mast, severed high above the bridge, crumpled and fell to hang against the starboard side with the control-top over the sea. Rigging collapsed like a steel and hempen web across the bridge and one big double-pulley block felled Henderson. The top of the second funnel disappeared, blasted out of existence and it seemed that the length of the upper deck was aflame. Smith was numbly aware that *Dauntless* was still turning, Jameson and Bright stood with him while Buckley stooped over Henderson. *Walküre* lay to port and she was so close the black bulk of her filled his vision. He croaked, "Fire!" He did not hear his own voice but Jameson saw him mouth the order and repeated it to the torpedo gunner in the waist.

Smith lurched across to the port wing of the bridge and stared aft, squinting against the smoke and the glare of searchlights and flames. He saw the port tubes and the gunner on his seat, saw one torpedo leap out into the sea, then the other. Guns flashed again on *Walküre* and he was thrown to the deck as the shells ripped into *Dauntless*.

She still turned. He pulled himself up by the screen, held on to it and stared across at *Walküre* as *Dauntless* slowly swung away so now the big cruiser was off the port quarter. It was nearly half-a-minute since the torpedoes were fired and at any second there would come another broadside from the big cruiser and *Dauntless* could not stand much more.

The sea lifted against *Walküre*'s side right under her bridge and a second later it spouted again below the solitary funnel the bomb had left her. The thumping explosions came deeply to him across the sea dividing the ships and the beams of the searchlights jerked away, wandered aimlessly about the sea as if the directing hands had been torn from them. Maybe they had. The salvo did not come, only a single gun fired and the shell shrieked overhead. *Walküre* was slipping astern of them now.

He shouted hoarsely, "Meet her! . . . Steer that!"

The searchlights went out and he peered blindly into the rain and the darkness that was broken by the yellow lick of the fires that roared aboard *Dauntless*. *Walküre* was lost in the night somewhere astern of them. He was certain she was finished but he had to be sure. While he listened to Ackroyd's report the torpedo gunner and his crew were loading the tubes again. When Ackroyd finished reading the long list from the smudged pages of his notebook, Smith summed up for him: "So we're afloat and under way and that's the best you can say."

He had to raise his voice above the roaring fires. Ackroyd nodded, the whites of his eyes gleaming through the grime and soot.

Smith said, "We'll attack again."

"Aye, aye, sir."

Dauntless turned and dragged herself once more towards her quarry, while Ackroyd's stumbling, exhausted parties still fought the fires aft and in the smoke-filled inferno below. Ackroyd went down to that inferno but paused briefly at the sick bay to shove his head in at the hooked-back door and ask, "How're things, Doc?"

Merryweather did not look up from the gash he was stitching, only jerked his head sideways indicating the crowded sick bay. And this was only where he operated, most of the wounded had spilled over on to the mess-deck. He seemed to work in a mist of air made thick with the smell of blood and antiseptic. "As you see. What's happening?"

Ackroyd answered, "We're attacking again." He pushed away from the door and was gone to his duties.

Merryweather whispered, "Jesus wept!" His gaze lifted and fastened on Adeline Brett where she knelt on the deck, her quick fingers completing the dressing on a man's chest. He smiled up at her weakly, grateful as she rose to her feet and drew the back of her hand across her brow.

Matthews, the cook, had brought a man in and sat him against the bulkhead clutching a makeshift bandage about his leg. As the cook made to leave Merryweather said, "Here, Matthews, take Miss Brett on deck but see her safe under cover."

"Aye, aye, sir."

Adeline protested, "Why? I'm perfectly all right. I—"

Merryweather cut her short. "Never mind what she says. She's not all right. Take her out of this if you have to carry her and get some clean air into her lungs." To himself he added, "We'll need her again soon. Or she might get a chance in a boat or a life-raft. I'll not keep her down here for the end of it."

The cook's big hand encircled Adeline's arm and she had to go.

Blackbird and the chaser were left astern; there was no point in exposing them again to *Walküre*'s guns and this time *Dauntless* would not have to search for the big cruiser. They saw the light of fires aboard her now and Smith stared at them as *Dauntless* crept towards her. Until he ordered, "Searchlight."

The beam swept out from above the bridge, settled on *Walküre* and edged along her length. She was listed to port and down by the head, already her deck forward was awash as far as the bridge. Boats were clustered at her side and filling with men, while other crowded boats pulled away from her. They were launching life-rafts. Her ensign still flew but no gun fired.

Smith said quietly, "Slow ahead both."

The little way *Dauntless* had fell off until there was barely a ripple at her stem as she edged in towards *Walküre* and the boats.

Buckley said, "If you'll let me have that jacket, sir. It's a bit of a mess. I found this one in your sea-cabin." He held Smith's best jacket and said apologetically, "Nothing much left o' the cabin aft, sir."

Smith nodded, dragged off the filthy, soaked garment and pulled on the other, shoved his hands in his pockets and found the letter. He took it out, frowning, then remembered. Braddock's broad hand was scrawled across the envelope: "Cdr. D. C. Smith.' He broke the seal, took out the single sheet of paper and held it up to his eyes. In the spilt light from the searchlight's beam he read:

I could not tell you this before you set Edwards ashore to lead the attack on Lydda because I would not add the burden of this knowledge to the others you already bear. But Edwards is the cousin I mentioned. He will, no doubt, contest your grandfather's will . . .

There followed reassurances but Smith crumpled the letter into a ball in his fist and threw it over the side. Braddock was mistaken; Edwards would not contest the will because he lay dead by the railway track outside of Lydda. So Smith would inherit after all. Edwards his cousin, of the same blood? Selfish, ambitious, wild – there could be a lot of Edwards in himself. But it was all irrelevant, unreal. This was reality, this shattered ship of his, the big sea running and *Walküre*'s boats pitching as *Dauntless* slipped down to them.

Lofty Williams came from the wireless office aft, climbed the twisted ladder to the bridge and handed the signal to Smith. "From the admiral, sir."

Smith read it and lifted his eyes, saw them all on the bridge watching him and said, "The Australians have taken Beersheba."

There was a moment of silence then Jameson said without expression, "Oh, good."

It was not just good but tremendous news. This was the victory for which they had all suffered. Allenby had secured the pivot on which he would turn to roll up the Gaza-Beersheba line, other victories would follow and maybe now, soon, this bloody war would end. Jameson and the others were just too benumbed to take it in. There would be a celebration, but later.

They also had gained a victory but paid an awful price. Smith looked from the blank, white face of the boy Bright, aft along the torn length of *Dauntless* smoking under the rain, then across to where *Blackbird* and the U.S. Submarine-Chaser No. 101 were coming up out of the night. There were men on their decks and the deck of *Dauntless*, staring silently at the stricken, sinking *Walküre*. There was no cheering. Adeline Brett stood a small, lonely figure seen in the shifting light from the flames, the pale blur of her face turned up to the bridge.

Smith thought they had all paid. So long as he lived he would remember the red dust coating Taggart's battalion and the yelling madness of their night attack at Lydda, the roaring rush of the Australians' charge falling like a hammer on the Turkish column. The cold-blooded, calculating courage of Edwards, and Chris Pearce flying Delilah in at masthead height to ram the bomb into *Walküre*'s heart.

He did not give a damn for the estate or the name that went with it but he had known from the start that this campaign would make or break him and he had not broken. He moved to his high chair by the bridge screen and pulled himself stiffly up into it. "Make to *Blackbird* and the chaser: 'Stand by to recover survivors.'"

Buckley came with a blanket and hung it around his shoulders but Smith did not notice as he sat hunched under the rain. *Dauntless* was not finished, nor was he.

At five p.m. on October 31st, 1917 the 4th Brigade, Australian Light Horse captured the fortress of Beersheba with a cavalry charge, probably the greatest and last of them all.

And at noon on December 11th, 1917 Allenby, the cavalry general walked into Jerusalem, a conqueror going on foot like a penitent.